NOW IT'S *YOUR* TURN . . .

on *Juneau,* Commander Douglas Scott Graham stared at the image on his monitor screen in horror and disbelief, hardly able to watch but equally unable to tear his eyes away.

He was watching a ship die, a sight all too common for a Terran Confederation Navy officer in this thirty-fifth year of continuous warfare with the Kilrathi Empire, but that didn't make it any easier to watch *Dover* coming apart under the incredible bombardment generated by the Kilrathi carrier the two Terran ships faced.

Kruger wanted revenge, he thought bitterly. *I hope it's worth the price we're paying.*

When the Kilrathi carrier battle group had launched a raid on planet Landreich, every ship in the region had been summoned to intercept them before they could return to Imperial space. The running pursuit had knocked out three of the five . . . but the carrier and her escort were still formidable foes when the two Terran cruisers had moved in to engage.

The proof of that was on his monitor. The Cat carrier was pumping everything she could fire into the unfortunate *Dover.*

"Christ, look at her," someone said behind Graham. "She's a goner for sure. . . ."

"Back to your post, spacer," Graham snapped.

The monitor flashed as explosions ran along the spine of the crippled *Dover.* For an instant the flare of light was blinding before the computer cut in the compensators. One moment the ship was whole. The next she was shards of wreckage whirling away in all directions, ship and crew alike consumed by the fearsome energies unleashed by the concentrated Kilrathi attack.

Graham swallowed. Now it was *Juneau*'s turn . . .

THE WING COMMANDER SERIES

WING COMMANDER™
FALSE COLORS

WILLIAM R. FORSTCHEN
ANDREW KEITH

FALSE COLORS

This is a work of fiction. All the characters and events
portrayed in this book are fictional, and any resemblance
to real people or incidents is purely coincidental.

A Baen Books Original

Baen Publishing Enterprises
P.O. Box 1403
Riverdale, NY 10471

ISBN: 0-671-57784-0

Cover art by Gary Ruddell

First printing, January 1999

Distributed by Simon & Schuster
1230 Avenue of the Americas
New York, NY 10020

Printed in the United States of America

• PROLOGUE

> *"Better Death with claws extended than Life without honor."*
>
> from the Fourth Codex
> 18:35:3

Flag Bridge, KIS *Karga*
Near Vaku VII, Vaku System
1335 hours (CST), 2669.315

Admiral Largka Cakg *dai* Nokhtak gripped the arms of his command chair as the ship shuddered under the impact of multiple torpedo hits and the red lights flickered in protest. "Damage report," he ordered tautly, studying the Kilrathi *Hyilghar* in front of him with a stern eye. Young, proud, with a stiffly erect bearing and green eyes gleaming against his tawny fur, the staff officer was the very picture of a young Kilrathi warrior. He wore his beard and mane short in the most recent court fashion, and his fangs gleamed in the dim orange light of the flag bridge.

"Lord Admiral, neither the command bridge nor the secondary control center respond." The young officer's voice quavered a little, but he kept himself under rigid

1

control. Largka allowed himself a moment's pride. It was his sister's son's first deep-space assignment, his first brush with the God of the Running Death, and *Hyilghar* Murragh Cakg *dai* Nokhtak was bearing up with courage and honor. "The launch bays have ceased operation to repair damage to the flight control computer, and the port side hangar deck is blocked by debris. With the previous damage to the starboard hangar deck, we cannot retrieve the fighters we have already deployed. Structural integrity in the stern section between bulkheads fifty and seventy-two is down by better than seventy percent. We have lost long-range sensors, interstellar drive, and the main tactical computer. Backup systems are functional but overloaded. Defensive weaponry is operable, but without the tactical computer must be directed manually. Offensive weapons are still functional, but with intermittent power failures . . ."

Largka waved his nephew to silence. "That is sufficient," he said quietly. "Neither the Captain nor the Exec is available?"

Murragh extended a clawed hand palm-up, the empty hand of negation. "Neither bridge is in contact with the rest of the ship," he said. "I fear both took direct hits. Nhagrah *ko* Lannis is the senior officer, but he is Chief Engineer, not fit for a combat command . . ."

The Admiral made the grasping gesture of understanding. "What of the apes?" The ship shuddered again as if to emphasize his question.

"Both cruisers are concentrating on us now that the *Frawqirg* is out of the action, Lord Admiral," Murragh said. "At last report one of them was showing definite power drops and was trailing atmosphere at a rate that indicated imminent structural failure. That was before the sensors went off-line. The other cruiser is also damaged, but to a lesser extent."

"And your assessment of our options, young *Hyilghar*?" he asked quietly, maintaining a rigid calm to counter the grim situation. "An exercise for a young officer."

Murragh didn't answer right away. Finally he spoke. "We cannot run. Our chances of defeating both ape ships are small, given the extent of the damage. The fighters we have deployed already are running low on fuel and ammunition, and they cannot resupply while the hangar bays are down." His eyes met his uncle's. "What other option is there save to die with honor?"

Largka showed his teeth. "What option, indeed?" Inwardly his heart was filled with pride, knowing Murragh could meet the final race with the Running Death with the true Kilrathi spirit. But pride was balanced by rage. They had come so close to victory, but it had eluded their grasping hands by less than a claw's-length. "Return to your post, *Hyilghar*," he said quietly. "And reflect on this . . . you have done well, young Murragh. Your entire clan would be proud today . . . as I am."

He turned back to the bank of readouts and monitors, most of them blank, that were supposed to allow him to direct a multi-ship deep-space battle. Irony tasted bitter in Largka's mouth. He had argued for months that he should be given a battle command instead of being confined to a staff job on Kilrah, and always his cousin Thrakhath had said there was no available command large enough to sustain the honor of the Imperial Family. Largka had appealed directly to Thrakhath's grandfather, the Emperor himself, protesting that he would take any squadron, however small or unimportant.

And the Emperor had granted his request. A tiny raiding squadron operating on the fringes of the war zone between humans and Kilrathi, one of the new supercarriers and a scratch supporting battle group of only four escorts. And those had fallen one by one during the disastrous raid on the world the humans called "Landreich." First the two cruisers, then the destroyer *Takh'lath*, and finally the escort *Frawqirg*, caught by the two Terran cruisers and badly damaged before *Karga* could secure from jump and assist him. The crippled escort had last been seen shaping an orbit for the inner moon of the oversized gas giant Vaku, a marginally habitable world where they might manage a landing and await a rescue . . . if the Kilrathi won the engagement in space.

But it was clear that wasn't the likely outcome of today's battle. Without escorts, even a supercarrier was vulnerable to a sustained attack by conventional warships. Carriers weren't supposed to fight in the thick of the fray. *Karga* had been forced to do just that, though, and it would take a miracle for him to pull through.

But before he died, the carrier would give a good account of himself against the apes. Largka vowed to make the Terrans remember Vaku, one way or another.

"Concentrate fire on the lead Terran cruiser," he ordered. It was strange to be making tactical decisions again, fighting a ship instead of directing a whole squadron. But with both the carrier's control rooms out of operation, his flag bridge was the closest thing to a tactical control center left on *Karga*. "Ignore the other one . . . but kill that ape cruiser!"

"As you order, Lord Admiral," one of his aides acknowledged.

Largka studied his monitor screen with the chill calm of a warrior determined to fight to the bitter end.

Engineering Control Center, TCS *Juneau*
Near Vaku VII, Vaku System
1342 hours (CST)

Commander Douglas Scott Graham stared at the image on his monitor screen in horror and disbelief, hardly able to watch but equally unable to tear his eyes away.

He was watching a ship die, a sight all too common for a Terran Confederation Navy officer in this thirty-fifth year of continuous warfare with the Kilrathi Empire. Plenty of ships had been lost over that decades-long span, but that didn't make it any easier to watch TCS *Juneau*'s consort, *Dover*, coming apart under the incredible bombardment generated by the Kilrathi carrier the two Terran ships faced today.

Kruger wanted revenge, he thought bitterly. *I hope it's worth the price we're paying.*

The two cruisers were part of a Terran Confederation task force operating among the frontier worlds in loose cooperation with colonial military units and semi-autonomous planetary governments. The most prominent of these was Landreich, neither wholly independent nor fully cooperative under the leadership of its maverick president, Max Kruger. Kruger had reluctantly played the role of cavalry-to-the-rescue during the Kilrathi assault against the Sol system three years back, and now when Kruger sneezed there was a scramble among Confederation leaders to see who could hand him a handkerchief the fastest. So when the small but deadly Kilrathi carrier battle group had launched a raid on Landreich itself, every ship in the region had been summoned to intercept them before they could return to Imperial space.

The running pursuit had knocked out three of the

five Kilrathi ships . . . but the carrier and her escort were still formidable foes when the two Terran cruisers had spotted them jumping into the Vaku system and moved to engage.

The proof of that was on his monitor. Ignoring *Juneau* entirely, the Cat carrier was pumping everything she could fire into the unfortunate *Dover*. Under that intensive bombardment, the cruiser wouldn't last long. Graham could see the rippling of shields burned through by energy beams, and the Confederation cruiser seemed to stagger under wave after wave of missiles from the carrier and the swarm of Kilrathi fighters that clustered around her.

"Christ, look at her," someone said behind Graham. "She's a goner for sure. . . ."

"Back to your post, spacer," Graham snapped. "Chief, get these slackers back to work *now*, or they'll have a lot worse than the Cats to answer to."

"Aye aye, sir." Chief Ellen Quinlan responded smartly. "All right, you sons-of-Cats, you heard the man! Eyes on your consoles and heads in the game! And if any of you aren't afraid of what an officer might do to you, just keep in mind what *I'll* do! Do I make myself clear?"

Graham hid a chuckle as the engineering control center grew suddenly quiet and thoroughly businesslike under the Chief's stern glare. A stern, hatchet-faced CPO of the old school, Quinlan could generate more sheer terror than a whole squadron of incoming Cat fighters. She was also one hell of a good engineer.

The monitor flashed as explosions ran along the spine of the crippled *Dover*, bringing Graham's attention back to the fight. For an instant the flare of light was blinding before the computer cut in the compensators. Even then, it was difficult to distinguish details. One moment *Dover* was whole. The next she was shards of wreckage whirling away in all directions, ship and crew alike consumed by the fearsome energies unleashed by the concentrated Kilrathi attack.

That left *Juneau* and the Cat carrier alone under the mottled light of Vaku. Cruiser against carrier . . . and that carrier had just done in a Terran cruiser in one furious assault.

Graham swallowed. Now it was *Juneau's* turn.

Flag Bridge, KIS *Karga*
Near Vaku VII, Vaku System
1348 hours (CST)

Admiral Cakg *dai* Nokhtak bared his teeth in defiance as the Terran cruiser broke apart. *Victory is still possible!* he told himself. If *Karga* could just put some time and distance between himself and the surviving Terran, they could effect repairs to the jump engines and escape back into Imperial territory, where songs of this day's action would be sung for eight-eights of years to come.

"Target the cruiser's engineering section," he ordered, keeping his voice level and firm despite the urge to let the emotions inside him run free. "Helm Officer, take us in closer to Vaku."

"Lord Admiral . . ." The staff officer who had suddenly found himself acting as helmsman for the crippled supercarrier was almost visibly shivering as he questioned his superior's order. "Lord Admiral, the shields are already weak, and the radiation from this star . . ."

"Will kill us in minutes if they fail," Largka finished the sentence for him. "Nonetheless, you will carry out my order. I want a tight hyperbolic orbit that will take us through the plane of Vaku's ring system. If we can cripple the Terran ship's engines, the ring debris and that same radiation you are afraid of will serve to mask a course change as we move out of their range. This will give us our chance to break off this fight."

"You would run away from battle, Lord Admiral?" That was Baron Grathal *nar* Khirgh, whose official title of Fleet Intelligence Officer masked his real position as the Imperial Family's spy and political officer aboard the carrier. "The Prince would not like to hear that one of his noble cousins chose to run rather than fight."

The admiral half-rose from his chair, unsheathing the claws of his powerful right hand before he forced himself to ignore the insult. "Thrakhath would be more concerned still to hear that I lost a supercarrier in battle with the apes," he said through tight lips. "Once we have broken off the action and made repairs to engines and flight bays, we can come back and deal with that cruiser. Right now the important thing is to preserve the *Karga*."

He sank back in his seat, but his eyes remained locked on Khirgh's until the Intelligence Officer gave a reluctant grasped-claw gesture and turned away.

"Course laid in, Lord Admiral," the Helm Officer said, sounding nervous. Largka couldn't blame him. No one wanted to get involved in court politics at the best of times, and certainly not when a battle was raging around them.

Damn Thrakhath and his idiot followers! The Emperor's grandson had consistently mismanaged the war against the Terrans, and no small part of that mismanagement was the way he'd treated the nobility that should have been the mainstay of Imperial support. Thrakhath's policy of using court favorites as watchdogs over nobles he didn't trust only magnified the rifts in the Kilrathi war machine. Even if he managed to win the final victory he was always touting, Thrakhath might very well fall to the sharp claws of the factions he had created.

And perhaps a member of the Imperial Family who had distinguished himself in battle might hope to take advantage should the Emperor's favorite grandson stumble. . . .

"Execute course change," he ordered, pushing his bitter thoughts from his mind and focusing once again on the battle unfolding beyond the supercarrier's bulkheads.

"I have targeting solutions on the Terran cruiser," the Acting Weapons Officer announced. "Locking energy batteries on the engineering section. . . ."

"Fire all batteries!" the admiral ordered.

Bridge, TCS *Juneau*
Near Vaku VII, Vaku System
1351 hours (CST)

Unimaginable energies battered at the cruiser as the Kilrathi supercarrier loosed its barrage. Captain Ekaterina Tereshkova tightened her grip and closed her eyes for a moment as she felt her beloved cruiser shuddering under blast after blast from the Kilrathi ship's main guns. She had seen what had happened to Captain Fowler's *Dover* when the Cats had turned their full power against that ship. She wasn't going to let them do the same thing to *Juneau*.

"All batteries, fire!" she grated. "Give me everything you've got, Guns!"

"Aye aye, skipper," her Fire Control Officer responded. On the monitor screen in front of her, lasers stabbed back at the Kilrathi carrier, probing the kilometer-long ship's weakened defenses.

How much more punishment can the Cats take, anyway? Tereshkova wouldn't have believed it possible for the Kilrathi ship to hold out this long. Even a Kilrathi carrier wasn't supposed to be able to handle a stand-up fight with Terran cruisers. Their primary weapons were the fighter squadrons they carried, and with a few exceptions they hadn't been able to launch fighters with their hangar decks crippled in the first exchange of fire. But whoever was skippering that carrier was as brilliant as he was stubborn.

The cruiser lurched again, the red bridge lights flickering and then going out as power was interrupted. After a long moment a backup power source kicked in, but there were plenty of dead consoles around the bridge . . . and the ones that were still registering were lit up with warning lights.

"Heavy damage to the rear shields," her XO reported, gripping a stanchion with one hand and holding his earpiece communications link in place with the other. Commander Lindstrom's voice was matter-of-fact, as if he wasn't really a part of the chaos that had erupted on the bridge after that hit. Tereshkova's eyes flicked from one station to another, taking in the body of the FCO slumped across his board and the young commo officer kneeling beside his chair trying to give first aid.

"Armor's gone from sections sixty-four through seventy-one," Lindstrom went on. "Maneuvering drives are off-line. Fusion generator's still functioning, but we've got multiple ruptures in the power grid. Damage control crews are re-routing now, but we don't have weapons power until we get the grid hooked up again. Estimated repair time is ten minutes. Shields are still holding except around the burn-through point. Graham's deploying portable shield units to protect engineering from radiation effects."

"Repair estimate on the drive?" Tereshkova snapped.

Lindstrom looked grim. "An hour . . . maybe more."

"We don't *have* an hour, Commander," she said quietly. "Tell Mr. Graham—"

"We nailed him! We nailed the bastard!" The shout from someone on the far side of the bridge brought a wave of cheers from the stunned crew, and Tereshkova turned in her chair to study her monitor screen again.

The computer-enhanced image showing there was subtly different, but it took a few seconds for her fatigue-numbed brain to interpret what she was seeing. She raised her eyes to meet Lindstrom's again, and this time she had a savage smile on her lips.

"Her shields are down," she said. "She's helpless out there. . . ."

"And us with no weapons power," Lindstrom replied with a frown.

"But without shields, Mr. Lindstrom, those Cats are going to fry in a matter of minutes," she said. "They're even closer to Vaku's weird star than we are, and that means they're getting a full broadside of radiation sleeting right through their hull as we speak. Unless they get their generators back on-line pretty damned soon, they're all dead meat over there . . . unless they surrender and let us try to extend our own shields around them."

"Let 'em fry," Lindstrom said harshly. After thirty-five years of warfare people didn't talk much about compassion for the enemy. Not after the losses inflicted on Earth herself, or the plague on Locanda, or any of the other atrocities the Kilrathi had carried out over the years.

But Tereshkova shook her head. "We'll give them a chance to surrender, Commander," she said. "Just think about the propaganda value of leading that big sucker in to port back at Landreich . . . with her surviving crew as prisoners. It'll be the biggest thing since Ralgha *nar* Hhallas defected. Might give some people the idea it's worthwhile keeping up the fight a little while longer. God knows we've had few enough victories, large or small, to boost morale back home." She turned again. "Lieutenant, let someone else look after Mr. Martinez. Get back to your post and put a message out to those Cats. Surrender, and we will impose our shields against the star's radiation until they can get their damage control sorted out."

"Aye aye, Captain," the communications officer said.

Tereshkova slumped back in her chair. It was almost over. . . .

Flag Bridge, KIS *Karga*
Near Vaku VII, Vaku System
1356 hours (CST)

"Surrender! Would the apes see us dishonored? Would *you*, Lord Admiral?"

Largka Cakg bared his teeth at the Fleet Intelligence Officer but did not reply. His eyes found Murragh, and he gestured his sister's son forward. "Status?"

"Shields are down and cannot be restored short of a full-scale overhaul, Lord Admiral," Murragh said. "Lethal radiation dosages will be reached within the next ten cycles; it is already too late for many in Engineering or who have already received significant doses of radiation previous to this. We still have maneuvering drive and limited weapons availability, but we cannot run from the radiation fast enough to save the crew, and we cannot fight the cruiser with the weapons we have left."

"And the apes?"

"Damage assessment suggests they have lost their maneuvering capability. There would appear to be gaps in their power distribution grid. Their shields are intact except in their Engineering section. We have no way of estimating the extent of their damage, Lord Admiral, save by observation, and they may be holding back. . . ."

Largka cut him off with a claw-grasp. "Without other capital ships we cannot even abandon ship and hope to survive. Lifepods would shield us from the radiation for a few hours at best, but that would be insufficient without other ships to perform search and rescue. Nor do we have adequate powered craft to evacuate the entire crew with the launch bays out of action. A few lifeboats are all that can escape; the rest of *Karga's* crew will die without shields."

"Would you actually consider surrender to the apes?" Khirgh demanded, snarling.

"No, Lord Khirgh, I would not. Murragh, pass orders for the Cadre to evacuate in available lifeboats. Senior officers to remain at their posts, but get the designated Cadre out. The inner moon of Vaku is marginally habitable, and we saw *Frawqirg* heading there when they broke off the action." The Cadre—fifty specialist officers and petty officers out of the five thousand aboard the supercarrier—would survive to carry their individual skills back to the Fleet. "You will act as my deputy, Murragh," Largka added. "Take charge of the Cadre until you meet a senior line officer to pass the command to."

"But my place is here—"

"You are the last of our branch of the Clan," Largka told him. "You must survive to carry on the Clan's name and honor. There is no shame in obeying orders."

"There is no shame," Murragh repeated formally. "I obey."

As Murragh hastened from the flag bridge Largka slumped back in his chair, trying to control the reflexive movement of his fingers and claws. He did not want any of his crew to see him betray weakness at this of all moments.

By the God of War, they had come so *close*. And now the whole crew was condemned to a slow and agonizing death, because of a lucky shot by the ape cruiser.

There was nothing left now but to let *Karga* end his service in glory.

"Helm, plot an intercept course with the Terran ship. Get us everything you can from the engines. We will ram the apes if that is the only way to ensure they don't see home again. Engineering, coordinate with the helm. I want self-destruct systems rigged to explode the ship as we reach the cruiser. Full destruct—reactors, ordnance, auxiliary generators, munitions and fuel stores . . . everything rigged to the computer destruct program."

"Yes, my Lord." The engineering officer looked shaken, but raised no word of protest.

"Communications, I will record a message."

"Ready, Lord Admiral."

Largka paused for a moment in contemplation before speaking into the microphone at his side. "This is Admiral Largka Cakg *dai* Nokhtak. *Karga* is the last ship of the squadron, and we have lost shields while passing close to an anomalous brown dwarf in the Vaku system. As a result, lethal dosages of radiation will soon render the ship's crew dead, something the apes who have attacked us could not do themselves."

He paused, seeing the orange jungles of Kilrah again in his mind's eye. One last hunt would have been pleasant, but the God of War demanded otherwise. "Even in death we have a last chance to grasp the enemy in our claws. Our last surviving opponent appears incapable of maneuver, and I have ordered an intercept course. We will destroy the ship once it is close alongside the Terran cruiser, so we will not go to the afterlife without a proper escort of our dead and defeated foes. Weapons stations should continue to fire as they are able, until the end. We die for the glory of the Empire, and to honor the hero whose name our vessel bears. Remember the words of the Tenth Codex: *Even in Death there can be Victory!*"

He signaled to the communications officer that he was finished. "Have that announcement broadcast on all internal comm channels," he ordered. "And send it by hypercast with the appropriate codes inserted, so that Governor Ragark knows *Karga* has carried out his final duty to the Empire."

"Yes, my Lord."

Largka contemplated his tactical monitor, content in the knowledge that his death, and the deaths of these valiant warriors, would not be in vain.

Bridge, TCS *Juneau*
Near Vaku VII, Vaku System
1400 hours (CST)

"God damn it, that bastard's changing course and powering up his maneuver drives!"

Tereshkova called up the tactical plot and quickly confirmed Lindstrom's report. The Kilrathi supercarrier was changing vector, all right . . . and the projected course would bring them straight in to an intercept with the *Juneau*.

"You don't suppose the Cats are coming alongside so we can extend our shields around them, do you?" someone said behind her. "Maybe their comm system's down and they can't accept the surrender offer."

As if in response energy pulsed from the carrier's forward turret. "If that's a surrender, I'm a Cat pacifist," Lindstrom said. The cruiser's screens handled the incoming fire, but Tereshkova could see that the shield reserves were getting weaker by the minute.

"What about the maneuver drives?" she asked. "Any progress getting them back?"

"Negative, skipper," Lindstrom told her. "Graham says half the section's fused together back there. We're not stepping out of the way on this one."

"Estimated time to course intersect?"

"Five minutes, Captain," the helmsman reported crisply. He might have been commenting on the weather back home.

"We can't blow them up . . . we can't get the hell out of the way." Tereshkova met Lindstrom's eyes. "Ever see any statistics on the survival prospects of a cruiser getting rammed by a supercarrier?"

He shrugged. "Not that I remember," he said with a sour, gallows humor smile. "And I doubt it would matter much if we could survive a collision. If that Cat over there realizes that his people are going to cop it from this weird brown dwarf's radiation anyway, he's liable to order the destruct systems armed. That way he gets us even if we don't collide. Probably takes out any last-minute lifepods we dump, too."

"Options?" Tereshkova knew what they were, but she had to hear Lindstrom confirm them. When the safety of her crew was at stake, she wouldn't overlook any possibilities.

"We sit here and fry," he said. "Or we pray for a miracle

with the weapons or the drives . . . and fry if we don't happen to get it." He paused. "Or we sound Abandon Ship. Lifepods can handle the radiation for a little while, and if we deploy our shuttles now they should be able to round up most of the crew and get them to a safe distance before the dosages become critical. There'll be casualties. A lot of them. And long-term survival's another thing entirely."

"There's a habitable moon in this system. That's something."

"And a flock of Kilrathi, too. The fighters that were cut off from their hangar deck, and that escort that withdrew. They could still be a threat."

"They're a possible problem." She jabbed a finger at the tactical display. *"That's* a threat." She sighed. "Sound Abandon Ship, Mr. Lindstrom. And download the navigation data on that moon to all the shuttle computers. Better make it fast—that Cat's not going to juggle his schedule just to let us finish the job."

"Aye aye, skipper," Lindstrom said. "Permission to take the bridge during the evacuation?"

"Denied," she said harshly. "You get to your lifepod. The captain's supposed to go down with the ship. I'll ride herd on the old girl while the crew gets clear."

She turned away from Lindstrom and studied the monitor again, unwilling to let him see the emotion in her eyes.

Slowly, ponderously, the two blips on the screen that represented the Terran cruiser and the Kilrathi carrier began to move toward one another, and there was nothing Captain Tereshkova could do to stop it.

Flag Bridge, KIS *Karga*
Orbiting Vaku System
1413 hours (CST)

"Lifepods. The apes are escaping in lifepods."

Largka heard the anger in Khirgh's voice and wondered at the intelligence officer's blind hatred. Why did so many Kilrathi—Thrakhath's followers in particular—nurse such enmity for the Terrans? They were brave fighters, tenacious in battle even when the odds were against them. Hadn't the hero Karga himself won glory for honoring a brave but outmatched warrior who had challenged him in battle? Perhaps if the Empire had accorded a status higher than that of prey to the humans the war would not have stretched on so long.

"Let them," Largka said calmly. "They can burn slowly in the radiation of the brown dwarf, or quickly in the explosion of the *Karga*. Even if they escape, they will be marooned on the habitable moon, and some of our warriors are still there. We have achieved our purpose, regardless."

"At a high cost, Admiral," Khirgh commented.

"You would have preferred to evacuate with the Cadre?" That was a sneer. There were no political repercussions left for Largka now, no more need to pretend to support the Emperor, or Thrakhath, or their toadies.

"I know my duty," Khirgh snarled. "But you cannot deny the cost of this exercise."

"If your precious Prince had planned something more worthwhile than a mere raid to be avenged for what the humans on Landreich did at the Battle of Earth, if he had given us sound objectives and the forces we needed to achieve them, rather than sending us out

with blunted fangs, this 'exercise' might have had a better
outcome. But instead Thrakhath has thrown away this
squadron as he has thrown away so many other warriors
and ships, for nothing but his own vanity. One day it
may be that he will throw away the Empire itself. And
perhaps my sister's son will still be alive to claim the
throne as the last surviving member of the branch of
the Imperial *hrai* worthy of holding it."

"Treason!" Khirgh surged toward Largka, claws
extending. "The Prince was right about your treacherous
ambitions!"

Largka rose from his command chair, drawing his
ceremonial dagger. His thrust met Khirgh's rush, and
blood pumped from the intelligence officer's slit throat.
Khirgh's claws grasped ineffectually at Largka's chest
before Thrakhath's agent sagged to the deck. The
admiral studied the body for a long moment, but there
was no savor to the kill.

"Lord Admiral," one of the bridge crew said, voice a
little unsteady after witnessing the short but savage clash
between the two officers. "Lord Admiral, the cruiser's
shields are failing!"

He jerked his attention to the monitor. Minimum
sensors had been restored, and they could read the wild
fluctuations in the energy levels powering the cruiser's
defensive grid. A rapid string of energy pulses from
Karga's forward batteries played across the Terran ship's
bow, and suddenly the sensor readings showed the
shields entirely down.

The next barrage tore through the Confederation
ship like claws through soft flesh. On the main
viewscreen he could see the rippling series of explosions
as every system overloaded at once and the cruiser
came apart.

So . . . there would be no collision, no need to count

on the self-destruct system to ensure the Terran ship's destruction. *Karga's* foe was already dead.

But the countdown to destruction would go on. His ship and crew were already dead as well, thanks to the shield failure and the radiation sleeting through the hull. Best to deny *Karga* to those who might find him drifting out here, derelict, a prize to be claimed and dishonored.

With one foot he rolled the body of Khirgh away from his command chair and sat down once again. "Time to self-destruct?" he demanded.

"Two minutes, Lord Admiral." The voice was calm and resigned. There was one officer, at least, ready to meet a warrior's death.

The time passed slowly for Largka as he meditated over the familiar words of the Fifth Codex. *Honor shall flow to the warrior who does his duty, for his Clan shall earn glory by his deeds. Honor shall flow to the warrior who meets death in battle, for his name shall be remembered. Honor shall flow to the warrior who strikes down his foe, for he shall win victory for his people . . .*

"Eight seconds . . ." someone said. Largka heard another crewman quoting the Codices, and felt a swelling pride within. They had all done their duty . . .

A long moment later he realized the count had passed zero, but nothing was changed. "Report," he snapped.

"The computer has gone off-line, Lord Admiral," the engineering officer said. "Self-destruct sequence cannot be completed. I do not believe we could even trigger it manually. There is too much damage to internal systems."

"*Vraxar!*" he swore. Was he to be denied the chance to take *Karga* out in one last moment of glory? Would he preside over a crew of the dead and dying, like the Wandering Conquistador of Kilrathi legend?

No . . . that was too much to ask.

"Communications Officer! Can you at least put me on internal channels? Or must I shout a message to the crew?"

"Internal channels, Lord Admiral."

Largka licked lips gone dry and summoned up the will to speak. "This is Admiral *dai* Nokhtak. Our self-destruct system has failed. The ship has won a glorious victory over the Terrans, but all estimates indicate that we have already received lethal dosages of radiation. Repairs are impossible without the support of a base or a fleet tender; by the time we could accomplish anything on our own we would all be dead anyway."

He paused. "Any crew member who wishes to take his chances in lifepods is welcome to do so. Some of our comrades may still be alive outside the ship and able to render aid. For myself, I choose the only honorable option, *Zu'kara*. Any who wish to do the same will do honor to their *hrai*, seeking a clean death in the moment of victory. Follow the dictates of your own consciences. That is all."

Largka sensed the emotion in the flag bridge. *Zu'kara*—ritual suicide—was the ultimate expression of the warrior's creed. The Kilrathi warrior took his own life if he or his clan stood to be dishonored, or to enhance honor when the odds were hopeless and there was no prospect of either survival or a warrior's death in battle. It was not a decision to be made lightly.

The admiral ignored the currents of uncertainty that ran through the bridge around him. He took up the knife he had used to kill Khirgh, knelt beside the command chair, and placed the point of the blade directly above his heart.

Honor shall flow to the warrior who is true, to his hrai, to his comrades, to his people, and to himself, for only the true warrior shall know the gods hereafter.

His last thought was of the warriors under his command. He wished them all a chance at glory in death.

Then he drove the point of the dagger home, and felt the blood running free.

Shuttle *Juneau Delta*
Vaku VIIa, Vaku System
1747 hours (CST)

The overloaded shuttle bucked and shuddered as it descended through the roiling atmosphere toward the planet's surface. Donald Graham held on to the stick and fought to keep the craft on course as it bled off speed, all too conscious of his precious cargo. Sadness vied with relief within him as he contemplated the planet below. Three of the cruiser's shuttles had escaped the *Juneau*'s destruction, and they had collected enough lifepods en route to pack each of the craft with survivors. But many more had died, including Commander Lindstrom and the entire contingent aboard Shuttle *Alpha*, caught by the last explosions that had consumed *Juneau* while trying to rescue a cluster of lifepods that hadn't won clear of the ship.

Three shuttles packed to the gills . . . maybe a hundred men and women, all told, out of the cruiser's complement of three hundred sixty. It was hard to even think of the loss of two-thirds of his shipmates.

But for the moment Graham couldn't afford to let emotion tear at him. He was the senior surviving officer left out of the *Juneau*'s wardroom, and he had a responsibility to the survivors. The main job at the moment was to find a safe place to land and pray the conditions on the surface of this miserable planet wouldn't be too harsh. It was listed as "marginally habitable" in the navigation files, but his sensor readings didn't look promising.

A few degrees off his heading, the sensors were registering a concentration of metal and a few sporadic energy readings. That would be the Kilrathi survivors who had made it down earlier, from the damaged escort ship and whatever fighters and escape vessels had managed to get clear of the carrier. His first impulse was to put plenty of distance between his survivors and the Cats.

Then Graham considered again, and moved the stick to bank left and line up on the sensor readings.

He had no way of knowing what had happened to the Cats. They might be strong enough to be a real threat to the human survivors, in which case a quick overflight before they realized there were humans in the area might be the one chance Graham would have for estimating the danger. And if they were in worse shape than the *Juneau*'s survivors, there was always the chance the humans could overpower them and make use of whatever equipment and supplies they had on hand. After all, the shuttles carried plenty of people, but little else. They needed food, water, shelter . . . just about everything, in fact.

The shuttle broke through a cloud layer and Graham saw the wreck of the Cat escort ship spread out below. They'd come down hard, no doubt about that. Close by were a handful of shuttles and a line of fighters drawn up on a reasonably smooth stretch of ground. Figures were racing back and forth across the open plain, some stopping to point or raise clawed hands to the sky in defiance.

Graham swallowed, his eyes on those fighters. If they took off . . .

He reached for the control that would activate the shuttle's weapons pod. Kilrathi had never been prone to surrender, even in the face of overwhelming odds. But that ragtag group on the ground looked confused and unready to fight. Could he force them to surrender?

Or persuade them that they had to work together with the human survivors if either group was going to see their homes again before the brown dwarf's strange radiation filtered through the clouds and killed them slowly.

• CHAPTER 1

> *"Fortunate is the Warrior who meets Death in Battle; no true Warrior should die in bed with his claws sheathed."*
>
> from the Second Codex
> 3:18:12

Shuttle Port Three, Moonbase Tycho
Luna, Terra System
1228 hours (CST), 2670.275

Commodore (Ret.) Jason Bondarevsky leaned against the railing overlooking the reception area for Shuttle Port Three and shook his head in dismay. It was hard to believe so much could change in a matter of months, but the evidence was there before his eyes. It was the end of an era . . . or perhaps it was the start of a new one. Jason Bondarevsky wasn't sure he liked either option much.

"Credit for your thoughts, skipper," a soft contralto voice spoke up from behind him.

"Don't waste your money, Sparks," he said, turning to meet the newcomer. Lieutenant (Ret.) Janet "Sparks" McCullough was dressed in civilian clothes, though like

Bondarevsky she was entitled to wear the Terran Confederation Navy uniform if she so desired. Her taste, though, ran to plain coveralls, the garb she'd been comfortable with ever since she'd started out in the service as an enlisted technician. Since then she'd risen through the ranks, and later earned a commission, but Sparks still had a taste for the nuts and bolts of technical work, and dressed to suit that taste.

Still, even her baggy coveralls couldn't hide the fact that she was an attractive woman, though she often seemed determined to ignore that fact completely.

"Seems strange to have this mausoleum so empty," she said. "You think they're going to sell the whole place off for scrap, or what?"

"Wouldn't put it past them," he said.

The last time he'd been here the decades-long war with the Kilrathi Empire had still been raging on, and Moonbase Tycho had been a busy hub of the Terran war effort. That had been only ten months ago, when the fortunes of war had been anything but smiling upon humanity. Bondarevsky had been rotated back to Tycho suffering from multiple wounds suffered during the desperate battle when the Terran Confederation's monster weapons platform, *Behemoth*, had been destroyed by the Kilrathi after a traitor had betrayed details of its weaknesses to the Empire. The *Coventry*, flagship of his beloved destroyer squadron, had been heavily engaged in the fighting and nearly torn apart before the whole thing was through.

Back then, Bondarevsky had been sure the end was near for all Mankind. After a war that had gone on for so long that most of the combatants had grown up never knowing peace, the Kilrathi had been poised for a last strike that would have knocked Earth's defenses out and left the Empire unchallenged in this part of space.

The air of desperation at Tycho Moonbase had been palpable.

And then, abruptly, everything had changed.

Bondarevsky's gaze sought out the oversized video rig that dominated one wall of the reception area. He remembered watching the ISN news update while he and Sparks awaited the arrival of Admiral Geoff Tolwyn's shuttle . . . the reports, carefully slanted by a worried Confederation government but all too clearly conveying word of a string of fresh defeats on the frontiers . . . the woman sitting beside him who cursed the Kilrathi and the Administration with equal vehemence as she listened to the newscaster . . .

And then came the bulletin. A daring raid with an experimental planet-busting bomb had penetrated deep into Kilrathi space, to the Imperial homeworld itself, and when the bomb went off it literally shook Kilrah apart. The Emperor and his power-hungry grandson had perished along with swarms of their subjects, and the shocked survivors of the Imperium had sued for peace, a concept alien to their warrior natures until that stunning moment of utter defeat.

That moment had changed everything. The peace talks had dragged on before a treaty was finally signed at Torgo, but from the moment of Kilrah's destruction everyone had known the war was over at last. Bondarevsky remembered how the same woman who'd been cursing had started cheering, hugging and kissing everyone in sight. She'd embraced him so tightly that his shattered arm had hurt like hell, but in the general euphoria it hadn't seemed very important. Mankind had won a splendid victory, and with the end of the fighting the citizen-soldiers of the Confederation could lay down their weapons and return to the plow, to the ways of peace.

Looking at the shuttle port now, Bondarevsky wondered

if they hadn't been far too hasty in their rush to renounce a lifetime of fighting.

The Confederation had started demobilizing even before the final details of the treaty were hammered out at Torgo. Ships were decommissioned; soldiers, spacemen, and marines were mustered out in droves. The Confederation's military machine was transformed in an incredibly short time.

He'd stood through plenty of ceremonies, heard more high-minded speeches than he'd ever thought he could endure. *Thank you . . . credit to the Service . . . conspicuous valor in action against the Kilrathi . . . heroic dedication to duty . . .* But in the end it had been clear that the Confed Navy wasn't looking for heroes any more. They wanted peacekeepers, timeservers, administrators and bureaucrats, men and women who knew how to carry out policy and show the flag, not fighters who would push the envelope in the name of winning at any cost. Bondarevsky hadn't bothered to wait for the Navy to let him know his services wouldn't be needed any longer. He'd put in for retirement, with a courtesy promotion to commodore, a half-pay pension, and the prospect of a long and frustrating recovery from his wounds.

He looked down at his right hand and flexed it, frowning. The doctors hadn't been able to save the arm, and the bionic replacement still didn't feel like it was really a part of him yet. But he'd been pronounced fit two weeks earlier. If the war had still been on, he'd have been bombarding the brass with daily requests for a chance to return to active duty, and devil take the physical therapist's recommendations. But Bondarevsky wasn't in the Navy any more. *He* didn't belong any more.

Too many changes . . . In Tycho Moonbase, working on a complement less than a quarter of the wartime establishment. In the Confederation Navy, beating swords into plowshares with dizzying speed.

And in Jason Bondarevsky, who'd looked forward to the day the war ended for most of his life, but found he wasn't equipped for the peacetime existence he'd always hoped for.

Sparks followed his glance to the plastilimb arm and gave him a quirky half-smile. "Afraid the warranty is running out?" she asked. "Don't worry about it, skipper. You've nearly got it now. All you need is some more practice."

"If I do, it's because of your help, Sparks," he said. She'd been aboard *Coventry* during the last battle as Damage Control Officer, and she had led the party that had saved his life after the Kilrathi missile had struck the flag bridge, killing the other six people in the cramped compartment. Bondarevsky would have perished with the others, from blood loss or decompression or lack of oxygen, if it hadn't been for her quick thinking that day. And when he'd taken retirement after the treaty was signed she'd left the service as well, looking after him during his convalescence and overseeing his physical therapy. "I don't know how I'd've made it without you."

She shrugged and grinned, her very best "Aw, shucks" routine. "The way they were downsizing the fleet, skipper, I wouldn't have lasted long anyway. During wartime a maverick can come up to officer's country through the cargo hatch the way I did, but nobody wants you around in peacetime unless you're an officer and a gentleman . . . or lady, as the case may be. I figured you needed the help."

He studied her for a long moment. Sparks had served with him for a long time now, ever since the days of the *Tarawa*'s deep penetration raid on Kilrah back before the Battle of Earth. The relationship between a fighter pilot and his crew chief was almost always incredibly close, because the pilot put his life in the crew chief's hands every time he took his craft out of the hangar. The two had hovered on the edge of a romance for a time following the death of Bondarevsky's first love in *Tarawa*'s raid, but he'd pulled back from anything serious. Not only was it a bad idea for a ship's captain to have a dalliance with one of his officers while on active service, but Bondarevsky hadn't been willing to risk losing another Svetlana. Since that one brief kiss a few years back, he and Sparks had been friends unwilling to risk anything more.

But one way or another Bondarevsky had always placed absolute trust in Sparks, a trust that had carried over after she'd earner her commission and moved on to other duties. Somehow, though, he'd never really considered what drove her. Fact was, Sparks could have stayed in the service without any trouble at all. After the devastating battles of the decades-long Kilrathi war, technical officers with her talents were much in demand even with the Fleet's downsizing program. But she had elected to follow him into retirement in the seaside home he'd purchased in Odessa . . . and now into what amounted to a self-imposed exile.

An announcement over the PA system cut short his reverie before he could say anything further. *"Attention, attention, Landreich Shuttlecraft* Themistocles Alpha *now docking at Shuttle Port Three."*

"That's us," he said quietly. "Got your gear?"

Sparks nodded as Bondarevsky hitched his kitbag over his shoulder and turned toward the lift that would take him into the reception area below. She followed him along the empty catwalk, and somehow the fact that she was there made it easier for Bondarevsky to make the short but monumental trek.

He'd put one era behind him. Today it was time to start a new one.

The security doors leading into the shuttle bay still hadn't been opened when the two officers reached them. Bondarevsky couldn't tell if that was because the work crews were short-handed, or because of some perverse desire on the part of those in authority to make the new arrivals wait before they could gain admission. Landreich was still regarded as a haven for outlaws and criminals, even though the frontiersmen there had made the difference between victory and defeat when the Kilrathi attacked Earth itself and a Landreich squadron had turned the tide when everything seemed to be coming apart.

The news was full of continuing problems between the Confederation and Landreich these days. The colonials refused to accept Terran authority; the Confederation accused Landreich of deliberately provoking trouble with their neighbors on the frontier, including the newly peace-loving Kilrathi. Knowing President Kruger as Bondarevsky did, it was a sure bet that Landreich would never back down, right or wrong.

Maybe that was why he'd accepted Landreich's offer of employment. They could be an exasperating bunch, but one and all they were the kind of people he could relate to, fighters who never backed down from a challenge, and threw out the rule book and winged it when they were in a furball.

A marine sergeant behind the desk at the security door cocked his head and raised one white-gloved hand to his earpiece receiver. Then he touched a stud on the console in front of him and stood up, drawing himself to attention. With his crisp dress uniform and his precise motions, he might have been an android responding to a carefully-composed protocol program.

The officer who stepped through the opening doors was a contrast to the wooden-featured sergeant in every possible way. He was young—probably not yet twenty standard years—and he was anything but stiff and solemn as he stared around the shuttle port with wide eyes and a broad, easygoing grin on his open but weather-beaten features. His shock of ginger hair was longer than Confederation regulations would have permitted, and there was a cheerful spark in his eyes. As for his uniform . . . well, the less said about that the better, Bondarevsky decided. Landreich had never had the money, time, or inclination to organize their military forces into anything as rigid as the Confederation's, and they generally relied on what they could steal, scavenge, salvage, or buy on the cheap when it came to uniforms and equipment. Bondarevsky recognized elements of the young officer's uniform as coming from Confed supplies, probably salvaged from *Bannockburn* or one of the other Terran ships that had operated in Landreich space back in the old days. But the man's jacket was decidedly nonregulation, looking like something out of a holo-vid Western—leather, with plenty of pockets and old-fashioned buttons running down the front. The youngster wore a pistol on one hip, and the holster and the protruding butt of the weapon itself had the look of frequent use. Had they been like that when they'd come to this young man? Bondarevsky had a feeling that was something he shouldn't take for granted. Young he might be, but growing up in the Landreich with the constant threat of Kilrathi attack only one of many dangers a colonial faced had a way of making a kid grow up fast . . . and dangerous.

The Marine saluted him stiffly, and the newcomer returned it with a casual, offhand flourish. "At ease, man, at ease," he said, the lilt in his voice fitting his appearance.

"They tell me there's a pile of forms I'm to be seeing to, so the sooner you turn me loose on 'em the sooner me and my mates can start putting in some shore leave."

"Excuse me, er . . ." Bondarevsky knew from his shoulder patch that the youngster was an officer, but he couldn't spot anything that looked like rank insignia.

"Harper," the young man replied, turning his easy smile on Bondarevsky. "Aengus Harper, Lieutenant in the Navy of the Free Republic of Landreich, at your service, sir."

"Jason Bondarevsky, Lieutenant. I'm—"

"The Bear himself!" Harper exclaimed. "Should have recognized you from your pictures! After Old Max, you're one of the biggest names back home, you know. Pleased to make your acquaintance, sir, right pleased!"

Bondarevsky was a little taken aback. He wasn't used to the younger man's tone, which hovered somewhere between mocking respect and outright hero worship. "I was supposed to meet one of your passengers, Lieutenant," he said slowly. "Admiral . . ."

"Richards, of course. Never you fear, sir, he'll be along in a minute or two. Is it true what they're telling me about you joining up with us, sir?"

That earned Bondarevsky a look from the sergeant. Evidently that was what it took to break through their famous iron reserve—the word that one of Terra's naval heroes was thinking of joining the renegades of Landreich.

"Nothing's been signed yet, Mr. Harper," Bondarevsky told him. "But Admiral Richards seemed to think it was something I should look into . . . and I have to admit the offer is tempting." He gestured toward Sparks. "This is Lieutenant McCullough. She's also interested in a new career."

"Is that young Bondarevsky?" The voice was as strong

and well-modulated as Bondarevsky remembered it, and he turned to see the thin form of Admiral Vance Richards striding towards him from the open security door. Unlike Harper, he wore a full-dress uniform that was everything a senior officer of an interstellar power deserved, dazzling silver trim against midnight black with a rack of decorations, from both Terra and the Landreich covering his breast. But the man inside the uniform hadn't changed much in the last four years, since he'd served as Bondarevsky's CO in the campaign that culminated at the Battle of Earth. If the last wisps of hair on his nearly bald head were a little bit thinner, and his gait was a little slower, he still had the fire in his eyes that had always marked him out from those around him. "It's *good* to see you again. From the reply you sent last month, I wasn't sure you'd be here."

"Back then I wasn't sure myself, Admiral," Bondarevsky told him. "But I've had time to think about your offer, sir. And it's a hell of a lot better than signing on a merchant ship or piloting shuttles for PanSystem Passenger Service."

Vance extended a long, slender hand. For a moment Bondarevsky hesitated to take it. He was embarrassed by his bionic arm, which didn't quite look or feel as natural as advertised, and he still had to concentrate hard to use it for fine manipulation. But after a moment he took the Admiral's hand in his plastilimb fingers and carefully shook it. The sensors in his palm and fingertips told him that Vance had lost none of his unexpected strong grip since the last time they'd seen one another.

The Admiral met his eyes with a serious look. "I heard about what happened on *Coventry*. It must have been hell when they told you about the arm."

"Yes, sir," he said, dropping into a formal military

tone to hide the emotion those words triggered inside him. "Yes, sir, it was."

Richards looked away. "I know, Jason. Believe me, I know. Everyone lost somebody to that damned war."

In the awkward pause that followed Bondarevsky found himself wondering what the Admiral was thinking about from his own mysterious past. Vance Richards had been the chief of Naval Intelligence for the entire Confederation before taking "retirement" to head up the secret mission that had put Confed ships, including Bondarevsky's old carrier, under the command of the Landreich during the months leading up to the Battle of Earth. His life had been shrouded in secrecy for years, and he never talked about himself. But the bleak tone of his voice hinted at losses of his own.

"If I might be remindin' you, Admiral," Aengus Harper broke the mood with a light tone, "it's late for your appointment you are. And you'll have to be seeing that flock of VIPs afterward."

"Thank you, Lieutenant," Richards said with a faint smile. "And to think I invested all that money in a portable computer secretary."

"I'll not delay you, Admiral," Bondarevsky said. "I assume we'll get a chance to see you on the ship later?"

Richards shook his head. "I'd like it if you'd join me, Jason," he said. "I think you'll be interested in my . . . appointment. Someone you haven't seen for a while, I'd imagine."

"As you wish, Admiral," Bondarevsky responded.

"You'll have to get out of practice with all the formalities, lad, if you're going to join the Landreich. Don't forget, our President's a wanted mutineer and our fleet would likely lose an engagement with a squadron of target drones. Isn't that what you told me, back when we first got a look at Kruger's little corner of the frontier?"

"Things change, Admiral," Bondarevsky said with a grin.

"Your luggage, sir?" Harper asked before he could turn away. "So I can see to getting it stowed while you hobnob with the great?"

Bondarevsky indicated the kitbag he'd set down beside the desk while waiting for the security doors to open. "It's all yours, Lieutenant," he said. "Sparks, if you could go with Mr. Harper, I'm sure you can get us settled in by the time I get back."

"Aye aye, skipper," Sparks responded. "I'll take care of things for you.

"Just this, sir?" Harper asked, raising a sardonic eyebrow as he took the kitbag. "You cut your ties with the Earth an' all, heading out for a new life on the frontier, and all you care to take is a single kitbag? They say the Spirit urges us to travel light, sir, but I'm thinking this is a mite extreme."

Bondarevsky shrugged. "*Coventry* took a direct hit in Officer's Country during the battle, and there wasn't much left of my personal effects. Since then . . . who has the urge to gather a lot of junk, when you've lived your whole life out of a flight deck locker?"

"Well, sir," Harper said, studying him with an appraising eye, " 'tis plain you'll be fitting in with the rest of us poor but honest colonials. Some of the lads were afraid you'd turn out to be a pompous twit, all rules and regulations and such-like debs."

That made Richards smile more broadly, despite the mild profanity. "Debs"—from debris—was one of those swear words that had entered the lexicon as a result of the war. Most Confederation officers maintained an official air of disapproval when it came to swearing among their juniors . . . but Richards had been out on the frontier for years now, and evidently had cultivated a more relaxed attitude in the interim. "Well, Lieutenant, I'm glad our new recruit has your full approval. I'll leave you to your duties."

"Aye aye, sir," Harper told him, but the gleam in his eye was mocking.

As they walked together down the concourse Bondarevsky heard the older man chuckling. "Pity young Mr. Harper didn't know you when you had *Tarawa,*" he said. "Maybe he would have had a . . . less charitable view of you back then."

"Implying I was a pompous twit, Admiral?"

"Not precisely. But I can recall that you weren't exactly impressed with the way old Kruger ran things. And you didn't hesitate to let him hear about it. He still talks about you, you know."

"I said what I had to say, sir," Bondarevsky told the admiral, bristling.

"That, my dear Jason, is exactly why he still talks about you," Richards said. "And why you're still just about the only Confed officer I've ever heard him speak of with anything remotely like approval." He paused. "I've seen the young lady before, I'm sure, but I can't place her."

"One of my officers on *Coventry,* sir," Bondarevsky said. "Before that she was a petty officer crew chief on *Tarawa.* You probably remember her from back then."

"And she wants to join the FRLN too?" The admiral raised an eyebrow. Bondarevsky remembered that he had a reputation for frowning on loose morals in the people under his command, a legacy of long service in Intelligence where concern over security gave rise to a strong desire to avoid scandal of any sort among sensitive personnel. Was Richards afraid there was some improper relationship between him and Sparks?

The thought made him want to smile. "She's a top-notch techie, Admiral," he said quietly. "And I owe her more than I could ever pay back. I figured Kruger's crew could find a place for her holding together some of those old tubs of theirs."

Richards shrugged. "Oh, I'm sure of that. Just so long as there aren't any . . . entanglements. Things are going to be tricky enough without introducing any extra distractions."

"I can assure you, Admiral, that entanglements are about the last thing I'd want right now, myself. You can count on my full attention, sir. But if you have any doubts, I'll tell her I didn't have any authority to suggest she sign on with the Republic."

"That won't be necessary, Jason," Richards said. "Even if you were involved with her . . . sometimes my new-found casual Landreich face slips and I revert to type. You'll have to put up with it sometimes, I'm afraid, if you're going to be working with me again."

The admiral changed the subject to ask for details about the *Behemoth* fighting and *Coventry*'s brush with the Kilrathi. From long experience of Richards and his secretive ways Bondarevsky didn't ask where they were going or who they were supposed to meet. Instead he answered the older man's questions, and the talk shifted to postwar politics and the question of defense policy as they continued to walk through the long, empty corridors. It was no surprise that Richards took a dim view of the situation that had developed in the three months since the signing of the peace treaty.

"I'm telling you, Jason, the Confed government won the war and then turned right around and lost the peace," Richards said angrily. "Instead of making sure the Cats finally got the idea of what it really means to surrender, those dumb bastards pulled back at the last minute and left so damned many loopholes I wouldn't be surprised to find they were right back where they started in another ten or twenty years."

"Admiral?" Bondarevsky fixed him with a surprised look. "Everything I heard about the treaty sounded pretty damned good." He hesitated. "And if we'd made the terms any harsher we might have ended up with another Versailles."

"Twentieth Century, right? You were always the history buff."

"Yes, sir," he answered. "World War One. The Allies toppled the Germans and then imposed an impossible peace settlement on them. Twenty years later they were at war again, and one of the big factors was the German anger over the way they'd been treated. When the Second World War ended, treaty terms to Germany and Japan were a lot less restrictive, and both powers evolved into stable allies for the Western powers."

"Yeah," Richards said. "I've studied the period too, lately. Max Kruger likes history as well, you know. Well, there's a big difference. After World War Two the Allies moved in on the Axis powers. Occupation. Foreign aid. Enforced development of Western-style democracies. But the Confederation didn't do that with the Kilrathi, Jason. We wiped out their leadership and damn near destroyed their entire culture when we took out Kilrah with the Temblor Bomb. But we didn't offer anything constructive to replace what they lost. Since the end of the war the Kilrathi clans have been allowed to do pretty much whatever they please, and what a hell of a lot of them please involves trying to put together petty clan-run states that don't care about the treaty at all. There've been raids all along the frontier, and the

Confederation doesn't do a damn thing about them. That's my real reason for being here, you know. Max Kruger wants me to deliver another protest to the Confed government over the latest string of Kilrathi raids across the Landreich border. Not that it'll do a damn bit of good."

"You're sure the government won't act?"

"We've got our sources, Jason. Fact is, the level of collective guilt inside the government is so damned high right now that I doubt they'd stop a Kilrathi fleet if it raided Terra right now."

"Guilt, sir?"

Richards nodded. "Over using the Temblor Bomb. Think about it, Jason. It wasn't quite genocide—blowing up one planet isn't going to wipe out a star-faring race as widespread as the Kilrathi, after all—but any way you look at it we took out a hell of a lot of innocent civilians just to get rid of Thrakhath and his doddering grandfather. And the effect on the Kilrathi culture . . . I've seen copies of some of the studies made when the strategy of going after Kilrah was first hatched, and most of them predicted the Kilrathi race wouldn't be able to weather losing their cultural center nearly as well as they've managed. Even so, the effects are serious. We took out their Emperor, their homeworld, their religious and cultural shrines, most of their major clan leaders and everything they recognized as holding their civilization together. What we've got left out there are a bunch of angry warriors who are likely to become barbarians of a sort . . . but barbarians who still have plenty of spaceships and high-tech weapons to use when they decide it's time for revenge." Richards stopped and looked at Jason with bleak eyes. "But what the Confed leaders are seeing doesn't go that far. They're just looking at the short-term effects. And they're bending over backwards to not seem to be kicking the Kilrathi while they're down. Did you notice how quickly the media started calling the peace accord the 'Treaty of Ko-bar Yagar'? It was originally announced as the Treaty of Torgo. That's their name for the system, even though they only captured it from us near the end of the war. Originally they were supposed to be out of there in six months, but rumor has it they've been given an indefinite extension on pulling out. And meantime we use their nomenclature 'to preserve the dignity of the Kilrathi people.' " He gave an undignified snort.

"You're starting to sound a lot like President Kruger, Admiral," Bondarevsky commented. "You haven't turned against the Confederation entirely, have you?" Inwardly he couldn't help but feel disturbed by the old spymaster's words. They dovetailed with his own reservations about the direction the Confederation had taken since the war . . . and he respected Vance Richards too much to simply dismiss the man's opinion.

"There's plenty who'd say that's exactly what I've done, Jason," the old man said softly. Every day of his sixty-five-plus years was evident in his tired voice. "But the fact is, I'm still doing the same job I was doing when we took the Free Corps out to the Landreich. The best hope for old Terra is a strong defense on the frontiers, especially now when the Confederation seems determined to drop the ball. Out there in the Landreich Max Kruger's trying to hold the line, and I figure if I can help him, I'm still doing my part for Earth as well." He fixed Bondarevsky with a steely eye, and all at once seemed to gather his old energy again. "What about you? You had your doubts about joining us, but you showed up here anyway. What kind of a life do *you* want to lead, now that the war is over?"

"Admiral, I respect you too much to lie to you,"

Bondarevsky said slowly. "For a while all I wanted was to see the war over, but once it was done with I found out I don't really know what to do with my life. Maybe if Svetlana had made it . . ." He pushed aside that memory, too. "So I decided to take you up on your offer of a job in the Landreich because it looked like the closest thing to the old life I was likely to find. Now . . . I don't know what to think any more. To hear you talk, the war might as well not be over at all. But I can't say if my motive is selfish, or if I can share the vision you're laying out, or what. If you're looking for sincere converts, maybe I'm not your man after all."

Richards smiled. "I'm too cynical to want converts, my boy. I'd rather put my faith in enlightened self-interest. It pays better dividends in the long run. I don't care about your motives, as long as you're willing to get back out there where you belong and make sure the Kilrathi don't cross the frontier again."

They had reached the door of one of the base VIP lounges, and Richards gestured for Bondarevsky to precede him into the large, opulent room. Like so much else in Moonbase Tycho it was almost empty, and the figure seated at the table near the center of the room caught his eye immediately. A stocky man with a shock of graying hair and the aquiline features of a born aristocrat, the figure wore the dress uniform of a Confederation rear-admiral and had decorations every bit as impressive as the ones Richards wore. He stepped forward with a welcoming smile on his face, extending his hand, his words coming in the clipped British accent Bondarevsky remembered so well.

"Vance! Good to see you again, after all this time. You still like the rustic life on the frontier?" Then he turned to Bondarevsky with an equally hearty greeting. "And you, my boy. I'm glad to see you, too."

Again he had to force himself to take the other man's hand in his bionic grip. "It's . . . good to see you again, Admiral," he said, trying to hide his surprise.

He hadn't thought to see Rear Admiral Geoffrey Tolwyn again, certainly not at a Confederation military base. Not Tolwyn, the man who had come so close to losing the war . . . the man whose *Behemoth* project had shattered a Terran squadron and cost Bondarevsky his command and his arm.

The man whose court-martial had been a sensation across the Confederation, and whose acquittal had aroused indignation on nearly every world in the human sphere.

• CHAPTER 2

> *"Fang and claw, sharp eyes and alert ears and the nose of a hunter, these are the tools of the Ideal Warrior, but they are as nothing without the spirit and heart of a fighter."*
>
> from the Fifth Codex
> 10:23:05

VIP Lounge, Moonbase Tycho
Luna, Terra System
1310 hours (CST), 2670.275

Jason Bondarevsky studied Admiral Tolwyn as they all took seats around the table and punched in their drink orders on the small keypads in front of them. Over the years Bondarevsky had come to regard Tolwyn as one of his most powerful navy patrons, a man willing to recommend him for promotions and important assignments and generally helping along his career. Ever since his attack on Kilrah and the mission Tolwyn had staged against orders to pull him out Jason felt as if his very life was owed to the Admiral and it was debt he would never forget. He'd always looked up to the man, even when one or another of the admiral's schemes

44

was putting him squarely in the line of fire somewhere out on the Kilrathi frontier. But, like most of the rest of the Confederation, he'd been stunned to find Tolwyn masterminding the *Behemoth* project. And when it was all over, the collapse of the plan and the high cost Bondarevsky had personally paid had certainly colored his opinion of the man who'd been so important to him for so many years.

"So, Vance," Tolwyn was saying, "how was the trip in?"

"The usual," Richards told him with a grimace. "When I retired from Intelligence I was used to quarters you could stand up in. Ever since I got out to that benighted frontier all I ever get to travel on is destroyers or cruisers, and they've got just about enough room to *think* about swinging a pet cat . . . but only if you want to risk banging your head when you think it."

Bondarevsky joined in the laugh, but he could still remember how good it felt to have a ship, any ship, around him. He'd loved the little *Coventry*, fast, responsive, and maneuverable despite the minor inconveniences of her small size.

"I watched your approach on the monitors," Tolwyn said. "Cruiser?"

Richards nodded. "LCA. She's the ex-TCS *Andromache*. Now the *Themistocles*, if you please. Old Max has discovered the fine art of historical pretensions. Cruisers get named after famous military men who ended up in exile." He smiled. "The Republic picked the ship up for a song and refitted her from bow to stern. Crash job . . . Kruger's got a team of specialists ready to turn around anything we can buy, salvage, or cobble together in a few weeks, and he's pushing everybody hard to build up the fleet ASAP."

"So he still figures it'll come to a fight, then." Tolwyn

made it a statement rather than a question. There was a brief lull in the conversation as a waitress brought their drinks. Richards didn't answer Tolwyn until she had gone back to the bar.

"No question about it, Geoff. Things are even worse than when I talked to you last time. The whole damned mess looks like it's coming to a head out there in the next few months, and we need you more than ever."

Tolwyn gave a grim nod. "I figured as much. I may be out of the mainstream these days, but I still have my sources. And the facts are there, no matter how hard the government is working to ignore them."

"So you're ready to come aboard, then? No more excuses?" Richards gave Tolwyn a sour look. "You know we could have used you three months ago."

"Back then I still thought I had a career, Vance. I thought the court-martial would clear me completely and let me get back to work."

"You *were* cleared, Admiral," Bondarevsky said quietly.

Tolwyn gave him a bleak look. "Oh, the verdict was 'Not Guilty,' son, but that isn't the same as being cleared. Not by a long shot. You should know that if anyone does."

He thought back to the aftermath of the *Gettysburg* mutiny and gave a reluctant nod. Back then it had been Bondarevsky on trial, and even after the court pronounced he'd done the right thing his career might have fallen apart then and there. But Tolwyn had come to his rescue then.

Perhaps he owed the same kind of support to the admiral now, no matter how bad things had looked the day *Behemoth* went to debris.

Tolwyn was still talking. "Hell, I'm surprised they acquitted me, now that I look back on it. I had the weapon that could have won the war, and I just plain blew it. If it hadn't been for Paladin and his Temblor Bomb—and our old friend Blair—the Cats would be squashing the last resistance down on Earth right about now. And I'm too damned old to go down fighting in a guerrilla resistance. We were lucky we stopped the furry bastards when and where we did . . . and I'm sorry to say I didn't have much to do with carrying it off. I'd . . . kind of wanted to be in on the kill." The admiral looked toward the big window that overlooked the floor of Tycho, an unfathomable expression in his eyes.

"There were some other things we were developing," he said softly, "other things that at times I'm not really sure of, but they would never have been ready in time."

"Such as?" Richard's asked casually.

Tolwyn looked up, smiled and shook his head. "On hold now, so of no consequence unless they might be needed later on."

That made Bondarevsky frown again. It seemed so out of character for Geoff Tolwyn, one of the most decent men he'd ever met, to be involved in a project that would have led to mass genocide. *Behemoth*, a massive weapons platform designed to destroy an entire planet, would have killed countless noncombatants on Kilrah if it had been unleashed. The Temblor Bomb had done the same thing in the end, but that had been the brainchild of General James "Paladin" Taggart of Special Operations, an outfit that fought under the unofficial motto "Any Path to Victory." Tolwyn had always seemed more like a gentlemanly officer of the old school, willing to do what had to be done to win, but always trying to stay on the right side of the line that marked the difference between civilized warfare and mere slaughter.

"Well, Geoff, you're past all that now," Richards said

softly. "You've got a new start to look forward to out in the Landreich."

"I thought I saw in the news, sir, that you didn't take retirement," Bondarevsky ventured, feeling unsure of himself. It was awkward trying to make small talk with Admiral Tolwyn. The man had been his mentor and patron for years . . . but he'd also committed some terrible blunders lately, and it was hard to know which of his two sides he was talking to now. "Did you change your mind?"

Tolwyn shook his head. "Not exactly. I'm officially still on the Admiral's List, but it's been made very clear that I'm not likely to see so much as a Supply Depot command for the foreseeable future. I'm on an extended leave, as it were . . . *very* extended. And free to take up other positions, so long as I'm available if our lords and masters should suddenly decide I'd be useful. I feel like a fighting Admiral after Napoleon was defeated, beached on half-pay."

"Don't you figure that's just what they'll do, if they hear you're heading out to Landreich?" Richards demanded. "You've made a lot of enemies over the years, Geoff, and you could be handing them the perfect opportunity to land you in some real trouble."

Tolwyn shook his head. "Not bloody likely," he said. "First off, I've accumulated enough leave that I can take my time coming back even if I do get orders to report. But the fact is, even the ones who're out for my blood will be just as happy to see the back of me." He gave a quiet sigh. "I'm just not that important any more, Vance. I spent all my clout on *Behemoth*, and then I blew it."

"Then you should make the break final and resign, Geoff," Richards told him. "Come out to the Landreich and get a brand new start in life."

"You know me, Vance," Tolwyn said. His broad, weathered face had the stubborn expression Bondarevsky had seen a dozen times in the middle of a battle, the look of a man determined to see it through his way or not at all. "I like to keep my options open. Right now there's nothing to tie me to the Confederation. I'm as effectively retired as I would be if I'd sent my papers in. But some day things could be different . . ." and his voice trailed off.

"So you're telling me you're still not really committing to the FRLN, is that it?" Richards' voice held a note of irritation. "Kruger isn't going to be happy, Geoff. He doesn't like people with divided loyalties."

"Well, he doesn't have to like me," Tolwyn said. "But that's the only way I come aboard, Vance. If you guys really want me, those are the terms. I won't run out on you when you need me . . . but I have to be able to keep my options open. I'm still loyal to the Confederation. Someday there might be something I can do to make up for what happened with *Behemoth*, and I aim to be able to be there for it."

Richards shrugged. "If that's the way you want it, Geoff," he said. "I just wish I understood what it is you think is going to change around here."

Tolwyn gave him a tight-lipped smile. "You're the intelligence man, Vance. You find out, and I'll tell you if you've got it right."

Bondarevsky looked from Richards to Tolwyn, sensing the strong undercurrent of unspoken thoughts and emotions. He agreed with Richards . . . he wished he knew what it was that Tolwyn was holding back. After the *Behemoth* disaster, he was worried about Tolwyn's possible performance. His management of that last campaign had been a poor job compared to the operations Bondarevsky had seen him involved in previously. If he'd lost his edge, would he be able to get it back? And how did his secret plans for the future enter into it all?

As if aware of the younger man's scrutiny, Tolwyn turned to meet his gaze with ice-blue eyes. "You're quiet, Mr. Bondarevsky," he remarked. "How much do you know about the situation out in the Landreich?"

"Not much, sir," he said. "I've learned to take the news reports with enough salt to fill up a hangar deck, but aside from a few dark hints from Admiral Richards I can't say I really know what's going on out there . . . or how we're supposed to be a part of it all."

"You're smart to ignore TNC, at least," Richards commented. "Did you catch that report by Barbara Miles last night?"

"The pirate raid story?" Tolwyn asked.

"Yeah." When Bondarevsky shook his head Richards leaned forward in his chair with an intense frown creasing his forehead. "According to the news channels, there was an attack on Ilios last week. Heavy casualties in the district of Dardania, property destroyed, several industrial centers put out of operation for weeks, maybe months. All very deplorable." His frown deepened. "And it's true, too . . . except that what they described as a 'pirate raid' was actually an attack by Kilrathi operating out of the Hralgkrak Province. We have proof, damn it, and we've shown it to the Confederation ambassador and sent details to the Joint Chiefs and the Office of Confederation Security and the goddamned Confederation Peace Commission. But they've passed the word to TNC news to play up this 'pirate' angle, and the Kilrathi don't get into the reports at all."

"You told me once that you've had some real pirate problems, too," Tolwyn said. He shifted in his chair. "I suppose there's just enough truth in their stories so that they can justify their position. And they'll tell you it's no good rocking the boat with the Kilrathi, or some such. Right? They've staked everything on the Treaty. If anyone outside the government got the idea that the whole Treaty was virtually a dead letter, the President wouldn't stand a chance. I doubt he'd get the luxury of impeachment proceedings."

"Maybe so," said Richards. "But Ilios was the most recent colony to join the Landreich. And it's one of our leading industrial worlds. Damn it, Geoff, things are getting serious out there. Except for a couple of raids back and forth, the Cats never saw any reason to press the attack against us. Our stretch of the frontier was too far away to be important to the main course of the war. But now that the Confederation's knocked out Kilrah, independent clans all through Cat space are striking out on their own—and their side of the frontier is as fresh and untouched as ours. Which means they have the strength to be a real threat, and they see the Landreich as easy pickings without the Confederation to back our play."

"So some Cat clan chief is playing at empire-building," Bondarevsky said. "And he's chosen the Landreich to be his first big conquest."

"Exactly," Richards said. "We're pretty sure the Haka Clan is behind the troubles we've been having. Ukar *dai* Ragark, the Governor of Hralgkrak, was no friend to Thrakhath and the Emperor when they were alive. He owed his particular position at the edge of nowhere to the fact that he was openly critical of the way Thrakhath conducted the Battle of Earth. Now that they're dead he's been turning up the propaganda to claim that the Empire only lost in the end because of incompetence and cowardice in the Imperial Palace."

" 'We were stabbed in the back,' " Bondarevsky said.

"What's that?" Tolwyn asked.

"Just a line out of the history books," he answered. He glanced over at Richards. "After World War I . . . the argument Hitler used to rally Germany behind his call for a new government that would restore the country's greatness."

"That's just about the line Ragark is taking," Richards said. "And pretty damn successfully, too, according to the reports we've been seeing. Ragark has a fair-sized battle fleet, plenty of ships that didn't see much combat action during the war. Fortunately they're mostly about the same as what we have in the Landreich, older ships that weren't good enough for Thrakhath's command. But they're enough to give Ragark some muscle, and he's set himself up as the warlord who can give the Kilrathi something to replace what they lost with Kilrah, a new spirit of victory. It's even taking on religious overtones . . . Kilrah perished because the Emperor lost touch with the old ways, the Word of the Codices, all that. It's powerful stuff . . . and with neither an Emperor nor a homeworld, a lot of Kilrathi are eating it up."

Bondarevsky looked down at the tabletop for a long moment. "Something doesn't make sense, though," he said. "Why should the government shift the blame to human pirates? I mean, all our dealings have been with Melek, haven't they? He formed the caretaker government after Kilrah was destroyed and negotiated the treaty afterwards. Why can't the Confederation take action against this Ragark as a renegade Kilrathi?"

"Who knows what goes through the minds of those bastards?" Richards said with a shrug. "Could be they're afraid the great unwashed masses can't tell a good Cat from a bad Cat. Lord knows the propaganda effort for the past few decades has certainly been devoted to peddling the message that the only good Cat is a dead one. Hell, our one genuine Cat hero turned out to be a traitor in the end."

Bondarevsky saw a spasm of emotion pass over Tolwyn's face. Ralgha *nar* Hhalles, the Kilrathi pilot who had joined the Confederation years ago, had been the spy who betrayed the secrets of the *Behemoth* to the enemy. And Tolwyn had trusted the renegade completely . . .

"I think it goes deeper than that," Tolwyn said quietly. "I think there are elements in the Confederation who would be quite pleased to see a Kilrathi warlord absorb the Landreich."

Richards gave him a look. "Now, Geoff, you know I'm no fan of the government. But, come on! You don't really think they're setting us up deliberately?"

"Well . . . maybe not," Tolwyn said, but he had that stubborn look again. "But you have to admit that the way things are going there's not much chance of Confederation intervention out in your stretch of space. And I've seen the same intelligence estimates you have, Vance. Ragark's forces can gobble up the Landreich for breakfast once he gets moving. The only thing that's likely to save your hides right now is the Cats' lack of cohesion without the Imperial system directing things. So whether it's deliberate or not, I'd say you've got plenty to worry about."

"*We've* got plenty to worry about," Richards corrected him. "We're in this thing together . . . unless you're backing out after all."

"I'm with you, Vance," Tolwyn snapped. "I've got just as many good reasons for wanting to help the Landreich as you do. Maybe one or two more."

There was an awkward moment of silence as the two strong-willed admirals regarded one another thoughtfully. Bondarevsky took the opportunity to change the subject.

"Couldn't you take your evidence straight to the people, Admiral?" he asked Richards. "Let them know about the Kilrathi involvement? Surely the Confederation government doesn't control every news channel."

"Maybe not all of them, but all the ones that matter, son," Richards told him gruffly. "And at any rate, the propaganda effort's being stepped up against us, lately, too. We're agitators, troublemakers, a threat to the success of the Treaty. When we complain about Kilrathi violations, we're simply trying to stir up trouble on the border. If we take any kind of aggressive action ourselves we're deliberately provoking an interstellar incident. So any evidence we presented would be discredited as a fabrication before the report was off the air."

"Then what's Kruger planning?" Tolwyn asked.

"What you'd expect from Old Max," Richards told him with a grin. "He's going to take the bull by the horns. Fight the Cats with everything he's got, carry the war across the frontier into Ragark's territory if he has to . . . anything he needs to do to keep them off-balance until the Landreich can deal with them. And Confederation protests be damned."

"But if this Ragark's naval force is so much better than what the Landreich has, how can Kruger hope to fight and win?" Bondarevsky fixed a questioning stare on Richards. "Even Kruger's not crazy enough to buck the odds if the outcome's certain defeat."

"Well, he's building up the Navy as fast as he can. We've been buying up every warship we can get our hands on as fast as the Confed decommissions them. We've got an experienced team of salvage experts working on each ship as it comes in. And we're recruiting officers who can make a difference . . . in case you hadn't noticed."

"It isn't much, sir," Bondarevsky said, frowning.

"Old Max has some other schemes in hand, son," Richards told him. "Believe me, we're going to hand out some surprises. You'll find out more once we get to Landreich. Max'd skin me alive if I let out any of his little secrets, especially here. You know what he thinks of the Confederation."

"Kruger always plays things close to his chest," Tolwyn said. "But whatever he has in mind, it isn't likely to be easy . . . or safe. You know, don't you, Jason, that this campaign's going to be dicey. Maybe more dangerous than anything you've been in before . . . and you were in a couple of the worst fights the Confederation faced. I hope, when everything's said and done, that you won't hold anything against me."

"Against you, sir?" For a moment, Bondarevsky thought Tolwyn was referring to the *Behemoth* battle and the wounds he'd suffered aboard *Coventry*, but Richards quickly set him right.

"Didn't you know, son?" he asked with a raised eyebrow. "It was Geoff here who first brought your name up as a possible recruit. Max and I both liked the idea, of course, but we wouldn't have even known you were available if he hadn't suggested you be brought aboard." He raised his glass. "So . . . here's to comrades in arms."

"May we all gather together again when the fighting's done," Tolwyn added, touching his own glass to Richards'.

As Jason Bondarevsky silently joined in the toast he wondered just how much chance there might be of Tolwyn's wish coming true. Facing a powerful new enemy on Mankind's most distant frontier, outnumbered and without Confederation backing, this time it didn't look like there was much hope of coming out alive.

But at least he could go out fighting, doing something positive instead of wasting away, one more retired hero in a society that didn't want his kind reminding them of the dangers they'd so recently faced.

Bondarevsky found himself looking forward to a chance—any chance—to see action once more.

Warrior's Hall, Brajakh Kar
Baka Kar, Baka Kar System
1855 hours (CST), 2670.277

"The last one is here, Lord Haka."

Ukar *dai* Ragark *lak* Haka turned from his contemplation of the scene outside the window to return his young aide's arm-to-chest salute. "Very good, Nerrag. I will be there shortly. See to the refreshments."

"Yes, my Lord." Nerrag *jaq* Rhang saluted again and hastened to the door. As the young officer left him alone, Ragark permitted himself a brief baring of his fangs. *How they all feared him!*

He turned back to look out the window again, savoring the thought of eight-eights of the fleet's senior officers kept waiting for his arrival in the chamber below. In the days of Thrakhath and his idiot grandfather the Haka *hrai* had been in disfavor, and Ragark had been forced to lead by compromise, conciliation, and petty chaffering with other leaders whose status might be lower but whose favor in the eyes of the Imperial Court made them too powerful to ignore or overawe. Now the Emperor and his heir were dead, and Ukar *dai* Ragark ruled his province of the Empire with unbreakable talons.

Power at last. After too many eights of years the Haka Clan had the power it deserved . . . Ragark had the power *he* deserved. With the Imperial Family gone, the clans would start the age-old scramble for control all over again, and this time the Haka would be poised to win the Imperial Throne itself.

To think that there were religious-minded fools who believed the loss of Kilrah meant the end of the Kilrathi as a people! The Kilrathi had traveled the stars when the dirty apes of Terra had lived in wattle-and-daub houses and fought with blunt-edged weapons. They were the rightful inheritors, not of a single world but of the entire Empire, and if orange Kilrah was gone, they could make any world the new hub of a glorious imperial state. This one, now . . . he had viewed Baka Kar as a place of exile when Thrakhath had "awarded" him the governorship of Hralgkrak, but it would make a suitable capitol for the Haka Dynasty.

The view through the window showed him a world not unlike Kilrah. The vegetation was a deep purple, rather than the red-brown of Home, but the jungles that surrounded *Brajakh Kar*—the Fortress of the Dark—were just as lush and full of game. The planet was an old colony, with everything needed to be self-sufficient . . . and it was the center of a province of eight-eights of other worlds all replete with the resources to fuel his lunge to destiny.

Thrakhath had treated him lightly, once. Now Thrakhath was beyond his vengeance. But when Ukar *dai* Ragark took his rightful place at the head of the reborn Empire, he would make sure that Thrakhath and all of Thrakhath's clan were erased from the annals of the Kilrathi people. Only Ragark and his heirs would remain.

He turned at last from the window and walked slowly toward the door, careful to hide the limp he'd suffered since childhood. Not that anyone was likely to remark on it, not like they had when it had prevented him from becoming a warrior. No one dared call attention to his shortcomings now. But Ragark was too proud to betray weakness. He had schooled himself to hide the physical handicap, as he had learned the arts of government and of war to carve himself a place despite the scorn of his peers.

The lift took him down a level, from the meditation chamber to the Hall of Warriors where his fleet captains waited nervously. When he entered the room they stood in unison, saluting and raising the battle-call of the Haka. That made the blood surge through Ragark's veins. By the War God, he could lead these warriors to victory!

A table stood at the front of the Hall, under a large monitor screen. Ragark settled his small but stocky frame into the lone chair and watched as the others sat. These were the officers who controlled his warfleet. Some had slighted him in the past; they would pay when he no longer needed them. Some had been his willing allies or servants from the very start. They would enjoy the fruits of victory with him. Many others were nonentities, like so many of the military and political officers consigned to this backwater province during Thrakhath's day. Their fate would depend upon their performance in the days and months ahead. Ragark didn't intend to let any officer long survive the kind of mistakes that had cost Thrakhath victory time and time again during the war with the Terrans.

But one and all were needed now, and with their aid the name of Haka would be feared once more.

"Today we will begin to put in motion our new campaign against the apes," Ragark began with a show of teeth. "The probing actions we have already conducted along the frontier with this 'Landreich' have given us the intelligence we need to consider a campaign in strength against them. It will not be as Thrakhath would have had it, quick and ill-conceived. We will carry out our conquest step by step, taking care that our position remains secure throughout. But in the end, we will have the ape worlds for our own."

"And their Confederation?" That was Akhjer *nar* Val, the captain of the province's flagship *Dubav.* "We know they can make new Temblor Bombs. Do we not run the risk of losing more worlds to them?"

He favored *nar* Val with a long and penetrating look. *Dubav's* captain had an impressive battle record; he'd commanded a carrier at the Battle of Earth, and had received an Award of Valor for a single-ship action with a human escort carrier the next year. Ragark needed him, at least for the moment, to add some seasoning to a battle fleet roster that had few enough genuine combat veterans. But while *nar* Val was deemed apolitical, he had a conservative streak in his character that made him one of the cautious ones, one of the officers who looked on lost Kilrah with fear and despair. That could be a problem some day.

"The Terran Confederation is satisfied with the peace the traitor Melek has signed with them." That brought a few angry mutters from the assembled officers. Melek had been no more than Thrakhath's chief lackey, yet after Kilrah's destruction he had arrogantly assumed the power to negotiate with the enemy, as if a low-born servant of the Imperial House could presume to the Throne itself. Melek called himself "Chancellor" these days, and pretended to have control of the Empire, but Ragark wasn't the only clan leader or senior officer to ignore the upstart's claims. "They want nothing more than to disband their military forces and go back to the decadence they enjoyed before they encountered us. This Landreich that stands in our way is an offshoot, a breakaway association of colonies with so little loyalty that they refused the guidance of their own mother planet and formed their own government in defiance of the Confederation . . . and the cowards of Terra let that defiance stand. There is no reason for the Confederation to take an interest in what we do out here. At least, not until it is too late."

Ragark paused before going on. "In any event, we will soon be acquiring a powerful new accession of strength which will once and for all put us in a position to dominate the apes. I have recently had the final confirmation. Jhorrad is coming here to offer his claws and fangs to our service."

A muttering sprang up around the room as Ragark's words sank in. Dawx Jhorrad had become something of a legend in the Empire in a few eights-of-days. Already a hero of the Battle of Earth, with two capital ship kills to his credit in that one engagement, it was the story of his odyssey after the destruction of Kilrah that sparked the imaginations of the Kilrathi people. Jhorrad had refused to bow down to Melek when the Chancellor claimed caretaker authority and began negotiations. Instead he'd taken his ship out of orbit and set out into self-imposed exile, fighting off attacks by Melek and various jealous warlords at every turn. It had taken some judicious bargaining for Ragark to convince him to come here to Baka Kar, but it would certainly be worth it.

Dawx Jhorrad . . . and his ship. What a ship he was! Ragark allowed himself a moment's baring of fangs. With Jhorrad's mighty *Vorghath*, there would be nothing to stop Ukar *dai* Ragark from subduing the Terran apes and the fragmenting empire alike.

He stood up and leaned on the table, his eyes wandering across the assembly. "Victory against the apes of this Landreich will prove that the Terrans are not some kind of gods or demons, despite what they did to the Homeworld. The other clans will see that we can lead them to victory, and they will join our cause. Melek will fall by the wayside, and the Empire, reborn, will again bestride the stars!"

"Haka and Victory!" someone shouted. Others took up the chant, until Ragark raised his arms to call for silence.

"Victory it will be, my lords. But first we must plan our campaign. The apes must feel our fangs poised at their throats. Only then will the Kilrathi retake our appointed place."

He sat down again and activated the monitor to show them the plans for their first move, but Ragark had trouble concealing the joy that burned inside.

The long days of frustration and exile were over. The day of the Haka was at hand.

• CHAPTER 3

> *"Of all the weapons of the Warrior, it is the
> mind that elevates mere fighting to glorious
> Victory."*
>
> from the First Codex
> 6:34:14

Wardroom, FRLS *Themistocles*
Deep Space, Terra System
0447 hours (CST), 2670.278

There was something about being aboard a ship
underway that made Jason Bondarevsky feel alive again.

Three days had passed since Admiral Richards had
arrived at Moonbase Tycho. Now his mission to Terra
was done, and the Landreich cruiser was shaping a
course for home. For Bondarevsky's new home, out
on the frontier.

Like all vessels throughout human space, the ship
operated on the same Terran Standard Time (CST),
derived from Greenwich time on Earth, that was in
use at Tycho, but Bondarevsky had been used to a
different schedule from his stay in Odessa these past
few months, and the shift in time zones had left his

body clock out of step. So despite the hour—right in the middle of the Second Dog Watch, what some of Bondarevsky's flight school comrades had referred to in days gone by as "zero-dark-thirty"—he was wide awake and restless. The lighting had been reduced to simulate night, and there was little activity on board except in the bridge and engineering sections, where the duty watches kept an eye on the vessel's progress toward the jump point where *Themistocles* would make the interstellar transit to Barnard's Star, the first leg of the long journey ahead. Bondarevsky had finally given up trying to sleep and had come to the officer's wardroom for a cup of coffee.

Although he was alone in the middle of the ship's night, he could feel the throb of power through the deckplates, the tiny fluctuations of the ship's inertial dampers as the helmsman corrected the acceleration curve. Even traveling as a passenger aboard someone else's ship beat spending his time planetbound. That much, at least, he could enjoy. He only wished he could switch off his brain for a while instead of worrying about the future.

Admiral Richards had returned from his meeting with Confederation representatives in a grim mood. They had been as unhelpful as ever, demanding that the Landreich rein in the "hotheads" they accused of stirring up trouble on the frontier. That had been roughly what Richards and Tolwyn had expected, of course, but that didn't make it any easier to accept. The Landreich was effectively on its own. War was only a matter of time, given the Kilrathi ambitions in that part of space and the dogged character of President Max Kruger.

And Jason Bondarevsky was heading right into that war.

He still had no idea what Kruger and Richards had planned for him, though it was plainly a combat role rather than some staff job. Richards was as close-mouthed as always, and Tolwyn was no better. Not that Bondarevsky spent much time in Tolwyn's company. There was a chasm between them that started with the *Behemoth* debacle but went wider and deeper than that. Geoff Tolwyn had changed since the old days, and not for the better. He was even more secretive than Richards, and there was a determination in his manner that worried Bondarevsky. He was like a gambler who had lost everything but lingered at the table hoping that one last role of the dice would change his luck, plotting and planning ways to stay in the game without regard for the potential pitfalls or consequences.

So Bondarevsky didn't have an outlet to vent his hopes and fears. He might have used Sparks as a sounding board, but long habit made it impossible for him to discuss the affairs of admirals with a lieutenant who had risen from the ranks. You didn't voice your doubts about flag officers with juniors.

Instead he'd turned inward. He spent most of his time immersed in research, trying to catch up on developments along the frontier since his last posting there. Things had changed quite a bit since he'd been part of the Free Corps that had been secretly loaned by Terra to Max Kruger's Navy to help secure the Landreich in the days preceding the Battle of Earth. Whatever his upcoming combat post might prove to be, he would have to know the situation in detail.

He studied the porta-comp on the table in front of him, ignoring the panoramic view of deep space spread out in the window that dominated one end of the wardroom. The holographic map displayed above the computer showed the sector of space known as the

Landreich . . . the next battlefield, it seemed, in the ongoing struggle between two interstellar powers.

Landreich had started as a single colony world located at the extreme limit of human-settled space, nearly twelve hundred light-years from Terra. The frontier out there was far from the direct line between Terra and Kilrah, and fighting in the region had always been in the nature of a sideshow by comparison with the major fleet actions of the war. Raids back and forth across the ill-defined borders had been the norm through much of the war, and neither side put their best men or ships into that part of space. It was regarded as a backwater region, of no great strategic importance.

During the opening moves of the war, the Kilrathi had launched a campaign in the sector, but the Confederation high command had recognized it for a diversionary effort and refused to reinforce the tiny squadron stationed at Landreich. Max Kruger, a reject from the Academy and smuggler who had flown a recon team into Kilrathi territory and discovered the impending move towards war, had helped to organize the defense of the system. He had crash-landed on a Kilrathi base planet and had driven them to distraction with his commando raids on their base. Finally stealing a Kilrathi frigate, he had made it back home and was hailed as a hero. His next action was typical of the Landreich, an action which catapulted him to the presidency of the system while at the same time earning him a court-martial and condemnation as a mutineer.

The Confederation had sent out a heavy cruiser with orders to act as the flagship for a Home Guard fleet of ships pressed into service from the Landreich's small local militia. The Confed commander, not used to the freewheeling ways of the frontier, had rubbed Kruger and others the wrong way with his spit-and-polish ideas of discipline. Their response had been simple, straight-forward, and entirely predictable: they had seized the cruiser, kicked the officers and anyone who didn't want to go along with them off, and then set off on a raid deep into Kilrathi territory with their newfound firepower. It had taken three years, but finally Kruger had destroyed the Cat base that had coordinated Imperial activity in the sector.

When the Terran government ordered his arrest and removal from Landreich, it had sparked a bloodless coup that had resulted in the expulsion of the Confederation's governor and his staff, a declaration of independence, and the election of the hero of the hour to the post of President and Commander-in-Chief of the Free Republic of Landreich.

Other frontier worlds had followed suit as it became clear that Terra had no interest in protecting the remote frontier region. By the time Bondarevsky had served there, the Free Republic extended across a volume of ten parsecs, holding eight major colony worlds and a number of outposts and settlements. It was known as "the Landreich" to distinguish it from the planet where everything had started, but Max Kruger was still the President. That had been an awkward situation indeed, to have the chief executive of a sovereign republic listed as a wanted fugitive from the Confederation. For the most part Terra ignored the break-away republic, and Kruger in turn followed a policy of looking out for the Landreich and otherwise staying clear of the war.

But when the Kilrathi had proposed a truce with the Confederation, Admirals Richards and Tolwyn had detected indications that the Empire was plotting something. The Kilrathi had set up a chain of bases through the "unimportant" Landreich sector, intending them as staging points for their all-out assault on Terra.

Acting in secret at the orders of the Confederation President and the Joint Chiefs of Staff, the two admirals had transferred a battle group from the Confederation Navy to the Landreich, the "Free Corps" of "volunteers" pledged to support the human colonists threatened by the Kilrathi incursions. Jason Bondarevsky had commanded the escort carrier *Tarawa* in that campaign. During their operations around the Landreich the Terrans had discovered the true nature of the Kilrathi plan, and Bondarevsky had pressured Kruger into dropping his stance of ignoring the Confederation and leading his fleet to intervene at Terra at the height of the fighting there.

That had made Kruger a hero, for a time, and there was no more talk of his past misdeeds. But after the Battle of Earth things had lapsed back into their old patterns. The Free Corps had been withdrawn from the Landreich's service, and Kruger had gone back to more or less ignoring anything that didn't threaten his own borders. A handful of Confederation ships were posted to the sector again and a Confederation diplomatic presence was established, but Kruger was too canny and far too stubborn to allow himself to be swallowed up by Terra once more.

Since those days the Landreich had expanded some more, according to Bondarevsky's map. There were fourteen colony worlds owing allegiance to Kruger, and the frontier was nearly twenty parsecs across now. The Landreich had become a genuine power in the region, albeit a minor one. The problem was, the old Imperial province that bordered it, Ukar *dai* Ragark's sectors, had better than twice the planets, population, and ships. Even the Landreich's accelerated naval expansion program would be hard-pressed to field an effective defense if the Kilrathi came across the frontier in force.

"Ah, burnin' the midnight oil, I see." The bantering voice of Aengus Harper disturbed his contemplation of the computer map, and Bondarevsky looked up to meet the young officer's mocking eyes. "'Tis late hours you're keeping, sir . . . or early ones."

"It seemed a good time to get some study time in," Bondarevsky said. "What's your excuse, Mr. Harper?"

The lieutenant spread his hands and grinned. "I always try to rise a mite before my watch, to get an hour or two in on the flight simulator before the wardroom gets busy." He indicated the simulator compartment at the far end of the wardroom. Half game, half training tool, flight simulators were popular diversions aboard ships in deep space, where boredom hung heavy on long voyages between the stars.

"Every morning?" Bondarevsky asked. "That's a hell of a lot of sim time, isn't it?"

"True enough," Harper said. His expression turned wistful. "The truth of it is, sir, I want to keep in top form, in case an opportunity should arise for a transfer to a fighter wing."

"You've had flight wing training?" Bondarevsky studied the younger man closely. He gestured to a chair, and Harper sat down across the table from him. "How did you end up a shuttle jockey? If you don't mind my asking."

"A sad tale, that," Harper replied. "I fear my scores in flight school were only just borderline. Not the technical side of it. I could fly rings around my classmates. Word of honor on it. But . . . 'tis sad but true that the Devil puts temptation in the way of mortal man, and some of us just lack the rectitude to resist as we should. They say I set a record for the number of demerits earned by one officer in any class, and as a result my standing was knocked down. This was before we had many openings for pilots, before we started acquiring escort carriers from the Confed boyos. So I missed out when the first round of flight wing berths was being filled, and drew shuttle duty instead. And bad luck has been keeping me away from the action ever since. I put in for transfers, but by the time this old tub gets to port all the new vacancies have gone to new pilots, and I stay where I am."

"That's a damned shame, Lieutenant," Bondarevsky said. His sympathy was genuine. There was nothing a born pilot hated more than to hold back on the sidelines and watch others do the job he knew he could do better. Bondarevsky had gone through the same thing a few times. "I'd offer to help, but I don't have the faintest idea of what kind of assignment I'll be drawing myself, so my promise might not be any good to you."

Harper gave him a grin. "Well, sir, I can't hold you to anything . . . but it's eager I'd be if you *could* find a chance to get me a fighter of my own."

"Just so you don't go running up demerits in an outfit I'm in charge of," he told the lieutenant sternly. "I know that fun and games are supposed to be the natural perks of any fighter jock, but not when it might put a unit of mine in danger. You follow me?"

"Ah, sir, that was when I was still a lad," Harper said with an even broader grin. "I've learned to be more . . . selective in seeking out my entertainment, since I've reached my maturity and all."

"Yeah, right," Bondarevsky said. "You're a wise old man now, eh, Harper?" He paused. "Look, Lieutenant, if it doesn't throw you too far off your sim schedule, let me buy you a cup of coffee. I'm trying to get a handle on conditions in the Landreich, and I'd like some input from someone who knows it. Could you do that for me?"

"With pleasure, sir," Harper said. "But I should warn

you that I haven't seen or heard all that much. A shuttle pilot doesn't exactly move in the rarefied atmosphere of admirals and commodores, you know. And all I really know is Tara, and maybe a little about some of the stations I've been on since I signed up."

"Even that much would be a hell of a lot more than I've got now," Bondarevsky told him. "I haven't been in the Landreich since the Free Corps campaign, and a lot can change in four years. And even when I was there, I didn't have much of a chance to get a feel for the Free Republic."

The younger officer helped himself to a cup of the hot, bitter coffee from the vending machine near the table, then returned to his chair. He regarded Bondarevsky with an uncharacteristic solemn expression. "What can I be telling you, then, sir?"

"Tell me a little bit about yourself, first, Mr. Harper," Bondarevsky said. "Give me a junior officer's view of the situation in the Landreich."

Harper shrugged. "Not much to say, sir, really. I told you already that I was born on Tara. We were one of the first colonies to join Landreich in the succession movement, back when the confees decided we weren't worth the effort to guard. I joined up after my father was killed, when a Cat raider blew his freighter out of space. Lied about my age, too, I'm afraid. At sixteen you can't see yourself waiting two years for anything, and I wanted the chance to give those Cats back a little of what they'd give us."

"How far back was that?"

"Ten years it's been, sir. I had just graduated from flight school when Himself took the fleet to Terra in '66."

"Himself?"

"The President, you know. Old Max. I wanted to be

a part of that run so bad I could taste it, but I was flying shuttles between Landreich and Hellhole."

"You should be glad you missed it. A lot of good people died out there."

"Ah, but many a deserving young officer came home with a promotion, too, I'm thinking," Harper returned. "At any rate, it's mostly been quiet since, except for that raid the Cats mounted late last year. A carrier battle group actually got as far as Landreich itself, but the fleet chased them off again."

"That must have been right near the end of the war," Bondarevsky commented.

"I suppose it was, sir." Harper shrugged again. "Fact is, we don't really figure the war is over. If anything, things are worse now than when Kilrah was still around and old Thrakhath was calling the shots. He thought the same way the confees did about our stretch of space, I guess. The Imperial province facing us was a dumping ground for rejects and castoffs, ships and Cats alike. The leaders were usually nobles who were out of favor with the Imperial Government but too important to deny a posting. The ships were mostly third-line, and the crews were either still getting their spacelegs, or recovering from a hard stint in the main Theater of Operations, or sometimes they were oldsters past their prime but still serving in the Navy."

"That's probably the only thing that kept your people alive," Bondarevsky said. "No insult intended, Harper, but if this had ever become a primary target area, I doubt if the Free Republic's Navy could have stood against some of the stuff the Cats were throwing at us."

"True enough, sir, true enough," Harper said. "When they launched that raid last year, they built their squadron around one of their supercarriers. Damned big, she was, I tell you true."

"But you beat her off?" Bondarevsky couldn't keep a note of incredulity out of his voice.

"It took everything we had, but we did it," Harper said. "The Cats lost a couple of ships, and when they found us waiting over Landreich they contented themselves with a long-range orbital bombardment and then headed for the jump point. Our intell boffins said they were supposed to teach us a lesson in return for our helping the confees at Earth, but I don't think their hearts were really in it. 'Twas a damn-fool idea anyway, supercarrier or not. Even if they'd done what they set out to do, what would it have accomplished anyway? They might have chopped up Landreich pretty bad, just like they did Terra before the relief fleet arrived, but the rest of the Republic would still have been there . . . and it wouldn't have made much difference to the course of the war elsewhere."

"Is the carrier still there?" Bondarevsky asked. "If the Cats still have a supercarrier in these parts and they decide to make a serious attempt against the Republic, that one supercarrier would be a more serious threat than most of the rest of their fleet, especially if they've been relying on junk Thrakhath didn't want for the primary theater."

"As to that, who knows?" Harper's shrug was eloquent. "We had a message that a couple of confees caught up with the big bastard somewhere out in the Disputed Zone, but they never came back. On the other hand, word is the raiding squadron never went home either, if the intelligence reports that've leaked from on high are anything to be trusted. I guess both sides ended up as debs, more's the pity for your confee boyos."

"Well, at least the Cats aren't waving a supercarrier in our faces," Bondarevsky said. "That's something."

"Aye, it is, but I'm thinking it might not be enough this time, sir. Not by a long shot. We're used to standing on our own two feet out here, but I'll confess to you, sir, that I wish Admiral Richards was bringing back word that Terra was willing to back us." He mustered a grin, but Bondarevsky could see that Harper was forcing the cheerful expression. "Fact is, we've never been completely on our own, even when the confees put us at the bottom of the list of strategic targets. We always figured we'd get help if we truly needed it—your Free Corps, or something like it—and that made facing the Cats a mite less frightening. Now, though . . . we really are on our own this time out, and I'm wondering if it's any of us at all who'll be seeing home again after it's done with."

Unbidden, an image of the wrecked bridge of the *Coventry* flashed through Bondarevsky's mind, with the dead sprawled across their consoles and vacuum tearing away the air with an audible shriek. But he thrust it away. "Some won't make it, Harper," he said quietly. "But if we can stop the Cats, even the ones who don't come back will have counted for something."

Presidential Palace, Newburg
Landreich, Landreich System
1624 hours (CST), 2670.292

The Presidential Palace was said to be the largest residence on Landreich, and Bondarevsky was prepared to believe it. On his last tour along the frontier he'd never actually been here. In those days Kruger had led his people from the front, setting up a presidential command post at the Landreich base on Hellhole when he wasn't playing squadron commander from the bridge of a warship. It was a lot easier picturing the hard-bitten Kruger going into action than it was to envision him in the palatial surroundings that greeted Richards, Tolwyn, and Bondarevsky on their arrival. *Themistocles* had barely made orbit when word came for the three to see Kruger in person. Lieutenant Harper's shuttle had carried them straight into the Palace Compound, and from there they'd been conducted inside, passed from one staffer to another until they had finally been led to the reception chamber outside Kruger's office.

"A moment, please, gentlemen. The President is in a meeting, but he'll be able to see you shortly."

Bondarevsky nodded courteously to the slender, elderly man who had been introduced as Kruger's Chief of Protocol, a soft-spoken and gentlemanly sort who seemed completely out of place anywhere within twenty light-years of Max Kruger. Admiral Tolwyn didn't respond to the man at all, seemingly wrapped up in his own thoughts. Richards gave the aide a cheerful smile. "Don't worry about it, Karl," he said. "Knowing how Max feels about meetings, I'd be willing to bet we won't have long to wait."

As if to confirm the admiral's statement, there came the clear sound of raised voices through the massive double doors that led from the reception area to Kruger's private office. After a moment, the doors were flung open. Max Kruger himself stood to the left side, gesticulating wildly as he spoke in a loud and thoroughly unpresidential tone of voice.

"Freebooters and pirates, my ass! How many more Cat attacks will we have to put up with before you bastards back in Confed get it through your thick heads that these raids don't have a damned thing to do with pirates! I've had it, Williams! If you confees don't know how to deal with Cats, I sure as hell do, and be damned to the Treaty and everything else! We won't stand still for any more raiding!"

A second man, portly and dressed in the formal suit that was virtually a uniform of the Confederation Foreign Service, walked ponderously out of the office, turning to face Kruger from the middle of the reception area.

"You can rant and rave all you want to, Mr. President," he said calmly, his voice surprisingly thin and high-pitched for such a big man. "But the facts are as I have presented them. The Confederation cannot allow human worlds, even your so-called Independent Republic, to act against the provisions of Ko-Bar Yagar. To the Kilrathi, a human violating the treaty is a human violating the treaty. They will blame Terra for your indiscretions out here on the frontier. If you continue to lash out at the Empire because of your inability to deal with homegrown troublemakers, you risk destroying everything we fought thirty-five years to achieve. Before we allow that to happen, we *will* take action ourselves. If you don't want to find yourselves facing a Confederation battle group with a marine expeditionary force prepared for combat, I would suggest you moderate both your tone and your actions. Your declaration of independence was accepted twenty years ago because we had too many other commitments to waste time and resources dragging your Colonial rabble back into the fold, but things are different now, and if that's what it takes to protect the peace with the Empire that is exactly what we will do. Good day, Mr. President . . . and please think over what I've said. For your own good. And the good of your people."

Kruger's assistant looked from the President to the diplomat with an expression of uncertainty, but when Kruger didn't respond he stepped forward. "If you'll follow me, Mr. Williams, I will show you to the door."

As they left, Kruger couldn't resist a parting shot. "Lard-assed file-shuffling confee bastards think they can push around Max Kruger, do they? I was fighting the Cats out here on the frontier back when the whole gang of console commandos was still going to some la-di-dah university learning how to claim a spending increase was actually a cut so the voters would give them the chance to play god." The President's words were muttered, but just loud enough for Williams to catch them. Bondarevsky saw him falter, his chubby face flushing red, but the man kept control of himself and followed his guide through the outer doors.

When Williams was gone, Kruger looked around as if seeing his new visitors for the first time.

"Still the master of tact and diplomacy, eh, Max?" Richards said with a lazy smile. He turned to Tolwyn and Bondarevsky. "Clark Williams is the local liaison to the Confederation Peace Commission. Ever since he came out here he's pretty much run roughshod over Ambassador Phelps, who's getting near enough to retirement age to prefer not to mess around with the airlock controls. Unfortunately, I'm afraid Max here just can't find common ground when he gets together with Mr. Williams."

"Make light of it if you want, Vance," Kruger growled. "But that fat bastard isn't going to keep me from defending the Landreich. We'll fight the Cats and the confees too, if we have to." He paused. "But this isn't the way to greet old friends, is it? Come on in to the office."

He led the way through the inner doors. Inside, Bondarevsky had to hide a grin as he got a look at the way the office was furnished. The computer and communications gear was functional and efficient, but the desk was piled high with a clutter of papers, and the chairs and couches had a comfortable but thoroughly battered look. Plainly Kruger favored surroundings that fit his rough-and-tumble image.

"So . . . the famous Admiral Tolwyn. It's been, what? Almost five years now, right?" Kruger shook hands with the admiral. "Since we last met."

"Right after the Battle of Earth, Mr. President," Tolwyn answered gravely.

"And Mr. Bondarevsky." Kruger took his hand, frowning for a moment as he realized it was artificial. "The voice of my conscience made flesh, or so it seemed back in those days. A lot's . . . changed since then, eh, boy?"

"You could say that, sir," Bondarevsky replied stiffly. "But some things are still the same. You've still got Cat problems, and it looks like we're still here to help you with them."

Kruger cracked a smile. "Same old Bear," he commented. "Grab seats, people. Anybody want a beer?"

That almost made Bondarevsky smile. The President of the Landreich was a true man of the people, with common tastes and a tough, practical outlook on life. Bondarevsky could still remember storming in to his office on Hellhole one day after a tough mission, furious at the sacrifices his people had been forced to make in the name of protecting the Free Republic. Richards had urged Kruger to decorate Bondarevsky, and the President had casually given him the highest award the Landreich could bestow, plus a promotion, then tossed him a beer. It had been plain enough that Kruger had regarded the beer as the more tangible reward.

Richards accepted a can from the President's small, battered office refrigerator, but Tolwyn and Bondarevsky declined. All four men settled into seats before Kruger resumed the conversation.

"I read over the report you sent by hypercast, Vance," he said. "Anything you couldn't say there?"

"Not a damn thing, Max," Richards said. "The crap you've been getting from Williams comes straight from the top. The Confederation's just plain ignoring our complaints, and it looks like we're being thrown to the Cats. If we fight back, they might decide to come and stomp on us themselves, just like the man said."

"No, there's not really much chance of that," Kruger said. "Here's the way I've got it figured. Melek's trying to hold the Empire together while they figure out who should be the next Emperor. If he protested our fighting with Ragark, it might goad the confees into keeping us from fighting. But Melek and Ragark hate each others' guts. I'd say Melek would rather we stopped Ragark for him here so he didn't have to face off with him later for control of the Imperial heartland. No, the confees will let Ragark have us . . . and as far as everybody's concerned, the odds are all in his favor right now. Check?"

"Check," Richards said. "That's the way it would probably play out . . . unless we come up with something big. What about it, Max? *Have* we come up with something big?"

"The biggest . . . I hope. We've got a damned good lead, Vance. All that we have to do is see if it's feasible."

Tolwyn stirred beside Bondarevsky. "Would someone mind putting the visiting team in the picture here?" he demanded. "Or are you two going to talk in riddles all day?"

Richards grinned. "Sorry, Geoff. We've hardly dared say anything straight out about this even in private. Have either of you heard of the *Karga*?"

"It was one of the ships that raided Landreich late last year, wasn't it?" Bondarevsky responded, remembering his talk with Harper. "A Kilrathi supercarrier. I understood it was driven off by the FRLN, and presumed destroyed in battle with a pair of pursuing Confederation cruisers." He couldn't help but put a slight emphasis on the word

Confederation, just to remind Kruger that he owed Terra something despite all his present problems with the Confederation government.

"Still a man for doing homework, I see," Kruger said. "That's right, Mr. Bondarevsky. *Karga* was probably the best ship in the Cat fleet operating along this front . . . certainly the biggest and the most modern. Not one of those monsters Thrakhath deployed against Earth, but almost as big and probably as mean. The admiral assigned as battle group commander was a cousin of Thrakhath's. But they threw her at us with precious little support and a battle plan a kid could have predicted. Nobody was entirely sure what happened to the carrier and her last surviving escort. We were afraid for a while that she'd managed to destroy the two confee pursuit ships and escape back to Baka Kar, but Vance's intelligence net couldn't discover anything about her, and one of our informers claimed to have picked up a fragment of a message that said she was getting ready to self-destruct."

"She must've been hurting pretty bad," Tolwyn said. "Not even the most fanatic Kilrathi captain orders a self-destruct unless he's well and truly in the bag."

"Right," Richards said. "Well, the way we figured it, that was the last we'd seen of the *Karga*, and good riddance. The battle fleet the Cats have mustered out there has carriers and escort carriers enough to knock us out of action by themselves. If they had a supercarrier on top of everything else I'd just go ahead and start learning to speak Cat, because we wouldn't have a snowball's chance on Hellhole to fight *Karga* and all those other ships together."

"That's what we thought," Kruger said, "until last month."

"We got the news from a frontier scout looking for salvage out on the border," Richards said. "We've been scrounging for anything we can find, and paying top dollar. This gal—her name's Springweather or some such—was checking out the Vaku system when she registered one goddamned big source of magnetic readings . . . and an automated beacon."

"*Karga?*" Tolwyn asked.

"We're pretty sure of it," Kruger responded. "The beacon was on a Kilrathi distress channel, but the coding was garbled by radiation. It was coming from orbit over a brown dwarf, so you can figure the kind of havoc that was screwing up the comm channels. The scout didn't get close enough to eyeball it in case the Cats were active, but she got all the readings she could through that junk and brought 'em straight back here. And our people have been going over them in detail ever since."

"You've had a report?" Richards asked.

Kruger nodded. "Mass about right for the *Karga.* Power signature low, but some of the harmonics match readings we got in the fights we had with her before she disappeared. Orbit is highly elliptical, and likely to decay before too long. No life signs, but we can't be sure if that's accurate with all the rads. And you have to figure that if the ship's intact at least some of her crew could have survived. Somebody had to light off that distress call."

"Unless her screens went down after a power failure," Bondarevsky mused. "Radiation would've killed everybody aboard in a few days or weeks if the screens were down—hell, they'd've run up lethal dosages in a few *minutes*, but it wouldn't have been a fast death."

"That's what we've been thinking, too," Richards said. "Think about it! That supercarrier's just floating out there in space. If she can be put back into commission . . ."

"A damned tall order, Vance," Tolwyn said. "You don't

know how badly damaged she is . . . and working with alien engineering's bound to give us no end of problems."

"But if it *was* possible," Bondarevsky said softly, "we could sure as hell use a supercarrier when the bad guys come calling."

"If we can put her back in service . . . and before Ragark rolls over us or the Confederation changes policies again and decides we're a threat to the peace," Richards said. "Geoff's right, it *is* a tall order. But it's something we have to try. And you gentlemen are going to be involved . . . under the leadership of your humble servant, of course."

"What do you have in mind?" Tolwyn asked.

"We've been getting pretty good at salvage ops, Geoff. Have a whole team that can work miracles. We're going to take a battle group out to the Vaku system and take a look at that wreck. If there are any Cats still out there, we'll take them down. Then we'll put the salvage team aboard and see what we can do. Assuming we can reactivate her, I'll command *Karga*'s battle group as senior admiral. You'll be skippering her, Geoff. It's a step down from leading a fleet, but we need talented ship-captains a hell of a lot more than we need senior flag officers. Interested?"

Tolwyn leaned forward and gave a nod, more animated than Bondarevsky had seen him in a long time. "Just point me to the bridge," he said. "If that thing'll fly, I'll take her anywhere you want to go!"

Richards chuckled. "Easy does it, Geoff. If this doesn't pan out, you're likely to end up commanding some outpost . . . Hellhole, maybe. And we still don't know if we've really got any hope of making it work."

"And me, Admiral?" Bondarevsky asked.

"You'll have to take a cut in grade too, Jason," Richards told him. "But I think it's a job you'll be able to sink

your teeth into. Wing Commander, with an acting rank
of captain and all the pilots we can scrape together to
fly off that oversized tub."

"Odds are she won't be carrying much that'll fly, sir,"
he pointed out. "If she went down fighting, her
squadrons would have been deployed."

"We'll shuttle in fighters if we have to," Kruger said.
"We're sending you out in our one large carrier, the
Independence. Once you've decided what you need,
the carrier will bring in additional birds to fill out your
complement just as fast as we can get them mobilized."

Bondarevsky nodded slowly, his mind already racing
ahead to grapple with the problems he knew would
face them on the salvage mission. But while he was by
no means confident of success on the venture, given
everything that might go wrong, he realized that this
was just the kind of challenge he'd been looking for.
Win or lose, he'd put his best into it.

"That's the plan in a nutshell, gentlemen," Richards
concluded. "*Karga's* just waiting for us out there. She's
named for a Cat folk hero. His story reads something
like David and Goliath, except Goliath's the good guy
and David gets beat to a bloody pulp. But in honor of
it, we've designated this as Project Goliath. May it be
successful!"

"Hear, hear," Kruger said, clinking his beer can against
the admiral's. "The battle group's almost assembled,
so you'll be leaving in a day or two. Start thinking of
anything you think we'll need . . . or anyone, for that
matter. Goliath has top priority. And God help us all if
you fail out there."

• CHAPTER 4

> *"Brave comrades are the Warrior's most
> cherished gift."*
>
> from the Fifth Codex
> 2:17:38

Shuttle *Independence Alpha*
Orbiting Landreich, Landreich System
1447 hours (CST), 2670.298

"We're ready to begin final approach now, sir. Would
you like to be tryin' your hand at the trap?"

Bondarevsky turned to look at Aengus Harper across
the narrow confines of the shuttle cockpit. "It's been a
while since I flew a shuttle, Lieutenant," he said. "And
onto an unfamiliar carrier deck . . ." Despite his words
he was sorely tempted. Taking the stick on a spacecraft,
even a slow-moving, antiquated shuttle, would be a taste
of everything Bondarevsky had lost in the last few
months and years. But he was out of practice, and it
wouldn't do at all for the newly appointed Wing
Commander of the Goliath Project to crack up the first
time he tried to make a landing . . . and on someone
else's ship at that!

"Maybe 'tis not so unfamiliar at that, sir," Harper told him. "If you'll be lookin' at your monitor . . ."

Bondarevsky glanced down at the display in the center of his console. The shuttle was taking them up to the *Independence*, the pride of the Landreich fleet. Admirals Richards and Tolwyn, together with a small Cadre of staffers, were riding in back, but Harper had extended the invitation to Bondarevsky to join him in the cockpit for the flight. It was the young lieutenant's way of thanking him for wangling him a spot on his personal staff, with the promise of an assignment to the Goliath Project Flight Wing if and when such an organization materialized. With the priority status President Kruger had granted the operation, it had been easy to arrange Harper's transfer from *Themistocles*.

For an instant he didn't see anything special on his monitor, but then Bondarevsky did a double-take. He knew the ship that was framed in that screen, knew every line and curve the way a man might know his lover. Even the regular pulse of the ID beacon was familiar. Every one had its own special character, and Jason Bondarevsky had learned this one by heart in years gone by.

"*Tarawa*," he said softly. It wasn't just an escort carrier of the same class . . . it was *Tarawa* herself.

"Aye, sir, that it is," Harper said with a grin. "We picked the old girl up for a song when the confees started scrapping the fleet. She wasn't in very good shape, I'm afraid . . . but Old Max turned his salvage crew loose on her, and now she's ready for action."

Bondarevsky didn't respond. He was studying the magnified image on his monitor, thinking about all this old ship had come to mean to him.

He'd served as Wing Commander on her maiden voyage, and back then he'd been critical of the old girl. Terra's desperate need for carriers at a crucial stage of the war had prompted some unknown naval procurement officer to make the decision to take nine transports under construction and convert them in midstream into escort carriers, and the compromise design had been less than efficient in a lot of ways. But he'd come to love the makeshift carrier. On that first tour he'd loved and lost Svetlana . . . carried out the deep-penetration raid on Kilrah . . . seen the captain and bridge crew killed when a Kilrathi missile took out her bridge, leaving Bondarevsky to take command and lead the battered carrier out of enemy territory.

Tarawa had still been his for the Landreich expedition and at the Battle of Earth, too. It had been hard to give her up afterwards, when he took command of DesRon-67 and hoisted his broad pendant aboard the *Coventry*, harder still when he'd learned *Tarawa* had been crippled in a clash with the Kilrathi just a few weeks later. Bondarevsky had assumed she'd been scrapped . . . but here she was, after all these years, with a new name and new colors, but the same old *Tarawa* despite it all.

"She's a tricky approach," he said, trying to keep the excitement out of his voice. "The entrance to the flight deck is narrow . . ."

"The shuttle is yours, sir," Harper said, a twinkle in his eye. "Seeing as you're the old hand at this, and all." He released the joystick, and Bondarevsky tightened his grip around his own stick automatically.

"The shuttle is mine," he acknowledged. A thrill surged through him. It had been a long time since he'd had his own craft to handle and the flight deck of the old *Tarawa* inviting him to come home.

"*Independence Alpha* to *Independence* Landing Control." Bondarevsky spoke crisply into his flight suit radio mike, and the years fell away. "Ready for final approach now. Vectors are matched and I have you on my navscreen."

"*Roger, Alpha,*" the voice of the landing signals officer crackled in his ears. "*You are go for final approach. Change vector and start your run when you're ready. Watch for traffic. Two Rapiers, outbound, one supply shuttle in holding orbit. Confirm please.*"

Bondarevsky checked his radar scope. "Roger that, *Independence.* I have all three on my scope. Commencing final approach maneuver . . . now."

Bondarevsky nudged the throttle and kicked in the steering jets to settle the shuttle into the groove that would bring her over the approach deck at the escort carrier's bow. He allowed himself a momentary frown as he was forced to overcorrect; a shuttle was a lot less responsive than a fighter, and he was out of practice in making a trap on a carrier deck with any bird at all.

The carrier was visible through the viewscreen now without computer enhancement, swelling as the shuttle swept towards her on a precisely calculated course. Bondarevsky could pick out her forward armament bristling around the approach deck, a quad-barreled neutron gun flanked by mass drivers and anti-torpedo batteries. But he didn't linger on the sight. There was too much to do to bring a small craft in on the deck of a carrier in space, and it took all of a pilot's attention to do it.

In the old days of atmospheric flight, aircraft carrier landings had been considered the most difficult operations a pilot could attempt, but now that carriers were used in deep space those old atmospheric fliers were commonly held to have had it easy. Despite advances in computers and electronics, it still took the inborn skill of a talented pilot to get exactly the right feel for handling a bird. And a zero-g approach under power was a hell of a lot harder to manage than an old-style aircraft carrier trap, with tiny differences in inertia or thrust adding up to giant-sized headaches for the pilot and the flight control crew alike.

"One degree starboard," the LSO told him calmly. *"Reduce your angle of attack . . . good. Very nice, Alpha. Reverse thrusters . . . steady . . . Call the ball."*

Bondarevsky studied the looming approach deck until he made out the shape of the Ehrenberger Optical Approach Signal above the entry port. It helped a pilot establish his final vector by giving him a set of lights to line up on. With a practiced eye he gauged his course. *"Alpha,* shuttle, ball, forty-three point seven percent," he said, identifying his craft's designation and type, the fact that he had the optical signal in sight, and the shuttle's power reserves, all by the book.

"Roger ball," came the imperturbable reply.

The shuttle was moving very slowly now as it closed toward the carrier. This was the trickiest part of a carrier landing. If the pilot didn't have a perfect line on the port, he'd plow straight into a bulkhead and destroy his bird . . . and a fair chunk of the carrier, too. Too much thrust was bad even if the alignment was perfect, because once through the opening you ran out of maneuvering room quickly inside. But too little speed had its own difficulties.

That, as Bondarevsky had often remarked to non-pilots in countless late-night drinking sessions, was why the flyboys got the big bucks and most of the glory.

He steered through the narrow opening of the carrier's entry port, remembering how he'd once regularly cursed the naval architect who had designed it. Passing through the energy airlock, the shuttle was abruptly in atmosphere, but Bondarevsky had anticipated the change in the boat's handling characteristics and caught her deftly. The transition through the barrier had killed most of his remaining forward momentum, and Bondarevsky eased her forward to make a smooth touchdown right in the center of the landing deck.

"Shuttle *Alpha*, on the deck," he announced. "Powering down main engines."

"Nice job, Alpha," the LSO said. *"You're getting a 'Pass' on this one."*

Beside him, Harper chuckled. Squadron pilots aboard a carrier were graded on each approach they made by the LSO, and the results posted in the ready rooms. It was a form of competition designed to keep everybody sharp. "Passed" was the highest rating given out. Plainly the LSO didn't know that he had just graded a visiting Wing Commander.

"Thanks, Control," Bondarevsky responded. He saw the same humor in the situation that Harper did, but he couldn't help but feel a little smug at making the grade. After all, it really had been a lot of time since he'd handled a shuttle docking . . . and a long time since he'd negotiated the tricky approach down to *Tarawa's* deck. "*Independence Alpha* securing from flight stations. VIP party preparing to disembark."

He shut down the cockpit controls and glanced over at Harper. "Well, Lieutenant? I hope my performance was satisfactory . . . for an old man."

"Aye, sir, more than satisfactory," Harper said with a grin. "I'll fly alongside you any day, and that's a fact."

They unstrapped and left through the rear hatch that led into the passenger compartment, where the two admirals were just standing up while they continued a technical conversation about the design philosophy of Kilrathi warships. Other officers, staff members and a few techies—Sparks among them—held back, waiting for Richards and Tolwyn to exit the shuttle. The age-old rule of the high seas still held: senior officers were last to board a small craft, and first out.

Harper cracked the hatch. "They're ready for you, sirs," he said.

Richards led the way through the shuttle's hatch, followed closely by Tolwyn and Bondarevsky. The flight deck looked just the same as it had the last time Bondarevsky had been aboard, with bustling technicians hard at work on a number of planes close by, and a fresh team swarming toward the new arrival with an assortment of hardware to get the shuttle moved out of the way and into the maintenance cycle as quickly as possible.

They paused at the top of the door ramp. Right in front of them the organized chaos of flight operations swirled around a side party of Landreich marines in full dress uniforms. A bosun's whistle shrilled in greeting, and Richards started down the ramp.

The officer who advanced to meet him was dressed in a uniform several grades fancier than any Bondarevsky had seen in Landreich's navy, better than the one Richards had worn for his meetings with Confed VIPs at Tycho. There were gleaming captain's bars on his collar and plenty of gold braid just about everywhere else, and a patch on each shoulder carried the name *Independence*.

"Welcome aboard, gentlemen," he said. His accent tended toward the faint drawl of the Landreich aristocracy, and he seemed rather young for the responsibility of commanding a carrier. On the other hand, Bondarevsky himself had still been in his twenties when he took over command of *Tarawa*. It was just strange seeing another young officer taking the job. "My name's Galbraith.

Captain John Calhoun Galbraith, at your service. Welcome aboard the *Independence*."

The name rang a bell. He'd heard of Galbraith when he'd served in the Landreich before. The man's father was one of the wealthiest industrialists on Landreich, a robber baron who owned just about everything that was worth owning. His influence had ensured a smooth rise through the navy for his son, who'd commanded a destroyer when Bondarevsky had last heard of him. Galbraith was said to be competent enough as an administrator, and he'd never marred his combat record with a lost fight, but he was generally regarded as too soft and lazy to make a good combat skipper.

And now he was in command of the old *Tarawa*. What a comedown for a grand old lady . . . handed over to the man because Kruger needed the Galbraith family's continued goodwill to keep the Landreich on its feet.

"My senior officers," Galbraith went on with a casual wave at the cluster of faces behind him. "My XO, Commander Roth. My Chief Engineer, Commander Watanabe." He paused, looking at Admiral Tolwyn. "And you, at least, Admiral, should know my Wing Commander."

Bondarevsky suppressed a surprised exclamation as the last-indicated figure stepped forward.

"Kevin, my boy, it's good to see you," Admiral Tolwyn greeted his nephew in a tone that was pleased, but by no means surprised. So he had expected to meet Kevin Tolwyn out here in the Landreich. He might, Bondarevsky reflected ruefully, have mentioned something about it.

"Likewise, sir," the younger man replied. He looked much as Bondarevsky remembered him, short and stocky like his uncle, but with a baby face that belied his years of service as an officer in the Confederation Navy. He'd been one of the heroes of the Battle of Earth, but after he'd been declared Missing in Action in the final clash with Thrakhath's fleet and only recovered by the sheerest of chances the admiral had persuaded him to give up his flight status and become part of his *Behemoth* project staff.

Now he was here in the Landreich, wearing the insignia of a full commander and serving as the head of the flight wing assigned to the *Independence*, FW-105, the Liberators. Yet another old friend, Bondarevsky reflected, mustered for this new clash with the Kilrathi out here on mankind's most distant frontier.

Kevin Tolwyn caught Bondarevsky's eye and gave his familiar grin. "Glad to see you, too, Bear," he said. "And on the old *Tarawa*, too. Old home week, no less."

"Yeah, I'll say. I brought Sparks along, too."

"Hey, really? Doomsday's one of my squadron commanders. And there's a couple of others from the old days on board."

Bondarevsky didn't let his reaction show on his face. It seemed Richards and Tolwyn had been doing quite a bit of recruiting over the past few months. The situation was starting to remind him of that first Landreich campaign. Just what were they letting themselves in for this time around?

He didn't have a chance to reply, though. Galbraith, looking impatient, spoke up before Kevin Tolwyn had even finished speaking. "We're almost ready to break orbit," he said. "And the Presidential shuttle is due any minute, so that he can see us off properly. I hope you gentlemen won't mind if we cut the greetings back a little so that we can get the flight deck ready for the President's arrival. We have a great deal to finish."

"Of course, Captain," Richards responded casually. "If you'll just detail someone to show us to our quarters, we'll get out of the way until it's time to listen to Old Max and his words of wisdom."

"With your permission, Captain, I'd be glad to see our guests to their quarters," Kevin offered.

Galbraith frowned. "Job's a bit below your station, isn't it, Commander?" He assayed a brief smile. "Well, I suppose it won't hurt morale any." The captain waved a negligent hand. "You gentlemen let me know if I can be of any assistance."

Before any of them could reply, he had turned away to address his Exec, leaving the three new arrivals to Kevin Tolwyn.

"One of my men will see to the rest of the passengers," Kevin said. "I'll show you to the quarters we've set aside for you. I'm afraid they're not exactly up to standard flag rank issue."

"Give me a bunk and a computer terminal and I'll be happy as a Cat in a sandbox," Richards said. The elder Tolwyn grunted agreement.

The quarters were part of a refurbished section of the carrier. In Bondarevsky's day they had housed storerooms for munitions spares, but those stores were evidently in a new section two decks below the flight deck, allowing this expansion of available berths. "Old Max ordered the changes himself," the younger Tolwyn explained as he showed the first cabin to his uncle and the others. "Word is he expected to use the boat as his own personal flagship, and wanted the bunk space for his staff. But that all fell through, leaving us with extra VIP quarters no one expected to use until we got this new assignment."

Once the two admirals had been shown their berths, Kevin led Bondarevsky to another cabin close by. "All yours, Bear," he said with a smile, entering the keycode to open the door. "I know it's not the captain's suite, where you belong, but hopefully it'll do for the time being."

"It's fine, Kevin," Bondarevsky said. He tossed his bag on the bunk and did a double-take as something moved against the space-black blanket. "Well, hello, who's this?"

Tolwyn reached down and picked up a bundle of black fur. "The official *Independence* reception committee. Jason, meet Thrakhath. He's one of our ship's cats."

The black cat opened a pair of startling green eyes and studied Bondarevsky suspiciously. After a moment the cat started to purr loudly, obviously glad of the attention Tolwyn was giving his neck and ears.

Bondarevsky chuckled. "Thrakhath, huh? Does he know he's royalty?"

"Absolutely," Tolwyn replied, returning the cat to the bed. "He finds his way into just about every corner of the ship, usually through the ventilation system . . . though some of us think he can walk through walls when he wants to. But he's staked out this deck as his personal territory. If you don't want him slipping in here and bothering you, we'll install a screen he can't get through."

"Nonsense," Bondarevsky replied. "I can use the company." He paused, then looked Tolwyn in the eye. "It was a bit of a surprise finding you out here, you know. Your uncle didn't mention anything about it."

"He didn't?" Kevin frowned, then shrugged. "Well, you know how he's been lately. Won't let his right hand know what the left one's doing for fear it'll break under interrogation. Fact is, I've been here since just after the end of the war—stayed just long enough to see the court-martial verdict, then shipped out to sign on with Old Max and his gang of cutthroats."

"At the admiral's suggestion?"

"Yeah." Tolwyn frowned again. "I don't know what it is that's had him so worried, but he seemed to think it was a good idea for me to get out of Earthspace for a while. And Wing Commander on a Landreich carrier sure as hell beats being a major on the staff back home."

"How much do you know about the mission?"

"We're supposed to salvage a Kilrathi derelict that could be protected by hostiles," Tolwyn responded. "Should be an easy enough job." He paused, his innocent, open features reddening. "Look, Bear, you rank me six ways from Sunday even in the Landreich's Navy. I could step down as Wing Commander if you wanted to do something more than twiddle your thumbs on the flight out . . ."

"Forget it, Lone Wolf. You've earned the spot."

"It's just a damned shame they couldn't give you *Tarawa. Independence.* Whatever. Or at least her fighter wing. It's just . . . wrong for you to be a passenger aboard the old girl."

"Don't you worry about it," Bondarevsky told him. "Just seeing her again is enough for me. And if we end up trying to put that Kilrathi monstrosity back in business, I'll be glad enough of the vacation time." He hesitated. "But . . . look, Kevin, thanks for making the offer. It means a lot."

"I owe you big-time, Bear," Tolwyn told him. "When I signed on with you before the Kilrah raid I was a spoiled brat who didn't have any idea what to do with his life. You made me into a proper officer, and a pilot, and a man I don't mind seeing in the mirror every morning when I shave, and I won't forget that."

"Presidential Shuttle on final approach." The blare of the public address system kept Bondarevsky from having to respond to the younger officer's words. *"Welcoming party, lay down to the flight deck."*

"I suppose that includes VIPs," Bondarevsky commented.

"Well, it certainly includes Wing Commanders," Kevin said. "Question is, will our beloved Captain Gall-Bladder claim you and our two admirals as 'his' VIPs? He's very acquisitive, is our CO. A veritable interstellar pack-rat."

"You don't sound too happy with him," Bondarevsky commented as they started down the corridor together.

"Still a marvel of deduction, eh, Bear?" Tolwyn cracked a smile. "Let's just say that I'd like it if the skipper of this boat measured up to the standards of an earlier captain I might name. And I'm damned tired of being 'his' Wing Commander. In theory we're supposed to be equals under the Battle Group CO, but he makes me feel like I'm one of his daddy's lackeys."

"Since he's here and not in the Flag Officer's suite, I take it Admiral Richards isn't commanding the Battle Group."

"No. Old Max decided to make the derelict the hub for a separate squadron if and when she goes operational, and Admiral Richards'll be in charge of that. Admiral Campanelli's in charge of the *Independence* battle group, but he doesn't show himself much. The man's the senior flag officer on the fleet list, over seventy but still refusing retirement. And because he's the biggest war hero next to Old Max that the Landreich's got, nobody even *thinks* about easing him aside to let a younger man take over. He's a pretty good man even yet, but he's been sick off and on ever since I signed aboard, and lets Galbraith do most of the work running the battle group." Tolwyn grinned. "Might almost be better if Old Max did take to space again."

"Don't bet on it," Bondarevsky told him. "Your admiral might be old and sick, but Kruger's just plain crazy. I still remember the stunt he pulled to get us into the

Battle of Earth on time. Hit the last jump point at full speed. Half the fleet overshot the target jump point, and a couple of ships ended up with their bows twenty light-years from their sterns."

"It got you to Earth on time," Tolwyn pointed out.

"Yeah . . . but the man's still crazy. Doesn't care about the odds, or the possibilities. Just charges in with guns blazing, and be damned to anybody who gets in his way."

"Sounds to me like you approve of him, underneath it all," Tolwyn told him as they reached the lift that would take them up to the flight deck.

Emerging back onto the open area, they joined the two admirals at the fringe of the captain's welcoming party and watched the Presidential shuttle slipping gently through the force field to settle on the deck close by. Bondarevsky noted that the shuttle bore the name *San Jacinto*, after Kruger's old ship that he'd used to launch his mutiny and his subsequent career. He wondered what Richards thought of it. Vance Richards had been the young commander of Kruger's squadron when Old Max had committed his act of defiance. He sometimes claimed it was Kruger's act that had blotted his service record and earned him a transfer to Intelligence.

The shuttle door opened, and once again the bosun's whistle greeted the arrival of the VIP visitor. This time it was accompanied by a recorded band playing something stately and elegant, presumably some Baroque fanfare that was part of the normal greeting for Landreich's President.

Knowing how Kruger felt about ceremony of all kinds, Bondarevsky couldn't help but wonder what the Presidential reaction would be. Galbraith certainly knew that Old Max wasn't the kind to waste a lot of time on all the formal aspects of his office. Did he put on this display because he was helplessly wedded to the rigmarole? Or was he trying to remind Kruger that there were elements in the Landreich who regarded the presidency as something more than just a job?

Kruger stepped out of the shuttle hatch, looking around with a pugnacious but somehow wistful gleam in his eye. Young Tolwyn's comments about his intention of using the escort carrier as his own personal flagship struck a chord with other pieces of scuttlebutt Bondarevsky had heard over the last few days. Old Max wanted to lead this mission himself in the worst possible way, and he was bitter at having been thwarted in his plans.

Back in the crisis preceding the Battle of Earth Kruger had taken direct command of the Landreich fleet from the bridge of the destroyer *Blitzkrieg*. He'd also maintained a command post on Hellhole before the Kilrathi had bombed the settlement there. His flamboyant leadership style was best suited to leading from the front—preferably the forward element of the most advanced scout units of the fleet vanguard—and Kruger had played his role to the hilt.

But since that time, from what Bondarevsky had heard, Old Max was finding it harder to carry out his duties from the deck of a fighting ship. The worlds of the Landreich were a cantankerous bunch, peopled by stubborn, independent-minded folk who took a lot of governing. Having an absentee president tended to unsettle things in the capitol. That hadn't made much difference back when Kilrathi forces were running roughshod through Landreich space, but now that things were more settled Kruger's political advisors had turned up the pressure to keep him chained to his desk at the palace.

And this mission, as important as it was likely to be, was also sure to be a long and largely boring one. Surveying and salvaging a derelict ship was not the kind of life-or-death mission Kruger could point to as needing his personal touch, not when there were political problems to deal with at home.

Even so, it had taken Richards reminding Kruger that he was the only one who could keep Clark Williams and the rest of the Confederation embassy under control while the crisis continued to unfold to convince Old Max of the need to stay at his post like a good soldier instead of running around in deep space where he longed to be.

So that wistful look was genuine. Bondarevsky felt sorry for the man, whatever his personal eccentricities. Kruger was very much a man of action, finding it hard to come to grips with the idea that not all leadership involved the direct approach he favored. But facts were facts. As Bondarevsky had commented to Richards after one of Kruger's angry tirades on the subject, "He says the president of a frontier republic doesn't have to worry about protocol or formalities or little things like running the country. But if that's the case you'd be reading history books about Thomas Jefferson taking personal command of the *Intrepid* the day Decatur went into Tripoli harbor to burn the *Philadelphia*. The man still has the mind of a destroyer skipper trapped in the body of a head of state."

Kruger was still at the top of the ramp. He touched something at the side of his neck, the control, Bondarevsky realized, for a headset microphone and amplifier system. The President's words boomed out in the hollow space of the flight deck.

"Citizen-spacers of the Free Republic Navy! I've come up from planetside to see you off in person because

Independence and the squadron traveling with her have a task of potentially vital importance to carry out. On you, the brave men and women of the Landreich armed forces, on you, I say, rests the future of our small league of planets out here on the frontier. For years we've been under the threat of attack by the Cats, but our situation today, when a peace treaty supposedly protects mankind, is even more grim than it was in the bad old days before Secession. You may think that a salvage mission cannot be as important as a combat operation, but if you recover the vessel you are setting out to salvage and put it back into operation, it could very well turn the tide in our favor now and for years to come."

Kruger paused, then went on in a lower tone. "I know a lot of you think I exaggerate a mite from time to time, but this time out I'm telling it to you straight. The actions you take during this mission could determine the very future of the Landreich, maybe of all human worlds. And I know of no better body of people to entrust that responsibility to than the spacers and marines of the Free Republic Navy.

"Good luck to you all, and Godspeed."

Terran Confederation Embassy Compound,
Newburg
Landreich, Landreich System
1934 hours (CST)

"I wish to God I knew what that maniac Kruger was up to," Clark Williams said, taking a sip from his coffee cup and pausing for a moment to savor the Jamaica Blue Mountain blend he imported every month from far-off Terra. "You can bet it's something big, I'll tell you that much. With Geoff Tolwyn involved . . ."

"That isn't really such a surprise, now, is it, Commissioner?" Lorenzo Mancini leaned forward in his seat, looking intense. "After all, he's had contacts out here since he and Richards pulled that stunt back before the Battle of Earth, and it wasn't as if he had much of a future back home. Not after that *Behemoth* fiasco."

"No, this is something more than just Max Kruger lending a helping hand to some poor slob he thinks deserves a break," Williams said. He put the cup down with exaggerated care, every movement precise. "Kruger doesn't figure he owes anything to anybody. Just the opposite. He'd still like to have the Confederation government jump through hoops to thank him for 'rescuing' us at Terra."

His chair creaked a little as Williams leaned back, and he frowned. Commissioner Clark Williams was a man who loved order, efficiency, and smooth sailing. His office, the best in the Terran Embassy Compound, was furnished with the finest things he'd been able to bring in from Earth, and everything was neat and orderly. Nothing like Kruger's den in the Presidential Palace, he thought.

Mancini shrugged. "The man has a point, Commissioner," he said. "The Cats had broken through our last defensive line when Bondarevsky and the rest of Kruger's people showed up and forced them to break off."

"He's a criminal, an outlaw, and the most dangerous man in the sector."

"Precisely why the Landreich makes such a perfect staging ground for our little project," Mancini countered. He was a small man, easily overlooked, but he held the rank of Colonel in the Confederation Security Bureau, Terra's elite espionage and intelligence service.

He had other connections, too, that rendered him even more powerful, and Williams was inclined to avoid arguing with him.

"I suppose you're right," he admitted. "But with Tolwyn and Bondarevsky involved with Kruger again, I'm afraid our operation could run into trouble. Don't count Tolwyn out just because of what went on last year. The man's a tactical genius, and he very definitely does *not* agree with our position. The combination could spell trouble."

"You're certain Kruger has something special in mind?" Mancini was frowning. He was new to the Landreich station, and hadn't had much of a chance to get his information network working yet. Williams had heard that he was almost obsessive about not relying on any sources he didn't know personally.

"He flew up to the new escort carrier this afternoon to see the crew off in person," Williams told him. "Richards, Tolwyn, and Bondarevsky are all on board as VIP passengers. Rumor has it that the battle group normally assigned to the carrier has been augmented by a number of additional ships and several thousand personnel . . . a sizable commitment, you'll agree, for a struggling little republic like the Landreich. I say it's some mission Kruger has taken a personal interest in, and if that's the case, it could be something big."

"But you don't know what." That was a statement, flat and brusque, not a question.

"Our best guess is that Kruger wants to stir up trouble inside of Hralgkrak Province," Williams said. "On Nahaddar, for instance. The Nahad have been growing restive the last few years, and Kruger could see possibilities in stirring up a rebellion there. Richards with his intelligence background, Bondarevsky to organize an aerospace defense, Tolwyn as the resident strategic brain . . . if it's true what I've heard, that they're taking a troop transport and a factory ship with them, it would all add up. Start a rebellion on Ragark's flank, train, equip, and support local fighting forces, and throw Landreich forces in at a crucial moment in a typical Max Kruger banzai charge, and you've got the ingredients for a disaster out here. The last thing Terra needs is to see Kruger become an interstellar hero all over again. That's *not* what the plan envisioned."

"Then we need to take corrective steps," Mancini said calmly. "But first we need to find out if your guess is anywhere close to the truth. Don't we have any sources who could give us an inside look at what Kruger's up to?"

"Nothing inside his administration," Williams responded. "You know how loyal the rank and file are to their beloved hero. He's losing ground with the politicians on the Council, but as far as I can tell that only makes him less likely to share his plans with them. Hmmm . . ." He paused, trying to remember something he'd heard about the mission Kruger had dispatched. "One thing. There's a civilian ship involved somehow with the battle group. A tramp frontier scout out of New Plains or some such place. The crew would have had a few days worth of shore leave, and you can bet they wouldn't obey any orders to keep their plans a secret. *Somebody* will have talked . . ."

"Hard to trace," Mancini said. "You'll be sorting through idle gossip and useless rumors for months looking for anything significant."

"Not necessarily," Williams replied. "These frontier scouts operate on the fringe of the law at the best of times. Most of them have connections with our good friend Mr. Banfeld and his Guild. I think if there's anything worth knowing, Banfeld's already found it out.

All we have to do is make sure we offer the proper . . . inducements to win his cooperation."

"Then I suggest you get started, Commissioner," Mancini said. "If we're going to stop Tolwyn and his friends from complicating things out here, we have to discover what he's up to, and where, so that we can take steps to correct the matter quickly."

Williams smiled coldly. "I'll get on it. But I still think you should consider my other suggestion."

"Assassinating Kruger?" Mancini shook his head. "Too risky. The Cats don't operate that way, so you can't throw suspicion on them. And you risk setting him up as a martyr, both here and back home. Do that and you'll set us back even more than a Landreich victory against Ragark would. No, we keep our hands off Kruger for the time being. We harass him diplomatically, and stir up as much political trouble as we can, and take action to keep his underlings from putting one over on Ragark. But we leave Max Kruger alone. Let the Cats deal with him, when they bomb that pretty little palace of his into debris."

• CHAPTER 5

> *"There is no dishonor in caution, so long as the careful Warrior avoids the pitfalls of cowardice."*

from the Fourth Codex
16:12:21

Operations Planning Center, FRLS *Independence*
Deep Space, Oecumene System
1005 hours (TST), 2670.312

When Jason Bondarevsky had commanded the *Tarawa* many of the most important decisions controlling the ship and its missions had been made in the Operations Planning Center, a large chamber abaft the CIC complex, buried deep in the heart of the ship's superstructure. Where the Combat Information Center was all computer consoles and monitor screens, crewed by technical experts who monitored the flow of information from inside and outside the carrier constantly, the OPC was an island of calm. A large triangular conference table ringed with chairs filled most of the room, but aside from small computer keypads in front of each seat there were no banks of instruments, no readouts or tactical monitors or viewscreens. The bulkheads were decorated with artwork: a holographic portrait of the *Independence* in orbit over a blue-green planet; an old-fashioned painting of the *San Jacinto* fighting a Kilrathi ship at the Battle of Landreich; a holo-still of Max Kruger looking stern and wise, as if surveying the chamber with pride and benevolent interest in the proceedings. The flag of the Landreich dominated one entire wall, a white cross of Saint Andrew on a black starfield impaled by an upright sword, with the motto "Freedom Through Strength" below.

The three-D holo-projector in the center of the conference table showed the image of the Landreich squadron clustered near the jump point to Vaku, eight ships about to leap through hyperspace into the unknown. The assembled leadership of the expedition gathered around the table seemed strangely unaware of the importance of the moment, but Bondarevsky found it hard to think of anything else. In another day, Project Goliath would be fully under way, and there would be no pulling back once they were committed.

Bondarevsky had been in more than his fair share of pivotal battles, usually against overwhelming odds, but today he couldn't help but feel that this salvage mission was going to be no less important than all those combat actions. It was as much a gambler's throw as any engagement in space . . . and Bondarevsky felt oppressed knowing that there wasn't a great deal he personally could do to contribute to the outcome of the mission until others had made the preliminary judgments as to whether the operation was even feasible.

Admiral Vincent Camparelli, ramrod straight in his chair despite his age and the hacking cough that frequently interrupted his speech, raised a blue-veined hand and called for attention.

"I want to make sure everyone knows what's expected of them when we go through," he said, glancing over at Admiral Richards. "The overall conduct of the salvage mission may come under the authority of the Project Goliath staff, but until they actually go aboard the derelict—if it is a derelict—to conduct their initial survey, the operation is a matter for Battle Group Independence. Coordination of our efforts will be extremely important throughout, as I hope you'll all understand and agree." His dry, reedy voice might have belonged to an aging professor lecturing on military tactics at the Confederation Space Academy, for all the emotion the old man betrayed. But despite his frail appearance he seemed to have all the facts at his fingertips, and Bondarevsky thought he could still make out the firm and decisive mind that had led a Landreich fleet to victory over the Kilrathi nearly thirty years ago, back in the first days of the Secession crisis.

Glancing around the table, Bondarevsky found himself wondering about the others assembled there. In previous campaigns he'd known the men serving with him. They'd been squadron-mates or members of the same flight wing who lived and worked and played cheek-by-jowl every day; later they'd been fellow ship-captains from the same battle group, men and women of proven competence whose actions and thoughts became thoroughly known over weeks or months of duty on a distant combat station. But this group was largely composed of unknowns, at least as far as Bondarevsky and the other Goliath officers were concerned. It made him edgy to know he'd be depending on total strangers not just for the success or failure of the operation, but possibly for his very survival.

They tended to split into two groups, the Goliath team and the senior officers of the battle group. Though

Admiral Camparelli presided, it was clear that it was Captain Galbraith most of them looked to for direction, and that young CO was wrapped in an air of almost palpable superiority. From hints the man had let fall in conversation already it was plain that he considered this mission a milk run, a minor chore far beneath the dignity of the flagship of the Landreich fleet. Perhaps he was also conscious of the fact that *Tarawa*—no, damn it, *Independence*, Bondarevsky reminded himself bitterly— stood to lose that flagship status if the salvage mission was successful, and with Tolwyn destined for her command seat he might be feeling a little disappointed that his father's political machinations had secured him the escort carrier when this new vessel was waiting in the wings.

· The other three skippers of the battle group's fighting ships sat between Galbraith and Camparelli. So far they were little more than names and faces to Bondarevsky. Forbes of the light cruiser *Xenophon* was a blonde giant with a faint accent that reminded Bondarevsky of one of his old comrades, Paladin. Miruts Bikina of the destroyer *Durendal* was his complete opposite, a wiry black soldier of fortune from the colonial world of Azania who had joined Kruger's navy only a few years back, but quickly established an impressive combat record that had earned him rapid advancement. His reputation for competency boded well, but Bondarevsky wondered if a mercenary could ever be trusted as much as someone actually defending his home and hearth.

On the other hand, that was essentially what he and Tolwyn were, mercenaries for hire. Perhaps he'd have to adjust his way of thinking now that he wore the uniform of a captain of the FRLN.

The third captain commanded the destroyer *Caliburn*, a stunning red-headed woman named Pamela Collins.

Bondarevsky had noticed that most of the male officers of the battle group were so busy noticing her good looks that they didn't realize she had a string of single-ship kills on her service record that would have put most Confederation skippers to shame. He didn't have any worries as to how *Caliburn* would perform, at least.

Two more around the table weren't ship captains, but they were an integral part of the power projection abilities of the battle group. Colonel Bhaktadil Rai was commander of the *Independence*'s contingent of Republic Marines, a slight but sturdy man with light skin, fierce black eyebrows, and a prominent nose between dark Asiatic eyes. He was a descendent of the proud Gurkha warriors of old Terra, and took his heritage seriously. Even on duty he wore a turban instead of more usual military headgear—what he did when he had to wear full space armor was something Bondarevsky hoped to discover some day—and he carried a wicked-looking curved combat knife, a kukri, at his side. Beside him, Kevin Tolwyn looked uncomfortable wearing khakis instead of his flight suit, but like the marine he stayed quiet and let the others do most of the talking. The young commander had come a long way since Bondarevsky had first taken him under his wing right here aboard the old *Tarawa*.

There were also four non-combatant ships in the squadron, assigned specifically to assist in the Goliath Project. The transport *City of Cashel* was commanded by a dour reservist named Steiger. She had been designed to carry a full division of troops between worlds, but today was carrying nearly six thousand men and women who would serve aboard the supercarrier, together with the two hundred specialists from Kruger's prized salvage team who were represented by Armando Diaz, who had a brevet rank of major in the Landreich's army for the duration of the crisis. Diaz was dark, thin, and radiated enough nervous energy to run a medium-sized combat ship for a year or two, but he plainly knew his business. Whether or not he could surmount the extra obstacles of putting a Kilrathi ship into service again remained to be seen.

Diaz would be working closely with the captains of the tender *Sindri* and the huge factory ship *Andrew Carnegie*, a Mutt-and-Jeff pair whose names were Dickerson and Lake—Bondarevsky still wasn't entirely sure which one was which. Their commands, though non-combatants, would have the pivotal part in the Goliath Project, the tender serving as a deep-space repair platform for the supercarrier while the mammoth *Andrew Carnegie*, designed for semi-automated minerals extraction and fabrication work on unsettled frontier worlds, had been pressed into service to manufacture whatever the Kilrathi derelict might be lacking right on the spot.

The last member of the assembly was an olive-skinned, attractive woman, Wenona Springweather, from the planet of New Plains poised on the boundary between the Landreich and the Confederation. Settled mostly by a mixture of Native American tribes, the planet had tried to stay out of the political rivalry between Kruger's government and Terra, and Captain Springweather was typical of the frontier scouts who operated out of the free port at New Plains. Her scout ship, *Vision Quest*, was the only civilian vessel in the fleet. She was along to help the Goliath team locate and investigate the hulk she'd stumbled across . . . and, to hear her talk, to make sure that she wasn't swindled out of her finder's fee by the sharpies working for Max Kruger.

Springweather and the salvage specialists gravitated into orbit with Admiral Richards and Geoff Tolwyn,

seemingly at odds with the voices of authority represented
by the purely military members of the operation. As
for Bondarevsky himself, he was torn in his loyalties.
He sympathized thoroughly with the battle group officers
who had to plan for God alone knew what contingencies
out there in the Vaku system, but at the same time he
considered the supercilious Galbraith and his immediate
juniors a poor substitute for the combat veterans he'd
served with in the war. The worst of it, he thought, was
the fact that they reflected their maverick Commander-
in-Chief, Max Kruger. Bondarevsky was used to the
common bond between the officers in the Confederation,
products of a uniform academy training system and a
rigid code of conduct. Out here in the Landreich
individual eccentricities seemed to be the norm rather
than the exception, whether it was Galbraith's ultra-
fashionable uniforms, Bikina's unsavory mercenary past,
or Bhaktadil's old-fashioned adherence to the ways of
his Gurkha ancestors. It emphasized the almost amateur
nature of war out here on the frontier, and Bondarevsky
had never regarded warfare as a fit subject for amateurs.

But these were the men and women he'd have to
learn to work with, not just on the Goliath Project but
afterwards as well, whether the mission succeeded or
failed. The combat ships of the battle group, minus
Independence, were slated to become the supercarrier's
fighting force if the derelict could be recommissioned.

Bondarevsky hoped they'd all grow to understand one
another well before the time came when they had to
rely on each other in a combat situation.

He forced himself to focus back on the conversation
around the table. Camparelli had finished his opening
comments and slumped back into his chair, letting
Galbraith take over the operational briefing with the
assistance of the carrier's XO, Mary Roth, and Camparelli's

Flag Lieutenant, Commander O'Leary, who manipulated the controls of the holo-projector while Galbraith spoke.

"The deployment for the first stage of the operation is relatively simple," the carrier's skipper said languidly. According to Miss Springweather's reports—"

"That's Captain Springweather," the woman corrected loudly. "Just because I don't have one of Max Kruger's instant commissions doesn't mean I'm not captain of my own damned ship."

That earned her a look from Bikina as well as Galbraith, but the only response came from the senior officer, who cleared his throat. "Yes, of course," he said with an ingratiating smile. "*Captain* Springweather's survey of the system spotted the jump point closest to the derelict, roughly thirty thousand klicks away. It hooks up with the jump point here in the Oecumene system. My intention is to deploy *Xenophon* and *Durandel* first, to get an initial tactical scan of the area in case there should be any hostile activity around Vaku." His tone made it clear that he didn't expect any such thing. He was going through the motions, Bondarevsky thought, hoping to impress the brass with his thoroughness even though he really didn't see the point of going in expecting trouble. That probably wouldn't matter at Vaku, unless the Cats were preparing some sort of elaborate trap for the Landreich. But it could spell trouble later on if Galbraith carried that same attitude into a real combat situation.

Hopefully Bondarevsky would be far away if and when that came to pass. But poor old *Tarawa*—and any of his friends unfortunate enough to be aboard under Galbraith's command—might be in for trouble.

"Once the initial scan is completed, *Durandel* will relay an all-clear signal by drone through the jump point, and we will send in the rest of the battle group.

Independence will go through first and immediately launch her fighters to cover our approach and conduct a close-in examination of the target. Commander Tolwyn, I will expect the fighter squadrons to do a thorough job of sweeping the region in as short a time as possible. I do *not* want to keep the battle group waiting around on full alert for any prolonged period. If there is a danger to be dealt with, I want to be able to move as quickly as possible to deal with it. And if there's nothing to block our closer investigation of the Kilrathi carrier, I want to be able to close in and start the detailed survey job ASAP. Is that clear?"

"You won't have any problem with *my* people, Captain," the younger Tolwyn said, the slight emphasis his own sign of irritation at the captain's usurpation of authority over the flight wing.

"I trust not," Galbraith said, unruffled. "The order for the rest of the battle group will be *Sindri*, then *City of Cashel*, then the factory ship. *Vision Quest* and *Caliburn* will bring up the rear."

"Do we really need a rear-guard in an operation like this?" Pamela Collins asked. "It isn't as if we have any enemy activity to worry about in these parts."

"We'll do this by the book, Captain," Galbraith said. "If something should happen to one of the non-combat ships I want a destroyer on hand to deal with it. And I particularly require a civilian ship to be escorted at all times while under our protection." He darted another look at Springweather. "In any event, those are the deployment orders. I expect them to be carried out exactly as posted."

"Aye aye, sir," Collins said. "As you order."

"Once the battle group has assembled and the fighter sweep is completed the initial survey can begin. Colonel Bhaktadil will have command over this phase of the operation." He looked across at Richards, Tolwyn, and Bondarevsky. "In all deference to your ranks and reputations, until we're sure there's no threat on board that supercarrier I require the operation to be conducted strictly within the chain of command."

Richards gave him an easy smile. "Don't worry, Captain," he said. "I for one am happy to stay as supercargo for the time being. Just be glad Old Max didn't come along for the ride, though. I doubt you'd have much luck keeping him from taking charge. Or from stealing a lifeboat and crossing over to the derelict all by himself if he thought you weren't moving fast enough to suit him."

"Er, yes. Well . . . as long as the position is understood," Galbraith said. Bondarevsky hid a smile. Evidently Galbraith wasn't as free and easy as a lot of the Landreich colonials when it came to free expression about the Commander-in-Chief. "Colonel?"

The Gurkha Marine officer gave a curt nod. "Ten shuttles will board simultaneously at various key points on the supercarrier," he said crisply. "Each will carry two squads in full space armor and standard infantry weapons loads. I will be using both my own men and the marines assigned to *Karga*, off of the *City of Cashel*. These will be used to immediately secure the two bridges and the flag bridge, engineering, weapons control, and the flight deck. Investigation of other sections of the ship can be conducted later, but the key areas must be secured early on to avoid problems later if there should be any Kilrathi aboard."

"The odds are entirely against that," Diaz spoke up for the first time. "Judging from the power readings obtained by *Vision Quest*, there's no way they're sustaining any shielding. The crew would have fried."

"It's a precautionary measure, Mr. Diaz," Admiral

Tolwyn said. "In case the supercarrier's bait for a trap, for example. If the Kilrathi just wanted to draw us into an ambush, the derelict might have troops deployed aboard as soon as they saw us coming."

"And we don't necessarily know how accurate *Vision Quest*'s readings were," Galbraith put in. "No offense, Captain Springweather," he added hastily. "But you did conduct your investigation at long range, and there's no knowing if you might have missed something. Improvised shielding within the hulk, for instance, to maintain survivors . . . or an ambush force. Or other ships operating close alongside the supercarrier, using its bulk to shield their emissions."

Diaz looked uncertain. "I . . . see. Are you gentlemen seriously expecting Kilrathi in the Vaku system?"

It was Bondarevsky who answered. "Mr. Diaz, a good space officer always expects the worst. That way he's prepared if there's trouble."

Galbraith smiled reassuringly. "But in all probability, Mr. Diaz, this will just be a particularly large and elaborate exercise for the battle group," he said. "Don't worry about the Cats. The object of all this is to keep them from interfering . . . assuming they're anywhere within ten parsecs of here."

Richards spoke up. "Look, Captain, I do have one problem with everything you've put together here. I've been reading through your mission orders, and I see that you don't plan to let Goliath personnel go aboard until after you've secured the entire ship. That could take a day or two, given the ground you've got to cover."

"That's about right," Galbraith nodded.

"It seems to me that we could send elements of the specialty teams aboard right away. The initial points the marines are assigned to grab—control, engineering, weaponry, and flight—these are also the places where we have to conduct our initial observation of conditions aboard the ship. If we can't fix these, there's no point in going on. And no point risking our boys in securing the rest of the ship if we're not going to put her back in service."

"A squad of marines will have its hands full setting up a perimeter and looking for Cats," Galbraith said. "They shouldn't have to babysit a survey team at the same time."

"I'm sure the survey teams will have enough sense to sit tight inside the shuttle until somebody gives an 'all clear' and it's safe to go to work," Richards replied. "I'm not talking about carrying out a full-scale survey in the middle of a firefight, for God's sake. But if we can get started looking at conditions aboard right away, we can make a judgment about the next stage of the project a lot more quickly, and maybe save a lot of wasted time, effort, maybe even lives."

Galbraith rubbed his eyebrow with one elegantly-manicured hand. After a moment he nodded reluctantly. "Very well, Admiral. What exactly did you have in mind?"

"As long as you're bringing marines across anyway, have the pick of Mr. Diaz's men transfer to *Independence* before we jump," Richards said. "A small team will go on each shuttle. I'll go in with the group that secures the flag bridge, Admiral Tolwyn can take the main bridge or CIC, as he desires. Captain Bondarevsky will go in on one of the shuttles that takes the flight deck. I imagine Mr. Diaz would be best suited to handling engineering. We each get a crack at seeing what we'll be up against to get this big bugger back on-line. Agreed?"

No one argued, though Diaz, perhaps still worried about a Kilrathi presence on board, failed to look particularly excited by the prospect of going in with the marines.

Bondarevsky spoke up. "I'll want Sparks as part of my team, Admiral. She knows more about flight deck ops than full technical crews I've seen on some carriers."

"Pick your team as you wish, Jason," Richards said. "But be guided by Mr. Diaz as far as the salvage team personnel he thinks are best suited to your part of the operation." He looked around. "Anything else?"

When there was no response Galbraith took over once more. "Very good. Colonel, make whatever changes you need to in your assault plan to include the survey teams. I emphasize again that battle group personnel have full authority at all times. Our people have the final say in how things are done. Commander Tolwyn, you'll have to see to any changes the extra personnel will cause in the shuttle load specs, of course."

"Yes, sir," the younger Tolwyn responded, a don't-tell-me-my-job gleam briefly flashing in his eyes. "It'll be taken care of."

Bhaktadil spoke again. "Keep in mind that if the shielding *is* out aboard the derelict we will have a radiation problem to deal with. Space armor can protect personnel for a short time, and the portable shield generators we're loading aboard the shuttles will handle the problem for a while longer—but only over limited areas. Make sure the people you choose for your survey teams are used to suit work. Zero-g experience would be useful, too, if the grav systems have gone off-line . . ."

"I dare say we've more experience of this kind of work than you have, Colonel," Diaz told him. "Though I admit we've never operated outside of a dry dock facility before."

"That's where we come in," Dickerson—or was it Lake?—put in. "The quicker your gang gets things secured and calls us in, the sooner you'll have all the comforts of home, courtesy of the good ship *Sindri*."

The briefing session moved on to more detailed discussions of individual phases of the operation, and Bondarevsky leaned back in his chair and let the comments flow past him while he considered the mission. It seemed strange not to be in Kevin Tolwyn's position, planning for the flight wing's operation as the mission profile unfolded. Bondarevsky was eager to be something more than a VIP to be shielded by marines and kept out of the chain of command.

He was ready for action again.

Flight Wing Officer's Lounge, FRLS *Independence*
Deep Space, Oecumene System
1924 hours (CST)

The Officers' Lounge set aside for use by the Flight Wing had always been one of Bondarevsky's favorite places aboard the old *Tarawa*. Even after he'd gone on to become the captain of the ship he'd still managed to wangle frequent invitations to join the off-duty pilots in the large recreation area, even though there were those who claimed it was bad for a CO to socialize too freely with his crew. Bondarevsky had always maintained that it was good for morale for him to relax with his men instead of retreating into the isolation of the captain's cabin, and there was certainly an element of truth in the statement. It had done *his* morale no end of good, whatever impact it might have had on the rest of the ship. By nature a sociable man, Bondarevsky had never fully come to grips with the isolation imposed on a commanding officer.

Tonight Kevin Tolwyn had extended the invitation, part of a long-time ritual of theirs—toasting an upcoming mission with a few drinks the night before it was

scheduled to start. The lounge was much as Bondarevsky
remembered it. Evidently Armando Diaz and his men
hadn't seen any need for extensive renovations in this
part of the ship when they'd brought it back into
commission. There was a shabby, run-down atmosphere
about the room now, mildly depressing to Bondarevsky.
He had the feeling that he could walk over to the dart
board on the bulkhead beside the door and turn it over
to reveal the same dog-eared picture of Max Kruger
that had been a favorite point of aim for dartsmen back
in the Free Corps cruise.

But even so there was something right about being
here with Tolwyn and Sparks, sharing a quiet drink,
swapping old war stories or just pausing to stare out
the wide windows that dominated one wall with a
panoramic view of space.

Bondarevsky was watching a shuttle moving a few
hundred meters from the monstrous factory ship *Andrew
Carnegie*. Nearly totally automated, the factory ship
had a tiny crew to oversee operations, but frequent
personal inspections inside and out were the order of
the day to ensure that no trouble developed that wasn't
caught and acted on early. *Carnegie*—Bondarevsky had
heard that her nickname, "Old Carnage," referred to
a notorious accident on board ten years back that had
resulted in the deaths of most of her crew after a
catastrophic computer breakdown—was going to play
merry hell with the rest of the battle group's operation.
Ponderous and difficult to maneuver, she'd slow them
down tremendously in both normal space and jumps
through hyperspace, but she was too damned valuable
to abandon if they were caught in a firefight. In addition,
they'd have to find a ready source of raw materials to
keep her fulfilling her intended function, and the brown
dwarf's ring system had already been ruled out as being

mostly ice chunks lacking almost all the minerals needed
to turn out finished replacement components. Wrangling
over exactly how to ensure the big factory ship's safety
had taken up a large portion of the briefing earlier in
the day, and Bondarevsky still wasn't entirely happy
with the outcome. But Old Max had decreed that the
carrier was to be refurbished where they found it or
not at all, even though *Sindri's* captain had claimed
he could tow the derelict home to Landreich and save
a lot of headaches by getting her into a proper space
dock for her refit.

But it wasn't just concerns over how difficult it might
be to get the supercarrier back to civilization that had
dictated Kruger's decision to refit her in the field. The
longer they kept the project under wraps, the bigger
the surprise the Landreich would hand the Kilrathi if
and when they threw her into action . . . and the less
likely the Confederation would be to get wind of the
scheme and try to stop it. That was almost as important,
at this stage, with Commissioner Williams still making
threatening noises about Terran intervention in the event
of escalating hostilities out here on the frontier.

"You're looking particularly out of it tonight, skipper,"
Sparks commented after the silence had gone on for a
while. "You feeling okay?"

"He's just beat down by all the haggling, that's all,"
Tolwyn told her. "By God, I swear these Landreichers
have everything backwards! Their president wants to
lead fleets in action, and he's damned good at it, too . . .
while the fleet officers sit and argue more than any
bunch of worthless politicians who ever disgraced a
parliament! Do you suppose Landreich's ruling council
would make good fighters, Jason?"

He smiled without much humor. "Just look at Captain
Galbraith. His family damn near controls the council

back on Landreich. And he's sure waving the flag properly."

Tolwyn snorted. "Yeah, right." He looked at Sparks. "You think there's a spot for me in your techie crew on the new ship if I finally get fed up and go after the guy?"

She turned a sunny grin on him. "Why, surely, sir. Just as long as you remember to be careful of my planes."

"Oh, great," he groaned. "Somebody else who wants to take over our birds! Just what we didn't need."

"Hey, let's face it, Commander, those birds have always belonged to the techies. We just loan them out to you flyboys . . . and we don't let the spit-and-polish navy even get near them!"

"Don't tell our illustrious Captain Galbraith," Tolwyn said. "He thinks he owns the whole shooting match."

"When you figure it was probably his father's money backing Kruger when he started buying decommissioned ships from the Confederation, you can see where he might get the idea," Bondarevsky pointed out. "I always knew Max Kruger was playing things entirely too fast and loose back in the old days, but it's gotten a lot worse since then. He's let Galbraith and the other big money boys get a stranglehold on his government, and all because he couldn't be bothered with the petty details of playing president the way he was supposed to."

"You think it'll be a problem down the line, Jason?" Tolwyn asked. "I mean, some of us have burned our bridges back home, and if it falls apart out here too . . ."

"Keep your priorities in order, Kevin," Bondarevsky advised. "First we've got the Kilrathi threat to deal with. Then we've got to deal with the Confederation and whatever their silly little game is. It's only if we weather both those meteor swarms that we'll have to worry about the long-term health of Max Kruger's government. I figure the odds of it ever being a problem *we'll* have to cope with are long enough that we don't need to bother worrying."

"Cheery these days, isn't he, Sparks?" Tolwyn said.

"You don't know the half of it, sir," she told him.

"I call them like I see them," he said. "Tell me something, Kevin. Do you have any idea what's got your uncle acting so paranoid? He was always big on secret schemes, but since I met him on the Moon I've had the feeling he's got something really big going on, something he won't tell either me *or* Vance Richards."

Tolwyn nodded. "I know something's up, but I couldn't tell you what. All I know for sure is that getting me to sign up out here with Kruger's gang wasn't intended to further my career. It went against everything he's ever tried to do for me before. I invested half a lifetime in a Confederation Navy career and threw it out in five minutes because Uncle Geoff suddenly thought it was important I take this deal instead."

"Why?"

Tolwyn shrugged. "Beats the hell out of me. But I had the definite feeling he was worried about my safety . . . about my physical well-being. A couple of times he let slip things that suggested he thought Terra was not a very healthy place to be a Tolwyn for the next few years."

"Bad feeling from the court-martial, maybe?" Sparks suggested.

"Maybe," Tolwyn said. "But that was a nine-day wonder at best. Nobody'll ever forget it, and he made a few more enemies before it was all done with, but I just don't see it being a raging topic of controversy that would leave him worrying about our security."

"True enough," Bondarevsky said. "Well, look, Kevin, I'm not going to ask you to spy on your uncle or anything like that. But if you pick up anything you think I should know about, please pass it on. I respect the old man's judgment in most things, but ever since *Behemoth* . . ."

"Yeah. Ever since *Behemoth*." Tolwyn shook his head. "That was a goddamned shame. Screwed up from start to finish. To think that Hobbes was the one who betrayed him, too. One of the only two Cats I ever met that I would have trusted with my life."

"Whatever happened to the other one?" Sparks asked. "Kirha . . . the one I met in Britain when we were getting ready for the Free Corps mission."

Bondarevsky looked down at his empty glass. "You know he was bound by oath to Hunter . . . took the strongest possible Kilrathi vow to be the loyal servant of 'Ian St. John Who Is Also Known As Hunter.' Well, Ian bought it when we were out here. You remember, Sparks?"

She nodded sadly, and so did Tolwyn. Captain Ian St. John had been one of the old band of brothers . . . and the best friend a man could have on his wing in a furball.

"Kirha was shipped off to Ian's ranch Down Under for the duration. The brass was worried that he might get wind of what we were doing with the Free Corps operation, shipping ships and men out to serve with Kruger's boys while the Confederation was in the middle of those phony peace negotiations. I flew down there after the Battle of Earth to let Ian's folks know what had happened first-hand. I couldn't put that kind of thing in an internet bulletin, you know." He paused, staring down at the drink again, wrapped up in unpleasant memories.

"And?" Sparks urged. "Did you see Kirha?"

He shook his head. "No, I was too late. The news had got there ahead of me. And Kirha did the only thing he could do under the circumstances, given the vow he'd sworn. The big orange bastard took a knife and stabbed himself through the heart. *Zu'kara* . . . ritual suicide. Without his adopted clan leader, he was alone in a strange culture, and I don't think Kirha wanted to live without Hunter to lead him."

"Cats," Tolwyn said. "I can't figure them. Barbaric, stupid buggers if you ask me."

"You're wrong there, Kevin," Bondarevsky said sternly. "The Kilrathi have been civilized a lot longer than we have, and they're anything but stupid. Or else the war would have been over with a long time back, and without all the blood and pain we've had to invest just to fight them to a standstill. No, they just have a different outlook on things. If more of our political leaders would stop treating them as if they were humans in furry suits and start recognizing just how different their culture is, we might be able to deal with them better. Find common ground, even. It's only when you insist on holding somebody to your own narrow standards that you shut off all hope of ever reaching them. Hearts and minds and all that."

"I still prefer the old approach," Tolwyn said. "When you've got 'em by the balls, their hearts and minds will follow."

• CHAPTER 6

> *"The brave Warrior is not without fear. He is a*
> *friend of his fear, embracing it, intimate with it,*
> *but never allowing it to overcome him."*
>
> from the First Codex
> 10:21:18

Flight Deck, FRLS *Independence*
Jump Point Three, Vaku System
0717 hours (CST), 2670.313

Jumpshock!

There was something fundamentally incompatible
between living organisms and the realm of hyperspace,
not powerful enough to kill but strong and unpleasant
nonetheless. Nausea, dizziness, momentary disorientation, these were the symptoms of jumpshock, and
Bondarevsky experienced them all in good measure as
the *Independence* made the transition from the fringes
of the Oecumene system to the jump point nearest
Vaku's brown dwarf companion and the derelict's last
plotted position. He blinked, trying to focus his eyes
and get his bearings while fighting a feeling that
reminded him of the worst hangover he'd ever awakened

124

with. It didn't help that his vacuum suit, designed for salvage and construction work in space, was bulky, stiff, and unwieldy compared to the issue flight suit he was used to wearing. He had a momentary flash of fear that he was about to vomit, one of the worst experiences known to man when it happened inside a suit and at times fatal if one was out in vacuum and couldn't clear his breather. The wave of nausea passed and he breathed a sigh of relief.

Beside him Aengus Harper recovered more quickly, as younger men were apt to do. "My sainted mother always said that man wasn't meant to travel through space, and Lord forgive me but I said she was wrong," he said, his voice husky. "Remind me, sir, to let her know she was right."

Across from the two men, Sparks was already playing her fingers across the keys of the small holo-projector set up between their seats. Bondarevsky had never seen her suffering from the effects of jumpshock. There were some people who claimed to be immune, and at times like this Bondarevsky would cheerfully have killed any one of them.

"Looks like everything's going according to plan," she commented cheerfully.

Bondarevsky blinked again and peered at the computer-generated holographic image floating in the air. He could discern the blips that represented *Independence*, *Xenophon*, and *Durendal*, grouped around the jump point but already beginning to shape their course inwards, toward the oversized gas giant the derelict orbited. There was nothing registering in the projection that might have been their target, only the brown dwarf and its attendant moons.

"Where's our Kilrathi hulk?" That question came from Colonel Bhaktadil, seated beside Sparks. He didn't have his turban on today. Like the rest of them, he had his helmet ready at hand in the storage rack behind and above his seat, and his dark, curly hair looked all wrong somehow without its customary covering. "Don't tell me we've come all this way for nothing!"

The marine CO had elected to go in with the squads assigned to the flight deck of the supercarrier, since that was the largest single space they'd have to secure and investigate and hence required the most marines to take it. The marines and Bondarevsky's survey team were already strapped into the shuttle, ready to launch as soon as the all-clear was given by Kevin Tolwyn's pilots. Other shuttles ready on the flight deck were similarly manned and set for launch. Although they had plenty of time left before they were close enough to launch, Richards and Tolwyn had ordered them to be ready to go at short notice. Even if something dangerous was waiting for them in the Vaku system, the fighting ships of the battle group might be able to lead it away while the shuttles went in to size up the situation, so preparedness was the order of the day.

"Probably obscured by the brown dwarf," Sparks said. "You know the database better than I do, skipper. What do you think?"

Bondarevsky tapped a command into the projector controls and nodded as a trace appeared on the far side of the supergiant. "Yeah. That's the computer estimate of where it should be, given *Vision Quest*'s data on orbital characteristics." He switched it off again, leaving the original real-time plot. The four of them studied the projection in silence as long minutes passed. At least there was no sign of a hostile reception committee, he told himself. So far, so good . . .

Aft of the carrier the tender *Sindri* popped into

existence out of hyperspace, followed closely by the
City of Cashel. Up ahead the leading escorts were
spreading out to form a broader front, leading the way.
It would take some time before the rest of the battle
group came through. The huge factory ship's jump
engines were slow to charge up, and once she made it
into the Vaku system her sheer bulk would limit her
acceleration to a crawl. But they wouldn't be needing
the *Andrew Carnegie* soon. If the derelict couldn't be
salvaged, they wouldn't need her at all.

"Fighters launch! Fighters launch!" That came from
the comm channel, set to monitor squadron operations.
Bondarevsky had a momentary vision of what Kevin
Tolwyn must be seeing right now as his Raptor led the
way off the carrier's flight deck into deep space. He
wished he was out there, with a bird to fly and a solid
mission to carry out, instead of being cooped up in a
shuttle waiting for the chance to go aboard an enemy
derelict and survey it for damage. Bondarevsky wasn't
entirely sure he'd be much use at that anyway. For most
of his life he'd been learning how to inflict damage on
Kilrathi warships, not analyze it.

But his job wasn't out there any more. Best he came
to terms with that fact, no matter how distasteful it
might be.

Raptor 300, VF-88 "Crazy Eights"
Deep Space, Vaku System
0735 hours (CST)

Commander Kevin Tolwyn felt a surge of pure
adrenaline in his veins as his fighter cleared the flight
deck and steadied on course toward their destination.
"Raptor 300, good shot, good shot," he reported over

the comm system, letting the flight controllers know that he'd launched without difficulty.

"*Roger that, three-double-zero,*" came the reply. "*Captain says 'good hunting,' Commander. And be careful.*"

"Be sure to tell him I'll be careful not to scratch the paint," Tolwyn said. It was the kind of remark he could never have gotten away with in the Confederation Navy, admiral's nephew or not. The casual side of life on the frontier did have a few advantages.

He waited as other heavy fighters joined him in formation off the carrier's bow, taking the time to get the feel of the Raptor. The bird had been state-of-the-art fifteen years back, during the famous Vega campaign. Now it was fit for second-rate fleets like the Landreich's, though Tolwyn had found it to be a sturdy, reliable craft in practice flights. He hoped it would do as well in actual combat, if and when it came to that.

"*Lone Wolf, Lone Wolf, this is Doomsday. You copy?*" The radio call jerked him out of his introspective mood. The last of the Raptors had left the flight deck and joined him. It was time to get the mission under way.

"Five by five, Doomsday," he said. "You boys think you can keep up with me okay? Or should I hold back?"

"*Don't go asking for trouble, there, kid. You may be the Wing Commander now, but I remember when you were a wet-behind-the-ears newbie who didn't know a high-g turn from a hole in the ground.*"

Tolwyn chuckled. Etienne "Doomsday" Montclair was one of his oldest and best friends from back on the end run to Kilrah all those years ago. He'd been senior to Tolwyn then, a cocky veteran who tended to slam the new kid whenever the opportunity arose, but he'd been a damned good friend and a fine wingman. Unfortunately, Doomsday had been part of the Free Corps mission to the Landreich during the period leading up to the Battle of Earth, serving under Jason Bondarevsky on the *Tarawa* while Tolwyn was in the thick of the action with the Confederation fleet that faced the Kilrathi at Sirius and in the Solar System. As a result, and because of his high-placed connections, Tolwyn had shot onto the fast track and advanced more quickly in rank than Doomsday. So now he was senior to Montclair in this new navy, probably once again because of his uncle's influence, but Doomsday being Doomsday there was little chance of the Wing Commander getting a swelled head.

"Everybody stick to the game plan," Tolwyn ordered. "Babe, are you ready to make your run?"

"That's affirmative, skipper." The soft contralto voice of Darlene "Babe" Babcock answered him. *"Waiting for your orders."*

For a moment Tolwyn wished he'd strapped on a Hornet for today's mission, instead of picking the Raptor. Babcock's squadron, VF-12—more usually known as the "Flying Eyes"—was equipped with the Hornet light fighter, a fast, high-performance craft that was ideal for reconnaissance missions but limited in the fighting it could handle. Today they carried even lighter combat loads than usual to make room for a Mark VI APSP, a sensor pod containing a battery of cameras, imaging systems, and other survey gear that was normally used to conduct long-range scans ahead of a fleet or target identification runs in a planetary atmosphere. So Babcock would be taking her planes in low over the Kilrathi hulk to get a good look at the supercarrier ahead of the rest of them, while the heavier Raptors of Doomsday's VF-88, the Crazy Eights, waited to provide cover if they ran into trouble.

Tolwyn's instincts were still those of a combat pilot, and the recon mission had tempted him mightily. But though he still used his old handle, "Lone Wolf," he knew that his responsibilities as a wing commander ran deeper than satisfying his personal desires. Some wing commanders would have directed operations from the carrier's flight control center, but that would have been too much of a leap for Kevin Tolwyn. Instead he'd fly the support part of the mission, where he could sit back and oversee the whole operation but still get into the action personally if a furball developed.

It was the kind of decision he figured Jason Bondarevsky would have made . . . or at least he hoped so. It was hard to live up to the standards set by a man like Bondarevsky, but Tolwyn was determined to do his best.

On his tactical plot the white dots representing the Flying Eyes were beginning to sweep past the green symbols of VF-88, gathering speed as they accelerated at maximum military thrust. Tolwyn kept his eye on the screen, letting the Raptor maintain course and speed on autopilot while he devoted his full attention to the unfolding recon flight.

As the minutes crept past a new indicator came alive on the plotting board, a fuzzy red symbol that indicated a large and potentially hostile target.

"There she is," Babcock announced calmly. *"Tally ho!"*

"Maintain your watch," Tolwyn reminded her. "Don't get so wrapped up in the target that you miss any loiterers who might be planning to crash the party."

"Roger that. Snake, Lefty, you two are on high guard. The rest of you peel off according to the recon plan. Stick to your wingmen and make sure your cameras are hot. Go!"

"Good luck to you all," Tolwyn muttered under his breath.

Flight Deck, FRLS *Independence*
Deep Space, Vaku System
0805 hours (CST)

"Look at that thing," Bondarevsky said softly, almost reverently. "My God, just look at it. I've never really been able to just sit back and watch when one of these was on my screens. I was too busy dodging Double-A-S to do anything more than fly and fight."

Sparks had shifted from the tactical plot to a real-time computer-enhanced relay from the sensor pod mounted on the bow of Babe Babcock's Hornet. The four officers grouped around the three-dimensional display had almost lost track of time as they waited and watched, but now, at last, the fighters were getting a good view of the derelict spacecraft.

"*Seems kinda funny not to be locking on,*" one of the pilots said over the commlink, echoing Bondarevsky's sentiments.

"*Keep your eyes on your displays and your mind on the job, Drifter,*" Babcock growled. "*They're not paying us to sightsee out here . . . that's why God invented sensor pods.*"

"*Aw, Babe, you got no romance in your soul,*" Drifter replied in a mock-sad voice. Then, a moment later, he switched to a completely business-like voice and manner. "*You see the spike on the emissions readout?*"

"*Yeah. I copy it. Her shields may be down, but she's got power running through her grid. Not much, but power.*"

"*Stay focused, people,*" Kevin Tolwyn broke in. According to the latest position check, his Raptor squadron was still five minutes from the hulk, and Bondarevsky could hear a trace of nervousness in his voice. He knew the feeling, the fear that something could go down that would cost good pilots' lives while the support squadron was still killing off velocity to match vectors and join an engagement.

Sparks leaned closer to the display. "I'd say something blew up pretty damn close to her, skipper," she said. "See the pattern of damage along her forward hull?"

"Yeah." Bondarevsky frowned. "I don't think that's what did her in, though, Sparks. Doesn't look like the blast damage did all that much to any critical areas of the ship. Just breached the hull in about thirty or forty places, that's all. Her shields were already down when that happened, or nothing much would have got through."

"That's battle damage there, Captain," Bhaktadil said, pointing to the shattered blister on the forward part of the carrier's massive superstructure. That was the main bridge, Bondarevsky thought. "All the signs of a burnthrough on the shields and a fairly heavy missile strike following it up."

"Looks like our Cat friends had some unfriendly company, all right," Bondarevsky said. "Those two cruisers must have caught up with her and given her more than she could handle. Pretty unusual for a ship-to-ship battle to develop around a carrier, though. Her fighter screens should have kept cruisers at arm's length."

"Let me check something, skipper," Sparks said. Her fingers played across the controls, calling up the images from a different Hornet. "This is Hornet One-oh-nine," she said. "He's assigned to skim past the port side flight deck."

"Sweet Mother of God," Aengus Harper said out loud. "Will you look at that bit of a tangle."

The image being relayed now hardly looked like a flight deck entrance at all. The tangle of wreckage around the entry port was twisted and blackened, and beyond, only partially glimpsed as the Hornet flashed past, it looked as if the interior of the flight deck had suffered equally serious damage. Bondarevsky frowned. If they had to put all that to rights, it was going to take time and effort on a Herculean scale.

"Looks like this flight deck was knocked out," Bondarevsky said. "Might have been a lucky hit, or even a landing accident by one of the Cat pilots. Hard to tell."

Harper had a pocket computer terminal out. "The way I'm rememberin' the database, sir, it was the port side flight deck that was reported hit during the battle over Landreich," he said. "Aye, here it is, indeed. *Blitzkreig* scored on the old girl late in the battle by making an unexpected run in to point blank range and firing a barrage of torpedoes. Barely escaped the scrapyard herself, but Himself has a charmed life when he gets out there in the thick of it all."

That sounded like typical Kruger tactics, all right. Brilliant, unconventional, daring, and suicidal. "This is the starboard side," Bondarevsky said. "No wonder they got in a ship-to-ship duel. It looks like they went into battle with only one flight deck operating, and lost that early on. Probably to a pilot who blew a trap. If she only had a few birds out for scouting when she blundered into the two cruisers, it would have turned into an old-fashioned slugfest. And big as she is, that supercarrier doesn't carry all that much offensive weaponry."

"Enough to take out the two cruisers, though," Bhaktadil commented. "But not in time to save herself."

"We might find a bunch of her fighters intact in the hanger decks, skipper," Sparks pointed out. "Assuming they were snugged down there when the blast swept through the flight deck, and not already up and ready for an Alpha Strike."

"Maybe so," Bondarevsky said. "But it's too early to say. We'll have to eyeball it in person to know what's possible over there. Looks like it really is a derelict, not bait in some Cat tactician's trap, so I guess we'll be going across. But I don't like the looks of her. That battle damage is pretty damned extensive. It's not going to be easy to put her back in fighting trim again."

"Tell me, Sparks, me darling, is that computer gettin' any trace of the signal Captain Springweather picked up on her visit?" Harper gave a casual grin and a self-deprecating shrug, as if to apologize for bringing the matter up.

"Nothing," she said. "Not even a carrier wave."

"So . . . if there were survivors, they're either dead, rescued, or their transmitter's out," Bhaktadil said. "Radiation in an unshielded ship would play merry hell with her electronics. Probably fried most of the systems within a few minutes of the shields going down. Like taking an EMP from a nuke—even with internal armor as redundant protection against radiation surges, you've got about as much chance of keeping electronic components in service in that as a Cat has of keeping his claws sheathed on a hunt."

"Good point," Bondarevsky said. "So if someone *did* set up a transmitter at some point, or get one of the shipboard comm systems operating, it wouldn't have had much of a life expectancy."

"That's the way I figure it," the colonel agreed. "Frankly, I think it's confirmation that there aren't any survivors over there. If they did have a few compartments rigged with makeshift shield generators to block out the radiation, there's no reason why they couldn't have kept repairing their transmitter. The fact that it's silent now means there's nobody there to repair it. For whatever reason."

"Well, that's good news, at least." Bondarevsky studied the images in silence for a few moments. "I hope all our problems turn out to be this easy to deal with."

"Now hear this! Now hear this!" The voice of the carrier's Flight Control Officer rang through the shuttle. *"All shuttles prepare for launch. Repeating, all shuttles on the flight line and prepare to launch!"*

"Looks like the admirals have been reaching the same conclusions we have," Bhaktadil commented, showing startlingly white teeth as he grinned. "Now is when we start earning *our* pay, I suspect."

"If I know Richards and Tolwyn, and believe me I do, they'd have proceeded to this phase of the op even if every Cat in this part of the sector was swarming out there with guns blazing," Bondarevsky told the Gurkha. "They didn't bring us all this way to turn around and go home without seeing what's over there."

Inwardly he could only hope that their enthusiasm for winning a supercarrier for the Landreich wouldn't warp their judgment and blind them to what needed to be done.

The shuttle quivered a little as it rose from the flight deck on thrusters, but that was the only sign they were under power. It wasn't anything like a fighter launch, the sudden high-g thrust that leaked through the onboard inertial compensators and slammed you back into your seat as you leapt outward into the void. Slow and stately, the shuttle left *Independence*, fourth in line and followed by the rest of the survey contingent, shaping a course for the enigmatic hulk that circled Vaku's gas giant and drew the humans in like the lure of a Siren's song.

Starboard Flight Deck, ex-KIS *Karga*
Orbiting Vaku VII, Vaku System
0849 hours (CST)

Bondarevsky was glad that he was a passenger on this shuttle run, and not up in the cockpit trying to bring her in. They watched the approach in the holo-projected display, and he found himself holding his breath as they made the final cautious course corrections to clear the wreckage that partially obscured the entry port on the starboard side flight deck of the *Karga*. In some ways it would have been easier than a standard carrier trap, since there was no force field across the port to complicate the final seconds of maneuvering and no internal gravity fields to deal with once they were within the confines of the ship. But without guidance from the carrier, without a working optical signals system, and most of all without an unobstructed flight deck it was a tricky bit of flying to bring the shuttle aboard.

When they finally touched down and the shuttle pilot cut in the magnetic clamps and announced "Down and safe," Bondarevsky let out an audible sigh of relief.

He wasn't the only one. He'd forgotten they were all wearing full pressure suits and helmets now, and their radios picked up every breath. Even the hard-bitten Bhaktadil seemed happy that the flight was over and they'd made it in one piece.

"Marines!" the colonel said crisply. "By the numbers! Prepare to deploy!"

"Sir!" That was Gunnery Sergeant Martin, Bhaktadil's senior NCO. "All right, people, look lively there! Positions for boarding! Standard dispersal pattern! Move it! *Move it!*"

As the twenty-eight armored marines scrambled to take their positions by each of the shuttle's three exits,

Bhaktadil spoke in calm, even tones. "Remember, the gravity's off-line out there. You're operating in zero-g and no atmosphere, so make sure you take it into account. Keep your eyes open—and don't just look for trouble on the deck. Check all the angles, and then check them again. Understood?"

"Yes, sir!" came the reply, all the men speaking as one. Bondarevsky was impressed. Kruger's marines, at least, knew how to function as an elite unit should. They waited for the air to bleed off from the passenger compartment. In situations like this, a potentially hostile action in vacuum, no one wanted to waste time going through conventional airlocks, so in effect the entire rear compartment became one for the duration of the op.

"All right, you sons-of-Cats," Martin said at last, after the tone had sounded in their headsets to tell them they were in vacuum and the shuttle pilot was ready to open up the hatches. "Are you ready to earn your paychecks today?"

"Hoo-YAH!" the marines responded, loud enough to make Bondarevsky's helmet radio crackle.

"Ready to deploy, sir!" Martin told Bhaktadil.

"Mr. Ortega." Bhaktadil's words were directed at the shuttle's pilot. "Drop the hatches . . . *now!*"

All three hatches—rear, port, and starboard—swung open at the same time. Two of the six fire teams went out through each exit, the men diving through into zero-g and twisting right and left in turn, weapons ready. The lack of gravity extended those dives considerably, but they were expert at this kind of drill and used the handholds outside the shuttle to check their progress so smoothly that it looked easy, though Bondarevsky knew for a fact that it was one of the trickiest moves a man in zero-g had to make.

They kept their weapons at the ready until the deployment was complete and the shuttle was ringed by armed men, scanning their surroundings in all directions. Martin ran them through a roll call, and each man sounded off with an "All clear!" as he responded. Finally Martin reported to the colonel.

"Initial deployment complete, sir!" he said. "All clear."

"Very good, Sergeant," Bhaktadil said. "Two-Six, this is Marine-Six. Do you copy?"

Two-Six was the call sign of the lieutenant commanding the other squad of Second Platoon assigned to the starboard flight deck reconnaissance. The shuttle carrying his men had approached from the opposite end of the flight deck, over *Karga's* stern.

"*Copy you five-by-five,*" Lieutenant Kate Loomis responded. "*Both squads deployed. All clear.*"

"Very good, Two-Six. Proceed with phase two. Make sure your people don't mistake one of us for a Cat."

"*Phase two. Roger.*"

"Sergeant Martin, move them out. Expand perimeter to meet with the other squad. Stay sharp, people."

Bondarevsky and the rest of the noncombatant team remained inside the shuttle, following the progress of the marines by their radio calls and images relayed from their suit cameras, displayed now as flat pictures on their helmets' HUD screens. Switching from one marine's viewpoint to another as their careful, leapfrogging advance unfolded at an efficient but unhurried rate, Bondarevsky was able to get an initial idea of the situation on the flight deck long before the area was secured.

There was no doubt the flight deck had suffered terrible damage. Much of the interior around the entry port was filled with twisted wreckage, jagged chunks of the bulkheads torn loose in a pattern that could only have been caused by a fair-sized explosion right at the mouth of the portal. He could also make out what looked like a part of the fuselage of a Kilrathi Darket-class light fighter that had smashed up against one bulkhead, probably not the cause of the disaster but a victim sitting on the flight deck as the explosion ripped down the vast chamber. Details, though, were hard to pick up on the video images. They'd have to go in for a closer look to see the full extent of the damage.

Finally Bhaktadil called for phase three of the op. This was the signal that his men had secured the flight deck well enough for the survey team to risk deploying and getting to work. Of course, two squads weren't much to hold a compartment that stretched nearly the full 920-meter length of the carrier, much less probe all the possible places where the enemy might be hiding, but the first sweep had turned up no sign of the Kilrathi . . . none that were alive, at least.

The dead were another story.

Bondarevsky only gradually became aware of the bodies that littered the flight deck. There were dozens of them, some floating free, others trapped under wreckage. In many cases it was hard to be sure he was even looking at something that had once been alive. Many of the flight deck crew had been caught unsuited when the airlock field collapsed. Explosive decompression was no prettier an end to a Kilrathi than it was to a human being.

He fought back nausea as the impact of the dead grew. For most of his life Jason Bondarevsky had been trained to kill Kilrathi, and he'd been good at his job. But seeing this . . .

More than ever, all he wanted was an end to it.

"Survey Leader to Team Four," the voice of Admiral Richards gave him something other than bodies to

concentrate on, and Bondarevsky was relieved at the distraction. *"Progress report."*

"We've only just started our sweep, Admiral," Bondarevsky told him. "The techies are busy getting the portable shield generators in place so we don't have to worry about the rads. So far . . . general impressions only."

"You're taking your time down there, Jason," Richards said with a hint of irritation plain in his voice.

"It's a big flight deck, sir," he replied. "The jarheads only gave us the phase three go-ahead a few minutes ago."

"Right. Sorry. We've been at it for about half an hour up here."

"How does it look, sir?" he asked.

"Flag bridge is mostly intact," Richards told him. *"A little peripheral damage, but it was never hit in the fight."*

"Casualties?"

"God, yes." The admiral's voice sounded suddenly old. *"Looks like they had a full crew manning the stations here. Twenty or so, including Admiral Cakg himself. They're dead."*

"How?"

"Well, it looks like one of them was killed in a brawl. An old adversary of mine in the Intel game, Baron Grathal nar Khirgh. One of Thrakhath's favorite toadies. We wondered what the hell had happened when he dropped out of sight last year. From the looks of things he lived up to a long and well-deserved reputation for letting his mouth get the better of his brain, and somebody stuck something sharp through his throat."

"And the rest, sir?"

"Suicide, son," Richards said heavily. *"From the*

admiral right down to the most junior console jockey, they all suicided. The full-blown Zu'kara ritual."

"God . . ."

"Yeah, that was my reaction, too. The best I can figure they knew they weren't going to get clear of the radiation before they took lethal dosages, so they all decided to give it all for the glory of the Emperor." Richards gave a humorless, rasping chuckle. *"What a waste. The Emperor probably didn't last more'n a week or two longer than they did."*

"Down here it's battle casualties so far," Bondarevsky said. "The flight deck took a real pounding. I'm not too sure we can get it put back together, sir. It'll be a hell of a lot of work."

"Don't jump to conclusions yet. Do your survey. We'll compare notes later."

"Aye aye, sir."

Bondarevsky had just switched off the comm channel to the admiral when Harper attracted his attention. "Sir, I'm thinkin' we've got something strange goin' on here."

He made a graceful zero-g leap and crossed to where the lieutenant was working, a relatively undamaged area where a line of lockers overlooked one of the main elevators that lifted planes up from the hangar deck below. The doors were labeled in the familiar wedge-shaped Kilrathi script. Bondarevsky centered his suit video camera on one of the signs and cut in the computer imaging and translation program that operated in conjunction with the mainframe back aboard the shuttle. A moment later the computer overlaid the image on his helmet HUD with an English translation: Survival Stores.

"What've you got, Mr. Harper?"

"The locker's empty, sir. So are three more I've checked so far." He paused, but when Bondarevsky made no response he went on. "I've never heard of anyone not keepin' his survival kits stocked and ready on the flight deck, sir. One locker might've run out if they were passin' them out to pilots about to launch on a mission, but three in a row?"

Bondarevsky nodded inside his helmet. "I see what you mean. Might be we have survivors after all, plundering the supplies to stay alive."

"It's more than supplies, skipper," Sparks joined them, swarming along a line of handholds looking for all the world like a high-tech monkey climbing a tree. "Look over there." She pointed. "There should be fuel pumps and a rack of external environmental feeds over there to service a plane waiting for launch. You can see where it used to be, but it's gone. And not from battle damage, either. The blast effects didn't do much this far in. Somebody dismounted a couple of tons of servicing equipment and hauled it out of here."

"Survival gear I can see," Bondarevsky mused. "But what would a survivor want with that stuff? Unless he was trying to get a bird up . . ."

"Maybe somebody did," Harper said. "Packed up and left after the rest of the ship went belly-up."

"Doesn't make sense," Sparks said. "If they had a working plane, they didn't need to pack up the gear and take it with them. And where else on the ship would they have a plane to service that would make them come here and strip out this stuff?"

"The other flight deck?" Harper suggested.

"No, I already checked with the team there," Sparks told him. "Not only is it in even worse shape than this one, so that a launch or a landing is pretty near impossible for anyone but a particularly depressed lemming, but they're missing all signs of their support gear too. It's been stripped out, same as this."

"I don't like this at all," Bondarevsky said. "It's not so much a threat as a mystery . . . but I've never liked mysteries involving Cats. Too often they lead to one of their little schemes, like the fake armistice before the Battle of Earth or that elaborate espionage role they put together for Hobbes. Okay, good spotting, you two. Get back to work, and keep your eyes open. I'm going to have a chat with the colonel about the possibility of Kilrathi hanging around here."

He didn't have a chance to follow through on his intention, though. Before he could even spot Bhaktadil and Martin, his helmet commlink sounded an emergency tone.

"All teams, all teams!" Richards sounded tense. *"This is Team Leader. Return to shuttles and secure! Abort survey! Repeat, abort survey and secure aboard shuttles!"*

"All right, people," Bondarevsky called. "You heard the man. Get aboard!"

Harper, Sparks, and the ten-man team from Diaz's salvage group were already in motion, and Bondarevsky heard Bhaktadil issuing terse instructions to his marines on their tactical channel. He watched as his people started back for the shuttle in haste, and switched off all his comm frequencies except the command link to Richards.

"What's going on, Admiral?" he asked.

"The Hornets picked up an incoming bogie," Richards said. *"Moving slow, but on a course to intercept us in another fifteen minutes. They're not answering calls, and there's no IFF signal."*

"Any idea what it is?"

"Not a clue yet, but I'm not taking any chances. I've got Babcock and her wingman closing in for a visual ID, but I want everybody ready to clear out in case

that blip turns out to be a missile or an attack bird coming in to give us an old-fashioned Cat-style welcome."

"Good idea, sir," Bondarevsky said. "But I doubt it's a missile . . ."

"Maybe not. But I keep remembering that the bomb that took out Kilrah was small enough to be carried in the munitions load of a heavy fighter. And big as this old rustbucket is, she ain't exactly planet-sized."

• CHAPTER 7

> *"Honor is a thing to be cherished, but no true*
> *Warrior will place his honor above his duty."*
> from the Third Codex
> 7:12:05

Hornet 101, VF-12 "Flying Eyes"
Near Vaku VII, Vaku System
1031 hours (CST), 2670.313

Commander Darlene Babcock studied her tactical
display and tried not to be irritated with the voice in
her headset. She'd never been a big fan of backseat
flyers, but she wasn't in a position to say so when it
was one of the Landreich's senior admirals giving the
unwanted and unnecessary advice. So she watched her
screens, listened to the voice, and pictured Admiral
Richards sitting at the controls of a Kilrathi Darket as
her targeting reticule flashed red to announce a
successful lock-on. . . .

"Whatever that bogie is, Commander, leave it alone,"
Richards was saying. *"Commander Tolwyn is on his way*
with the Raptors. Your job is to identify the thing if
you can, and avoid combat unless it fires on you."

"Copy," she said tersely. "My computer's still trying to process the sensor data, but so far it hasn't matched the configuration to any Kilrathi design in the warbook."

"Commander, this is Bondarevsky," a new voice broke in.

Great, she thought. Another expert trying to fly the mission for me. "Keep it short, Captain," she said. "I'm closing to weapons range in a hurry, and I won't have much time for talking."

"Check your warbook again, but don't limit the search parameters to Kilrathi designs," Bondarevsky said. *"That could be a civilian ship like Vision Quest. Or a Kilrathi using a captured ship to fool us. Lots of possibilities that wouldn't be listed as Kilrathi ship types."*

She cursed under her breath. She'd been flying against Kilrathi so long she'd automatically screened out other ship types when she called up the warbook database. What a damn-fool stunt to pull . . . and with no end of important brass looking over her figurative shoulder, too!

Maybe backseat flyers had a place after all, she thought. "Roger that. Running warbook." She couldn't keep her embarrassment out of her voice.

"Don't be too hard on yourself, Commander," her CO said. *"The Bear caught me doing the same thing once when he was my Wing Commander and I was supposed to be the hottest new squadron CO in the Confederation Navy, so I figure you're in pretty good company."*

Babcock didn't respond to that. She was too busy frowning at the readout from her warbook screen. "Computer's ID'd the target," she reported. "It's . . . a Confederation shuttle, Type R."

"Not one of ours," the Wing Commander said. *"Landreich never picked up any of the new R-types from the Confed fleet."*

"Stay on your toes, Commander," Richards advised.

"*The Kilrathi have captured their share over the years. That could still be some kind of a Trojan Horse.*"

Bondarevsky's voice was thoughtful. "*Didn't they start refitting cruisers of the* Tallahassee *class with R-type shuttles last year?*" he asked. "*For search and rescue work, wasn't it?*"

"*That's right,*" Admiral Tolwyn replied. This was getting to be a regular chat line.

"Inside weapons range. Still no sign they even know we're here." She paused. "Visual in thirty seconds. Drifter, you hang back and keep an eye on them. If they get me . . . well, you know the drill by now."

She tuned out the conversation between the senior officers that was still going on over the commlink and focused all her attention on the approaching ship. It showed up as a bright light against the void, just another star, but swelled visibly as the range closed. For the past several minutes she'd been allowing the computer autopilot to gradually adjust her vector so that she would be able to quickly match course and speed with the target if that seemed wise. As they came closer, the differences in their vectors were going down fast, and the approach seemed to drag out.

Finally the other ship was clearly visible. It was a human design, all right, a little sleeker than the Landreich's older shuttle designs but clearly nothing like the multi-hulled knife-blade shapes the Kilrathi favored. As her Hornet flashed by she got a look at the hull, where blast damage had blackened parts of the fuselage.

"*Did you see that?*" Bondarevsky demanded. "*The sensor pod images . . . Sparks, play it back for me. Yeah . . . there. Those are* Juneau's *numbers on the bow.*"

"Survivors?" Richards sounded incredulous. "*We didn't pick up any trace of* Juneau *or her consort.*"

"Well, they could be human survivors," Bondarevsky said. "Or the Cats managed to pick up a trophy before the fight was over."

"Any sign of hostile activity, Commander Babcock?" Richards asked.

"That's negative, Admiral," she replied, swinging the fighter around on a course parallel to the shuttle. "I'm closing the range now. IFF's still not responding, and I'm getting nothing but static from my automatic hails. I'm not even sure he's spotted me."

"Electronics could've been fried," Bondarevsky said. "If he's been operating out here around the brown dwarf very long, a shuttle's shields might not have protected all the electronics too well."

"Yeah. Maybe."

Babcock trained one of the sensor pod's video cameras on the shuttle's cockpit and started boosting the magnification. There were figures visible inside, the images becoming clearer as she continued to adjust the zoom and cut in a computer-enhancement program.

"I see a man at the helm," she said. "Two men . . . no, second one's a woman. Humans. Looks like we found survivors!" As she spoke, one of the figures aboard the shuttle looked her way and plainly spotted her Hornet for the first time. After a moment a spotlight lit up over the cockpit, pointing toward Babcock's plane and flicking on and off in the standard semaphore code of the Terran Confederation. Her computer read the signal and provided a running translation.

TCS - JUNEAU - SHUTTLE - SURVIVORS - OF - ENGAGEMENT - NINE - MONTHS - AGO - WHO - ARE - YOU - INTERROGATIVE

She responded with the same primitive signaling method, identifying her ship and the Landreich navy.

THANK - GOD - NEED - ASSISTANCE - CAN -

YOU - LEAD - ME - TO - YOUR - SHIP - INTERROGATIVE

Babcock didn't answer right away. Instead she bucked the question up to Admiral Richards. If he wanted to kibitz while she was flying, she thought with a grim smile, the least he could do was take care of the tough decisions for her.

"*Not* Independence," came the admiral's reply. "*He's already on course for* Karga. *Tell him we'll meet him there.*"

"*Paranoia?*" Bondarevsky asked.

"*Most paranoids have real enemies, son,*" Richards said. "*This guy could be legit . . . or he could be a human captive with a Kilrathi laser pistol pointed at the back of his head. And if that shuttle turns out to be carrying something dangerous, like enough explosive to do some real damage . . . well, this old girl's already seen enough trouble that a little more won't make much difference.*"

She passed on the instructions to the pilot of the shuttle, who made a brief acknowledgment but sent no further messages. Shuttle and fighter continued on course, with Drifter's Hornet following at a discreet distance.

Darlene Babcock heaved a sigh of relief as *Karga* came in sight. It looked like she wasn't going to have to face the Cats today after all.

Starboard Flight Deck, ex-KIS *Karga*
Orbiting Vaku VII, Vaku System"
1040 hours (CST)

The Confederation shuttle came in through the stern end of the flight deck, where there was less damage, but the craft still maneuvered carefully. Watching the boat settling to the deck using magnetic clamps to hold her down in zero-gravity, Bondarevsky felt a sense of relief. Despite the admiral's continued fears of a possible Cat trick, it looked as if they'd been lucky indeed. It was rare for anyone to survive the loss of a capital ship in combat, but apparently some had managed it here at Vaku.

Still, they didn't take any chances. Bhaktadil had his marines deployed watching the shuttle, and most of the survey team was still strapped in and ready to fly at the first sign of trouble. Bondarevsky, accompanied by Harper, had persuaded the colonel to let him help greet the new arrivals. As the most recent ex-Confederation senior officer available, he might be able to elicit more information from them than the colonials could.

They waited for the shuttle to open up, and Bondarevsky passed the time studying the battered craft's hull. It had clearly taken quite a beating at some point. The plating along the port side was pitted and scarred, and several external weapons and sensor mountings were missing. There was no sign of a commlink antenna, either, which probably accounted for their inability to communicate. That bird was lucky to still be flying.

Then the port side hatch began to open, and the tension among the watching marines became thick enough for Bondarevsky to feel. A pair of humans were standing at the top of the ramp, clad in Confederation-issue suits.

Behind them, a bulkier figure moved, then another one.

"Cats!" one of the marines shouted, raising his rifle to the ready.

"Don't shoot!" someone called. "Don't shoot . . . they're friends!"

One of the humans, the man, climbed down the ramp.

He was wearing magnetic boots, and moved awkwardly, but it was plain he was trying to hurry before the situation got any worse. "I'm Commander Graham," he said. "Chief Engineer of TCS *Juneau*. The former TCS *Juneau*."

"Do all your friends have fur, Commander?" Bhaktadil asked.

"They're castaways just like us," Graham responded. "From two Imperial ships we engaged nine months back. One of them this carrier here. This is Jhavvid Dahl, Assistant Communications Officer of the *Karga*. And Mirrach *lan* Vrenes, Supply Officer from the escort *Frawqirg*. And my Engineering CPO, Ellen Quinlan."

"Don't get me wrong, Commander, we're glad to see you," Bondarevsky said. "But you have to admit the company you're keeping doesn't recommend itself to just anyone."

Graham shrugged. "When both groups made it down, we had a choice between fighting to the death or cooperating and staying alive. We decided we could always kill each other later, and we've been working together down there ever since. We struck an agreement that whichever side got here first, the others would surrender to with the understanding they'd be repatriated." He paused. "Believe me, friend, neither group would be here today if we hadn't teamed up. It's been rugged."

"Well, it's over now. I'm Jason Bondarevsky." He stepped forward, extending his hand.

"*First to Kilrah!*" Graham said, gripping it firmly through their suit gloves.

"It wasn't much of a movie," Bondarevsky said dourly. He still regretted letting himself be talked in to cooperating with the picture. Even now, it continued to haunt him. "This is Colonel Bhaktadil, Free Republic Marine Corps. And my aide, Lieutenant Harper."

"The fighter that escorted us in identified itself as Landreich Navy," Graham said, frowning. "But what are *you* doing out here, sir? A ConFleet officer . . . ?"

"A long story, Commander," Bondarevsky said. "For the moment, I hope you won't object to a little paranoia on our part. When you see Terrans and Kilrathi together on the same shuttle where neither group has any good reason for being alive in the first place, you get a little nervous. Colonel Bhaktadil would like to have some of his men look over your shuttle . . . just a precautionary measure."

"Hell, sir, for all I care you can strip it down to scrap and sell it to the Firekkans as trade trinkets. There're about two hundred people, Terran and Kilrathi, down on that moon who are going to see home after nine months in purgatory. That's the only thing that matters right now."

Wardroom, FRLS *City of Cashel*
Near Vaku VII, Vaku System
1822 hours (CST)

"So there we were, three shuttles packed full of survivors, coming in over the crash site. The Cat destroyer must've been worse damaged than they figured. Something failed on final approach, and that sucker set down hard."

Bondarevsky passed another cup of tea across the wardroom table to Commander Graham, who took it eagerly. Gaunt and drawn, the young engineering officer had spent most of the time since reaching what passed for civilization eating, drinking, and talking.

They had decided to send the *City of Cashel* to pick up the survivors on the moon, which Graham called

Nargrast. Apparently that was the name for one of the hells of Kilrathi mythology, and the description his Cat opposite number had provided of the place it was an apt name indeed. Nargrast, the planet, was a frozen waste, habitable only by a generous application of the word's definition. It was a massive world, about twice the mass of Terra, with a gravitational pull of nearly two gs and a dense oxygen-nitrogen atmosphere. A greenhouse effect allowed the planet to retain enough of the brown dwarf's energy output to keep it from being completely unlivable, and screened out the worst of the secondary radiation as well, but it also gave rise to fierce storms. Most of the survivors were sick from the overpressures and the cold, and they probably couldn't have lasted too much longer.

Now the transport was en route, and Richards had ordered Bondarevsky to accompany Graham and his party to arrange the rescue of the colonists, turning over the survey work to Sparks and Harper. *City of Cashel*, designed as a combat troop transport, was the logical choice for the job. She had plenty of space for extra passengers despite carrying the crew destined for the *Karga*, and her fleet of shuttles and assault craft could make a quick job of the evacuation of the planet's surface.

Bondarevsky was glad to get away from the Kilrathi carrier and its crew of ghosts and corpses. He doubted the Goliath project would have much chance of success anyway, and was glad the expedition could do some good, at least, by rescuing the castaways of the Battle of Vaku.

"Two of the shuttles mounted weapons pods, so we had a little bit of firepower available," Graham went on. "But the Cats weren't much of a threat. There were some survivors from the destroyer, but they were in a bad way. Some fighters had also put down there, Darkets and a pair of Strakhas. Those scared us, I've got to admit, but by the time they'd touched down they were out of fuel and weapons, so none of them even tried to come after us. And there were a couple of big lifeboats off the carrier, but they weren't armed either. I don't really know to this day when it dawned on me, but I decided to hold off opening fire until I had a parley with them. I know it was stupid, but I couldn't see slaughtering a bunch of refugees who were in the same boat we were, enemies or not."

Bondarevsky shook his head. "Not stupid," he said. "You may have just proved that we can get along with the Cats . . . if we find a common cause that's good enough."

"Yeah, maybe so. They're not near as bad as they're portrayed in the propaganda back home, either. Sure, they're tough, and they don't think like we do, but there're a few of them I'd gladly trust my life to. Have, in fact, several times over the last few months." Graham took another long swig from his cup. "Anyway, their leader turned out to be this youngster, Murragh. He came out to meet me on the open field away from the crash site, and even though he tried to bluster he sounded like a scared kid even through the computer translation. I think it had all been just too much for him to take in, the fight, the mess planetside, his first command . . . he seemed relieved to find out he didn't have to fight to the death like a hero out of one of the Kilrathi Codices. We struck a deal. Both sides would share the resources we had available—our manpower and their wreckage, basically—and we agreed that we'd pledge to let the other side return home if our side was the one that found us first. There've been a few clashes, of course, but I've seen as much fighting between members of the same species, human against human or Cat against Cat, as I've seen between the two groups. Mostly we don't have time for that crap. We're too busy trying to keep everybody alive."

Bondarevsky frowned. "You could have some problems with your deal, Graham," he said quietly. "The Landreichers might not think they have to honor an agreement struck between Cats and Terrans. Neither group's too high on their list of favorites right about now."

"You don't think there'll be trouble, do you?" Graham put down his cup and stared at Bondarevsky as if he'd grown another head. "I've given my word, sir. And that means everything to these people."

"I'll do what I can. I've had . . . a certain amount of experience making Max Kruger do the right thing. But it might take some time. Help me explain it to the Cats when we're organizing the evacuation."

"But what's the trouble? The war's over, isn't it?"

"You're pretty well up on current events for a castaway, aren't you?" Bondarevsky asked, eyeing him with interest.

"We managed to put together a hypercast receiver out of comm systems from the destroyer and our shuttles. Not a very good one, and we never had hopes of getting enough power to rig a transmitter planetside, but we could pick up traffic from both sides of the border when the atmospherics were just right and all our fingers were crossed. We heard about Kilrah."

"Any trouble?"

"Some mutterings. Fortunately the bulk of the able-bodied Kilrathi were Cadre from the carrier, hand-picked specialists loyal to the *hrai* of Nokhtak. They didn't care a whole hell of a lot for Thrakhath or the Emperor, and the general consensus seemed to be that whatever those two had brought down on Kilrah was their own damned fault. Some of the survivors from the fighter crews and the destroyer were a little less philosophical. Several killed themselves, messy show and I thought that might get the others going but Murragh calmed 'em down. He's got a great future in politics, that kid. Knew just how to push their buttons."

"Well, the war *is* over, at least as far as the Confederation's concerned. But there's a Kilrathi warlord named Ragark stirring up trouble on the border, and the Landreich's getting ready to fight back. So around here things haven't changed much, peace treaty or not, and your Cats will be treated as hostiles no matter how cooperative they've been with you." Bondarevsky sipped his own tea. "Like I said, I'll do what I can. Your bunch sounds reasonable. I doubt they'll want to throw in with Ragark. But if we can get back to business, tell me this. What were you people doing making runs out to that derelict with your shuttle missing half its systems?"

Graham shrugged. "Scavenging run. We used to make them regularly, gathering up supplies and gear we thought we could use planetside. One by one, though, our shuttles have been giving out on us. Even with the junk we've brought back from the flight decks of the *Karga* we can't keep a proper maintenance schedule on them, and spending so much time exposed to the brown dwarf's weird radiation, even with shields, has taken its toll on our electronics. The bird we were on this morning was the last one running, and it took over a month to get it back in service after we tore apart all the others for spare parts. We don't have decent sensors, a working commlink, or any of the original weapons mounts. We had to do our course calculations on a jury-rigged Kilrathi wrist computer and then feed the data into the navigation system manually, and at that we had to hope our figures for the *Karga*'s orbit were close enough to put us in the ballpark."

"You thought there was something on board valuable enough to take that kind of risk? I'd've thought you would have stripped all of the important stuff a long time back."

"He's a big ship," Graham answered, using the Kilrathi masculine pronoun for the carrier without even seeming to notice. "And the most important thing was to try to get our transmitter back on-line."

Bondarevsky remembered the report of a garbled signal picked up from the hulk when *Vision Quest* first investigated the system. "So you did get a hypercast system up and running."

"Well, not very successfully, I'm afraid," Graham said. "Had to cobble the whole thing together to run off of one of the emergency power circuits, and we could never get enough juice into it to do much. The background radiation pretty much jammed the signal most of the time, and the transmitter went down a few days after we got it running anyway. But by that time we weren't flying anything, so there wasn't much we could do about it."

"Couldn't you get the mains back on-line to get the power you needed?" Bondarevsky asked. If a Confederation engineer working with Kilrathi Cadre couldn't even bring one of the primary generators back on-line to supply power for a comparatively minor subsystem, it looked more doubtful than ever that the *Karga* could be salvaged as a spaceworthy fighting ship.

"Never tried," Graham said. "Nobody wanted to take the risk."

"Risk?"

"Yeah. Look, the Cats rigged that carrier to blow.

Computer self-destruct system. As far as Druvakh—that's the Cadre Computer Officer—could tell, the computer went off-line a few seconds before detonation. There's a good chance that the destruct command will kick in if the computer net reboots, so we've been staying as far away from the power and computer systems as possible. Even then, it's scary, let me tell you. You don't know what might make some back-up system kick in and start the countdown up right at the point where the computers crashed. Hell, didn't you guys have that figured out yet? You were on board him."

"You mean that thing is ready to blow?" Bondarevsky surged to his feet, hastening across the wardroom to the intercom terminal near the door. He stabbed at the keyboard, entering the code combination with savage haste. A face appeared on the screen.

"Comm Duty Officer," the man said, sounding bored.

"This is Bondarevsky," he said. "Get me a channel to Admiral Richards on the derelict, pronto."

"Sir, all communications off ship have to be approved by Captain Steiger."

"Damn it, man, I need that channel now! The salvage team . . ."

"Wait one, sir, while I see if the Captain can talk to you." The screen went blank, leaving Bondarevsky to curse furiously. Of course a transport ship that carried thousands of people at a time would require special regulations to handle access to the commlinks. Otherwise the outgoing traffic would be swamped with messages every time the ship passed a planet where some of the passengers had family or friends. They'd need to be especially strict given the casual attitude of the Landreichers to most matters of discipline. But this wasn't the time for a bureaucratic screw-up!

Karga was a ticking time bomb, and if the survey

crew tried to bring the mains on-line or bring the computer network back up as part of the damage assessment, the whole carrier could go up in one massive chain reaction.

He might already be too late. . . .

Combat Information Center, ex-KIS *Karga*
Orbiting Vaku VII, Vaku System
1838 hours (CST)

Geoff Tolwyn was annoyed.

He had strapped himself into the one seat that had somehow remained intact in the *Karga's* Combat Information Center, the combat bridge where the Kilrathi captain would have been stationed when he took the supercarrier into battle. It had taken heavy damage in that last fight, evidently from a hit to the adjacent section by a Confederation missile that had blasted through the bulkhead where the main sensor displays were mounted and sent a deadly hail of fragments across the compartment. There were bodies everywhere, including the Kilrathi captain's, and it was clear that none of them had lived long enough to suffer explosive decompression when the oxygen had rushed through the ruptured hull.

That hit had been devastating. Probably the loss of the fighting bridge had played a large part in the death of the *Karga*, he thought, feeling bitter at the Confederation's success. CIC was an almost total write-off, and from all accounts so were the navigation bridge and several other crucial sections of the carrier. The prospects of getting her back into commission again weren't looking good. Richards had already started talking as if the failure of the Goliath Project was a foregone conclusion.

Now Tolwyn watched his experts working at one of the few reasonably undamaged panels with a black scowl on his face. *Damn it all!* He raged inwardly. They had to make Goliath work. The alternative was unthinkable.

A spacesuited figure drifted through the rip in the bulkhead. Tolwyn recognized the markings on his suit. It was Diaz, who had left his team in Engineering to join the admiral in CIC.

"What do you think?" Tolwyn asked him urgently. "Can we tap their computer? It looks like we're going to need to get the net back on-line if we're going to have any chance of doing a full damage assessment."

"I think we can get access, at least to the ship's records," Diaz said, sounding abstracted. "That will give us schematics and maybe a picture of their damage control orders during the battle. I doubt we can get anything else yet, though. Certainly none of the automated repair systems, not until we get Engineering into some sort of shape. Even then . . . I don't know. It's not looking good."

"How long?" Tolwyn insisted.

"We'll try to reboot now, and see where it gets us. Even if it doesn't work the first time, we might get a better idea of what's needed just by watching how the system behaves."

"Then let's get moving," Tolwyn said. "We've got to get *something* on this bloody boat working!"

Diaz looked at him for a long moment. "Admiral, I hope you're not expecting miracles. My team's damned good, but they can't produce results to order if the ship is just too far gone to fix. And I believe that's what you'll find here. This carrier may not be salvageable. Period. No amount of wishing otherwise is going to make it so."

"Just try it," Tolwyn growled. "Do what you can, and spare me the bloody lectures!"

He tried to get a grip on his temper as the smaller man pushed off from the bulkhead and drifted over to the controls where the other technicians were hard at work. Tolwyn remembered how his temper had flared during the last stages of the *Behemoth* project, how he had pushed himself and everyone around him right up to the breaking point in his determination to finish the weapons platform and get it into service. Perhaps that had contributed to the disaster that had ended the operation before it had fairly begun. He had to regain something of his old equilibrium if he was going to avoid a repeat of those mistakes he'd made then. Was it almost a year now since *Behemoth*'s short and inglorious career? It seemed like only a few days had gone by, sometimes . . . and like an eternity other times.

"All right, people," Diaz was saying. Tolwyn knew he was speaking not only to his technicians, but for the benefit of a recording being made back on *Independence* of every step they took in the salvage process which would be reviewed later to look for mistakes or missed possibilities. "First computer reboot test. Report readiness by the numbers, please."

"Ready on panel one," someone said.

"Ready, panel two."

"Ready on the power grid," another voice added.

"All ready, Mr. Diaz," the team leader told his superior.

"Good. Then let's get started. Power to the—"

"*Karga, Karga, this is Bondarevsky on the* City of Cashel.*"* Bondarevsky's voice was as close to panic as Tolwyn had ever heard it, and he had seen the man fighting horrific odds time and again during the war. "*Karga, cease all salvage operations immediately!*

Repeat, cease all operations and respond to this call immediately!"

"Hold test!" Diaz snapped. "What's going on here, Admiral?"

"Let's find out," Tolwyn said. He switched comm frequencies to transmit by way of the relays aboard the shuttles that kept the survey team in contact with the rest of the battle group, the same channel they'd used earlier to monitor Babcock's encounter with the survivors. "Jason, this is Tolwyn. What the hell are you playing at?"

"Admiral, I strongly recommend you get everyone off the Karga ASAP," Bondarevsky responded, sounding relieved. *"I've just learned that the computer self-destruct system was activated aboard the carrier, and never shut down. A computer failure kept her from going up as planned, but there could still be the potential for activating the system again if you try to activate power or computer systems."*

"Self-destruct? Are you sure, Jason?" Tolwyn was torn between incredulity and relief. "If the computer went down, wouldn't that have purged the command from the system?"

"Not according to Commander Graham, sir," Bondarevsky replied. *"He worked closely with a Kilrathi engineer scavenging the carrier for parts and supplies. The Cats evidently back up their destruct system very thoroughly. Once the command is entered, it is embedded in the very deepest layers of the net. Without a deactivation code, there's no way to be sure of taking it out again. So if the computers come back on-line, even for a few seconds, you could find yourself at the end of a self-destruct countdown."*

Tolwyn looked across the compartment at Diaz. "Does this sound right to you, Major?" he asked.

"Possible, certainly," Diaz responded. "But I couldn't tell you if it's true or not. We haven't worked on a Kilrathi ship before, Admiral. This is all new territory."

"Wonderful," Tolwyn said caustically. "All right, Jason, we'll pull back until we can some up with a way to deal with this mess. Thanks for the call. You caught us in the nick of time."

"I'm glad, Admiral," Bondarevsky said.

"You copied that, Vance?" Tolwyn went on.

"Yeah." Even over the commlink from the flag bridge Richards sounded like a death row inmate after a reprieve. "I'm not going to ask how close you were to that computer test you guys were talking about a little while back. Okay, general orders to all survey personnel. Shut it down, reboard shuttles, and head for home. We've got some serious thinking to do before we go any farther." He paused. "If we go any farther."

Tolwyn let out a ragged breath. Another obstacle!

But, by God, he'd figure a way around it. Because they needed this ship, and he was determined they would have it, come what may. He looked around the bridge and finally smiled. If the plan within the plan ever needed to be used, learning mastery of how a Kilrathi carrier operated just might come in handy some day.

- **CHAPTER 8**

> *"The true Warrior perseveres against any and
> all obstacles, and gains the greater glory for his
> efforts."*
>
> from the Fourth Codex
> 02:17:06

Survivor's Camp
Nargrast (Vaku VIIa), Vaku System
0822 hours (CST), 2670.314

The arrival of the first of *City of Cashel's* shuttles
brought scores of figures, human and Kilrathi, surging
out onto the frozen plain. Watching a video monitor,
Bondarevsky felt his heart race a little faster at the sight
of them all. The humans were thin, clad in ragged
uniforms that didn't look able to cope with the cold
weather. Even the Kilrathi looked less than healthy.
All of Graham's descriptions had not prepared him for
the realities of the situation.

They had adapted to the climate as best they could,
using the shattered wreck of the *Frawqirg* as the basis
for makeshift shelters. But they had used dome-shaped
survival modules scavenged from the ship to supplement

the protection offered by the downed escort, so that they now had what amounted to a tiny village clustered around the twisted remains of the once-proud warship.

"God, what a mess." The comment came from Commander Alexandra Travis. She had been assigned to the *Karga*'s flight wing as a squadron commander, though as yet she didn't have any planes to command. She was an attractive woman, not very tall but with a face that reminded him of Svetlana's, framed by a helmet of short, lustrous dark hair, but behind her beauty was the heart and mind of a fighter. She had commanded a squadron of ground-based fighters prior to joining Goliath, and according to her files her squadron had consistently scored top honors in every exercise they'd taken part in. She had even turned down a job as an instructor at the Landreich's Fighter Training Center in order to stay on active duty.

Today Travis and other members of the nascent *Karga* flight wing who had been available aboard the transport were Bondarevsky's chosen deputies for the difficult task of helping to organize the castaways and get them off of Nargrast. It should have been a job for the marines, but all the marines working with Bhaktadil's force aboard *Karga*, and Richards and Tolwyn had been adamant about not redeploying them now that they were already committed. So flight wing pilots, who were already under Bondarevsky's direct command anyway, made the best sense as his landing party for this mission.

"You try scratching out a living in a garden spot like Nargrast, and see how good you look in nine months, Commander," Graham spoke up. He was struggling into a Landreich-issue parka.

"No offense, sir," Travis said. "I meant it as a tribute . . . I don't see how anybody *could* survive in all that."

"It was not easy," Mirrach *lan* Vrenes rumbled. His Confederation English was slightly accented, but easily understandable. His fellow Kilrathi, Dahl, knew little English and remained silent . . . an odd situation for a Communications Officer. Evidently, if Bondarevsky understood what he'd been told, Dahl was of lower birth than most Kilrathi officers, and had missed much of the basic education Cat nobles usually commanded— including a working knowledge of the chief language of their enemies. "I must admit that I was not in favor of working with humans at first . . . but I am sure we would not have survived without their help."

Graham opened the shuttle's rear troop door. It was an assault craft, designed for moving marines in and out of danger in the quickest possible time, and the whole back end of the shuttle dropped to form a ramp capable of holding an armored personnel carrier. Outside a crowd of humans and Cats surged forward, noisy and excited. Stepping to the top of the ramp, Graham held up his hands and the mob fell silent.

"We found a rescue ship," he said loudly. "They've come to take us home!"

"Whose home, ape?" a large Kilrathi demanded, pushing to the front of the crowd. Even from inside the shuttle, Bondarevsky could see he was powerfully built, though the fur of his chest had been burned away and his skin was a criss-cross network of scar tissue. That he was still alive and kicking at all spoke volumes for the Cat's toughness, and Bondarevsky had to fight the urge to reach for his laser pistol. "Whose home, I say!"

There was a muttered reaction from many of the Kilrathi in the crowd. But it died away as one of their number stepped out from among them and mounted the ramp to join Graham.

"Kuraq," he said, facing the scarred Cat. He spoke in English, as the other had. Graham had said that they mostly used English in the castaway's camp these days, since more Kilrathi knew that language than Terrans knew their snarling tongue. There were several Cats translating what was said, though, for the benefit of those who didn't understand. "Listen to me, Kuraq. When we first agreed to cooperate with Graham, we pledged then that whichever side found us, we would all go willingly."

The Cat paused. He was slimmer than most of his kindred, with an aura of authority Bondarevsky found startling in such a young officer. The human couldn't quite tell what his rank insignia meant, but thought they were the tabs of some kind of lieutenant. Yet he handled this crowd with an ease few admirals could have projected.

Turning to look at Graham, the young officer went on. "We also agreed, Graham, that the side whose people came first would do everything possible for the rest of us."

Graham nodded. "I haven't lost my grasp of it, Murragh," he said firmly. "We haven't had a chance to discuss it yet, but I'm sure Captain Bondarevsky and his people will treat the Kilrathi survivors with respect. I'll do everything in my power to make sure of that. Meantime, we've got a chance to get off this rock! I don't know about you Kilrathi, but I'd gladly live in a zoo if it was anywhere but Nargrast!"

There was some cheering, then, mostly from humans but with a number of Cats adding the peculiar monotone chant that was their version of approbation.

Graham led the young Kilrathi to Bondarevsky. "Captain, this is Murragh Cakg *dai* Nokhtak. He is the ranking nobleman from the Kilrathi half of our little community. Murragh, Captain Jason Bondarevsky, in the service of the Free Republic of Landreich Navy, formerly a Commodore in the Confederation fleet."

Murragh extended a hand, a very human gesture. "I have heard of you, Captain," he said formally as Bondarevsky took it. "Your raid on Kilrah was most daring."

"Er . . . thank you." Of all the things Bondarevsky had prepared for over the course of his life, meeting an urbane Kilrathi nobleman wasn't one of them. "Cakg *dai* Nokhtak. That was the name of the admiral commanding the *Karga* battle group, wasn't it?"

"My uncle," the young noble said proudly.

"I'm . . . sorry."

Murragh frowned for a moment, then suddenly nodded. "Of course. Your human concept of the sadness of death. My uncle fought a long struggle with the God of the Running Death, Captain, and he killed himself to the greater glory of our *hrai*. There is no sadness in that."

Beside them, Graham cleared his throat. "Could we save the philosophy lesson for later, O Great Prince," he asked with a sarcastic edge to his voice. "The natives are getting restless again out there, and these people have a lot of organizing to do."

The evacuation of the refugees promised to be an organizational nightmare, and it took hours for Bondarevsky to get things running smoothly. *City of Cashel* had plenty of shuttles of all sizes and descriptions available to carry out the program, but lifting capacity was never one of the Landreich team's concerns.

By far the most difficult thing was overcoming the transport captain's loudly voiced objections to taking on ninety-seven Kilrathi on top of the five-thousand-plus crew destined for the *Karga*. It wasn't numbers that bothered him, it was the idea of carrying Cats at all. Captain Steiger didn't like Cats, and didn't see why they should bother taking them off Nargrast, since if they got what they deserved they would all end up getting spaced for war crimes against the Landreich anyway. Bondarevsky finally had to invoke the full authority of the Goliath Project, while hoping that Steiger wouldn't realize that the discovery of the self-destruct system aboard the supercarrier made it more unlikely than ever that Goliath would actually be anything more than a passing notion.

Even after Steiger's cooperation was secured there were plenty of details to attend to. There were the sick and injured, for example. Nearly half the survivors were ill to some extent from the atmospheric overpressure and the bitter cold, and there were a number of Kilrathi still recovering from injuries received in the crash of the escort. Several members of both races were suffering from the lingering effects of radiation poisoning, as well. *Juneau*'s Medical Officer, Bruno Abramowicz, and *Karga*'s Cadre Surgeon Ghellen *lan* Dorv, had done the best they could, but their medical supplies were running low and conditions had been declining steadily. So Bondarevsky had to arrange for the worst of the Sick Bay cases to be evacuated first. Up on the transport he drafted *Karga*'s intended medical staff to work with *City of Cashel*'s chief surgeon and the two castaway doctors. It created additional friction with Steiger, but in the end Bondarevsky made his decision stick.

A further complication arose in the form of instructions from Admiral Tolwyn, who ordered him to conduct a thorough survey of the crashed escort while he was there. Accompanied by Travis, Harper, and Graham, Bondarevsky explored the interior of the

shattered vessel, recording everything possible with
portable computer-imaging rigs. He supposed that
Tolwyn wanted to salvage parts and spares from the
downed ship, though Bondarevsky wondered what good
it would do with the *Karga* barred to them courtesy of
the quiescent but still potentially lethal destruct order
ticking away inside its computer banks.

Still, he carried out his orders. There wasn't much
to see inside the escort. Graham and his colleagues
had pulled out most of the onboard systems and
stripped them down for parts themselves, leaving the
empty compartments to be used as quarters or
storerooms. Where they'd left systems in place, like
the auxiliary power generators, they'd made any
number of repairs using anything and everything at
hand. Bondarevsky had to credit the survivors with
plenty of imagination, but he didn't want to even think
about the number of ways Graham had put the whole
colony of survivors at risk by his improvised solutions
to technical problems.

Eventually, everything started to sort itself out. The
shuttles began arriving to evacuate the survivors, and
the technical survey was wrapped up. Bondarevsky
ordered some of the personnel intended for *Karga*'s
crew to come down to the planet's surface and continue
the work he'd started. They would cannibalize as much
as they could from the various Kilrathi systems, including
the intact fighter craft and the useless shuttles.

For himself, though, he was pleased when he could
finally take a shuttle back up to the *City of Cashel*. He
had stayed on the planet less than nine hours all told,
and he found it hard to believe that anyone could have
lasted nine months there and stayed sane.

Whatever was fated for the Goliath Project, he would
be glad to get back to *Tarawa . . . Independence*.

Council Hall, Government House, Newburg
Landreich, Landreich System
1830 hours (CST)

"The motion to adjourn has been moved and seconded!"
Max Kruger bellowed. "All those in favor, say 'aye'!" There
was a chorus of assent. "Opposed, 'nay'!"

There were probably nearly as many delegates in the
Council Hall who wanted to continue the debate, but
Kruger pounded the gavel. "In the opinion of the chair,
the ayes have it! This session is adjourned." He pounded
his gavel, wishing it could be on a few heads belonging
to members of the so-called Loyal Opposition. Muttering,
grumbling, arguing, the members of the Council of
Delegates began to drift toward the door. Kruger sat
down in one of the chairs beside the speaker's podium,
feeling exhausted. He would much rather have faced a
Kilrathi warship armed to the teeth and swooping in for
an attack than put up with another of these interminable
meetings of the Council.

Today it had been particularly bad. First there had
been the move to cut funds for the refitting of the
Landreich's newest carrier purchased from the
Confederation Navy, formerly *Saipan*, now renamed
Arbroath in honor of one of the earliest declarations
of independence in human history. The charge to block
the refit program had been led by Councilman
Galbraith's party, who seemed determined to keep
the military expansion program from getting any
further. Kruger had nightmares of what might happen
if they learned about the Goliath Project, especially
if it turned out the Kilrathi ship couldn't be refitted.
With the amount of money and personnel he'd
channeled into the effort, a failure would be enough
to bring the whole government down—if Galbraith

and his faction discovered what Goliath was all about. So far it was simply one line on the supplemental military appropriations bill, classified top secret. Enough delegates still supported the government—Kruger—to go along with his assertion that the project wasn't something to be discussed in open Council. But it would only take a few shifts in party alliances to open up Galbraith's demands for a hearing. . . .

He could only hope that Galbraith's son would remember his military oath and put the Navy ahead of his family's political ambitions. One of the key reasons for keeping the whole refit project compartmentalized in the Vaku system with only minimal contact to and from the capitol was the need for secrecy—not so much from the Kilrathi, though that was important too, but from Kruger's own political opponents at home. Sometimes they were a worse enemy than all the Cats from here to the Galactic Rim.

He'd overcome the budget fights by sheer force of personality. In the early days of the Republic he'd presided over the writing of Landreich's constitution, and Kruger had managed to give the Presidency considerable power. He or a chosen Speaker had to preside over all meetings of the Council, which gave the Executive Branch quite a bit of control over the direction of debates. But it was exactly that facet of the constitution that was forcing him to stay at the capitol now, when he really wanted to be elsewhere. Enough of Kruger's political supporters were dead or defected to make it difficult to find anyone he could really trust to run the meetings of the Council, but Kruger himself was still a voice many heeded.

But it made it hard to do his job as he perceived it. Max Kruger was a fighting man, first and foremost, and if he couldn't be leading a fleet into battle he at least felt the need to be supervising the defense of the Republic. His advisers had probably been right in urging him not to accompany the Goliath mission. Richards, Tolwyn, and the others would be out there for months if they had to refit the derelict, and there wasn't that much Kruger could do to justify being away from the capitol for so long. But he should at least have been able to take a battle group out for a tour of the frontier. Ilios, now . . . ever since the Kilrathi raid the planet had been growing increasingly strident in its demands for more support from the government, and the delegates of Ilios had been among his strongest supporters until now. If he could have paid a personal visit, shown the flag and put the defenses in order, he might have done some real good. But he was shackled by politics to this planet, this city, this god-awful Council Hall.

Max Kruger was getting heartily sick of politics. Landreich's political system was a lot like other aspects of its frontier society—loud, frantic, and lacking in dignity. Though Kruger was no respecter of dignity himself, he sometimes wondered how the Republic had stood this long when it was run by a group of determined individualists like the members of his Council of Delegates.

He straightened up from his chair and looked out at the tiered benches that dominated the floor of the Hall. Most of the Delegates were on their way out, still carrying on noisy and often violent speech as they elbowed their way out into the antechamber. It had only been a few months since one such passionate post-session debate had led to the senior delegate from Ilios pulling a knife on one of the delegates from Tara. Today passions were running nearly as high as they had that day, but so far there was no sign that anyone was considering turning a political debate into anything more fractious.

A stocky, richly dressed delegate met his eye from near the front of the Hall. Kruger suppressed a fleeting moment of distaste and stepped down from the platform to approach the man. He didn't like Daniel Webster Galbraith, but he couldn't let that stop him from being civil to the man. After all, he commanded more wealth and power than most of the rest of the delegates put together. And before his faction had parted ranks with Kruger's administration after Ko-bar Yagar, Galbraith had bailed the Landreich out of one fiscal crisis after another.

He owed the man plenty . . . and Galbraith wasn't the kind to let him forget it.

"Well, Max," the industrialist-turned-politician said with a genial smile. "Glad to see you can still shout down a delegate when you have to. Ismat Bayulkin isn't exactly noted for his restraint, after all."

"He had a point," Kruger said. "Damn it, Ilios really is hanging right out on the edge of the Cat frontier. But that's no reason to start trying to conduct naval operations from the floor of the Hall. I know they feel exposed. I just can't let people like Bayulkin think they can take charge of the armed forces by virtue of their political ranks."

Galbraith smiled. "Saving that sort of thing for yourself, eh, Max?"

Kruger felt a flare of temper building inside himself. "I could do a lot more good out there than I'm doing sitting here at home listening to all this endless talk," he growled.

"So? I'm not the one who asked you to stay put. That was your own party. Frankly, I'd be happier if you'd let us get on with governing."

"What is it with you, Dan?" Kruger demanded. "A couple of years ago you were ready to do whatever it took to make things work. Now you're the leader of the Loyal Opposition . . . except half the time you aren't even particularly loyal any more. What happened?"

"Peace happened, Max. Or weren't you watching the holo-cast that night?"

"Peace. Right. You think Ragark's going to give us any peace?"

"You've been holding up Ragark as the boogieman for so long that nobody even believes he's real any more." Galbraith was looking exasperated. "Yeah, they've violated our territory a few times. We've violated theirs, too."

"And Ilios? Was that a 'violation of territory'?"

"The confees call it piracy."

"So now you're listening to the confees?" Kruger glared at the man. "We have plenty of evidence it was Kilrathi on Ilios, Dan. Why won't you admit it?"

"Evidence can be faked. Or suppressed. There were plenty of indications of piracy in that attack on the outpost at Balthazar. But you were so convinced the Cats were involved you closed your eyes to the whole thing." Galbraith looked away. "I'm sorry, Max. Genuinely sorry. In your day you were just what the Landreich needed. A military man who could stand up to the Cats and the confees both . . . and a real live war hero we could all look up to. But times are changing, Max. We need a leader who doesn't drop everything to charge off after glory every time things get boring in the capitol. We need somebody who isn't fixated on fighting the Cats or insulting the confees. Statesmanship is what we need now, not gunboat diplomacy."

"So you think it's time to put me out to pasture,

eh?" Kruger shook his head. "You're wrong, Dan. It's still a dangerous universe out there. Now that the Confederation's out of the game we've got to look out for ourselves. All this nonsense your bunch has been spouting about defense cuts is worse than just bad. It's treason!"

"Treason? I'll tell you about treason!" Galbraith, normally so suave and urbane, was agitated now. "Treason is frittering away the Republic's cash reserves on all your new toys. What is it now? Four new cruisers and three escort carriers? Or are there more I haven't heard about yet? *Independence*, *Magna Carta*, *Arbroath* . . . do you have to buy up *every* carrier the confees don't want any more? And then there's this mysterious Project Goliath. You've had us voting funds for a damned pig in a poke! Don't you realize that we just don't have the money to spend on building up the fleet to the size you want? I made some godawful big loans to keep you afloat. If I called them in now, with the Treasury in the shape it's in, the Republic would fold."

"Is that a threat?"

Galbraith shook his head. "No . . . just a warning. I'm not the only one your government's in hock to, after all. But you know I wouldn't pull the plug like that." He sighed. "I'm a patriot after my own fashion, you know, Max. I gave you that money because back then I believed in what you were doing. And I wouldn't jeopardize the Republic just because I've parted company with you over policy."

"So you'll just keep on doing your best to run me into the ground, so you can pick up the pieces later, is that it?"

"I want what's best for the Landreich. I just don't happen to think you fill that role any more."

"I'm sorry to hear that, Dan," Kruger said slowly. "Because the fact is that I intend to keep right on doing what I think is necessary. And I'll run right over you and all your cronies if you get in my way."

"Maybe," Galbraith said quietly. "But don't underestimate the strength of a democratic government, Max. You might find yourself facing a vote of no confidence some day, just as soon as you slip up badly enough. And I think if the circumstances were right that you'd find a lot of people backing my position . . . enough to vote you right out of office."

VIP Quarters, FRLS *Independence*
Orbiting Vaku VII, Vaku System
0112 hours (CST), 2670.315

Admiral Geoff Tolwyn leaned back in his chair and rubbed eyes grown weary with fatigue. There was just so much to do, and so little time to do it in. And from the line Richards had been taking the last two days, the deadline for action was coming up fast.

Richards actually planned to drop the entire Goliath Project!

It was the discovery of the self-destruct system that had triggered the crisis, of course. Richards had cut off the survey work cold as soon as Bondarevsky had passed the word from the castaways as to the *Karga*'s potentially lethal surprise. Tolwyn had gone along with it at the time . . . but only with the idea of pulling back long enough to find a solution to the problem.

Instead it looked like Richards would pull the plug entirely. *Karga* would be bombarded until she blew up, to keep the Cats from ever recovering her, and the battle group would tamely return to Landreich.

All that Richards was waiting on was a chance to sit down with Bondarevsky and have him put in his own advice. Knowing Bondarevsky, Tolwyn assumed he'd be with Richards. He'd never been very confident in Goliath in the first place, and with the risk to the lives of everyone involved in the Project aboard a ship with an armed self-destruct system, Bondarevsky was almost certainly to vote in favor of packing up and heading for home.

It couldn't be allowed to happen that way. There were too many reasons why they *had* to put the supercarrier back in service. Reasons Richards and Bondarevsky didn't know about yet, and which Tolwyn was reluctant to share with them. If either of them turned out to be an agent of Belisarius . . .

Bondarevsky, now. Suppose he'd passed that "information" about the destruct program to them as a way to deliberately sabotage the project? The Belisarius Group would want the *Karga* kept out of the picture, and it was just possible they'd gotten to him . . .

Tolwyn shook his head angrily. He'd been living with this paranoia for too long now. It was making him mistrust everyone. Bondarevsky wouldn't sign on with a bunch of conspirators like the Belisarius Group. Surely Tolwyn knew him well enough to have that much faith, at least.

The problem was, he'd lost the ability to trust. Even old friends like Richards and Bondarevsky raised distrust in Tolwyn these days. It made it that much harder for him to gain the support of the people he needed to rally against Belisarius, because he couldn't be sure enough of anyone to really open up to them when he had to. His months of tightrope-walking had already cost so damned much . . .

But the Goliath Project represented a chance to change all that, and by God he was going to see it carried out, whatever the cost. *Karga* was a resource they simply couldn't throw away.

He returned his gaze to the computer monitor in front of him, a summary report from the teams that had investigated the hangar and flight decks of the supercarrier before the bomb scare had caused Richards to pull out. The preliminary findings indicated that both hangar decks were well-stocked with Kilrathi planes, exact numbers still not determined. Until they got a close look at them there was no telling how many would actually be able to fly, but if even half of them were put into service they'd be a valuable asset all by themselves. The *Karga* had been one of the newest and most modern carriers in Kilrathi service, and the planes she carried were all first-line models that could outperform the antiquated Confederation cast-offs the Landreich was forced to rely on.

Tolwyn scanned the report. *Light fighters, Darket-class, less than a squadron in the hangar decks but several more reported on the surface of the brown dwarf moon at the castaway camp.* The Darket was small and agile, even better for scouting duties than the Confederation Hornet. Individually weak in shielding, armor, and weapons, they were often employed in fighting pairs by Kilrathi pilots to excellent effect.

Medium fighters, Dralthi Four-class, probably two full squadrons, most craft in good condition. The bat-wing shape of the Dralthi Four was fearsome to behold in combat. Tolwyn could still remember watching in frustration as squadron after squadron of the evil-looking birds had swooped low over the *Behemoth* during the battle that had destroyed the huge weapons platform. They were slightly weaker than their modern Confederation equivalents, but compared to the Scimitars and Raptors of the Landreich's arsenal they were a deadly match.

Heavy fighters, Vaktoth-class, many missing from hangars. Perhaps an eight-ship Kilrathi squadron left, though this remains to be confirmed by closer examination of individual planes. Vaktoths were superior in every respect to the Landreich's Raptors. Even if they could only get eight of them in service, they'd be a powerful strike force for the carrier.

Heavy fighters, Strakha-class, approximately one squadron in very good condition. That was really something to take notice of. The Landreich so far couldn't field anything using modern stealth technology, but the Strakhas were capable of cloaked flight that enabled them to evade detection before they struck. Even in the Confederation stealth fighters, the new Excaliburs like the one that had dropped the T-Bomb on Kilrah, had been slow to reach the front lines and scarce as hen's teeth right to the end of the war.

Bombers, Paktahn-class, numbers hard to determine because of heavy damage to many individual units. Dedicated bombing craft were comparatively new to human flight wings, where the recent Longbow bomber was still a novelty. The Paktahn wasn't nearly as good as the Longbow, but like the stealth fighter the bomber was something the Landreich hadn't used at all . . . until now. If they could even get a few of these fit for combat action, they could greatly extend the Landreich's ability at power projection.

Electronic Warfare Craft, Zartoth-class, more than a full squadron apparently intact. Built on the same frame as a Vaktoth heavy fighter, the Zartoth was only lightly armed, but was crammed with electronics gear and electronic countermeasures. They were most useful when it was necessary to pinpoint and destroy enemy targets by detecting energy outputs, or when it was deemed advisable to knock out defending sensors or communications channels. The Confederation used larger EW vessels, corvettes, but Tolwyn had always thought the Kilrathi practice of deploying multiple Zartoths for the same role was a better way of doing the job.

Reconnaissance craft, Hrakthi-class, approximately one squadron in good condition. Unarmed and constructed from a modification of an older light fighter, the Salthi, the Hrakthi was intended purely as a scout craft. They possessed the ability to cloak, and were packed with sensors, but their combat worth was small. Still, the ability to study an enemy formation from close up without being detected appealed to Tolwyn.

Shuttles, various types, roughly four squadrons. The Kilrathi design philosophy emphasized dispersal and duplication of valuable assets to allow a force to suffer losses and still win a battle. They had adapted one basic shuttlecraft design for a number of different purposes. The Naktarg was the original version, an assault shuttle large enough to hold troops and small vehicles and armed with gatling lasers and anti-armor ground-support missiles. A Search and Rescue variant, the Rogharth, was not unlike the Type-R ConFleet shuttle that had carried the castaway party back to *Karga*, devoting space to a medical bay and extra sensors. Another intriguing type, as far as Tolwyn was concerned, was the Gratha, which was fitted for command and control duties. It carried a crew of six as well as room for a strike commander and his staff, and duplicated the tracking, communications, and tactical computer functions housed within a carrier's

Primary Flight Control center. They effectively increased the carrier's ability to control flight operations over long distances.

Finally, there was the Kofar shuttle variant, a flying munitions and fuel dump that could dock with a Kilrathi fighter in space and transfer fuel and missiles. Tolwyn had long argued that the Confederation fleet could have used a similar platform. Carriers, after all, were at their most vulnerable when they were in the process of rearming and refueling fighters in the middle of combat operations. Terran carriers could launch small tankers, but there was no provision for restocking a fighter's missiles without having it return to the flight deck. The Kofar extended Kilrathi planes' flight times dramatically.

Tolwyn shook his head. All those planes, enough to fit out something close to a full flight wing that was considerably more modern than anything the Landreich could fly, and Richards was actually thinking of throwing it all away! And that wasn't even considering the carrier herself, a marvel of advanced naval design far better than escort carriers like *Independence* and her sister-ships. Even if they couldn't make good all of the damage—and Tolwyn had to admit there was all too much to do before the battered vessel was ready for combat again—the Goliath team couldn't afford to ignore the ship's potential.

He shut off his computer monitor and stood up to pace back and forth across the cabin. Tolwyn knew with absolute certainty that Goliath had to go forward, but he wasn't sure he could convince Richards or Bondarevsky. They might not believe what he knew about the Belisarius conspiracy. And if they didn't, they could do more than just pull the plug on the carrier refit. They could keep Tolwyn from carrying on his personal war against the people who were planning the unthinkable back on Earth. He couldn't afford to lose an argument . . . he had to take some other kind of action.

And he knew what that action had to be.

• CHAPTER 9

*"There is no treachery greater than the betrayal
of comrade against comrade."*

from the Sixth Codex
16:33:17

Mess Hall C, FRLS *City of Cashel*
Near Vaku VII, Vaku System
0845 hours (CST), 2670.315

Commander Donald Scott Graham was conscious
of hostile eyes turned toward his table, but he forced
himself to ignore them and concentrate on his food
and his conversation. The relief of being rescued was
starting to turn into concern for what might come next,
but he was determined to enjoy the benefits of
civilization without letting anyone spoil his first day
off of Nargrast. But it took plenty of effort to ignore
the stares and the muttered comments. Plainly there
were fellow passengers aboard the transport ship who
didn't approve of his choice of breakfast companions.

Murragh Cakg *dai* Nokhtak evidently noticed the
hostility as well. "It would seem that my people are no
more popular with humans than yours are among

Kilrathi," he said quietly. "Perhaps I dealt less well than I thought, that day, when I agreed to entrust my people to your good will."

From across the table Jason Bondarevsky spoke up. "It's rude, but you can't really blame them. The Landreich still considers itself at war, and when the fighting's gone on as long as this you stop recognizing the enemy as individuals and start regarding every one you see as a threat. Having close to a hundred Kilrathi in for breakfast makes people a little nervous, that's all."

Murragh favored him with a close-lipped smile. "Believe me, Captain, I understand. Early on when we started working with Graham I had to persuade my people that the stories were not true that said that you apes liked nothing better than to kill and eat Kilrathi prisoners for dinner."

Graham and Bondarevsky both laughed.

"I'm beginning to believe that there are a lot more similarities between our two races than anyone would have thought possible," Bondarevsky said.

The transport ship was on the return leg of her mission of mercy, with the survivors from Nargrast safely embarked with their equipment and supplies. They'd left a detachment of spacers from the transport on the planet to study the crash site of the Kilrathi destroyer and the neighboring camp where the mixed bag of survivors had lived for nine Terran months. The Kilrathi fighters on the ground were particularly worthy of a closer look, and might be retrieved when the battle group was ready to pull out. The transport was scheduled to rendezvous with the rest of the Landreicher squadron in orbit near *Karga* within a few short hours, and Graham was glad of a chance to relax in one of the passenger mess areas. It had been a difficult two days.

The survivors had been glad to be rescued, no doubt about that, and had cooperated enthusiastically with the Landreich rescue effort. After the first confrontation with Kuraq, the Kilrathi had caused no difficulties . . . at least not until the issue of when they could go home arose. The news that the Landreich considered itself still at war with the remnants of the Empire and hence weren't likely to send a shipload of Cats back to the nearest Imperial colony had come close to causing a full-scale riot among the Kilrathi contingent. Once again young Murragh had proved his talents as a leader, calming them down with a few more well-chosen words. As Graham had told Bondarevsky earlier, the young Cat had a flair for leadership. He was only a *Hyilghar*—the word translated very approximately as a lieutenant, but with a modifier that implied staff rather than combat duties and some sort of special aristocratic social status Graham didn't entirely understand—but despite his youth and modest rank he handled Kilrathi combat veterans three times his age with a natural aplomb that Graham still found himself envying after all these months.

So the trouble had never quite materialized, but it had left a bad taste in Graham's mouth. The agreement he had made with Murragh should be honored, he felt, but he was afraid the Landreichers weren't going to see things that way. The hostile stares and angry asides the Cats drew in the mess hall didn't make him feel any better about things.

"I understand you've been monitoring developments outside the system," Bondarevsky said around a mouthful of bacon from his plate. "What do you make of the situation across the border?"

Murragh showed his fangs briefly. "Ukar *dai* Ragark is an ambitious governor who never felt properly appreciated under Thrakhath's rule. I think he would like nothing better than to see his *hrai* take the Throne. Not that they would keep it for long. He might win some short-term popularity by redeeming our pride with a victory or two, but that one won't know when to stop. Sooner or later he will overreach himself the same way our beloved Prince did, and that will be the end of him."

Graham chuckled. "You see, Bondarevsky, the Kilrathi even understand the finer uses of sarcasm," he said with a smile. "If you were looking for a fanatical follower of either Ragark *or* Thrakhath, I'm afraid you're going to be disappointed."

"Well, forgive me if I'm too obvious," Bondarevsky said, grinning. "But it's always nice to know where you stand."

"A sentiment from the Codices," Murragh replied. "You are forgiven your curiosity . . . though I would warn you to remember that the ape's questing hands are a sure route to trouble."

"And curiosity killed the cat," Graham added. Murragh laughed, a strangely human sound from a massive, fur-covered, cat-like creature with a flattened muzzle and sharp fangs. It always startled him to hear the Kilrathi laughing. They were so often depicted in Terran propaganda as dour creatures who took pleasure only in blood and death.

"So who do you support, in the new Empire?" Graham asked. "Chancellor Melek?"

"An honest *kil*, although he was a creature of Thrakhath's," Murragh responded. "His caretaker government at least does not assert a claim to the Throne itself. I imagine he will turn control over to the rightful Emperor when the time comes."

"The trouble is deciding who has the right," Bondarevsky

countered. "Every governor and petty warlord in the Empire is claiming to be the one leader who should take over as Emperor, in the absence of a legitimate heir."

Murragh didn't answer, but he was showing his teeth again. The fighting smile wasn't an expression of satisfaction or humor in a Kilrathi warrior. It meant the anticipation of battle.

"Ah, Bondarevsky, maybe you missed the significance of Murragh's full name," Graham said, stepping into the awkward silence. "The *dai* Nokhtak *hrai* is a distaff branch of the Imperial Family. Murragh here is a distant cousin of the Prince Thrakhath's . . . maybe the last one alive. His grandmother was sister to the late Emperor. That makes *him* a legitimate heir to the Kilrathi throne."

"What?" Bondarevsky almost stood up, taken aback by Graham's quiet announcement. "I didn't make the connection . . . I guess somebody mentioned Admiral Cakg was a cousin of Thrakhath's, and you . . ."

"I am his nephew," Murragh said quietly. "And possibly the only living *kil* with a claim to the Empire. As such, since you ask me whose side I am on, I can only say that I am wholeheartedly in favor of my own side."

Bondarevsky shook his head slowly, his expression a mix of wonder and embarrassment that made it hard for Graham to keep a straight face. "My God, I've just had breakfast with the rightful Emperor of the Kilrathi. My memoirs are going to be a bestseller, I just know it." He grinned. "I guess you never know who you're going to meet out here on the frontier."

Graham laughed. "Surprised the hell out of me, too, when I found out," he said. "And I thought all Cats were pretty much alike . . . until I started hanging out with royalty!"

VIP Quarters, FRLS *Independence*
Orbiting Vaku VII, Vaku System
1442 hours (CST), 2670.316

Jason Bondarevsky cradled his head in his hands and stared at the overhead above his bunk. It was good to be back aboard the escort carrier, the rescue mission completed, but now that he was back he couldn't help but worry about what the future might hold.

The leaders of the Goliath Project had spent a stormy hour that morning discussing the situation on the *Karga*. For the most part, the consensus was that it was hopeless to try to salvage the ship. That self-destruct system made the whole prospect entirely too dangerous, and the extent of the damage was such that it seemed unlikely they could get the ship back into fighting trim even if they could circumvent the computer's deadly last program.

Of them all, only Admiral Tolwyn had been in favor of going forward with the project, but he'd made up in vehemence what he lacked in support.

As for Bondarevsky, his worries centered more on what would come next. Kruger had recruited him with this Goliath scheme in mind, and now that it looked to be a dead letter he had to wonder if there'd be a place for him in the Landreich after all. There weren't that many decent military commands available, and somehow he couldn't see himself ending up as some supernumerary staff officer pushing computer keys for the greater glory of Max Kruger and the Landreich.

The door buzzer sounded, interrupting his reverie, and Bondarevsky raised his voice to order the computer to open it. Sitting up in the bed, he was startled to see Admiral Richards framed in the opening. The admiral held up a hand as he started to scramble to his feet.

"Don't get up, Jason," he said, looking weary. "May I come in for a few minutes?"

"Of course, Admiral. Please. Can I get you something?"

Richards pursed his lips. "How about a sane assistant?" he muttered darkly. "Or a laser pistol so I can shoot the *insane* one I've already got."

"Sir?"

"That idiot Tolwyn went over my head!" Richards exploded. "Got on a hypercast channel with Kruger and talked him into authorizing a go-ahead on Goliath. And all this *before* the meeting this morning!"

"What?" Bondarevsky couldn't believe the admiral's words. Even Admiral Tolwyn couldn't be so set on this operation as to ignore the danger of trying to work on the supercarrier. "That's impossible! That ship is a bomb waiting to go off. We can't hope to work on her. I assumed we'd launch a spread of torpedoes, cut our losses, and head for home base."

"That's what I planned on doing," Richards said heavily. "But Kruger's adamant. We're to use all means available to try to save the carrier, whatever the risks may be. That's a direct presidential order, no less."

"But Admiral Tolwyn's behind it?"

"That he is," Richards said. "I went stomping across to his cabin as soon as I had Kruger's message, and the bastard actually boasted about getting Old Max to come on board. Said it was too important to back off now, and then clammed up on me. I'm telling you, Jason, I just don't know what to do! Part of me wants to out-Kruger Old Max, invoke my superior rank over Galbraith and take us out of here no matter what our orders are. But . . ." He shook his head. "Damn it all, we've invested a hell of a lot in Goliath. It really was the best chance we had of evening the odds. I know how Tolwyn feels. I'd like to take a crack at it too. But not when repairing a single circuit could bring the self-destruct countdown back up and kill the whole salvage team. This is asking too damned much!"

"I agree, sir," Bondarevsky said softly.

"I didn't think Geoff Tolwyn had it in him, to be this callous about men's lives." Richards locked eyes with Bondarevsky. "You know, I heard a lot of nonsense about how he'd turned into a cold-blooded killer when he started work on *Behemoth*, but I wouldn't buy into it. Now I'm not so sure. Maybe when you've seriously contemplated genocide as an option a few more lives one way or another aren't going to matter any more."

Bondarevsky looked away, remembering some of his own thoughts about Tolwyn's involvement with *Behemoth*. But some perverse part of him rallied to the admiral's defense. "Sir, I don't like the sound of this any better than you do," he said slowly. "But I've known Admiral Tolwyn for a lot of years now, and I've never known him to do anything without a pretty damned good reason behind it. Maybe we should try to find out what the reasons are for this, too."

"You do what you like," Richards said. "I don't know if I can trust myself not to punch the bastard out the next time I see him."

Bondarevsky understood exactly how Richards felt.

VIP Quarters, FRLS *Independence*
Orbiting Vaku VII, Vaku System
1934 hours (CST)

Bondarevsky touched the stud by the door to Admiral Tolwyn's suite and waited with mounting concern. The admiral had not stirred from his quarters all afternoon, and now, when Bondarevsky had finally decided to seek him out, it seemed as if he wasn't planning on seeing visitors. There wasn't even a query from the intercom.

Finally, though, the door slid open.

The room was dark, with all the lights out except a single worklight by the computer terminal, and the glow of the monitor screen. But Tolwyn wasn't at the desk. It took a moment for Bondarevsky's eyes to adjust to the darkness and pick out the shadowy figure of the admiral slumped back in an easy chair facing the door.

"Sir?" Bondarevsky ventured, uncertain of himself.

"Come in, Jason," Tolwyn said softly. "I suppose Vance Richards sent you."

"He . . . talked with me earlier, sir, but it was my idea to come, Admiral," Bondarevsky said.

Tolwyn chuckled, but there was precious little humor behind it. "You missed your calling, Jason. You should have been a diplomat. What Vance did was rant and rave, scream bloody murder, and call me everything but a Cat-lover, right?"

Bondarevsky didn't answer that. "I came because I think it's a mistake to go ahead with Goliath, sir. A big mistake. You're putting hundreds, maybe thousands of lives at risk on a project that had damned little chance of success from the very start. And going outside the chain of command to Kruger instead of working on a report with Admiral Richards . . ." He paused. "I've known you for most of my adult life, Admiral, and I've always thought of you as a second father. But you've not been acting like the man I remember . . . not since *Behemoth*. And that scares me, sir."

"Sit down, Jason," Tolwyn said slowly. He waited until Bondarevsky had settled into a chair across from him before he went on. In the darkened cabin, his quiet, firm voice seemed almost unreal, like a ghost's. "I know all the reasons why Goliath should be dropped. Believe me, under any other circumstances I'd be the loudest voice calling for cancellation, no matter how much Max Kruger wanted his new toy. But I know a few damned good reasons for going on, too, and in my opinion they outweigh the ones in favor of dropping the project."

"What could justify risking so many people?" Bondarevsky demanded. "Come on, Admiral, you've been hiding things since before we left Terra. How can you expect any of the rest of us to go along with you if you won't let us in on the same information you're using to base your decisions on?"

Tolwyn didn't say anything for a long moment. "You can't just accept that I know what I'm doing? Once upon a time, Jason Bondarevsky would have followed me into Hell and back out of sheer loyalty."

"When I was still a newbie on my first deep-space assignment, maybe," Bondarevsky said. "Back then everything was simple. You pointed at the holo-map and laid out the mission, and I flew. Simple. But a lot's happened since then, sir. I'm not the same man I was fifteen, twenty years ago. And neither are you. *Behemoth* proved that."

"*Behemoth*." Tolwyn packed a world of contempt into that single word. "That's where everything started to go wrong, Jason. And like a fool I didn't see any of it coming until it was too goddamned late."

There was another long pause before he started speaking again. "All right, Jason, since you won't accept my word I guess I'll have to spell it all out. But you're not going to like it. Not one bit of it." He stood up and started to pace back and forth across the narrow confines of the cabin, a dark shape only half-seen in the dim light. "Remember the mess we were in after the Battle of Earth? All the Joint Chiefs were killed, most of them in that bombing the Kilrathi pulled during the peace talks, and Duke Grecko in the fighting. And the government was in chaos, too, when the President resigned because of his part in letting the Cats nail us."

Bondarevsky nodded, though he didn't know if Tolwyn could see him.

"The new government amounted to a coalition between all the major parties, and it showed. After we beat the Cats back from Terra we should have followed up with a strike that would have knocked them into the stone age, but instead we frittered away our strength against a string of useless targets until Thrakhath and his granddaddy had a chance to rebuild everything they'd lost and then some. When *Concordia* went down, that was the last straw. We'd fallen behind in ship building, and were starting to deploy miserable old carriers fit for the scrapyard in front-line sectors because our resources were stretched so thin. That was largely thanks to the Department of Industrial Affairs. The bureaucrats there were dragging their feet every time someone suggested a move that would cut a few corners and speed up production, and Secretary Haviland either wouldn't or couldn't put his foot down. But we were getting the same kind of trouble from half a dozen other cabinet people, too. It was a mess from start to finish."

Tolwyn paused. "I'd just been assigned to the Weapons Development Office when *Concordia* went down. I inherited *Behemoth* from Ubarov, who had the post before me. Frankly, my first reaction was to scrap the damned thing then and there. The design was all wrong, for one thing. It should have been mounted aboard a ship that could defend itself effectively . . . and one that had some legs, too, so it could maneuver in a combat situation. *Behemoth* didn't have either capability. And I didn't like the whole concept of blasting planets indiscriminately, either. It always seemed to me that the only thing that marked a difference between us and Thrakhath was that we had at least a modicum of morality on our side, and this was putting us on the very same level as him.

"But before I'd finished the review and made a final decision I had a visit from an old friend of mine that changed everything." Tolwyn fell silent, still pacing restlessly.

"Sir?"

"David Whittaker." Tolwyn paused again, as if the name alone conveyed everything he wanted to say. Finally he continued. "Dave Whittaker was a classmate of mine in the Academy more years ago than I care to remember. We were shipmates on our cadet cruise aboard the old *Albemarle*. The captain sent us down in a shuttle with a survey team . . . you know the drill, give the middies some responsibility on some jerkwater little planet where nothing can go wrong. Well, this time something did go wrong. My helm console exploded—they never did figure out why—during the landing approach. The shuttle crashed. I woke up blind and pinned in the wreckage, without my helmet and with sulfur dioxide fumes leaking in from the planetary atmosphere. Dave didn't have a helmet either, it had been crushed under a piece of the computer when we hit. But he stayed with me, got me out and helped me get to an emergency pressure bubble, breathing that god-awful stuff. I never would have made it if it hadn't been for him. We both pulled six months in the hospital, and Dave got a commendation and the Distinguished Service Award. We kept in touch, off and on, but I kind of lost track of him over the last few years, until he came to see me one night at my house off-base.

"It could have been old home week, but he didn't waste any time making small talk. Instead he launched right into it. He wanted to sound me out on behalf of some friends of his, military officers with long and distinguished service records who were sick and tired of the way the Confederation civil government was making a hash out of the war effort. He named a couple of names . . . important officers, men like DuVall and Murasaki. And they were just recent recruits, not part of the main organization. It took a few minutes for me to get it through my thick skull that Dave was talking about a military coup, about throwing over all of our service oaths and rising against the Confederation government!"

"What did you say to him, Admiral?" Bondarevsky asked.

"Well, what I should have done was say I'd sign on and find out more, but I didn't. I told him exactly what I thought of the idea of the military shaking loose of civilian control. I don't care how screwed up things are in a democracy, there's never an excuse for the military to run free of government control. Never! So Dave left, handing me a story about it was all just a vague idea and he was sorry he'd even broached it. But I knew he'd been serious. I guess my reputation for playing things my own way persuaded them that I'd be sympathetic."

"You could have been in a lot of danger," Bondarevsky said. "A halfway decent conspiracy would have had you killed if they thought you were a danger to them."

"I know. I think Dave was the only thing that held them back . . . that and the fact that I didn't do anything that could worry them."

"You mean . . . you didn't alert ConFleet Security?"

Tolwyn stopped his pacing and stood looking down at Bondarevsky. "I did not," he said flatly. "And for a good reason. One of the things Dave let slip when we were talking was the fact that Security is lousy with their people. They have a whole secret wing of the security forces, an agency I later found out is designated Y-12 on the TO&E. But they have agents scattered all through the structure. So who could I report things to? Anyone I contacted could have been part of it, even my best friends and oldest contacts. If Dave Whittaker was one of them . . ."

"You had Presidential access," Bondarevsky pointed out.

"And you know it takes time and several layers of bureaucracy to get a meeting, even to place a holo-call—not that I'd've trusted something like that to a holo-call, no matter how secure the line was supposed to be. The way I figured it, if I had made a move to see anybody I could be reasonably sure *wasn't* part of the plot I'd have been dead before I knew what hit me. So I pretended I believed Dave's disclaimers and did the only thing I could think of doing."

"What was that?"

"I threw everything I had into getting *Behemoth* operational, Jason. Everything. I pushed every man in my command past the breaking point, myself included, trying to get that goddamned weapon built and tested as fast as possible."

Understanding dawned. "To get the war over as quickly as you could," Bondarevsky said slowly.

"Exactly," Tolwyn said. "I figured the only way to head off a coup was to remove the only excuse the conspirators had. End the war by whatever means possible, and the civilian government wouldn't have be in a position to screw things up so much any longer. So I figured *Behemoth* was our best possible chance. If I'd've known about Paladin's Temblor Bomb project I would have thrown all my department's resources into backing him.

But his operation was strictly black, top secret all the way."

"So you pushed *Behemoth* as the best way to finish the fighting before the conspirators struck. I can see why you were under so much pressure . . ."

"Can you, Jason? Can you really?" Tolwyn's voice was suddenly ragged with emotion. "I don't know if anyone can understand what I was going through. Try to put yourself in my place. I was being forced to put my faith in a weapon I didn't really believe in, and the stakes weren't just victory or defeat any more. If we didn't stop the Kilrathi cold, one of two things would have happened. Either the Cats would have hit us so hard that we'd be joining the dinosaurs, or the conspiracy would strike and militarize the Confederation in the name of saving mankind. Either way, everything I believed in would have been gone. And on top of it all was the fact that it was Dave Whittaker who'd brought it to me. Damn it all, he saved my life when we were middies together, Jason, and yet he turned out to be part of this group that would actually consider an armed coup against our own government! I think that hurt me worse than when I lost my family."

Bondarevsky found himself picturing how he might react if someone close to him, Sparks or Kevin Tolwyn for instance, had approached him with such a concept. "Yeah . . . that must've been . . ." He trailed off. There weren't words for such a betrayal.

When Tolwyn spoke again, his voice had dropped until it was barely more than a whisper. "The real hell of it wasn't even Dave's involvement," he said. "God forgive me, Jason, but there was a part of me that was tempted to go along with Dave. The civilian government really was making a hash out of the war effort. In the right hands, a military government could have stabilized things long enough to deal with the Cats. It wouldn't need to be a tyranny, if the right people were involved. And Dave Whittaker should have been one of the right people."

"Then what stopped you from joining?"

Tolwyn's answer was oblique. "Back in the days of the Roman Republic, before the Caesars, the word 'dictator' didn't have any unfortunate connotations," he said. "A dictator was just a leader appointed for the duration of an emergency with broad military and civil powers. Did you ever read Livy, Jason? Cincinnatus was a simple country squire, but when Rome was in danger he left the plow to become the dictator until the crisis was over. Then he laid down the rods of office and went back to his simple rustic life. George Washington was the same kind of man, in the early days of the American republic." Tolwyn sighed. "But there aren't many men like Washington or Cincinnatus, Jason. Rome had Caesar and Pompey; America had Harold Jarvis back in the early twenty-first century. I was tempted to play Cincinnatus and defend the Confederation, but I'm damned if I'm going to help some ambitious bastard play Caesar!"

"I see your point, sir."

"Well, anyway, you know what happened. By the time we got *Behemoth* operational I was so tied up in knots over everything that I tried to carry off the whole operation on sheer brute determination. Most of my people were on the thin edge of a nervous breakdown, and I wasn't far behind them. Otherwise we would have tightened security, and that damned Cat Hobbes would never have been able to get the details of the *Behemoth* to Thrakhath. Hell, there were officers aboard my flagship who were conducting a search for a spy long before I ever knew anything about it. Maybe if I'd been more conscious of anything beyond the need to get the job done I might have been able to help them find him before he screwed us all. But . . . I didn't. Thrakhath jumped the fleet and knocked out *Behemoth*, and that was all she wrote. Fortunately Paladin was there to pick up the pieces, and Chris Blair flew the mission that ended the war before the conspirators had a chance to move. I ended up with a messy court-martial and a career in ruins even after they acquitted me. But it was what happened after the court-martial that made me realize that I'd underestimated the bastards in the conspiracy after all."

"*After* the court-martial?"

"Just after. When I got home from the court appearance that last day, I found a message on my comm terminal. No video, just a voice using a distorter so it couldn't be recognized. All he said was 'We could just as easily have crushed you. Remember that we look after our friends . . . as long as they *are* friends.' "

"You think the officers on the court were in on the conspiracy?" Bondarevsky asked.

"I'm certain of it," Tolwyn responded. "Just as certain as I am that it was that same bunch who had Dave Whittaker killed four months ago."

"But why?"

"I did some digging, as quietly as I could, and found out that some of the conspirators were in it for a lot more than just the idea of saving us from the Cats. They call themselves the Belisarius Group. Some of the ringleaders have enjoyed the increased power they've acquired as a result of the war. Even under civilian authority, the military's been riding high lots of ways. They must have figured they would lose out on their perks once the peace was signed. I suspect the civil government might not have been as stupid as everyone thought, too. The indecent haste with which they started scaling back the armed forces tells me they were worried about a coup even after the war . . . and it turns out they had good reason to worry."

"But without the War there's no excuse . . ."

"Exactly." Tolwyn sat down again, leaning forward and talking now with an intensity that reminded Bondarevsky of the admiral's customary aura before a major engagement. "The conspiracy has penetrated beyond the military now, Jason. They've got people on the Peace Commission, in the Foreign Office, plenty of key places. And they are deliberately engineering a revival of the Kilrathi War so that there will be a sufficient threat out there to justify them seizing power and holding on to it."

"That's . . . that's a pretty powerful accusation, sir."

"It's true. I've been collecting information ever since the court-martial, trying to gather enough evidence of what's going on to stop them, but they've covered their tracks awfully well. I *know* a lot of what they're trying to do, but I can't *prove* very much of it." He paused. "As far as I can tell, their plan is to stir up trouble out here on the frontier. They're doing everything in their power to embroil Kruger in a fight with Ragark, knowing full well that Kruger doesn't have a snowball's chance in Hell of stopping a full-scale invasion. But at the same time they're not letting the truth get out back home. When the Landreich falls, it will be another 'sneak attack' by the Kilrathi. Ten major colonies and all the people on them will be martyrs to the cause of resisting the Kilrathi hordes once again. They know that a show of support early on will probably make Ragark back off. He's no fool. So there is a concerted effort to keep Kruger and his people from getting so much as a hearing back home . . . and at the same time, they're already setting things up so that the blame for the Landreich's fall will be laid at the government's doorstep. Who disarmed the fleet? Who failed to respond to Kruger's warnings? So they'll have another war, and it will look as if the inept civil government is to blame. The perfect conditions to carry off the coup."

"It sounds plausible, I suppose," Bondarevsky said, dubious. "But you're ascribing an awful lot of power to these people. What do they need a coup for, if they've already got such a long reach?"

"They're powerful, but so far they have to operate very carefully, and from the shadows. And they didn't keep all of their original membership when they started this new phase. I'm convinced Dave Whittaker died because he couldn't go along with this new plan." Tolwyn slumped back in the chair again. "At least I hope that's why. I'd like to think that, in the end, he really was the same man I remembered."

"But they still want to use you?"

"I think so. I'm pretty sure they see me as a figurehead to give their regime an air of respectability. And look how they've set me up for it! They can blame the court-martial and my subsequent disgrace on the short-sighted civilian government. When they sweep into power I'll be the military man who was the victim of the civilian leader's meddling, rescued and reinstated by the saviors of the Confederation."

"MacArthur," Bondarevsky said. "A lot of people would have supported him after he clashed with Truman in the Korean War."

"Exactly," Tolwyn said. "I suspect I'd only last long enough to give them time to get a grip on things. Then some 'enemy of the people' would assassinate me, paving the way for tighter control and more repression."

"They're still playing a dangerous game. You don't

have much left to lose by airing what you know."

"Ah, but right now I'm so thoroughly discredited that nobody would believe me without some damned convincing proof. And these people play dirty, Jason. Why do you think I sent Kevin out here ahead of me? I figured he'd be the first one they'd target if they thought I was getting dangerous to them. Out here they can't touch him. I think."

"Okay, I see all of what you're saying. But I'm still not sure where *Karga* fits in to all this, or why we should risk our people in what looks like a lost cause."

"Come on, man, *think*." Tolwyn sounded exasperated. "Terra's one hope is if the situation here in the Landreich doesn't develop the way the conspirators have planned it. If we can just hold Ragark back, stop his invasion scheme, we not only save the Landreich, we also buy time to fight the conspiracy. They can't mobilize without Ragark's fleet orbiting Landreich after a bloody campaign that violates the Treaty in a big way. And that supercarrier is our last chance to hold the Cats back. Without it, Kruger doesn't stand a chance. We *have* to get her back in service, Jason. Without her, we're not just looking at the end of the Landreich. We're looking at the fall of the Confederation to a pack of tyrants a hell of a lot worse than Thrakhath ever would have been. He would have exterminated the human race . . . but this lot will do worse. They'll extinguish everything we believe in, turn the Confederation into a tyranny, maybe ignite a civil war. Better to die fighting the Cats than to live to see a military junta deciding the fate of mankind."

Bondarevsky didn't respond right away. His eyes were on Tolwyn's shadowy figure, but he was focused on something infinitely farther away . . . Terra.

All the arguments against proceeding with Goliath

were still there. It would be dangerous even to complete the survey, much less to attempt to disarm the self-destruct system so they could start repairs on the *Karga*. And the job was going to be even bigger than they had supposed, given what they had seen so far. Just understanding enough of the Kilrathi design philosophy to know *how* to attempt those repairs was going to be murder . . .

An idea stirred.

"Maybe there's a way we can balance out the odds against us," he said slowly. "Maybe . . ."

"What do you have in mind?" Tolwyn asked, his interest clearly piqued.

"I just realized, sir, that we have access to a collection of genuine experts on Kilrathi ship design. They might be able to help us disarm that destruct system . . . and they could certainly help us with the repair job."

"The Kilrathi you picked up from the planet? Why should they work for our side?"

He thought back to his conversation with Graham and Murragh, and smiled. "Maybe this time, Admiral, it's us who'll be joining their side for a change."

"Go to it, then," Tolwyn said with a smile.

Saluting, Jason withdrew and Geoff turned his chair, the darkness enveloping him. There was so much more he could have told Jason; the fact that he had engaged in half-truths with a fighting officer he respected more than any other who had ever served under him was troubling. There was part of him that wanted to pull Jason all the way in, to reveal all about the Genetic Enhancements program that was the conspiracy within a conspiracy but he knew that Jason was too much of a straight arrow for that.

Tragic, so damn tragic, that in order to save what we love we so often have to destroy it. It was warriors like

Jason who had ensured that the Confederation survived when so many others had given up hope, or worst yet would knowingly destroy it for their ambitions yet what I contemplate will most likely be resisted by ones like Jason.

Is this my own ambition, my own vanity, Geoff wondered. It was a troubling thought. There was the constant gnawing strain that the G.E. project, the virus hidden within the bacteria of Belisarius, was perhaps the greatest moral outrage of all. Yet there was no longer an alternative. That was the hidden truth Whittaker had revealed in their meeting, a truth which he had kept from Jason. Belisarius was simply the Trojan Horse that would be destroyed, and then the real plan would be hatched.

And the Landreich, all the Border World systems. That was the conflict to come against either the Confed or the Cats, which would be the platform for the G.E. project to be unleashed. That was why this carrier had to be saved, to provide the nucleus of an effective resistance so that the wheels within wheels would later turn.

Geoff sighed and, reaching under his chair, he took the bottle which he had hidden when Jason had come in. Taking a long drink he stared off, wondering. I know Jason would say no if he knew all the truth. Does that tell me something? An inner voice whispered the warning that indeed, if Jason did reject it, his rejection meant it was wrong. And if it is wrong for him then is it for me? God, why am I doing this? He thought of the new ones who even now were secretly in training, pilots like Seether. Seether, what would Jason think of him, this new generation, this new breed of Overman which I am helping to create.

Overman—strange, Whittaker had told me to read

Nietzsche to find the hidden truth of the program. I did and I believed in spite of my moral outrage. That was the trouble, you could be outraged yet there was a terrifying logic to Nietzsche that could not be denied. The only answer to the logic of Nietzsche was the logic of a higher order of good that transcended his frightful world view. Thirty-five years of war in this universe had all but burned out the last idealistic dream of a higher order of good. There was, he feared, only one answer left—that if we are to survive in this universe we must be the Overman.

For beyond the Cats there were other enemies, far more terrifying, far more powerful and implacable. And if the Cats could come within a hairsbreadth of destroying us, what did that bode for humanity a hundred years from now? For surely they were coming and most assuredly we would be destroyed.

There was only one answer left, he feared, the answer of Nietzsche, of Whittaker, of G.E., of Seether. And I know I should have moral outrage, but that is gone, he thought sadly. That must be buried if we are to survive. He closed his eyes and drained the rest of the bottle.

• CHAPTER 10

> *"Glory is the outward measure of the Warrior's worth, but the knowledge of a duty fulfilled is the one true inward measure."*
>
> from the Fourth Codex
> 04:18:31

Operations Planning Center, FRLS *Independence*
Orbiting Vaku VII, Vaku System
1108 hours (CST), 2670.317

"I want to be perfectly clear on this, Lord Murragh. Are you saying you *can't* help us, or you *won't*?"

Bondarevsky could see the strain in Admiral Richards' face as he asked the question. After a hard evening's discussions between Tolwyn and Richards the senior admiral had finally agreed, albeit reluctantly, to go ahead with the salvage operation. It had taken every bit of Bondarevsky's patience and tact to get the two strong-willed warriors to unbend and talk it over, and in the end Tolwyn had been forced to give the same detailed account of the conspiracy back in the Confederation to convince Richards that *Karga's* recovery was absolutely essential to more than just the Landreich.

But after all that, it seemed Bondarevsky's solution to the problem of disarming the self-destruct system wasn't going to work.

The OPC seemed larger with only a handful of people present for this meeting. Instead of the full battle group and Project Goliath staff who were present the last time Bondarevsky had been here, today there were only five. Tolwyn and Richards were on one side of the triangular table, while Jason sat alone on a second side. Donald Graham and Murragh occupied the third. At the moment Graham was looking troubled, while the young Kilrathi prince's expression was enigmatic, unreadable.

"I am not sure that I mean either of those, Admiral," the *kil* said slowly. "I am certainly not unwilling to help. If you can put *Karga* back into operational status, make him a part of your fleet and use him to prevent Ragark from making a bid for the Imperial throne, I am glad to be of assistance. It is not as if I or any other *kil* have plans to salvage the carrier, or the means to make the attempt." Murragh leaned forward, fixing Richards with sharp, penetrating eyes. "As to my ability to help, that is less certain. I am not sure that there is anything I can do . . . but there may be. Much depends on circumstances."

"Commander Graham's report indicates that many of your survivors are members of the carrier's Cadre," Richards said. "It seems to me the questions are simple enough. Do any of them have the ability to shut down the self-destruct system? And, if so, will they do it if you order them to do so? I can't see where circumstances will change the answers to either of those."

Murragh made a hand gesture Bondarevsky wasn't familiar with. "You have misunderstood the basic nature of the problem, I fear, Admiral," the young officer said softly. "I seriously doubt if any member of the Cadre could release the self-destruct system. It is deliberately designed to be proof against the attempts of enemy borders to disarm it and carry the ship off as a prize. So the Cadre does not enter into the question at all."

"Suppose you tell us what *does* enter into it, then," Tolwyn said. Unlike Richards, who managed a degree of smooth urbanity in his dealings with the Prince, Tolwyn was gruff and plainly uncomfortable. He'd been fighting the Kilrathi for a long time, and Bondarevsky knew he found it difficult to accept that a Cat might be an ally—particularly after the treachery of Ralgha *nar* Hhalles and the cunning lies that had lulled the Confederation before the Battle of Earth. Yet Tolwyn knew that this young *kil* prince held the key to the successful completion of the Goliath project in his stub-fingered hands. The man must have been torn between conflicting emotions of doubt and hope.

"The computer system aboard *Karga* was subject to specific command codes known to the senior officers of the carrier and the battle group," Murragh told him. "The self-destruct system can be shut down using those codes."

"Surely you weren't senior enough to know them?" Graham demanded, glancing sidelong at the Kilrathi.

"No, the information was limited to senior officers. But I know my uncle kept a full record of those command codes on file . . . and as his aide I did have access to those files. It may be that I can recover the information and use it to disarm the destruct sequence. But there is a risk."

"How so?" Bondarevsky asked.

Murragh looked at him, his face expressionless but his eyes conveying irony. "The files are in the ship's computer. In order to reach them, we must bring a portion of the computer net back on-line. And in so doing . . ."

"Risk setting off the self-destruct system," Bondarevsky finished. "Wonderful. The perfect Catch 22."

"The . . . what?" Murragh asked.

"A Terran figure of speech," Graham supplied. "You need to do something before you can do something else that will allow you to do the first thing." He looked at Tolwyn and Richards. "It's possible, as I'm sure your salvage experts will tell you. But there's no way to predict what might set that flying bomb off. That's why we never seriously considered having Murragh try to find the codes while we were recovering supplies and equipment from the carrier. It just wasn't worth the risk."

Richards glanced at Tolwyn. "It seems that it is, now," he said with a sour look on his weathered features. "Can you coach one of our specialists to do the job, Lord Murragh?"

The young *kil* shook his head, a human gesture he'd picked up from Graham. "No, that will not be possible. The files are open to me as an authorized member of the staff of the Battle Group Commander. There are retinal patterns and other identification markers on file in the computer. Few Kilrathi could gain access, and certainly no humans. I will have to do the job myself."

Graham frowned. "You're a valuable asset these days, Murragh," he said. "Sending the rightful Emperor of Kilrah aboard an orbiting bomb isn't exactly the shrewdest move any of us could make. Isn't there any way around it?"

Murragh barked a laugh. "If you have cloning technology and twenty-one standard Kilrah-years to grow a duplicate I suppose we could work an alternative out. But barring that, I think the only reasonable course within our grasp is for me to make the attempt. As to the political implications of it all . . . well, until a few days ago I was not a factor in galactic politics, and few will note my absence if I am lost to the Empire now."

"You can be flip," Graham said, shaking his head. "But the fact remains that you could die over there. Damn it all, Murragh, I didn't look out for that flea-bitten carcass of yours all these months just to see you throw your life away on a crazy stunt like this. You know the situation aboard *Karga*. Even with the destruct mechanism shut down, repairing that hulk is going to take a hell of a lot of work—and in the long run I wouldn't be too sure it's even possible. Do you want to risk your life on something that might not be worth the effort in the first place?" Neither Graham nor Murragh had been filled in on Tolwyn's conspiracy information, so Bondarevsky understood how reluctant Graham would be to let his young Kilrathi friend make the attempt. As an engineer Graham knew better than most people just how much was needed to put things right aboard the *Karga*.

Murragh didn't answer right away, but kept his eyes on Tolwyn for a long moment. "The reputation of Admiral Geoff Tolwyn is well known within the Empire," he said at length. "He is known to us as a warrior in the deepest sense of the word, an honorable adversary. If you, Admiral, say that it is essential that you make this effort, I will accept that and do what I can. Your goals, at present, are mine. The Kilrathi people do not need a renewal of the war. We should have ended it a long time ago. But Ukar *dai* Ragark and his kind will see victory in battle as the only way to rally our race to their standards, and that will mean more fighting we can ill afford when our first need is to rebuild what we lost when Kilrah was destroyed. The Codices teach us that the first duty is to the Race, and even my claim to the throne is less important in this pass than giving you the means to stop Ragark before he rekindles the fighting. I will do what I can, and hope that it is enough."

Bondarevsky looked from the Prince to Tolwyn and back again. It seemed there was someone willing to take Tolwyn at his word.

Admiral's Ready Room, ex-KIS *Karga*
Orbiting Vaku VII, Vaku System
0721 hours (CST), 2670.318

"That's as ready as it's ever likely to get. If you ask me, though, we should all just turn around and head back to the carrier."

Bondarevsky shook his head inside his helmet before he realized that Graham couldn't see the movement. "I don't like this any better than you do, Commander," he said aloud. "But now that we've come this far I think we'd better go ahead and give it a shot. As long as Murragh agrees."

"I do," the Kilrathi prince said.

They had led a small team of volunteers aboard *Karga* to attempt to retrieve the computer codes from the admiral's day cabin adjacent to the flag bridge of the battered supercarrier. This time there was no marine security detachment. Murragh had to be there, of course, and despite his continued protests Graham had volunteered to come as well, either out of pure friendship for the prince or because he felt the need to continue sharing the danger with his erstwhile fellow castaway. Bondarevsky had decided that someone from the Goliath Project leadership needed to be part of the operation; they couldn't ask strangers to take risks they weren't willing to face themselves. A pair of computer specialists from Diaz's salvage team rounded out the boarding party. Kevin Tolwyn and Aengus Harper had volunteered to fly the shuttle that had brought them across, but Bondarevsky had ordered them away once the salvage team had suited up and crossed over to the derelict. He wasn't about to put those two at risk.

If things went sour, there was no sense in risking anyone who didn't have to be there. At that, he wished Graham had stayed behind, especially since the man continued to voice all the doubtful sentiments Bondarevsky was trying to keep from thinking of himself. But he'd proven himself invaluable since coming aboard, his engineering expertise doubly valuable because he'd acquired a working knowledge of Kilrathi technology and how to make it work with human gear.

"Well," the engineer said, "I guess it's true what they say. Insanity really is contagious. Let's get it over with."

"Are you ready, Mr. Mayhew?" Bondarevsky asked the senior of the two salvage crew computer specialists.

"Yeah. I'm pretty sure we've got this terminal isolated from the rest of the net." The technician didn't sound very sure of himself, but Bondarevsky sympathized with his plight. The Kilrathi design philosophy emphasized multiply redundant systems, and it was difficult to be sure they had disconnected the flag officer's personal computer from the rest of the network of computers that made up *Karga*'s system. "I just hope we've got the power connections right. If we've screwed something up on the conversion, it'll fry the whole unit and we'll be right back where we started."

"It's right," Graham said. "Believe me, I've jury-rigged enough combinations of ConFleet and Imperial hardware to know what I'm doing. Right, Murragh?"

The *kil*'s response had a mocking note. "At least you've improved since the first few times, my friend," he said.

Since they were reluctant to tap into the ship's power grid to activate the terminal, they had decided to use a portable power pack instead. But the power specifications for Kilrathi and Terran systems were different, and Graham had been forced to improvise an adapter—he called it a "Nargrast Special"—to make the link-up possible.

"Ready on the monitor," Kristine Voorhies said from the far side of the compartment. She had hooked a computer analyzer into another terminal, one still connected to the system, and was ready to track the behavior of *Karga's* network as they started to work. Hopefully she would be able to warn them if anything they did had an effect beyond the single terminal, but Bondarevsky privately doubted it.

"Power . . . now," Murragh said quietly, inserting a data chip in the receptacle beside the monitor.

"Power is on," Mayhew announced.

A yellow light came on beside the terminal, and after a long moment the screen glowed. Alien letters flowed across the screen.

Bondarevsky realized he was holding his breath, and forced himself to relax. He almost succeeded.

"The terminal is functioning," Murragh said quietly. His voice was calm and level, and Bondarevsky envied his control. For a young officer on his first deep-space assignment, he was one cool customer. If he ever did make it to the Imperial throne, he was likely to prove an excellent ruler.

"Now for the hard part," Graham muttered. "Cross your fingers, folks."

The Kilrathi computer network functioned differently from the systems used on Terran ships. Confederation computers tended to be highly centralized, fast, efficient, but vulnerable. Computer rooms were heavily armored and shielded, and a complete back-up system was installed in case the primary computer went down at a critical moment. On Kilrathi ships, though, numerous separate computers were linked together, like cells in a living brain spread out through the entire ship. Response time was slightly slower, but large chunks of the net could be knocked out without significantly impairing the computer functions of the vessel, and the network was capable of rerouting connections to bypass damaged or destroyed areas.

With Admiral *dai* Nokhtak's personal terminal isolated from the rest of the ship, they had no access to the network. That was exactly the way they wanted it, given the danger from the self-destruct mechanism. What they hoped they would be able to get at, though, was the terminal's own memory. Personal data and secret files were most likely to be stored locally rather than spread through the network, which meant that the command codes they needed to take control of the ship were likely to be in this computer.

At least that was what everyone in the Goliath Project hoped. Murragh was no computer specialist, and so far Richards and Tolwyn had chosen not to reveal what they were doing to the Kilrathi computer officer in the prince's Cadre, just in case that officer was less sympathetic to their aims than Murragh had so far proven to be. So there was no guarantee that they were right in their approach. All they could do was hope they would be successful.

Murragh punched a keycode combination into the terminal, his fingers a little clumsy and awkward because of the gloves of his suit. More characters scrawled across the screen, and the *kil* gave a satisfied grunt. "I'm in," he said curtly. "Time for security scans."

He made a hardwire connection between his suit and

the computer terminal, then hung motionless for long moments while the humans waited tensely. His suit's built-in medical monitors could provide the information the computer needed to identify Murragh as an authorized member of the admiral's staff with a legitimate reason for accessing the files.

In response to some query, Murragh recited a few words in the snarling Kilrathi tongue. Then, to the others, he went on in English. "The computer is processing the security data now. Stand by."

"Everything looks good here," Voorhies reported.

"Security clearance granted!" Murragh said. His fingers danced over the keyboard as fast as the gloves would allow them. "I'm starting the download."

They had agreed that the most effective way to obtain the information they wanted was to download everything they could from the admiral's secured files into the data chip, rather than searching for the specific material they wanted and quite possibly tempting fate a little too long. But the downside to this approach was the volume of material contained in the terminal's local memory, which took a long time to transfer . . . and, of course, the risk that the command codes might not be in the data they obtained, forcing another attempt later.

It seemed to take hours before Murragh finally announced that the chip was full, though Bondarevsky knew it was only a matter of minutes. The *kil* disconnected his hardwire lead, then carefully removed the data chip before gesturing to Mayhew to cut the power. The computer screen faded back to blackness.

"Bondarevsky to Shuttle. Ready for pick-up." It was pure relief to utter those simple words.

Flag Bridge, ex-KIS *Karga*
Orbiting Vaku VII, Vaku System
1218 hours (CST), 2670.319

"Ladies and gentlemen, the *Karga* is operational."

Bondarevsky held his breath as Admiral Richards uttered the words and then tapped a combination into the control board in front of him. There was a long pause in which the silence hung heavy. Then, suddenly, orange-tinged emergency lights flickered on in the compartment, and a bank of consoles lit up. The men and women of the Goliath team gathered on the flag bridge gave a ragged cheer.

Karga was alive again, if only barely.

Murragh had extracted the command codes from the data chip on the shuttle trip back to *Independence*, using a Kilrathi wrist computer that had been part of his gear on Nargrast. Overnight the salvage crew had returned to the ship in force to go to work on the computer system, bringing it back on-line long enough to purge the self-destruct order, then starting to work on basic systems repairs. The ship had emergency power now, a precious few instruments, lights, and the possibility of at least partial artificial gravity with a few more hours' work in Engineering. But before they got back to the job, Richards had ordered the Goliath personnel to suspend everything for a few minutes. All over the ship space-suited personnel, most of them from Diaz's salvage team but with the addition of a picked handful of the crew who had traveled aboard the *City of Cashel*, stopped what they were working on to listen to the general address comm channel.

With one leg hooked under a seat to hold him in place in weightlessness, Admiral Geoff Tolwyn cleared his throat.

"Attention to orders!" Aengus Harper announced

unnecessarily. There was no need. Everyone was silent as Tolwyn began to speak.

"To Geoff Tolwyn, Rear-Admiral, Free Republic of Landreich Navy," he began. "Sir. By direction of the President and the Admiralty of the Free Republic of Landreich, you are hereby requested and required to take up the charge and command of Landreich hull number 106, formerly designated KIS *Karga*, and to proceed to render all possible repairs to said vessel in order to render it spaceworthy . . ."

As the admiral's voice droned on, reading the formal phrases from a projected image on the HUD display of his suit helmet, Bondarevsky's attention wavered. The stilted ceremonial had an archaic feel to it, and he suspected that Max Kruger, a self-taught man who relished the odd bit of obscure antiquarian knowledge, had probably adapted it from some old Terran source. At first glance it might have seemed foolish to go through this ceremonial now, with so much to be done, but Bondarevsky recognized the reasoning behind it. Even though *Karga* wouldn't be capable of functioning as an independent unit of the fleet for a long time to come, she would soon be receiving most of her designated crew from the *City of Cashel*, men and women who would be facing the enormous job of refitting her from stem to stern. And in order for that crew to function, they must officially become part of a Landreich naval command. By "reading himself in" Tolwyn was establishing his legal authority as master of the *Karga*, the officer whose word would be absolute law as long as she was in space.

". . . nor you, nor any of you, will fail, at your peril," Tolwyn finished with a flourish. "Signed Maximillian Kruger, President and Commander-in-Chief, Armed Forces of the Free Republic."

The admiral paused before going on in a more conversational tone of voice. "We've overcome the first hurdle, but I won't try to hide the fact that we've got plenty of other problems to deal with if we're going to get this old girl into some kind of shape. With your talents and God's help I think we can manage it . . . we *have* to manage it, for the good of the Landreich and for the future of all Mankind." He fell silent again for a moment, then turned toward Admiral Richards. "Sir?"

Richards, in his turn, began to speak, reading from a prepared text similar to Tolwyn's. The phrases were different in places—" . . . charge and command of Admiral commanding Provisional Battle Group *Karga* . . . operational command of ships and vessels previously assigned to Battle Group *Independence* . . . lend all support to the repair and refitting of the ex-KIS *Karga* . . ."—but the intent was the same. By his words Richards was "hoisting his flag" as the CO of the battle group which would be built around *Karga*, always assuming the salvage effort was successful. *Independence* would remain technically under Camparelli and Galbraith, standing by to furnish protection for as long as she was needed. But the rest of the ships that had accompanied the escort carrier to the Vaku system would henceforth take their orders from Richards.

His orders read out, Richards declined to make any sort of speech. He merely paused, then inclined his helmeted head back toward Tolwyn. "Proceed with the project, Captain," he said quietly. They had agreed beforehand that Bondarevsky's reading-in ceremony would take place later, among his own people on the flight deck.

Tolwyn responded with crisp authority. "Let's get this show on the road, people," he said. "Survey details to commence operations immediately according to the prepared schedule. Notify *City of Cashel* we will be ready to receive shuttles whenever they wish to begin off-loading our people. And contact *Sindri*; tell Dickerson that we're ready."

The crew on the flag bridge was already in motion by the time the orders were given. Grasping a handhold near the rear of the compartment, Bondarevsky watched them turn to with a feeling of pride. Whatever happened in the weeks and months ahead, this was a good team, and if anyone could restore life to the shattered remains of the supercarrier, they could.

Bridge, FRLS *Sindri*
Orbiting Vaku VII, Vaku System
1232 hours (CST)

"Thrusters at twenty percent," Captain Charles Dickerson ordered. "Bring us in nice and slow."

Sindri was floating above and behind *Karga* in orbit around the brown dwarf, edging closer as the helmsman deftly manipulated the tender's thrusters to approach the derelict. After hundreds of years in space, the most difficult maneuver to carry out continued to be docking one ship to another, but *Sindri*'s pilot was skilled at close-in handling and Dickerson had every confidence in his ability.

Still, it was a time for crossed fingers and held breaths. Dickerson knew tender captains who relied on rabbits' feet for luck, though he scorned them. He preferred the sprig of Taran pseudo-clover he carried in his pocket.

"One hundred meters, closing," the sensor technician reported from his post behind the captain's chair.

"Approach profile nominal," Lieutenant Kaine, the first officer, added.

As if oblivious to it all, the helmsman manipulated his controls like a concert pianist giving the recital of a lifetime. The rate of approach slowed steadily as the tender moved closer, dragging out the maneuver until Dickerson was ready to shout in frustrated impatience.

Then the ships touched, so gently that the contact was hardly noticeable.

"Deploying magnetic grapples," Kaine announced. "We have positive contact!"

"Secure from maneuvering stations, gentlemen," Dickerson ordered, breathing out. "Set the special duty watch and begin tender operations. Engineer, shields to maximum power. And make a note in the log that we have docked with *Karga*."

"Damn it all, skipper," the helm officer said, "don't we even get a chance to smoke a cigarette?"

"Very funny, Clancy," Dickerson said, forcing down a smile at the helmsman's ancient joke. "Since you're not going to be doing anything on the bridge for a few weeks, what say you go over to the carrier and lend a hand with the salvage crew? I'm sure they'll benefit from your experience with helm systems. And your sense of humor, so-called."

Clancy gave him a grin. "Aye aye, skipper," he said cheerfully. Dickerson watched him leave the bridge wistfully. The challenge of taking part in a project as big as rebuilding a Kilrathi carrier appealed to him, but unlike the helmsman he had plenty to do right here aboard *Sindri*.

The tender was riding piggyback on the supercarrier's massive superstructure, clamped in place by magnetic grapnels. Her maneuvering drives were powered down now, but the massive banks of fusion generators that made up most of the tender's mass were still on-line. For the next several weeks, as the repair process swung into full operation aboard *Karga*, little *Sindri's* power plants would play an enormous part in the job.

Already *Sindri's* shields had extended around the supercarrier. They weren't up to combat standard by any stretch of the imagination, but they would protect work crews from the brown dwarf's strange radiation and put an end to the continual bombardment of tiny particles of matter against the derelict's hull. When their orbit took them through the gas giant's ring system once, which happened on the order of once every three days, the shields would also block all but the very largest chunks of ice from further damaging the ship. Already the unshielded Kilrathi hulk had taken a great deal of additional damage from multiple passes through the rings, minor hits by small pieces of junk, perhaps, but at orbital speeds the damage was magnified by kinetic energy unleashed by each of those hits.

Once the basic shielding was up, the engineers would set up a second set of shields specifically attuned to retain gases. Then the process of reintroducing an atmosphere on to the ship could begin. It would still be necessary for work crews to wear suits until the hull of the carrier had been fully patched, because of the constant danger of a shield failure that could open the ship to hard vacuum, but many of the most basic tasks of repair would be considerably easier with an atmosphere to work in.

Meanwhile, one hole in the carrier's superstructure would not be targeted for repair for a while, a small, jagged opening Dickerson had deliberately aimed for during the docking approach. This was now positioned directly below one of several airlocks leading out of engineering. Soon engineers from the tender would be running leads through this opening to hook into the *Karga*'s power grid and computer network. Although the supercarrier was still generating some energy, the repair job would eventually require her power plant to be taken off-line so the equipment could be examined and overhauled. While this was going on *Sindri* would provide the power for *Karga* to operate light, environmental controls, and artificial gravity, and to run through instruments as they were tested. At the same time they would be busy downloading the carrier's computer network. The Kilrathi computer files already had intelligence experts in the battle group salivating in anticipation of the potential data they might hold. Once the files were duplicated, the Kilrathi network would be fully purged and then brought back on-line with the programming and data files needed for the ship to operate as a part of the Free Republic Navy.

It would be a monster job, Dickerson thought. *Sindri* had been involved in similar work before, including the refitting of the *Tarawa*—now the *Independence*—a few months earlier. That had been a bear of a project, but this one would be worse. The damage to the Kilrathi carrier had been far more extensive to start with, and Dickerson didn't even want to think about all the problems of mating human and Kilrathi systems aboard *Karga*.

Still, he envied the techies who'd have hands-on work to do in the weeks ahead. The captain of the *Sindri* would have plenty of headaches and more demands on his time than there were hours in the standard day to deal with them, but he knew from experience that his work would be far less interesting or absorbing than the refit his ship was going to make possible.

"Captain," the first officer interrupted his train of thought. "Chief Engineer's compliments and could you

please get together with Admiral Tolwyn and Mr. Diaz
to settle the priorities on power demands? He says
they're both demanding more power than we can deliver
and neither one of them is willing to budge."

Dickerson sighed. They'd only been docked a few
minutes and the headaches were already starting. "Very
well, Mr. Kaine. Have Communications put the
gentlemen through to my ready room." He rose from
his seat. "You have the bridge, Lieutenant."

Operations Planning Center, FRLS *Independence*
Orbiting Vaku VII, Vaku System
0843 hours (CST), 2670.320

"I'm telling you, Admiral, my crew is not going to
like this. Frankly, I don't like it either. I didn't sign up
in the Landreich Naval Reserve to be some kind of
ferryman for a load of dead Cats, and neither did my
people."

The atmosphere in the escort carrier's OPC was
charged with tension today, and Jason Bondarevsky had
to force himself to keep from jumping into the argument
with an angry comment. Everyone connected with the
Goliath Project was exhausted after days of nearly
constant work, and in consequence tempers were frayed.
The daily conferences aboard the *Independence* to
coordinate work schedules and iron out conflicts were
apt to produce more confrontations than solutions, and
today's was a good case in point.

Vance Richards looked older than ever, tired and
drawn. He worked as hard as any man on *Karga*, perhaps
harder. His wide experience as Chief of Intelligence
for ConFleet during the war had given him wide contact
with Kilrathi technology, and he was the indispensable

man in directing the repairs. But the work was taking its toll, and Bondarevsky was beginning to worry that he'd burn himself out long before he had to take up his duties as battle group commander if and when the supercarrier really was put back in commission.

"Listen to me, Captain Steiger," the admiral said slowly. "I know all the arguments, but I'm not buying any of them. You have your orders."

Steiger looked stubborn, but didn't answer right away.

The Kilrathi dead were the issue today, specifically the disposal of the bodies of the carrier's crew. The grisly reminder of *Karga*'s last cruise had to be dealt with, and soon. Now that they had atmosphere and heat decay would rapidly become a major factor, and until those bodies were removed they would impede the repair work. The first major task Richards had ordered the crewmen brought across from the *City of Cashel* to undertake was the collection of Kilrathi bodies.

It would have been easiest to simply consign them to space. Human dead were normally given a burial in space, with a brief ceremony, a launched casket, and an honor guard salute. The thinking among most of the Landreichers seemed to be that anything that elaborate would be a waste of valuable time, and that the expedient thing to do would be to simply jettison those thousands of bodies and get on with the business at hand.

But that wasn't the way Vance Richards operated.

As he'd explained at the outset of the meeting, Kilrathi burial customs went back many hundreds of years, to a time long before the race had developed space travel. Descended from carnivore stock, the Kilrathi race as a whole was extremely territorial, and the religious Codices established the need for each *kil* to return to the land so that his spirit would have a range in which to hunt and explore throughout the afterlife. Of course space travel had forced some alteration to the ancient beliefs, but the Kilrathi still preferred to return their dead to solid ground, be it planet, moon, or asteroid, rather than allowing them to be consigned to the endless void.

So Richards had decreed that the nearly five thousand dead aboard the carrier should be given the kind of burial their religion called for—on Nargrast.

It was going to require a major effort to carry out those orders, though. The dead, now stored in the carrier's port side flight deck in vacuum and zero-g, would have to be moved aboard shuttles from the *City of Cashel* and carried to Nargrast, where the shuttles would ground, unload their grisly cargoes, and deposit the bodies in a series of mass graves to be excavated by ore extraction vehicles from the factory ship. Richards also intended to have a burial service read, to honor the Kilrathi casualties who had given their lives for their Empire.

The orders had drawn a few frowns around the table, but it was Steiger who resisted the most. His ship and crew would bear the lion's share of the burden, and like most Landreichers he didn't see any need to honor Mankind's most inveterate enemy.

The transport captain glared across the table, first at Richards, then at Murragh and Donald Graham, who had been invited to the meeting so that Richards could discuss plans for the burials with them. "I wonder if you'd be so considerate of all these Cat stiffs if you weren't trying to impress your new buddies," Steiger said bluntly. "Some of you may think it'll make a difference, but I tell you the Cats won't care one lousy bit if you bury them, shove them out the airlock, or shove 'em in the fusion plants. They'll still be back shooting first chance they get."

Richards half rose, than sank into his chair again. When he spoke he sounded more tired than angry, but Bondarevsky could read the fury behind his icy eyes. "I'll only say this once, Captain," he said flatly. "I don't care in the least what the Kilrathi think of me. I would have ordered a proper burial for those people if there wasn't a single Cat within a hundred light-years to see me do it. We've been at war for more than a generation, but in my book war is no excuse to abandon our principles, and I say anyone, man or *kil* or whatever, deserves to leave this life with dignity and according to his or her beliefs." His tone grew harsh. "Or would you prefer that we stuffed you or your men into the fusion reactors if you're killed while we're out here, Captain?"

Steiger flushed. "Damn it, Admiral, it isn't the same!"

"Yes, it is," Bondarevsky put in. "I agree with the Admiral. How can we pretend to be better than Thrakhath was if we show the same contempt for our enemies that he did?"

Richards nodded. "Exactly. At any rate, Captain Steiger, whatever the morals and ethics of the situation, I've made it an order, and unless you would like to be relieved and shipped back to Landreich in a ship's brig, you will carry out that order. Is that understood?"

There was a long pause before Steiger responded. "The crew won't like it," he repeated. "But . . . aye aye, sir."

Richards let out a sigh and slumped back in his chair. "Very well. I think we should take a break before we get on with the rest of the meeting. Shall we say half an hour?"

The Goliath staff adjourned, most of them making

their way to the adjacent compartment where the carrier's mess crew had set up a buffet table with coffee and an assortment of pastries. Bondarevsky remained seated, and so did Richards, who started checking over his notes on his computer terminal with the air of a man on the very edge of physical collapse.

Murragh and Graham stood and walked slowly towards the admiral. "Admiral Richards," Murragh said quietly.

Richards looked up. "Oh, yes, gentlemen. I think we've covered everything you need to be here for. I suppose you'll both want to go to Nargrast for the service?"

"Yes, Admiral, I know that I would, and all of my people," the Kilrathi prince said gravely. "But before we leave, may I thank you sincerely for your observance of our ways. It is . . . not something I expected. I fear that were the roles reversed few Kilrathi officers would have been so generous toward human dead."

Richards waved a hand vaguely. "What I said was true, my Lord," he said. "I didn't order it for your benefit."

Murragh gave a human nod. "I grasp that, Admiral. That is what is so impressive." He paused. "Admiral, I have been thinking, and talking with my friend Graham. I was of service to you in the matter of the computer, was I not?"

"Yes, of course," Richards said. "we couldn't have pulled it off without you. I'm not quite sure how I can repay you for it, but I assure you I'll move heaven and earth, and maybe even Max Kruger, to try."

"The desire for compensation does not motivate the Kilrathi," Murragh said calmly. "Any more than your decision in the matter of the dead was motivated by a desire for personal gain. We believe in doing our duty, living with honor, and facing our enemies with courage. But since I was of service to you, I believe I could be so again . . . if you will allow it."

"What do you mean?"

"Admiral, I do not know the details of your intentions for *Karga*, but it is clear you are attempting a major repair effort, presumably to put the ship back into service again." Murragh said it casually, but Bondarevsky was impressed. The Kilrathi had been kept as far out of the picture as possible for security reasons, but the prince obviously had the imagination it took to see where Goliath was heading.

"And if we are?" Richards was suddenly very much the ConFleet intelligence officer, wary and poker-faced.

"There are many dissimilarities in technologies to be overcome, whatever you are trying to do," Murragh said. "If you had the assistance of Kilrathi officers who knew his systems, your work would be speeded considerably."

Richards frowned. "I'm not sure . . ."

"If you accept, you will have each *kil*'s word of honor to support your work honestly and fully," Murragh said. "My people will not attempt to sabotage your efforts. I have already told Bondarevsky and Graham that I view your people as my allies against Ragark, who would set himself up as an usurper on the throne that belongs to my *hrai*. Cannot an ally assist an ally in a venture to their mutual advantage?"

Graham spoke up. "He's serious, Admiral. Hell, I wouldn't mind joining your little party myself, as a volunteer, since I'm not likely to be getting a ride back to Terra anytime soon to report in. And me and my guys and gals have a lot of experience in splicing Cat and Ape gear together without having it blow up in our faces. We're willing to help any way we can. And I think it would be to your advantage to have us on board."

Richards didn't answer right away, and Bondarevsky could see that he was wavering between the paranoia that went with his training and the hope that he might obtain precious help.

"I think you should consider it seriously, Admiral," Bondarevsky said quietly. "Let's face it, these folks could make all the difference in actually making this harebrained scheme work. Let's sign them up."

After a moment, Richards nodded. "I think you're right, Jason. Very well, Lord Murragh. Commander Graham. Welcome to the Goliath Project."

• CHAPTER 11

> *"No Warrior should fear honest labor, as no*
> *Warrior should shirk onerous duty."*
>
> from the First Codex
> 04:22:10

FRLS *Karga*
Orbiting Vaku VII, Vaku System
2670.321-355

They had plenty of volunteers from amongst the Nargrast survivors, both human and Kilrathi. All of Murragh's Cadre officers were eager to follow their prince's lead. That, Bondarevsky decided, was only to be expected. They were loyal to the *hrai* of his uncle, the late Admiral *dai* Nokhtak, and Murragh was now the last living representative of that clan in addition to being heir presumptive to the throne. Their branch of the *hrai* had long been rivals of Thrakhath's, so they had no great feelings of loss regarding their erstwhile war leader. As for Ragark, he was considered something of an upstart, and evidently wasn't thought of as a proper Kilrathi warrior at all. So the collection of Kilrathi experts were willing to mobilize at Murragh's word to aid the

231

humans in restoring the ship. Their comrades, crewmen from the crashed escort and a number of surviving fighter pilots off the carrier, were more suspicious. A few, taking their cue from the embittered Kuraq and others like him, refused to have anything to do with the hated "apes." They remained in open confinement aboard the *City of Cashel* while their comrades got down to work.

The Goliath Project staff needed all the help they could muster, and inside of a few days the assistance of Murragh's people was already proving invaluable.

Time after time it seemed as if they would not be able to get the job done, but time after time the men, women, and *kili* working on the *Karga* rose to the challenge and somehow made things work. Bondarevsky was continually amazed at the adaptability humans and Kilrathi could bring to bear when they tried. Slowly, painfully, it began to look as if the *Karga* would one day sail the void once again.

With the tender docked and the bodies rounded up and cleared, the first job was to repair *Karga*'s shattered hull. The ship had suffered major penetration damage in a score of places, and minor holes in countless other compartments. The tender's force fields allowed the carrier to retain an atmosphere, but the hull needed to be patched as soon as possible so that the energy expended on keeping the atmosphere from leaking away could be used for more productive purposes.

So the first order of business was brute-force space construction on a massive scale. It started with survey crews swarming over the hull, measuring, recording, locating the major breaks in the hull and transmitting detailed images of each to computer records aboard the dozens of shuttles detailed to support their work. The computers analyzed these records and produced detailed specifications for the sections of hull plating needed to fill the gaps. A pair of naval architects attached to Diaz's team pored over each of the computer models as they were completed, double-checking the work. Humans were far slower than computers, but it still sometimes took an organic mind to make sense of engineering designed for organic life, and despite the bottleneck created by these reviews Admiral Richards overruled Tolwyn and ordered the process to go on.

The factory ship *Andrew Carnegie* had settled into orbit close by the *Karga*. Swarms of smaller carried craft had been dispatched to Nargrast loaded with automated vehicles and small supervisory crews. They set up camp near the site where Graham and Murragh had settled with their castaways, the vehicles ranging outwards in search of needed raw materials according to a list provided by the computer analysis of the needed components and modified by Diaz's team where the computer parameters couldn't be easily met. Unfortunately Nargrast was poor in many of the elements that would have been best suited for the job, but there was plenty of iron ore, and that was still the basis of the most basic parts of the hull that needed repair.

The vehicles excavated and extracted ores where they were discovered, carried them back to base, and loaded them aboard the ships waiting there. A constant string of vessels operated back and forth between Nargrast and the *Andrew Carnegie*, endlessly feeding the insatiable demands of the factory vessel for the raw materials necessary for fabricating *Karga*'s hull plating and other requisite components. A landing party from Tolwyn's crew also worked over the remains of the escort *Frawqirg*, following up on the initial survey work Bondarevsky had done while rescuing the survivors.

Though badly damaged in the crash and far too small to provide all the needs of the damaged carrier, the escort was a useful source of parts and materials that otherwise wouldn't have been available.

Aboard the factory ship, the iron ore was smelted and processed, refined and re-refined to produce the durasteel alloy needed for hull plating. The computer designs obtained from the first surveys controlled the pouring, shaping, and cutting of the individual patches or replacement hull sections, and as quickly as they came off the line they were released into space, picked up by the one-man work pods carried aboard *Sindri*, and maneuvered into the proper places. The pods—essentially egg-shaped capsules with thrusters and manipulating arms, barely larger than a man—were supported by work gangs of spacesuited crewmen who wrestled the hull plating into position and then brought their plasma welders to bear to seal the new segments of the hull in place.

Space construction work was difficult and dangerous, especially on the scale required for Project Goliath. With so many crew members operating in spacesuits, there were bound to be accidents. A few inevitably forgot that weightless hull patches retained all of their mass and inertia in zero-g, and as a result there were casualties. Commander Katherine Manning, *Karga's* Medical Officer, was kept busy handling fractures and decompression sickness in the carrier's sick bay complex buried deep on the fifth deck of the superstructure. Fortunately little damage had occurred there, and the sick bay area was even air-tight, so she had less work to do to get her part of the ship up and running and could concentrate on taking care of the injured. But with power still limited and the unfamiliar Kilrathi medical equipment mostly off-line, Manning complained bitterly of having to perform surgery under primitive conditions, using a field surgery package normally used by marines planetside to fill in for the usual amenities that weren't yet available aboard *Karga*.

There were, of course, fatalities. The first major replacement to the buckled hull plating around the entrance to the starboard side flight deck proved particularly awkward, and when Crewman Chan misapplied thrust to his work pod at a crucial moment the result was three men dead, crushed between the new plating and the hull, and five other injuries. Chan was one of the dead, and his pod was ruined in the accident.

Bondarevsky, who had been supervising the work, wondered if Geoff Tolwyn wasn't more concerned at the loss of the pod than at Chan's death. It wasn't that the admiral was callous . . . he was merely consumed by the need to finish the job, a man so obsessed as to seem unable to perceive reality.

One by one, though, the major patches were welded into place. Other spacesuited crewmen worked their way painstakingly along the outside of the hull, using a liquid patching compound to fill in the smallest holes and marking those too large for their attention but too small for the major pieces. These were dealt with by follow-up crews armed with small plates that could be sealed over an opening and then spot-welded. By the time they were through *Karga*'s hull was a bizarre patchwork quilt, but she would hold atmosphere without the assistance of *Sindri*'s force fields.

Bondarevsky's role in the exterior work was limited to getting the flight decks repaired. Early on Richards gave him priority in the waiting list for patches and parts, since the faster the flight deck could be restored the more easily personnel and supplies could be

transferred aboard. For the first two weeks, until the
bulk of the patches were in place and the testing of
hull integrity was well in hand, the salvage team and
the crewmen working with them had to be shuttled
back and forth each day from the *City of Cashel*. It
was only after they could be reasonably confident the
ship wasn't going to suddenly lose atmosphere that crew
members could begin moving in to quarters on board
on a more or less permanent basis.

All these considerations meant that work on the
starboard flight deck was first on the list of things to
be done, with Bondarevsky in personal charge of the
details assigned there. The physical problems of
repairing the wrecked hull and deck plating didn't take
long to finish, but once that was over there were myriad
details to deal with. The force field airlocks at each
end of the flight deck had to be repaired and tested,
and the massive clamshell doors that sealed off the deck
when flight operations were not in train had to be put
in order so that the crews working inside didn't have
to rely entirely on the force fields while they were
performing tasks too delicate to be done in space suits.
Bondarevsky left most of the actual flight deck work
to the supervision of Sparks McCullough, who knew
more about the cycle of flight deck operations than
most of the Landreicher crew was ever likely to learn.
He concentrated on a related section of the ship, the
Flight Control Center, located on the deck below the
CIC where Admiral Tolwyn was hard at work attempting
to restore some semblance of order to the carrier's most
vital command and control systems.

The FCC was actually a whole suite of related
compartments, each individual chamber responsible
for one aspect of the supercarrier's flight ops. Central
to all was Primary Flight Control, the nerve center which

oversaw all of the fighters, bombers, and support craft operating off the carrier at any given time. Primary Flight Control was relegated to a fairly low position on the priority list of places to be restored to operational order, however, since it would still be a long time before regular flight ops were conducted off *Karga*. Instead, Bondarevsky focused on CSTCC—the Carrier Space Traffic Control Center—located directly forward of the Primary Flight Control compartment. CSTCC governed the operations of craft in space within five kilometers of the carrier, and oversaw launching and recovery of all craft. The compartment had received only light collateral damage from the hit that had blasted CIC, but this structural damage had to be made good before anything else could be done. Banks of instrumentation had to be removed in order to install bulkhead patches and deck plating in CIC, using lighter versions of the hull patches that had been applied to the ship's exterior. Then the instrumentation had to be returned, with each system being thorough checked and tested before being installed to ensure that everything was at least potentially in working order. Two of the most vital systems in CSTCC relied on repair work being performed elsewhere on *Karga*: the sensor arrays located near the top of the carrier's towering superstructure, and the communications system. Fortunately these were high on everyone's priority list, and Diaz had specialists tackling these systems almost from the very beginning. Still, it was over a week from the time the CSTCC was physically restored until the first tests of ship's sensors and communications, and two more days went by after that tracking down a series of small but disabling glitches.

In fact, the computers came on-line before the sensors were fully working, and that was accounted a minor miracle by anyone with more than a smattering of computer knowledge. Given the vast differences in design philosophy between human and Kilrathi technicians, it had been touch and go for a time. In fact, it wouldn't have been possible to get the computer systems up and running at all without the active assistance of Hrothark, the Kilrathi Cadre Computer Officer who worked with Diaz's experts to modify their code to something the Kilrathi computers would recognize as usable. Fortunately the computer network was designed not only for redundancy and flexibility, but for a high degree of self-programming. Once Diaz and Hrothark introduced the basic directives into the system the computer net itself did most of the work of developing operating systems. Still, the sheer number of different jobs the computer had to oversee in order for the ship to work required a great deal of programming time, and even after the computer system was on-line and functioning programmers were continuing to introduce new routines as they became necessary. Computer control for environmental systems was introduced first, followed by sensors, communications, and the ship's power grid. But minor errors continued to be almost constant reminders of how much they had to do, from the periodic shutdown of gravity and light in the crew quarters on Deck Six to the fault that caused the entire computer system to crash every time someone tried to send a passenger lift to the ship's recreation section.

When at length the CSTCC came on-line, Bondarevsky was ready to turn control of the section over to Commander Juliette Marchand, who had been designated as the carrier's Space Officer, more often referred to as "the Boss." Marchand, like Bondarevsky, came from the Confederation Navy. She had previously served aboard the TCS *Ticonderoga*, but had drawn a court-martial and dismissal from the service for willfully assaulting a superior—the Confederation Secretary of Defense, no less—after the man had interfered with her disciplinary decision with regard to a subordinate during an inspection of her carrier soon after the Battle of Earth. A small, dark-haired woman who tended to wear coveralls emblazoned with the motto "Boss," Marchand was nothing short of brilliant when it came to handling CSTCC operations, but she had a short fuse and a habit of regarding "her" bailiwick as a private fiefdom, not to be interfered with by anyone, even the Wing Commander who rated as her nominal superior.

Under Marchand's iron hand, the starboard flight deck entered normal operation three weeks after the repair job began. But Bondarevsky's job had only just begun. Traffic Control could control the launch and recovery of small craft from the flight deck, but there was still plenty of work to be done. The three massive elevators that raised and lowered planes from the cavernous hangar deck beneath the starboard flight deck had to be overhauled before the carrier could pretend to be more than a platform for outside craft to land on. Unfortunately two of them had been seriously damaged, one by the hit that had crippled the approach deck, the other by Graham's scavenging missions, who had adapted some of the equipment that operated the aft elevator for use in repairing their planetside shuttles. By ruthlessly scrounging for parts from Graham's gear and the remains of the aft elevator they were able to make a start at fixing the forward one, but it was slow going at best and would leave them with just two working elevators on the starboard side. Bondarevsky knew from long experience that this would severely handicap flight operations in a combat situation, when a fast turn-around of planes was essential to maintaining the carrier's battle capabilities. He tried not to think too much about what they had deduced about *Karga's* last battle, since confirmed by Murragh. Limited flight operations had left the supercarrier unable to stand against a pair of cruisers which otherwise would never have been able to approach close enough to be so much as a nuisance.

There was one bit of good news, though. In the process of getting the elevators and the hangar deck back into operation Sparks was able to pass on the report that many of the Kilrathi planes in the starboard side hangar deck were useable. Each flight deck had its own hangar area, so the starboard side represented roughly half of the complement of aerospace craft on board. Out of sixty-four fighters, bombers, and support craft allocated to the starboard side, thirty-seven were arrayed in their storage bays and appeared undamaged. There were also seven Darket light fighters and four Strakha stealth fighters on the surface of Nargrast, bringing the total up to forty-eight. The port side hangar hadn't produced nearly as many craft in any kind of shape to fly. Evidently these had taken greater losses during the raid on Landreich, and less than twenty were reported as spaceworthy. But other damaged craft would be useful sources of parts when they had to start getting the flight wing into active service.

Bondarevsky was less sanguine when he considered the problems of training Landreich and ex-ConFleet pilots to use Kilrathi planes, and bumped a request for simulator programming and hardware repair up on the Flight Wing's priority list.

Sparks was happy, at least, at the prospect of getting her hands dirty tearing down Kilrathi planes and then putting them back together so they could start flying. But Bondarevsky had to hold her back. By this time the starboard flight deck was starting to cycle regular flights on and off the carrier, and even the refueling and repair equipment was starting to come back into play. But with all this accomplished, they had to turn their attention to the port side and start all over again.

In the meantime, work was proceeding in other parts of the ship. The flag bridge, which had never been seriously damaged, was back in operation on a limited basis early on, and as more and more of the shipwide systems came back on-line the role of the crew manning it expanded. This was the domain of Admiral Richards, who spent most of his time poring over the intelligence files extracted from the computer during the reprogramming process. With the addition of Murragh's experts he was no longer needed to explain every bit of Kilrathi technology to the salvage team or the carrier's crew, which meant he was under much less strain now. But he continued to drive himself to become as familiar as possible with the ship, and to keep himself fully updated on the strategic situation that faced the Landreich.

Tolwyn, meanwhile, started in on CIC, cheerfully working side-by-side with the lowest-ranking technicians to tear down control systems and put them to rights. The Combat Information Center had been damaged by the same hit that had crippled Primary Flight Control, but there wasn't as much destruction here as on the navigation bridge four levels up and all the way forward on the carrier's superstructure. That section was given a few rough patches and then given up as a bad business, to be repaired later as time and resources allowed. A working CIC would allow *Karga* to maneuver and fight, and that was all Tolwyn wanted of her. Each day, Bondarevsky was impressed with the change in Tolwyn's bearing and attitude. The demands of making the repairs work had narrowed the admiral's world so that he no longer spent so much time worrying about conspiracies and the interplay of politics and war across the whole of human space. Instead he had a job to do, something that he could measure day by day, and the way he threw himself into it was a positive inspiration for the rest of the officers, crew, and outside specialists.

Most of the other officers were up to the challenge, too. Diaz and his people performed miracle after miracle despite the technological difficulties of working with Kilrathi gear. Contrary to popular belief, the Cats were by no means backward or primitive; they had been in space longer than Mankind, though their technology wasn't far ahead of the Confederation's in any major respect. Nor was their equipment simpler or more rugged despite the common conception back home of the Kilrathi as brutal and violent. Many of their systems were surprisingly fine and delicate, though of course there were differences in the size of components that reflected the larger bodies and hands of the builders. But it was differences in basic design philosophy that gave the specialists most of their headaches. Kilrathi naval architects believed in redundant and diversified systems, and not just for computers. They frequently designed subsystems that could back up not one but several radically different primary functions, which made it hard for Diaz or his people to point to one single place and say "There is the backup for the system we're working on." It made it difficult to know when backups were on-line, and almost impossible to discard any components, no matter how little they seemed to have to do with any particular ship's function, without extensive testing, physical tracing of connections, and heated discussions among the experts. Sometimes the Kilrathi Cadre could help out, but not always. Fifty specialists covered a number of critical fields of expertise, but they were not ship-builders, and their specialties were often in areas removed from the nuts-and-bolts design process.

By the time Bondarevsky was getting ready to tackle the port side flight deck, the carrier was close to functioning as a ship again. She had computers, sensors, environmental systems, and communications up and running. Of her eight laser turrets, six were back on-line thanks to the heroic efforts of Lieutenant Commander Dmitri Deniken, the Tactics and Gunnery Officer. The other two probably wouldn't function again this side of a keel-up repair at a major spaceyard, but Deniken had managed to come up with arcs of fire that covered the entire ship. He also had hopes of getting the numerous point-defense turrets working again once they managed to track down a computer glitch that made the automatic intercept function useless.

The one area where repair work lagged behind was Engineering. Commander Kent, the chief engineer recruited by Kruger for the project, was another ex-ConFleet man, but turned out to be something of a plodder. The wild leaps of imagination and creativity needed to come up with improvised solutions to unexpected problems simply weren't for him. His by-the-book overhaul of the fusion power plants fell further and further behind schedule as he ran into trouble balancing the magnetic containment fields badly stressed by the final battle and the effects of long neglect and interaction with the brown dwarf's radiation. Finally Tolwyn, furious at the continued delays, had relieved him of duty after a blazing row. His choice to replace Kent was little short of brilliant. Donald Scott Graham, late of TCS *Juneau*, became *Karga*'s new chief engineer. It was highly irregular—technically the man was still on active duty with the ConFleet, though they didn't know he was even alive. But Tolwyn himself retained his admiral's authority, and as ranking Confederation officer in the star system accepted Graham's resignation from the service, placed him in the inactive reserve, and then swore him in as a Landreich officer. Hopefully they would be able to sort out the paperwork later. In the meantime, though, *Karga* acquired a Chief Engineer who knew exactly how to go about the recommissioning job. Many of his solutions to problems skirted the regs in more ways than one, but they got the job done. Slowly, the engineering department began to catch up with the others as Graham took hold of his new responsibilities.

The end of the year was fast approaching, with two months of work behind them, and the Goliath Project crew could look back at solid progress. But the work ahead remained daunting. They had the second flight deck to put back into service, and all of the Kilrathi planes to check, overhaul, and put into action—if and when they could get pilots trained on the craft. Graham had the fusion plants back on-line and was working on the shield generators, but these were in particularly bad shape and were likely to be slow. In the interim they continued to rely on *Sindri* for anti-radiation shielding, but the tender's extended shields couldn't handle combat conditions, and until they could put up a reliable combat-rated force field the carrier wasn't anything more than a particularly large and unwieldy dock floating in space. And as yet nothing had been done about her engines, maneuver drives and the hyperspace jump system.

Still, it was progress, more than Bondarevsky, for one, had ever believed possible at the outset. Another few months and they might actually have a fighting ship.

If, in fact, Ragark gave them another few months.

Operations Planning Center, FRLS *Karga*
Orbiting Vaku VII, Vaku System
1445 hours (CST), 2670.356

It was a measure of their progress that they now could hold their conferences aboard *Karga*, rather than assembling aboard *Independence*. The Operations Planning Center for the supercarrier was located adjacent to the admiral's ready room and the flag bridge, and was considerably more impressive than the escort carrier's cozy conference room. In the center of the large chamber was a holographic projection tank that could display anything from tactical dispositions of a squadron to starcharts of entire sectors. Seats rose in tiers on all four sides of the oval compartment, allowing senior officers from several ships in a battle group to attend the briefing at the same time. Each person had a computer terminal attached to his seat which allowed him to call up details from the holo-tank, and there was an excellent intercom system that allowed everyone, no matter where he or she was in the room, to take full part in the discussions.

Jason Bondarevsky had chosen a seat near the top tier by the door, well out of the way. He'd learned to watch and listen at these conferences, but saved his input for times when he could tackle Richards or Tolwyn in private. Too many voices arguing over priorities or procedures was a sure recipe for chaos, and the Goliath staff had proven this on more than one occasion over the last two months.

Richards was in the place reserved for the Kilrathi admiral, near the head of the oval in a private box seat something like a small throne. Tolwyn had a less impressive version of the same accommodations at the other end of the holo-tank, the spot where a Kilrathi intelligence or political officer would have been accommodated in an Imperial vessel.

The rest of the room was well-filled. This particular conference was far more extensive than the usual daily briefings, including officers from other ships of the battle group as well as the carrier's department heads and other important members of the team. The progress made to date had allowed Richards to convene this meeting to begin a new phase of the project.

"All right, people, the sooner we get started the sooner we can get out of here." Richards' voice came through clearly over the intercom headset Bondarevsky, like the rest of the assembled staff, was wearing. The original Kilrathi earpieces had been too large and bulky for humans to use, so Lieutenant Vivaldi, the Communications Officer, had raided the *City of Cashel* for a supply of marine tactical transceivers. Murragh and his fellow Kilrathi wore the original gear. They were clustered on one side of the holo-tank, a block of nonhumans who somehow seemed out of place now on their own ship. "Mr. Bondarevsky. Status?"

Bondarevsky cleared his throat. "Primary Flight Control will be on-line this afternoon, or so Mr. Diaz has assured me." He glanced toward the salvage specialist, who gave a little self-satisfied nod. "That means that by tomorrow morning we'll be able to start pretending we're a real carrier. If the sensors behave themselves, we should be able to track anything in this part of the system, although I'm still worried about the interference from the brown dwarf's strange radiation. A brown dwarf just isn't supposed to cause this much trouble. And the ring system still drives our sensor probes crazy."

Richards smiled. "Why should the sensors be any different from the rest of us?" he demanded. That raised a few laughs, from humans and Kilrathi alike. "Excellent work. With PFC and the starboard hangar deck up and running—and Mr. Deniken's weapons in place—this boat can start looking after herself. Commander Tolwyn?"

Kevin Tolwyn nodded. "Your capacity will be limited for a time, but I'd say you won't need us to look after you . . . if you have the planes to fly your own patrols."

"Exactly." Richards frowned. "I'm not about to start using our Kilrathi planes yet, not until Mr. Bondarevsky's training and simulation program is running. In the meantime, by the power invested in me by our beloved leader, Old Max, I am hereby ordering half of the *Independence* Flight Wing detached for duty aboard *Karga*."

Galbraith was quick to react. "Now wait just a minute, Admiral," he said. "I don't think—"

"Spare me, Captain," Richards cut him off. "I've already discussed the matter with Admiral Camparelli. And you know my orders give me broad discretion for requisitions of this type. At any rate, you'll have replacements waiting for you at Landreich when you head back there next week."

"Head back?" Galbraith frowned.

"That's the point to all this," Richards said. "Old Max made it quite clear that he wanted *Independence* back on active service again just as soon as we felt we didn't need her for protecting Goliath any longer. Well, we have guns and we have a flight deck. With half a flight wing we can handle most standard operations, and when we get our people trained on the Kilrathi birds and get the other flight deck up to speed we'll have everything we need here to protect ourselves. *Independence* is to make her way back to Landreich to link up with a new battle group. You can make good your shortages of planes there."

"I . . . suppose that will work out all right," Galbraith said.

"Good. Commander Tolwyn, you may assign whichever of your squadrons you see fit, of course, though I would suggest that you balance the two wings as best you can. Consult with Mr. Bondarevsky. I'll approve whatever TO&E the two of you come up with."

"Aye aye, sir," Kevin Tolwyn said, turning a brief grin on Bondarevsky.

"Do you see any further difficulties in starting flight operations, Captain?" Richards asked, looking at Bondarevsky.

"No, sir," he replied. "Nothing major, at least. Starboard side'll be crowded for a while, with all those Kilrathi birds in the hangars, but there's a fair amount of room to spare. Luckily the Cats built this tub with the idea of having to operate all their birds with one crippled flight deck."

"Too bad for them they didn't actually do it," Marchand said from here place a few seats down from Bondarevsky. "You may not think it's a major problem, sir, but as far as I'm concerned juggling all those planes is going to be a nightmare. How soon until we can start shifting a few of the Kilrathi junkheaps over to port side?"

"Probably a couple of weeks, Boss," Bondarevsky told her. "Until then, you'll just have to make do. I've seen you work. You'll handle it."

"Good," Richards said. "Now, Mr. Graham, what's our schedule on shields and drives?"

"That same couple of weeks, sir," Graham replied. "That is, if we don't run into any more trouble with the shield generators. I'm not happy about their power consumption. I'm pretty sure the battle damage was a bit more than the initial surveys showed. There was a hell of a lot of energy soaking through the whole system when *Juneau* and *Dover* hit the old girl, and I don't think Commander Kent's first estimates took into account the overload factor."

"From here on out, Commander, I think you should have priority on all resources," Richards said. "I'm not happy sitting on a ship that can't break orbit and can't defend herself in a combat situation. I know we're off the beaten track here, but a Kilrathi raiding squadron could ruin our whole day. Any comments?"

No one argued with the decision, though Bondarevsky could see several department heads looking grim. Too many jobs, too few resources, that was the story of the Goliath Project from start to finish.

"All right, other points." Richards consulted his computer terminal. "Damn, it's printing out in Kilrathi again. Armando?"

Diaz keyed a command into his terminal, and after a moment Richards gave a faint smile. "That's better. Actually, I can read Kilrathi. Last week I think it was giving me Gaelic."

"Probably got confused by Lieutenant Harper's folk-sing in the rec room," Bondarevsky suggested. "I know I did."

"Be that as it may," Richards said. "Hmm. *Vision Quest*, I think, should head back to Landreich in company with *Independence*. Unless you think there's anything else for you here, Captain Springweather?"

She shook her head. "You took care of the money. That was the important part. And I have the survey data from Nargrast. That could fetch a few credits on the minerals market. But if I stay here much longer I'll be losing money hand over fist."

"That would never do," Richards said blandly. "By all means head for home with *Independence* next week.

I'll see to it that the Navy gives you a free maintenance overhaul when you put in at Landreich."

Springweather smiled, an expression that always put Bondarevsky in mind of a cat studying a trapped bird.

"Next item . . . Captain Galbraith, I'm also requisitioning your marines." Richards held up a hand to forestall the inevitable protest. "Same reasons as before, with some added points. The colonel and his men know this ship inside and out after their part in the early surveys. In addition, they have Nargrast experience, and we'll still be conducting mineral extraction work there for some time to come. Once again, we need them here, and you'll be able to pick up replacements at Landreich. Colonel? Any problems with that?"

Bhaktadil shook his turbaned head. "Not on my part, Admiral," he said. "I think my boys and girls are getting used to things over here." He looked more pleased than the reverse. Probably, Bondarevsky thought, he was looking forward to getting out from under Galbraith's thumb. And he would be the ranking Marine officer aboard, commanding a double-sized contingent.

"Very good, then," Richards said. "That clears my list. Now, who wants to talk about anything?"

"Sir?" Lieutenant Mario Vivaldi, the Communications Officer, put up a hand.

"Yes, Lieutenant?"

"Sir, Christmas is coming up, and some of us were wondering . . ."

Richards smiled. "I think I can safely say that we'll be on a holiday watch rotation for Christmas, Lieutenant. Father Darby was already in to see me the other day to discuss religious observances. We've got a good cross-section of faiths represented in the Chaplain's Office, so I'm pretty sure you'll be well covered spiritually. Anything else you need, I'm sure we can provide."

"If you want a tree, you're welcome to try the ones on Nargrast," Graham said with a grin. "Of course, they've got trunks as big around as this compartment and don't reach as high as the overhead, and they give off fumes that smell like something died, but they're green . . . sort of."

"Pass," Aengus Harper said.

"Any other questions before we get down to the regular business?" Richards asked. "No? Then the squadron officers are free to go, unless they want to sit around and listen to a lot of technical garbage. Mr. Clancy, I want you to go over the ideas you brought up last night concerning the improvements to the helm station. You've already got the thing cross-patched so many different ways I'm afraid to even think about powering up the engines, for fear of where we might land . . ."

And so the work went on.

• CHAPTER 12

> *"There is no such thing as a battle without honor, though it is possible to encounter an honorless foe."*
>
> from the First Codex
> 02:28:10

Flight Wing Lounge, FRLS *Karga*
Orbiting Vaku VII, Vaku System
1925 hours (CST), 2670.358

"Break left! Break left!" The voice in Bondarevsky's helmet receivers was urgent. *"Come on, Captain, you can nail this guy!"*

Bondarevsky pulled the joystick hard over, rolling to the left and trying to spot his quarry. The Strakha bucked and kicked as if it resented the very idea of a human pilot flying it, but he fought the controls and forced the fighter into the turn. He reached for the sensor controls to narrow the focus and try to get an accurate position estimate on the cloaked enemy fighter he knew was closing in for the kill, but a split second too late he realized he'd instinctively reached for the spot where they would have been located on one of the Ferrets he'd flown back in his days as *Tarawa*'s Wing Commander. The sudden realization made him try to shift in mid-reach, but that sent his bionic arm into a feedback spasm.

The delay was fatal. The enemy Strakha decloaked bare meters off his starboard side, and the red flash of incoming fire washed through Jason Bondarevsky's cockpit.

The buzzer going off in his ear made him wince and grind his teeth. The cockpit opened up, revealing a crowd of men and women surrounding the simulator unit. Money was changing hands as they paid off their bets. Bondarevsky blinked in the glare of the lights.

"Bang, you're dead," Doomsday Montclair announced from the other simulator cockpit, climbing out with the aid of a pair of his squadron's younger pilots.

"I noticed," Bondarevsky replied dryly. "I've got to hand it to you, Doomsday. You haven't lost your edge."

Montclair grinned. "Didn't let them promote me out of the cockpit, skipper," he said. "But don't sweat it. You'll get the moves back. And if you don't, I'll be around to bail out your sorry ass!"

That sparked laughter from the audience. Bondarevsky started to clamber out of the cockpit, and Harper and Sparks were quick to help him. The simulator modules were cobbled together from a combination of Confederation and Kilrathi technology, mostly the former. The Kilrathi had less use for detailed simulations of flight missions than human pilots did. According to Jorkad *lan* Mraal, the senior pilot from the Nargrast survivors who had been working with Sparks on building the modules, the Empire preferred live-training exercises with real ships, real maneuvers, and live ammo.

Jorkad was there now, looking out of place amidst the revelry of the Flight Wing's Christmas party. The

Christmas holiday was something the Kilrathi couldn't quite grasp. The message of "peace on Earth, good will toward men" was so alien to their way of life that they simply had nothing to compare it to. But a *kil* enjoyed a good party as much as any human, and Jorkad seemed to be developing a special fondness for eggnog.

"I was studying your performance, Captain Bondarevsky," he said gravely. Jorkad was always studiously correct and formal. At first some of the members of the wing had assumed it was a mask for some underlying hostility to the humans, but on closer acquaintance the general consensus was that Jorkad was just naturally serious and punctilious all the time. "Your instincts are good. But I fear your reactions have been somewhat slowed by your injuries. The artificial arm . . ."

"Is a problem sometimes, yes," Bondarevsky said, feeling impatient. He still didn't like discussing the plastilimb, especially not with a Cat. "I'm getting the hang of it."

He wasn't good at reading Kilrathi expressions, but he thought Jorkad's look might have been the Cat equivalent of a frown. "I believe that Hrothark and I could design an interface that would connect your arm directly into the controls of the fighter," he said. "It is possible that you could substantially improve your performance by having many of the onboard systems essentially controlled by thought—or at least by the muscular impulses associated with specific actions, such as operating sensors or firing weapons."

"Thanks, but no thanks," Bondarevsky said.

Jorkad studied him curiously. "I do not understand. Why would you reject something which could give you an advantage in combat? Particularly when it turns a current handicap around and makes it an asset instead?"

Bondarevsky shrugged. "I don't know if I can explain it, my friend." He held up his arm. "Look here. You can see that the limb is designed to look as much like a biological arm as possible. It would be a lot more efficient, and cost-effective too, for that matter, if it wasn't built this way, but you'll find most people prefer artificial limbs that don't *look* artificial."

The Kilrathi pilot gave a very human head nod, at the same time making the Cat grasping gesture that stood for understanding.

"The thing is," Bondarevsky went on, "a lot of us don't like to be forced to admit to something like this. I've got a machine doing the work of a limb, and I'm damned glad to have it, but I'd far rather have the original. And the last thing I want is to lose my humanity more than I already have by plugging myself into my cockpit like one more onboard system. I learned to fly by my gut, and I'd rather keep on doing it that way even if I have to work a little bit harder at it. Do you understand?"

"I believe I do, Captain," Jorkad said slowly. "Your sentiments are reminiscent of some of the passages in the Seventh Codex. You've given me much to think about."

"Glad I could help out," Bondarevsky muttered as the Cat pilot stalked away in search of a refill for his empty cup of eggnog.

"Well, well, Jason Bondarevsky trading philosophy with a Cat. I never thought I'd live to see the day." The crowd parted as Kevin Tolwyn approached, trailed by a junior lieutenant carrying a large, bulky box.

"I've swapped that kind of stuff with stranger types than him," Bondarevsky said with a smile. "In fact, I'm looking at one now."

Tolwyn's expression was one of mock horror. "I'm wounded! To be insulted so, and by my own dear mentor! Maybe I'll just call off this whole Christmas thing right here and now."

"Christmas thing?" Bondarevsky frowned. "Please tell me you didn't . . ."

"Oh, don't worry, I'm not going to give *you* anything." Tolwyn grinned at him. Bondarevsky had never been much for celebrating Christmas, beyond putting in the expected appearances at the festivities held by the people in his command. Born and raised on Razin, a distant frontier world settled by Russians of mostly Eastern Orthodox religion, Bondarevsky had been brought up to celebrate Epiphany, the baptism rather than the Nativity of Christ, and even yet he still was apt to keep the Twelfth-Night holiday rather than the more traditional Christmas Day. He and Kevin had a long-standing tradition of not exchanging presents until Epiphany. "No, I brought over a gift from all of the Liberators to all of you . . . whatever it is you're going to call yourselves. Lieutenant, if you please . . ."

His assistant stepped forward and set the box down on the table. "Open it up, Jason," Tolwyn said.

He looked at the box for a long moment, half-expecting some kind of prank. Then he noticed that the lid of the box was pierced by half a dozen small holes, and that piqued his curiosity. Just what was Tolwyn up to, anyway?

Bondarevsky lifted the lid and looked inside. There, almost invisible in the shadows, a pair of green eyes regarded him curiously.

"Thrakhath!" he said. He reached in and lifted out the black cat, who responded by rubbing on his chin and purring loudly. That set off laughter from the officers clustered nearby. "Kevin, are you sure about this? I had the idea Thrakhath was kind of a favorite of yours. This one, at least."

Tolwyn grinned. "Yeah, I like him a lot better than I ever liked the one from Kilrah, but there's a dozen cats on *Independence* to keep our rodent population under control. And we thought you guys could use a mascot over here. Given your new home and all, it just seemed like a good idea."

Bondarevsky put the cat down on the table, but kept petting him. "Just as long as he doesn't cause as much trouble as his namesake . . ."

"Oh, he'll cause a *lot* more than that." Tolwyn grinned again. "And he'll bring bad luck to anybody who crosses his path. Like Ragark and his Kilrathi . . ."

"Or the confees!" one of the pilots called from the back of the watching crowd. "Or anybody else who gets in our way!"

Tolwyn looked embarrassed. "Anyway, Merry Christmas from the Liberators to . . ." He trailed off. Bondarevsky's command had been officially designated as FW-137, but it didn't have a name as yet. The carrier hadn't even received a formal Landreich Navy name yet.

"The Black Cats!" a voice from the crowd declared loudly. Commander Alexandra Travis came forward and stretched out a hand to scratch Thrakhath behind the ears. The animal looked satisfied with himself and redoubled his contented purring. "What do you say, Captain? What better name for a Flight Wing operating off a Cat carrier, with Cat fighters, and probably in Cat space, sooner or later?"

There were plenty of comments from the others, and they all sounded favorable. Bondarevsky nodded. "All right, the Black Cats it is." He paused. "Mr. Harper, I am hereby appointing you as Chief Cat-tender, with all the duties and responsibilities that traditionally go with that post. And somebody else is going to have to explain all this to Murragh. I sure as hell don't want to tell him we've got a house pet named after his cousin."

"To hear him talk," Travis said, "house pet would be a step up from what Murragh's people think of their ex-Prince." She grinned. "But you know *we'll* be bad luck to anybody who crosses *our* path!"

Tolwyn and his aid stayed on for a drink, then left to catch the tail end of the Christmas party aboard their own ship. Soon after they had taken their leave Bondarevsky stopped at a side table to refill his drink, and encountered Travis once again.

"So . . . you lost your simulator duel, huh?" she said. "The legend has feet of clay after all. I lost ten credits on you, Captain."

"Sorry, Commander," he said with a faint smile. "If I'd've known you were betting on me I would have worked harder."

She returned the smile. "Or bet against me and thrown the fight deliberately," she said, arching one eyebrow. "Seriously, though, how did it feel? Do you think it's an accurate simulation of a Strakha?"

Her interest was understandable. Alexandra Travis had been designated as squadron commander for VF-401, one of the new fighter squadrons being organized aboard the supercarrier. Once she and her pilots finished training, they'd be flying the squadron of Strakha fighters salvaged from the Kilrathi planes on board. Her previous experience had been confined to the Raptor heavy fighter, and they had little in common in terms of handling with the Cat Strakhas.

Bondarevsky was impressed by her record and by the skill she'd displayed getting her squadron in shape these last few days. Of all his new squadron commanders she was the one who seemed most in tune with him, her mind often following the same leaps of imagination that his own did as they discussed the ways and means of making the Flight Wing work.

"I don't know how accurate it is," he said, "but Sparks and Jorkad seem to think it isn't too far from the real thing. If it's anything like the simulator, the Strakha's going to be heavy going. Big and mean, but not exactly subtle . . . except for the stealth technology. I guess the Cats figured they had a cloak, so why bother making the thing nimble too? Takes some getting used to when you've come out of the high-maneuverability school."

"Sort of like trying to fly a shuttle after a stretch of duty with Hornets," she said, nodding.

"Well, not quite that bad, maybe," he said, remembering his landing on *Independence* and how clumsy the shuttle controls had seemed. "I figure with enough sim time it won't be too much of a problem getting these Cat planes down cold. I have to admit, though, that it's pretty strange thinking of how to use them in combat, and not just how to beat them."

She laughed. "You could say the same thing about this whole operation," she said. "A year ago a Cat was just something to shoot at. Now I'm starting to understand how they think . . . and it's starting to scare me. Sometimes I wonder how we managed to hold them off so long. They sure as hell know how to build a carrier."

Bondarevsky nodded. "I know what you mean. And working with the Cats from Murragh's bunch . . . they're not exactly what we always thought they were, are they?"

Before she could reply they were interrupted by a chord from Aengus Harper's guitar. The young lieutenant had found himself a perch on one of the tables and taken the battered-looking instrument out of its case. For a moment he contented himself with strumming chords, apparently at random.

"Well, the Bard of the Spaceways is at it again," Bondarevsky commented with a smile. "What's it going to be tonight, Lieutenant? More of your old Irish rabble-rousing songs?"

"Ah, now, sir, should I be playin' such things and ignoring the spirit of the season?" Harper replied with his easy, charming grin. "No, tonight I'll not be speakin' of the Gaels and their long struggle for freedom, more's the pity. Instead I thought I'd give you a Christmas song me auld mither taught me when I was just a lad."

He started picking the strings with practiced skill, closing his eyes and starting to sing in a soft, pleasant voice. It was a song Bondarevsky hadn't heard for years. The crowd was rapt as the young Taran sang the story of the child Jesus and his scornful playmates in Egypt, and the miracles that alarmed their mothers.

Thinking of the work they'd done on *Karga*, Bondarevsky couldn't help but think the lieutenant's choice was deliberate . . . and apt. They'd all worked their share of miracles out here on the edge of the frontier, and after this holiday was past they'd be right back in the miracle-working business once more.

Lutz Mannheim Starport, Newburg
Landreich, Landreich System
1039 hours (CST), 2670.364

"There's a visitor at the airlock to see you, Captain. Do you want to see anybody?"

Captain Wenona Springweather looked up from the computer terminal on her desk at her First Mate, who stood just inside the door of her day cabin with an apologetic look on his face. "Does this visitor have a name?" she asked irritably. Two solid hours had gone

by since the *Vision Quest* had grounded and Landreich
Port Authority officers had swarmed aboard each
armed with questionnaires and computer forms that
she had to fill out personally, it seemed, before the
scout ship could secure permission to berth at the
starport at all, much less apply for the free overhaul
Admiral Richards had promised her before the start
of the voyage.

She suspected that Captain Galbraith was behind
the extra attention she was receiving. He hadn't been
at all happy with the scout ship's performance on the
way home. Springweather couldn't help it if her jump
coils had worn through coming out of hyperspace at
Oecumene, and the cycle time for an interstellar hop
was running anywhere up to five times as long as it
should. If Galbraith had sent over the parts and
technical experts she'd asked for when the problem
first developed she could have put the problem to rest
then and there, but Galbraith wasn't the sort of Navy
man who'd extend a helping hand to a frontier scout.
So *Vision Quest* had slowed *Independence* down, and
now it seemed Galbraith was exacting his revenge by
inflicting petty bureaucracy on her. At this point a visitor
would be a welcome relief . . . unless he turned out
to be another bureaucrat.

"I'm sorry, skipper, but he wouldn't give a name. Looks
like a merchant skipper . . . a prosperous one, by the
cut of his clothes. Said he had a business proposal for
you."

She grinned. "When have you ever known me to turn
away the chance to make a credit or two, Frank? Send
the gentleman up, by all means."

Springweather managed to finish going over the
Customs Manifest, appending her retinal print to the
computer file just as the visitor arrived at her door.

He was a tall, gaunt man with dark hair and a down-turning mustache that made him look like a pirate right out of a historical holo-vid romance. His eyes, studying her, burned with the intensity of a man with a mission.

She stood and rounded the desk, extending a hand. "I'm Wenona Springweather. Captain, for what it's worth, of the *Vision Quest*. My Mate tells me you've some business for us. How can I be of service?"

"My name is Zachary Banfeld," he said, taking the hand.

Springweather's eyes narrowed. That was a name she'd heard before. But she had never expected to meet one of the most notorious men on the frontier.

Banfeld was the organizer and leader of a group that called itself "The Guild," a loose association of ship-captains and businessmen from a dozen worlds along the frontier, and not just within the Landreich's sphere of influence. Ostensibly they were civilians who had banded together for mutual protection and support during the war, but in fact rumor had it that they were much more than harmless merchants. Pooling their funds, they had bought weapons to arm their merchant ships, and even managed to acquire a small, antiquated escort carrier and some Confederation fighters. All this was supposed to be used to convoy merchant traffic along the dangerous frontier trade routes, but there were stories that suggested Banfeld's Guild operated as privateers—some said outright pirates—raiding shipping and remote planetary outposts and selling the proceeds at a substantial profit.

He seemed to sense her reaction to his name, and gave her a thin-lipped smile. "My reputation no doubt precedes me, Captain, but I assure you I'm not at all the way I'm portrayed on the holo-casts. Neither Robin

Hood nor Blackbeard . . . just Zack Banfeld, trying to do my job."

"And that job is?" She let a hint of ice creep into her tone. Wenona Springweather was as mercenary as any frontier scout, but her motto had always been to steer clear of the war and everything it represented. Banfeld, on the other hand, took entirely too much interest in conflict.

His smile turned wolfish. "Why, simply turning a profit, Captain," he said. "And, if I can, helping out the small shipowner from time to time."

"Such as now?" she asked. "What sort of help did you have in mind for me?"

"Just a chance to make a large sum of money in return for a few small bits of information," he said blandly. "About the work you've been doing the past several weeks."

"My last two trips have been classified by the Landreich government," she told him. "They've been employing me as a consultant, and you must understand that I couldn't go around selling secrets."

He shrugged. "It's fairly well known by now that you found a Kilrathi derelict. That news has been circulating around the bars for weeks. I'm . . . interested in learning the details, though. If the government is no longer interested in this ship, it might be an excellent source for parts, equipment, that sort of thing."

"And if the government *is* still interested?"

"Then I may still be able to turn a profit. Providing supply transport, for example, to and from the hulk. That sort of thing. I can't really say how The Guild might get involved until I know more details. But if I could obtain a little inside information, I'd not only know what to offer, but maybe I could get an inside track on the bidding."

"As far as I know, the government's not using civilian contractors out there," she said. "I was there because I found the thing in the first place. But the rest seems to be entirely a Navy operation. I'm sorry, but I don't really think I can help."

His eyes flashed for an instant. Then the smile was back. "Come, come, Captain. You haven't even heard my offer. Fifty thousand for your information, and a ten percent share of any profits I might turn from it."

"Fifty thousand . . ." That was substantially more than Max Kruger had paid her for the original information about the *Karga*. Tempted, she turned and walked to the far side of the office, gazing out the small transplast porthole over her desk at the busy starport outside. Finally she turned back, shaking her head. "I'm sorry. I can't help you."

"You're afraid I might misuse the information?" He was frowning now. "Look, from what you say the government is already there, and from the size of the battle group that went out and didn't come back with you and *Independence* I'd say they were protecting this derelict pretty damned well. What am I going to do? Sell the story to the Cats? Even if they were interested, they couldn't do much without mounting a damned big raid, and by the time they did anything the Navy would be ready for them. Anyway, dealing with Cats is hardly ever profitable. And I swear all I'm trying to do is make a good business move ahead of the pack."

She studied him for a long moment, her thoughts prey to conflicting emotions. Despite his reputation Banfeld had generally played the part of a patriot during the war, though he'd also turned a handsome profit at the same time. She didn't really think he'd betray anything she told him to the Kilrathi. And fifty thousand credits . . .

Her eyes came to rest on the computer terminal where she'd been poring over the Landreich's forms and endless bureaucratic garbage. What did she really owe the government now, anyway? She'd done the job they'd hired her to do, led Richards and his men to the *Karga* and then wasted months hanging around waiting for them to decide to pay what they owed her. And Galbraith had treated her ship and crew like so much debris the whole trip back. If she chose to make some extra money off her find at Vaku, how would that hurt Max Kruger or his lackeys?

Fifty thousand credits . . .

"I'd want a contract, Mr. Banfeld," she said at last. "Not that I don't trust you, but . . ."

He smiled again, his eyes burning hotter. "I anticipated the need, Captain. Shall we go over it now?"

Terran Confederation Embassy Compound,
Newburg
Landreich, Landreich System
1315 hours (CST)

"We have them, Commissioner. We have Richards, Tolwyn, and Kruger! All we have to do is decide how to deal with them."

Clark Williams regarded Colonel Mancini with a sour look. "Not more of your rumors," he said. "More barroom gossip about Kilrathi ships abandoned in the sector. I've had just about enough of hearing all the drunken speculations of the bums who hang out at those places down in Startown."

"Not a rumor this time, sir," Mancini said. "This time we have the information straight from the source. *Vision Quest* landed this morning."

"What?" He sat upright, his chair creaking under him. "Got the Springweather woman in here as soon as possible! We'll squeeze everything she knows out of her . . ."

"That won't be necessary," Mancini said. "Fact is, one of our agents spotted her arrival and moved on his own initiative. Tied her up aboard ship by persuading the authorities to give her more than the usual share of Inward Clearance nonsense, and then moved in for the kill." He smiled. "It's amazing how much you can get when you combine greed and frustration in one package."

"Well? What did your agent get?"

"I'll let him tell you himself." Mancini touched a stud on his shirt sleeve, activating a tiny communications device. "Send him in."

The door opened a moment later to admit Zachary Banfeld. "Ah, Commissioner," the newcomer said pleasantly. "Good to see you again."

Williams nodded. "And you, Mr. Banfeld. It's been . . . what? Two years now?"

"Since that little situation on Freya. Yeah." Banfeld smiled as he took a seat beside the CSB colonel. "That was quite a nice little operation, as I recall."

Williams studied the man assessingly. Here on the frontier Zachary Banfeld was regarded as something between a romantic highwayman and a black-hearted pirate, depending on who you asked, but no one suspected that he was also a freelance agent of the Confederation government. The Guild really did do legitimate business, organizing merchant convoys and taking on contracts to ship needed materials through spacelanes no other civilian trader would willingly travel. And it sponsored privateering raids, hitting vulnerable targets and looting them for resale later.

Banfeld's people also dabbled in black market deals, arms smuggling, mercenary operations, and training local militias to handle combat situations.

Behind all these dealings, though, Banfeld also took on odd jobs for the Confederation from time to time, especially in the last few years. He had been recruited, not only by Mancini's CSB, but by the other, more shadowy organization that Williams and Mancini both belonged to—the Belisarius Group. And he had been a useful tool on several occasions of late, when Belisarius needed to flex its muscles out here on the frontier without any direct Confederation involvement in frontier affairs. Guild ships had staged a few raids on Landreich outposts to confuse the issue after Kruger had started complaining of Kilrathi incursions, for instance, leaving clear-cut evidence of human pirates at work. And they had raided into Kilrathi space as well, to keep the pot boiling and to make it look as if Ragark was being provoked into action by Kruger and his "irresponsible warmongers."

Zachary Banfeld was a man with a mission. He had grown rich and powerful along the frontier by exploiting the war between humans and Kilrathi. With the end of the war his shadow empire was threatened, and he wanted nothing more than to see the fighting start again so he and his could get back to their business of profiteering, privateering, and pirating. Fortunately, that goal was perfectly in accord with the needs of the Belisarius Group.

"All right, Mr. Banfeld, the Colonel tells me you have information we can use." Williams smiled coldly. "What have you found out?"

"The stories about the government finding a Kilrathi derelict were true, after all," Banfeld said. "A supercarrier that was caught in a battle but not quite destroyed, out in the Vaku system. Kruger's expeditionary force went there with the idea of recommissioning the ship and adding it to his fleet. Apparently the job is well in hand." He went on to describe the situation as Springweather had explained it to him.

When he was done, Mancini summed it up. "So what we have here is a supercarrier that could alter the entire balance of forces in the region if it completes repairs and joins the FRLN. But for the moment she's still weak. Her combat shields still aren't operating, and she only has half of a flight wing for protection until their pilots train on the Kilrathi planes they're salvaging."

Williams frowned. "That ship could ruin everything we've been working for," he said. "The only alternative I can see is to take it out of the picture now, before it becomes operational."

"My thoughts exactly," Mancini said. "Mr. Banfeld, I think your strike force might be of use to us once again. Do you have enough information to do the job, or should we arrange for a more . . . thorough talk with the good Captain Springweather? I could have Y-12 pick her up and interrogate her further, if you wish." Y-12 was the designation of the Belisarius Group's covert operations unit. Mancini held the rank of colonel in that organization, as well as the Confederation Security Bureau.

"She gave me everything I need," Banfeld said. "Even to the fact that they're having trouble with their sensors in the ring system around the gas giant. And more than that. They're still getting the bulk of their shielding from the tender. Take that out and *Karga* has no shields. That's how her first crew was killed, stuck in orbit with no screens against the radiation and no engines to pull them clear in time. All I have to do is hit that tender, and we've solved the problem."

Mancini smiled thoughtfully. "And if you can minimize the damage to the rest of the ship, we might put a crew of our own aboard her. Think what a nice job a Kilrathi supercarrier raiding a few outlying colonies could do to turn up the war fever a few more degrees."

Williams shrugged. "That's a nice thought, but I'd rather be sure the carrier's out of action. If it comes to a choice, don't hesitate to blow it out of space."

"I'll be sure to stick to the appropriate priorities, Commissioner," Mancini said. "Count on it."

"You've never let us down yet," Williams said. "All right, you've both done an excellent job. Especially you, Mr. Banfeld." He paused. "You said Springweather reported some Kilrathi were working with the Landreichers?"

"That's what she said. Rescued from a habitable moon in the system, apparently." Banfeld made a dismissive gesture. "She didn't know much about them. She wasn't at too many of the briefings, and Richards and Tolwyn mostly kept her in the dark about the details of what was going on. But apparently they were survivors from the fighting who escaped before the end of the battle, and they were grateful enough to the Landreichers to help them with the repair job."

"I don't like it," Williams said. "A *kil* doesn't work with a human without a damned good reason, and they wouldn't think gratitude was reason enough to show a bunch of humans how one of their carriers was put together. Something's rotten here. I'd like to know what."

Mancini shrugged. "If our friend Zachary is successful, it will be a moot point," he said. "The Cats will be as dead as Richards, Tolwyn, and Bondarevsky. That's all that really matters."

"I suppose you're right." Williams sighed. "But it would have been interesting to know what could make a *kil* cooperate with a human. It would be useful if we could recruit a few agents on the other side of the border."

"We're doing fine as we are, Commissioner," Mancini avowed. "The Cats are easy to manipulate without having to get them as buddies. Or at least the ambitious ones like Ragark are. Everything's falling into place. All we have to do is make sure that this carrier doesn't disrupt the plan."

Williams nodded. The Belisarius Group was dedicated to rekindling the war between the Confederation and the Empire, and so far the plan to make it happen out here in the Landreich was going smoothly. In the two months since Richards and his expedition had been gone the raids had increased in frequency and scope, sometimes helped along by Banfeld's pirates. Kruger was facing a political crisis at home, too, brought on by Councilman Galbraith's faction and their demands for a larger say in government affairs. They were hamstringing Kruger's attempts to increase his defense budget, insisting on pouring more money into domestic programs instead. And Kruger, being Kruger, was only making the situation worse by his stubborn attempts to prove he could run the Landreich without the support of his own Council. With luck the internal problems would be coming to a head just about the time Ragark finally moved in force. The Landreich would be overrun, and the Confederation would have to step in to stabilize the threatened frontier.

Yes, it was coming together nicely, the whole Belisarius operation. They'd named their group for the famous Roman general who had fought brilliantly for an emperor who had no military talent of his own, only to be betrayed by the suspicious ruler when it seemed likely the legions would offer him the Imperial purple. Belisarius had been a fool not to take his army and march on Constantinople to seize the throne for himself. The Belisarius group was determined that they would not allow the same kind of betrayal by civilian authorities at home to ever take place. They would do what Belisarius should have done—strike first, take power, and ensure the future of human civilization. If they had to sacrifice Max Kruger's Landreich along the way . . . well, that was a small enough cost to pay.

Banfeld broke in to his reverie. "When do you want us to hit them?" he asked.

"I want you to move as quickly as you can," Williams told him. "We want to nail Tolwyn and Richards before they have a chance to get the carrier in any better shape than it already is. And we want to make sure we hit them hard."

• **CHAPTER 13**

> *"Among the pillars of victory, the first and greatest is the art of the unexpected, for it is by surprise that the Warrior achieves domination on the field of battle."*

> from the Second Codex
> 04:18:21

Combat Information Center, FRLS *Karga*
Orbiting Vaku VII, Vaku System
1447 hours (CST), 2671.011

Admiral Geoff Tolwyn settled into his captain's chair and thought once again how good it felt to be in command of a ship again.

The thought had occurred to him more than once since the beginning of the Goliath Project, but it still hit him every so often that he was fortunate to have a second chance like this one. For all of his reputation as a strategist and a brilliant fleet commander, Tolwyn had always secretly felt that it had been a mistake to give up his first and greatest love, ship command, in favor of the wider responsibilities of a ConFleet admiral. People often talked about the "loneliness of command," but the fact was that a captain knew his ship, officers, and crew far better than a flag officer could ever know his battle group or fleet. The decisions you made sitting in the captain's chair were translated into instant action, for good or ill; an admiral's orders filtered through layers of subordinates and were never so immediate or so personal.

Even with the back-breaking work of refitting *Karga*, Tolwyn had found these past months among the most worthwhile he'd ever been through. For at least this brief period he had felt truly alive again, the pressures, the worries about other things secondary. Indeed, they were following their chosen course, the other things—that was a machine all ready running, just waiting for the moment to be unleashed. If anything, these weeks out here had been a final respite, a rekindling of older days before the events of things to come were finally shaped and unleashed. It was something special to see the battered derelict come alive again bit by bit, and to know that he had played a part in making it all happen. A decisive part, in fact, given the way he'd been forced to maneuver Richards and Bondarevsky into going ahead with the project.

Whole days had gone by in which he'd never even thought about the Confederation, or the conspiracy, or his career. He wished, sometimes, that it could always be like that, but tempting as it was to throw himself wholeheartedly into the service of the Landreich he was still committed to serving Terra any way he could. Getting *Karga* back into service was the only way he could help right now, but when the time came he'd leave Kruger's navy and go home to carry on his struggle over fresh battlefields.

"Ring System transit coming up in fifteen minutes, sir." Lieutenant Clancy, the helm officer from *Sindri* who'd been helping out with the refit had the conn today.

There were a whole series of tests scheduled for *Karga* to attempt, and Clancy knew the helm and navigation systems better than any of *Karga's* regular crew.

"Thank you, Helm," Tolwyn said. He keyed the intercom pad at his arm. "Engineering, are you ready?"

"As ready as we'll ever be, sir," Commander Graham's voice responded. "I *think* the generators will stay online this time."

"Do your best, Commander," the admiral told him. He touched another key. "*Sindri*, this is *Karga*. Shield test commences in thirty seconds."

"*Roger that,*" *Sindri's* captain replied. "*Thirty seconds.*"

Tolwyn watched the event countdown roll by on his monitor. As it hit zero, the lights flickered in CIC for a moment, and the ship's status board beside him came alive with multi-colored lights as Graham switched on the shield generators and a whole new part of the ship awakened from a year-long slumber. At first the lights were a mixture of red, green, and amber, but slowly the red lights went out as section after section adjusted to the new configuration of the power grid and the shielding subsystems.

They'd been through this before—three times, in fact. Each time the shields had gone down almost immediately. Tolwyn hoped they wouldn't have to go through a fourth failure and another week or two of tracing connections and bridging weak spots in the shield emitter arrays.

Seconds crept by like hours, and the shielding held.

After two full minutes, Tolwyn activated his intercom again. "*Sindri*, my board shows green. Shields are nominal."

"*That's confirmed*, Karga. *Looking good from here. I'm switching our shields to stand-by mode . . . now.*"

And *Karga* was generating her own protective field

at last, unaided by the tender still riding her superstructure like some kind of bizarre metallic symbiont.

"Engineering," Tolwyn said. "Good work, Commander Graham. I think this time you've got it."

Graham's reply was pessimistic. "They're holding, sir, but I'm not real happy with some of these readings. There's still something wrong with the power flow to the upper superstructure emitters. I'll need to do some more work before I can guarantee any kind of combat-rated shields."

"But in the meantime we don't have to depend on *Sindri* just to keep from frying," Tolwyn said. "And that counts for a lot. Keep me appraised, Commander."

"Aye aye, sir," the engineer responded. "We'll try to maintain shields through the ring transit, and see how they do. But don't start thinking about cutting the cord just yet. We need *Sindri* to fall back on if a glitch develops."

"Ten minutes to ring transit," Clancy announced.

"Anything on sensors, Mr. Kittani?"

Karga's First Officer, Captain Ismet Kittani, was peering over the shoulder of the technician on duty at the sensor panel. He straightened up slowly and turned toward Tolwyn with an aura of finicky precision Tolwyn found irritating. But the man had an impressive service record as CO of a destroyer, and although his personal style clashed with Tolwyn's he'd done some good work in the refit project.

"We are still not getting reliable readings through the ring plane," the swarthy Turk from Ilios said gravely. "We will have to do something to improve sensor performance before we attempt any sort of active operations."

Tolwyn frowned. The sensors, like the shield generators, had become one of those on-going problems that seemed to take up increasing amounts of refit time that should have been going into less essential systems by now. "We'll get them when we can." He activated the intercom system again. "Flight Wing, from CIC. Captain Bondarevsky, we will be entering the ring system in nine minutes. What's your status?"

"*Four Hornets on patrol,*" Bondarevsky replied. "*Four Raptors on Alert Five.*"

"Very good. Please have your fighter patrol take position ahead of us. They might not be able to help much, but I'd like some eyes out in front, just to avoid what happened last time." On the ship's previous ring transit two days earlier a particularly large chunk of ice had very nearly hit the ship, and Tolwyn didn't want a repeat of the threat today. Not while Graham's shields were still not fully reliable.

He checked the status board again, pleased to note that the shields were still holding steady despite the chief engineer's concerns. Despite the problems that continued to crop up, he was still confident of success. With luck they'd soon have the shields permanently on-line, and maneuvering drives ready to lift them into a better orbit before the next time their present elliptical path brought them back through the rings again.

With luck. . . .

Hornet 100, VF-12 "Flying Eyes"
Orbiting Vaku VII, Vaku System
1454 hours (CST)

"*Watchdog, this is Kennel. Put a couple of your birds four minutes ahead, same orbital vector. And keep your eyes peeled for anything big enough to be a bother.*"

"Kennel, Watchdog. Copy. Viking, we'll take point.

Lefty, Drifter, you two maintain your position." Babe Babcock accelerated her fighter to the new vector, settling in ahead of *Karga* with her wingmate close by. She was feeling irritable today, the result of a whole string of petty frustrations that had started with the hot water heater in the squadron's ready room showers going belly-up just when she wanted to use it that morning and culminated in the discovery that her regular Hornet had earned a down gripe from Lieutenant McCullough and had been pulled from the flight line to have a navicomp fault repaired. As a result she'd been forced to take out Hornet 100, the fighter normally reserved as a back-up craft and designated for use by the Wing Commander when he chose to fly a mission with the lesser mortals of his command.

She didn't like Hornet 100. The target lock system was slower than it should have been—though it was still within acceptable tolerances, a good pilot knew the difference in a combat situation—and it was fitted with an APSP rather than the extra pair of missiles she would have preferred to mount. But it would have taken too long to reconfigure the fighter's load, so she'd taken the fighter despite her preferences. After all, it was another routine patrol, more practice than anything else—for the carrier's flight crews as much as for the Flying Eyes.

She was starting to regret her new assignment to the *Karga*. She'd liked duty aboard the *Independence*, and had regarded Kevin Tolwyn as the best kind of Wing Commander, a CO who was willing to delegate responsibility to his squadron leaders and let them have their own heads most of the time. Bondarevsky, her new Wing Commander, might have been a big-time war hero and an intelligent, capable officer, but he was a hands-on type of leader who wanted to have a part in anything and everything going on around him. It made Babcock uncomfortable to know that he might turn up to look over her shoulder any time, any place, always ready to offer an opinion or point out an alternative.

But more than the change in personalities, duty aboard *Karga* wasn't exactly what she'd signed up for. The crew and officers' quarters were still a long way from being refurbished, and recreational facilities were something between horrible and nonexistent. And the daily flight ops were becoming something of a joke. Vaku was a backwater even among backwaters, and *Karga's* endless orbit was a study in monotony. The pilots who had come across from *Independence* weren't even involved in much of the refit work, since they had to do flight duty, so they didn't even have the technical challenges the rest of the crew faced to keep them fresh.

Babcock was starting to think she ought to volunteer for one of the squadrons designated for the Kilrathi birds. At least then she'd get a crack at extensive combat simulations, instead of nothing but routine patrol work.

"Come on, skipper, we're coming up on the rough spot!" The voice of her wingman, Lieutenant Eric "Viking" Jensson, brought her back to reality. *"One minute."*

"Copy," she said. "Stick close to my three, Viking."

"Close enough to reach out and touch you," he replied, drawing his fighter in tight beside hers.

"You do and you'll be up on charges," she said sweetly. "Again." Viking was a big, blonde, handsome Dane who'd grown up on Terra but drifted out to the frontier after being turned down by the ConFleet Academy as unsuitable officer material. He'd done better on Landreich, but three times in a relatively short career he'd landed in hot water by making unwelcome advances to female officers. If he hadn't been a naturally brilliant fighter jockey he would probably have been cashiered long since. Still, despite his reputation, Babcock was glad to have him in the squadron . . . as long as he knew where to draw the line in his personal pursuits.

They were coming up fast on the arbitrary "edge" of the gas giant's rings. They were impressive by any standards, out-showing even Saturn in the Terra system, but though they extended for thousands of kilometers outward from the superjovian world, they were less than a hundred kilometers thick. Made up of ice ranging in size from dust up to chunks like small boulders, the density of the ring field was fairly low, so that ships could pass through without much danger of major collisions. Unshielded, *Karga* had passed through the rings hundreds of times since being damaged, and had collected only a few extra scars as a result.

Still, a ring system wasn't exactly a pleasant place to fly. Particles of debris clouded sensor scans and confused computer imaging systems, and an unlucky encounter with a substantial ice boulder could ruin your whole day. It was particularly bad here and now. Normally a carrier had enough sensor arrays and sufficient computing power to compensate for the inhibiting effects of the rings, but *Karga*'s systems still stubbornly refused to resolve the data gathered into anything useful. That meant she and Viking had to be doubly careful making the transit. And they also had to be the eyes for the carrier. If they picked up anything large enough to be a threat, they'd have to deal with it. *Karga* still couldn't maneuver away from danger under her own power, and her point-defense batteries couldn't fire as long as the sensors weren't able to distinguish individual targets.

"Here we go!" Viking called. *"Hornet one-oh-six, feet cold!"* That was pilot's slang for approaching any airless chunk of rock or ice, up to and including small planets.

They passed the boundary set arbitrarily by the navicomps. At first there was no noticeable change, but then the particle density began to rise until Babcock felt like she was flying in atmosphere. Although the rings were not very thick, the supercarrier's orbit was at a very low angle from the plane of the rings, and it took nearly half a minute on that vector to pass through them. As abruptly as they'd entered the orbiting ice cloud, they were through.

And, all at once, the threat tone sounded loud in Babcock's ears.

Bridge, Guild Privateer *Bonadventure*
Orbiting Vaku VII, Vaku System
1458 hours (CST)

"Targets! Targets! Two targets, bearing zero-zero-two by zero-one zero! Range ten thousand, closing."

Zachary Banfeld rose from the captain's chair and crossed to the tactical control officer's position. "What are they?" he demanded sharply.

"Mass is just under fourteen tons each," the TACCO reported. "Length 'prox twenty-five meters . . . warbook calls them Hornet fighters."

"Hornets." Banfeld didn't bother to hide the contempt in his voice. Obsolete light fighters from ConFleet's old stock didn't pose much of a threat to his squadron.

"They will be posted as patrol craft," Gedi Tanaka

commented. He was nominally the captain of the privateer, a one-time Confederation Fleet officer who had been discharged for failing to prevent a Kilrathi raider from knocking out three ships in the convoy he'd been assigned to escort. Despite that blot on his record he was a fine tactician and a capable leader, and he had flourished since coming out to the Landreich and joining the Guild. "There will be heavier fighters ready to respond to an attack."

"But not enough to stop our attack," Banfeld replied. "Not if we can get the first blow in by surprise."

He checked the tactical plot. *Bonadventure* had settled into orbit well ahead of the *Karga*, keeping the rings between the two ships. Springweather's information had made mention of a sensor glitch, and that was just the thing he needed to achieve complete surprise.

His orders from Williams were to destroy the supercarrier, but Banfeld had no intention of doing so if he could possibly knock it out without severely damaging it. Those Landreichers had worked hard restoring the ship to something like working order, and he fully intended to take advantage of their hard work. But to take out the ship's shields without causing collateral damage he'd needed an edge, and the obscuring rings had given him just what he wanted.

Bonadventure was the perfect ship for the mission, and she was ready to strike. Originally a bulk ore carrier, she'd been taken over by the Landreich government ten years back and refitted as a sort of makeshift escort carrier, with a single flight deck and a capacity of no more than twenty carried fighters. Before she was finished the Landreich Navy had pronounced her hopelessly outclassed for combat service against the Empire, and the project had been abandoned. But the orbital shipyard where she'd been building had belonged to a member of the Guild, and Banfeld had paid to have her completed and crewed as the largest of his fleet of privateers. Though she might not be able to face a stand-up fight with a Cat battle group, she was an excellent convoy escort . . . and an equally effective raider.

Against an enemy with no drives and dependent on a tender's thin-stretched shields, *Bonadventure*'s fighter contingent would be more than adequate. Striking with surprise, they'd have the tender's shielding battered down before the carrier could scramble its available fighters, and that would be the end of the fight. Banfeld could sit back and wait for the supercarrier to fall into his hands, intact and ready to have her refitting completed by the Guild.

Of course, Mancini and Williams didn't have to know if the supercarrier was captured. Let them think he'd been forced to destroy it. They were pleased to call him one of the best agents of Y-12, but in fact Zachary Banfeld remained his own man. It was convenient— and lucrative—to work with the confees from time to time, but in the end what mattered to Banfeld was preserving the balance of power out here on the frontier. He'd take down the Landreichers before they could put a ship into service that would force Ragark to back down . . . but later it might be the Cats or the confees who needed to be cut off before they became a threat, and with the *Karga* he'd be nicely placed to do whatever was needed to keep the fires of war stoked high.

Banfeld smiled. He enjoyed the dangerous game he played, balancing opposing sides and growing wealthy from the profits. He imagined Ragark would offer a tidy sum for information about Murragh, the *kil* Springweather had claimed was the heir to the Imperial

Crown. He'd kept that bit of information from Williams and Mancini, figuring that Ragark would pay more than they would. How much would it be worth to the warlord to have this rival eliminated? With luck, Banfeld would have a chance to find out. But, as he'd told Springweather, he wouldn't be telling the Cats about *Karga*. That was too valuable a secret to let Ragark discover. For now, at least.

The tactical plot showed the wedge of fighters shaping their course toward the oncoming Hornets . . . and the supercarrier that would soon be coming through the rings. *Bonadventure*'s sensors were tracking the supercarrier well enough. They were top-of-the-line modules salvaged from a Kilrathi cruiser, coupled with a computer imaging program he'd picked up from the ConFleet by way of a black market source who had an inside line to the CSB. He smiled at the thought. According to Springweather that was just the sort of thing they were doing aboard *Karga*, cobbling together different technologies to produce an effective compromise between Cat and human systems.

Banfeld knew he'd feel right at home when he sat on the bridge of the supercarrier. . . .

Hornet 100, VF-12 "Flying Eyes"
Near Vaku VII, Vaku System
1459 hours (CST)

"We have multiple targets! Repeat, multiple targets!" Babcock strove to keep her voice level. "Looks like a cruiser and . . . twenty small craft. Maybe fighters."

"*Nonsense*," Viking argued. "*A cruiser can't carry that many fighters.*"

"Look at your warbook, you dumb Dane," she flared.

"Those are reading as Broadsword heavy fighters . . ."

"Confederation fighters?" That was Bondarevsky, back in Primary Flight Control. *"What are twenty obsolete Terran fighters doing out here?"*

"Beats the hell out of me, Captain," she replied. "What I want to know is what the hell I'm supposed to do about them? Do I wave, ignore them, or spit?"

There was a long moment of silence before Bondarevsky replied. *"They're not Confederation Navy. Broadswords are out of service except with Reserve Wings. And they're not Landreichers, unless somebody's forgotten to update our own warbook files."* He hesitated again. *"Your ROE is to consider them potentially hostile, but engage only if fired upon. Repeat, fire only if they fire first. I'm launching the Alert Five birds and putting the rest of the Wing on scramble now. Just in case."*

"Thanks a lot," she said sourly. Fire if fired on, indeed . . . as if two Hornets could fight off twenty Broadswords under any circumstances.

"The bandits are accelerating," Viking reported, sounding cool and professional. Whatever his personal shortcomings might be, he was all business in a crisis. *"I make their vector an intercept with* Karga.*"*

She checked her navicomp. "Confirmed. You copy that, Kennel?"

"Roger. Break off and pull back to join the rest of the patrol. Stay close to the boat and we'll give you support from the laser turrets."

"Two bandits breaking formation!" Viking broke in. *"They're coming after us!"*

"Break formation!" Babcock ordered. "We can outrun them!"

The Broadswords opened fire . . .

Primary Flight Control, FRLS *Karga*
Orbiting Vaku VII, Vaku System
1500 hours (CST)

"We are under fire. Repeat, we are under fire!"

Bondarevsky turned from the communications console. "Why aren't those Raptors up yet?" he snapped.

"First one's launching now," Boss Marchand replied evenly. "How do you want to handle the rest of the deployment? It'll take time to get the other birds from the Eyes and the Eights up and prepped. They've already started their maintenance rotations . . ."

"What's the status on the Kilrathi planes?" Bondarevsky asked. They had scheduled a practice launch of the recovered Imperial fighters for later in the day, the first flight for the pilots who had been taking simulator training these last two weeks.

Marchand didn't even hesitate. "The Strakhas were scheduled first up," she said. "They're ready to go. Five minutes to get the first two up on the flight deck and ready for launch. After that . . . call it four more every three minutes. The Dralthis and the Vaktoths will take a little longer."

"Do it," he ordered. "Scramble the Strakha squadron! And make sure one of the first two is one-zero-zero."

"You're taking her out yourself, sir?" Marchand asked.

"Yeah." Bondarevsky was already heading for the door. "You think I'd send those people out there to fight in ships they've never handled before without going out there myself?"

Marchand gave him a long, thoughtful look. "Some would," she said curtly. Then, "Good luck, skipper."

Combat Information Center, FRLS *Karga*
Orbiting Vaku VII, Vaku System
1502 hours (CST)

"One minute to the ring field, Captain."

Tolwyn clenched the arms of his chair and watched as the forward viewer began to grow hazing from the gradual thickening of multi-hued ice dust. Somewhere up ahead a small swarm of hostile fighters was bearing down on his ship, but he was helpless to fight them for the moment. Blind and unable to change course, *Karga* could only ride out whatever was coming at them. The patrol fighters wouldn't be able to stop the attackers, and the rest of Bondarevsky's planes would take time to launch. The enemy, whoever they were, would get at least one punch in before *Karga* cleared the ring field and the Flight Wing went into action.

After that, though, they'd be fighting an even battle. Or so he hoped.

"*Captain,* Durendal *and* Caliburn *are moving to support us, but it will be at least ten minutes before they can get into the game.*" That was Richards, calling on the private line from the flag bridge. "*I've ordered* Xenophon *to keep station with the* Carnegie *and the* City of Cashel. *I know it isn't likely, but I don't think it's a good idea to leave them open to attack. It looks like we're on our own for now.*"

Tolwyn gave a tight nod. "Looks that way, Admiral," he responded. "We'll keep them busy until the tin cans can get here, don't you worry." He turned from the intercom screen. "Deniken! Are your weapons on-line?"

"All laser turrets ready, sir," he said. "Point defense off-line until we get the sensors up again." He sounded apologetic.

"Stay on top of it." He glanced at Kittani. "Get Damage

Control ready, Exec. And alert Doctor Manning that she may be getting some casualties down there." Tolwyn didn't like to think about that. Sick Bay was still not up to anything like ConFleet standards, and Manning could be handling combat injuries under appallingly primitive conditions down there if the carrier took any serious damage.

"Aye aye, sir," Kittani replied.

"Engineering, this is CIC. Will your shields keep on holding, Mr. Graham, or should I order *Sindri* to go back on-line?"

"Won't matter much one way or the other, Captain," Graham responded, sounding harried. "*Sindri*'s shields might stop a mosquito—if it wasn't too mad. I'd say we've a better chance with our own. They might not be able to take a whole lot of pounding, but they're better than what the tender could put out . . . while they last."

"The shield generators have priority, Engineer," Tolwyn said grimly. "I don't care if you have to splice wires together by hand. I want those shields to stay up. Understood?"

"We'll do our best," Graham said.

"Entering the ring field," Clancy announced.

"Get ready, people . . ."

"Targets! Targets! Targets!" Deniken chanted. "Just came up on the screens. They're close . . ."

The effective range of the sensors in this mess of ice was barely a kilometer. The enemy fighters were right on top of them.

"Incoming fire," Kittani said. "Beams and missiles!"

Tolwyn braced himself, ready for the worst.

Broadsword 206, Guild Squadron "Raider-One"
Near Vaku VII, Vaku System
1504 hours (CST)

"Firing!" Winston Drake hit the trigger to release a
full salvo of beam weapons, then followed up with a
pair of salvaged Kilrathi Image Recognition missiles.
According to the mission profile the pilots had gone
over during the outward voyage, the target ship would
have only minimal shield power available, and a rapid
string of laser hits would weaken the force fields long
enough to allow the missiles to penetrate. Each of the
privateer fighters in the two Broadsword squadrons
would make an identical run, and the cumulative damage
from so many tightly-packed attacks was sure to overload
the target's capacity to protect itself and destroy the
target completely.

That was the plan . . . direct and simple. But his
sensors were giving him a different story from the
predicted profile. The attack wasn't going anything like
the computer simulations they'd run back on the
Bonadventure.

The beams were striking the intended target area,
but the shields were absorbing them easily. And the
two missiles detonated harmlessly, their hellish energies
barely causing a ripple in the force field.

"Damn!" he said aloud. "Damn it, those shields are
stronger than they're supposed to be!"

"*Continue your run,*" Zachary Banfeld ordered. "*If
it takes a little more effort to bring the shields down,
so be it. Just knock out that tender!*"

Bridge, FRLS *Sindri*
Docked with FRLS *Karga*, Vaku System
1504 hours (CST)

"Those bastards are targeting us!" Dickerson added a few more colorful comments.

"Calm down, Captain," Tolwyn said over the commlink. *"What's your status?"*

"If we hadn't been letting you run your own field, we'd already be debris," Dickerson said harshly. "As it is, we're draining power fast. Our generators weren't built to cycle fast enough for combat conditions. We've got lots of reserve power, but we're losing ground."

"This is Richards," the battle group commander cut in. *"Captain, cut loose your grapnels and get under way. With our fighters joining the part and the carrier clearing the ring system I think we can keep the bastards occupied while you make good an escape. If you stick where you are, one of them could get through and take you out."*

"But, Admiral, if your generators go down . . ."

"Never mind that! This is not what your crew signed on for. Get them clear!"

"Aye aye, sir," he said reluctantly. Dickerson wanted no part of a battle, but he felt guilty at leaving the carrier to fend for itself. He'd been monitoring the same instruments Graham was watching from the carrier's engineering decks. *Karga* could replenish her shield reserves far more quickly than *Sindri* could, but the generators weren't balanced properly. Sooner or later the strain of maintaining them at full power would cause the whole system to collapse, and the supercarrier would be wide open to whatever the hostiles sent her way.

And if the shields were knocked out for a prolonged

period, radiation would do all the killing the enemy needed.

But he had the admiral's orders . . . and the lives of his own people to think about. "Mr. Kaine, cut us loose," he told his first officer. He glanced at the empty pilot's chair. Clancy was on his own. Luckily they wouldn't need his fine touch for the kind of maneuvering they were about to perform. "You take the helm, Kaine. Get us the hell out of here!"

Broadsword 206, Guild Squadron "Raider-One"
Near Vaku VII, Vaku System
1506 hours (CST)

The carrier was clearing the ring system by the time Drake killed his original attack vector and swung around for a second run. He was cursing under his breath as he locked in the target coordinates. The first bombardment was supposed to have penetrated the shields and destroyed the tender perched on the back of the carrier's looming superstructure. That would have spelled victory then and there.

Now the privateers would have to go back in against an opponent ready for them. They wouldn't have the advantages of obscured sensors and masked point defense weapons. And the sensors showed fighters had started launching from the starboard flight deck of the ungainly Kilrathi ship. That would complicate things.

But even though the Landreichers had been working on that monster for months now, Drake had seen the pitting and scarring along the carrier's hull. A ship that badly damaged couldn't put up much of a fight, not against two squadrons of determined men willing to do whatever it took to get the job done.

He lined up his targeting reticule on the tender, then cursed as it lifted clear of the ship and accelerated outward. His sensors showed the carrier still had shields up. That explained the unexpected strength of the tender's shielding, then. The carrier didn't need the tender's support any longer.

Drake followed the tender. His orders were to destroy it, and destroy it he would, attached or separated. Putting the tender out of action would still leave the carrier at their mercy if they could batter down her shields as well.

He lined up his shot and opened fire with everything he had. . . .

Hornet 100, VF-12 "Flying Eyes"
Near Vaku VII, Vaku System
1506 hours (CST)

"I've got one on my six! Give me some help!"

Babcock scowled and accelerated as Jensson's desperate call crackled in her headphones. Retreating toward the safety of the carrier had proved to be no safety at all, not with those Broadswords circling and swooping in like birds of prey stooping low over their victim. Most were concentrating on attacking the tender, but the attackers didn't pass up a chance to take a shot at the Hornets if they came in range.

Viking's Hornet was being pursued by one of the Broadswords. Both ships were plunging straight in towards the carrier, rolling from side to side as the enemy pilot tried to match Jensson's evasive maneuvers. Viking's acceleration curve was all wrong, far too slow, and Babcock caught a glimpse of twisted metal along the rear of the port side wing. He'd taken a hit, then, and now he'd lost the one advantage of a light fighter over a heavy one—speed.

"Keep them guessing, Viking, while I get into position," she said coolly, dropping her fighter behind the Broadsword and arming her heat-seeking missiles. The target reticule seemed to take forever to center on the Broadsword, and Babcock remembered again how she'd wished she could have strapped on her own plane today instead of this one.

Then the diamond on her HUD display glowed red to indicate a target lock, and Babcock opened fire with both laser cannons and both heat seekers, a single powerful strike. She hoped it would at least get the other pilot's attention.

But even as she fired, the Broadsword was opening up as well. Beams stabbed at the weakened rear shielding of Viking's Hornet, and moments later missiles detonated. It was small consolation to see her own missiles batter right through the Broadsword's shields and rip through a weak spot in the armor around the main engine . . . not when Viking's Hornet disappeared in an expanding cloud of debris at almost the same instant.

Babcock swore. She hadn't liked Eric Jensson, but he had been one of her pilots. Now he was gone.

The threat tone sounded in her ear. Another Broadsword had decided to join the party to help the one she had just crippled. And it had just acquired a target lock on her fighter.

She rammed the throttle full forward on her main engine, and prayed she could out-fly this new menace before she joined Viking in whatever Valhalla dead fighter jocks ended up in.

Strakha 800
Near Vaku VII, Vaku System
1508 hours (CST)

Acceleration pushed Bondarevsky back into his seat as the Kilrathi fighter leapt from the deck, hurled clear by a powerful linear accelerator catapult. Internal gravity compensators absorbed most of the g-force, but not quite all, and for a moment Bondarevsky reveled in the feel of it. Too much time had gone by since he'd made his last catapult launch.

There wasn't time to think about it, though. Clear of the flight deck, he cut in his main engine and pushed the throttle forward to full military power. The Strakha was handling remarkably like the simulator version he'd flown time and again since Christmas. Maybe, just maybe, the squadron's training time would count for something out here after all.

"Strakha Eight-zero-zero, good shot! Good shot!" he called, setting course toward the nearest of the enemy fighters.

"Strakha Eight-zero-niner, good shot," he heard just seconds later. It was Harper, who'd insisted on flying as his wingman. Boss Marchand must have been cycling the catapult faster than ConFleet safety regulations would ever have allowed, rushing to get the Kilrathi fighters into the battle before the Hornets and Raptors were overwhelmed.

"Bard, this is Bear," he said crisply. "Go to stealth mode."

"Copy," Harper responded, all his banter gone, replaced by a cold, professional manner. *"Engaging."*

Bondarevsky flipped a switch, and to all intents and purposes the Strakha fighter vanished.

Kilrathi stealth technology still wasn't fully understood

in human circles even yet, despite having been studied and adapted for use in the latest ConFleet ships, from Excalibur fighters up to recon ships like the old *Bannockburn* that James Taggart had commanded out here in the Landreich during the Free Corps campaign. The twin generators mounted under the fighter's ventral fin created an area of distortion that bent most radiation, right up through the visible spectrum, right around the hull. A small amount was allowed to leak through— otherwise the pilot would be as blind to the outside universe as his enemies were to him—but the narrow band opening was constantly remodulated by a random computer program so that it took a lucky observer to spot a cloaked ship. But it also took a lot of power, and a Strakha couldn't stay cloaked very long under combat power requirements.

Right now, though, Bondarevsky was glad to be in the cockpit of a Strakha. These unexpected and unknown enemies had pounced on the carrier with little warning. He intended the counterstroke to return the favor.

Up ahead, his sensor display had picked out a hot and heavy engagement between a Broadsword and a Hornet that was weaving and dodging for all it was worth. Bondarevsky increased his acceleration. "Bard," he said. "We've got a furball at zero-three-one by zero-four-four. Let's see if they like gate crashers at *their* party."

"Right with you," Harper replied.

The Broadsword was losing ground as the Hornet accelerated away, using the full advantage of speed and maneuverability, but despite the opening range the Broadsword pilot was keeping up a heavy assault with lasers. Some of them were scoring hits. The Hornet's shields and armor weren't likely to hold long against the heavier, more modern fighter's firepower.

But the Strakha was newer and heavier than the

Broadsword. Bondarevsky smiled coldly as he started his attack run, powering up his meson guns as the Strakha hurtled toward the pursuer. As the range closed he cut the stealth generators.

It took several seconds for the fighter to decloak, and during that time he couldn't fire his weapons. But he'd timed the maneuver almost perfectly. The Broadsword was looming close ahead when the veil of energy shimmered around the Strakha and it became fully visible again. The targeting reticule on his HUD flashed orange, and Bondarevsky hit the trigger.

Both meson guns opened fire at close range, battering through the Broadsword's shields and peeling away armor in a fury of raw energy. For good measure Bondarevsky launched a ConFleet-issue Pilum FF missile. It struck the weakened Broadsword and detonated in a brilliant fireball.

"Never thought I'd be glad to see a Cat fighter turn up like that," Babe Babcock said. *"Whoever you are, drinks are on me when we get back to the barn."*

"No problem, Commander," he replied. "Head for home, and round up your other pilots on the way in. This is no place for your Hornets."

"Aye aye, sir," she responded.

A pair of Broadswords had changed vector to support the fighter he'd taken out, and now it was Harper's turn to decloak suddenly and score a kill. Bondarevsky followed the other Broadsword as it veered off. He could sense the shifting fortunes of the fight. The tide was turning in *Karga*'s favor as more fighters joined the battle. Deniken's gun turrets were lending a hand, two, firing streams of coherent light that blazed furiously against the darkness of space. Bondarevsky saw one Broadsword caught by the carrier's Anti-Aerospace fire. It vanished, torn apart by the Double-A-S.

"All right, Strakhas, let's get them!" That was Commander Travis, her voice exuberant as she led the second pair of Kilrathi fighters into the fray.

"Let's concentrate on driving them off, Commander," he said dryly.

"Hey, come on, skipper, I just want to get a little live-fire practice with this thing!" she responded.

"Quite a wee shield maiden we've got, I'm thinking, sir," Harper said, dropping back into his brogue. *"Or maybe an Amazon?"*

"Whatever," Bondarevsky said, worried that his pilots were getting too excited by the thrill of the fight. "Right now—"

All at once something flared so bright that his cockpit went opaque to protect him from the glare. When he could see again, he was horrified.

A Broadsword had scored a direct hit on *Sindri's* engines, and the tender had been literally torn in half by subsidiary explosions. The little workhorse ship that had made *Karga's* refit possible was gone.

Stunned, Bondarevsky couldn't find words for long seconds, and it was plain he wasn't the only one. After a few heartbeats Travis spoke, and her voice was ragged and flat now, totally unlike her high-spirited tones of less than a minute before.

"They're breaking off, Captain," she said. *"Looks like their mother ship's spotted the two destroyers coming up and sounded the recall."*

"Do we pursue?" Harper asked.

"Negative." Bondarevsky forced mind and mouth to work again. Much as he would have liked to go after the pilot who had taken out *Sindri*, the flight wing couldn't go charging off after their retreating foes. There could be other dangers lurking nearby, and the fighters were needed to stand guard against another attack.

"Negative. We've done our job. Let the tin cans do theirs. Commander, form up your squadron and maintain a patrol in force until we're sure the bastards are done with us." He switched channels. "Kennel, Kennel, this is . . ." He suddenly realized that the abrupt nature of the crisis had taken them all by surprise, so that the Strakha squadron hadn't even been assigned a code-name for the mission. "This is Bondarevsky," he went on at last. Commlink security wasn't particularly necessary right now anyway. "Get one of the Cat Kofars prepped and fully loaded. I want our people to be able to take on fuel or reloads without going back down to the deck, until we're sure there won't be another attack."

Boss Marchand responded in person. *"Twenty minutes, sir,"* she said.

"Roger that." Suddenly Jason Bondarevsky felt very tired. The Black Cats had won their first victory, but it didn't seem much like a triumph.

• CHAPTER 14

> *"Honor the heroic dead, for their deeds are
> worthy of remembrance."*

from the First Codex
10:14:64

Operations Planning Center, FRLS *Karga*
Orbiting Vaku VII, Vaku System
1821 hours (CST), 2671.011

Admiral Geoff Tolwyn glowered from his position at
the foot of the oval holo-tank, the good mood of just a
few hours earlier shattered by the attack on the carrier.
Someone had attacked his ship, and he wanted nothing
more than a chance to strike back. But it was unlikely
he'd have that chance any time soon.

"Shields are still holding well enough," Commander
Graham was saying. "If the bastards had made a couple
of runs against us, they might've strained the generators
past their limits, but we were lucky. All we took was
collateral damage. But with *Sindri* gone we're going
to want to rethink the repair schedule. Either we get
the drives working so we can put this boat into a higher
orbit, or we try a tow from *Xenophon*."

"Towing something this size is a risky proposition," Admiral Richards said slowly. "I think I'd rather do it under our own power. Can you get the drives on-line?"

"On a crash-priority program, I'll have us able to change orbit inside a week," Graham said. "But it means pulling everybody off all the non-essential repair work. We have to virtually rebuild the maneuvering drives from the deck up, which means a lot of work for the *Carnegie.*" He gave a thin smile. "So I'm afraid the repairs to the hot water heaters on Deck Eight are going to have to wait a while."

"We'll live with it," Richards said. "Geoff, what do you think?"

Tolwyn was still frowning. "It all depends on whether we've driven them off for good, or if they're just off regrouping to hit us again. As Graham says, we can't handle a full-scale attack, and without *Sindri* . . ."

"Yeah," Richards nodded. "Yeah, without *Sindri*, we fry if the shields go down for more than an hour or so. Just like the original crew."

"Their intentions must depend on their resources," Bondarevsky said from his usual place in one of the upper tiers of seats. He looked tired and grim. "If we knew who they were, and what they were after, we might have a clue as to whether they'll be coming back any time soon."

"Not Kilrathi," Tolwyn said. "Not Landreich or Confederation, either, the way I figure it. Mercenaries?"

Captain Bikina of the *Durendal* stirred. "Mercenaries have to have an employer," he said. "And I've never heard of mercenaries with a carrier, even a ramshackle job like that one." His contempt for their erstwhile foe was plain in his tone. The carrier had gathered in its surviving planes and fled at the approach of the two Landreich destroyers.

The other destroyer captain, Pamela Collins, cleared her throat. "I don't know who they're working for now. But I know who designed that carrier."

"Who?" Richards demanded. He seemed angry. Probably, Tolwyn thought, he was frustrated that he didn't have access to the intelligence information he was used to having. That was often the difference between a staff posting at home and a command in the field. And it had been a long time since Vance Richards had held a combat command.

"There were plans for an improvised carrier like that one in the Landreich Navy several years back," Collins told them. "I was up for a spot as T/G Officer on the prototype. But the Council did a study that proved the design wouldn't be worth putting into action against superior Cat fighting ships, so the whole project was scrapped before the first boat was completed."

"I remember that flap," Forbes of the *Xenophon* said. "'Twas a big brawl in Council. Auld Max almost ended up with a vote of no confidence over it all, until Danny Galbraith talked him into shutting down the program."

"What happened to the prototype, then?" Bondarevsky asked.

"I heard it was bought up by a consortium of shipowners for use as a convoy escort."

"Zachary Banfield's gang of pirates," Richards said, sounding disgusted. "I should have thought of him. He's got fingers in every pie from here to Sirius, and he's completely without loyalty to anything or anyone except his own profit margin. Somehow he found out there was a nice fat derelict out here just waiting to be taken over, and he tried to move in on it. But when he saw he wasn't going to get it cheap he cut his losses and bailed out."

"If that's the case he's not likely to come back," Bondarevsky said.

"I'm not so sure," Tolwyn said slowly. "He had inside information. Nothing's more certain. All the orbital elements, and details of *Sindri's* part in the repair work. Probably at least a hint of our sensor and shield problems, judging from how the attack was mounted. I think we're up against more than one greedy privateer. Somebody who could collect all that data on us and then bring Banfeld in to act on it."

Richards looked thoughtful. "Maybe so," he said, frowning. Tolwyn recognized his expression. It was the one Richards usually adopted when he thought Tolwyn was being overly paranoid. "But the fact is we took out five of his Broadswords. A quarter of his force in one engagement, and that was when they had the element of surprise. Banfeld's too smart to try again, whether he's working for himself or somebody else."

"Whether they try again or not, we'll be ready next time," Bondarevsky said. "I'm increasing our patrols and bringing the rest of the Black Cats on-line as quickly as possible. If Commander Graham isn't going to monopolize all the workers and the entire output of the *Carnegie* I figure we'll have the port flight deck up and running in three or four days, and Sparks tells me she's got most of the Kilrathi birds that we're ever going to get running just about ready to start flying."

She nodded from her seat beside the Wing Commander. "We'll actually have an oversized flight wing by the time we're through," she said. "At least by ConFleet standards. *Karga* originally carried a hundred and twenty-eight planes of all types, in sixteen of their standard eight-plane squadrons. Eight of those were fighter squadrons—two each of light, medium, heavy, and stealth craft—with two more of bombers, and six support squadrons. Support planes, command and control birds, attack shuttles, and so on."

McCullough glanced at her computer monitor. "Here's how we're looking to stack up," she said. "We have four squadrons from the *Independence* wing. That's eleven Hornets in the Flying Eyes, twelve Rapiers, and twelve Raptors. That makes thirty-five ConFleet-type fighters, just about half of a standard wing."

"I wish a few of them had been available today," Deniken growled.

"They were out there, Lieutenant," Bondarevsky shot back. "We lost a Rapier today, and almost had the CO of the Eyes taken out too. And one of the Broadswords we got was killed by one of the Raptors from the Crazy Eights."

"They caught us at a bad spot in our maintenance schedule," McCullough added. "That *won't* be happening again."

"What's the story on the Kilrathi planes?" Richards asked. "You said you can get most of them up this week."

She nodded. "Here's how it stands. We have one squadron of Darket light fighters, and a couple of working birds in reserve if you're not too fussy about how you define 'working.' Both squadrons Dralthi Fours, medium fighters. Apparently they never got into action at all during *Karga's* raiding mission, and they didn't suffer any losses. We're short one plane to make an eight-ship squadron of Vaktoth heavy fighters, but there's an extra Strakha that I'm fitting out as the CO's bird for that outfit. A full squadron of Strakhas, of course. They did a damned fine job out there today. And we've managed to cobble together a full squadron of Paktahn bombers, although there's a couple of them that are going to be maintenance-intensive for a while. Jorkad tells me the Paktahns got pretty badly chewed up in the fighting near Landreich." She checked her list again. "We're also able to fly full squadrons of each of the noncombatant types, and we've even got spares on most of those. Forty fighters, eight bombers, twenty-four miscellaneous noncombatants from the Kilrathi side of our stocks, though of course their squadron sizes are based on eight birds instead of twelve. Even so, seventy-five fighters makes a pretty damned impressive aerospace wing."

"And these will be ready for normal duty in a few days?" Richards asked.

"Well . . ." Bondarevsky cleared his throat. "Most of the pilots have had at least some sim time. The Strakhas performed well enough. I'll be happier after everybody's had a chance to get the feel of their birds, but with an intense cycle of flight ops we ought to get everybody up to snuff fairly soon."

Graham shifted. "You said you'll need some men and resources for all this. Just how much do you absolutely have to have? Because I wasn't kidding about needing crash priority to get the drives back in operation."

"I'm sure we can work out a compromise, Commander," Bondarevsky said wearily. "But much as we need to get the engines working and get this tub into a safer orbit clear of the brown dwarf's radiation, we also need to be able to rely on both flight decks to get our fighters into play faster. That was the big bottleneck this afternoon. Half the Strakha squadron didn't even clear the flight deck before the bandits were running. We've got to have a faster response time. Next time around it might not be a bunch of pirates in a half-improvised carrier coming at us. If the Cats found out we were here and sent in a supercarrier of their own, we'd be dead meat."

"The two of you can hash out a work schedule tomorrow morning before our regular meeting," Richards suggested. "Captain Lake, maybe you could be there too?"

The commander of the factory ship inclined his head.

Richards looked around the chamber. "If that's all, I think we should probably call it a day . . ."

Tolwyn met his eyes. "The memorial service," he said quietly.

The battle group commander nodded. "Right. We'll be holding a service for the *Sindri's* crew at twenty-one hundred hours tonight on the flight deck. I'd appreciate it if all department heads were there, and anyone else who cares to come. I know those of you from other ships will want to hold your own observances, but representatives would be welcome. This has been a blow to morale, despite the fact that we beat the attackers off, and I think it would be a good idea for the whole battle group to demonstrate out solidarity and determination before we get on with the next stage of the project. Agreed?"

There was a murmur of approval from the assembled officers. Richards stood slowly, looking his full age and more today, and turned to leave. Tolwyn watched him thoughtfully. He was beginning to wonder if Vance Richards was really up to the strains of leading a battle group after so many years behind a desk.

Flight Deck, FRLS *Karga*
Orbiting Vaku System, Vaku System
2112 hours (CST)

Bondarevsky tried not to sway from sheer fatigue as he stood in ranks together with the other senior officers and listened to *Karga's* ranking chaplain, Commander Francis Darby, somberly reciting the words of the memorial service to the assembled crew on the flight deck and all around the carrier over the internal video channels. It was principally for the thirty-two crew members aboard the *Sindri* when she was destroyed, but Bondarevsky, at least, considered it a send-off for Lieutenant Jensson as well. And tired as he was, he wanted to honor the memories of the dead the best way he knew how.

How many times had he done this over the years? He'd watched more good men and women die than he could ever hope to remember, and it never got any easier. Tomorrow he would have to write the letter to Jensson's widowed mother back home on Terra. He'd barely known her son, transferred to the supercarrier less than two weeks before his death. What could he say to comfort her?

He remembered how he'd felt the day Svetlana died. There was precious little comfort to be given when a loved one was killed in action.

Darby finished speaking and nodded to Harper, who stood poised by an intercom station. The young Taran touched a button and the recorded sound of a great bell tolled out. The gathered officers and enlisted personnel on the cavernous flight deck stood in respectful silence as the bell rang thirty-two times, slowly, mournfully. One stroke for each man and woman aboard FRLS *Sindri*.

When the bell had faded, Harper hit another control, and called up a recording of "Amazing Grace" played on bagpipes. Sparks operated another set of controls to wheel out an empty coffin bearing the name of Eric Jensson. It rolled to the edge of the force field at the stern end of the flight deck, paused for a moment, then lifted on thrusters to drift through the opening and out into the void. A team of Bhaktadil's marines raised their laser rifles to their shoulders to fire a last salute.

Bondarevsky was a little bit surprised to find his lips

moving in a silent prayer for the dead man, the first battle casualty of the Black Cats.

The coffin drifted from view, the marines shouldered their arms, and "Amazing Grace" faded away. Geoff Tolwyn stepped forward to replace Darby and stood for a long moment in silence, surveying the audience.

"The loss of a ship in combat is always a tragedy for the people left behind," he began at last. "Especially when the ship was never intended to fight in the first place. Those of us who are trained to warfare regard it as our job to protect the noncombatants from harm, and failure weighs heavy on us all when we find that all of our efforts, however heroic or determined they may have been, have turned out to be to no avail.

"*Sindri* was destroyed today because an enemy saw it as a way to get at us. They believed that it was the tender's shields that were keeping us alive, and they targeted her with the deliberate intention of rendering us helpless. Every analysis of the battle that we've run only reinforces that statement. We were lucky enough to have our own shields up, thanks to Commander Graham and his engineering staff, but the attempt could easily have been successful. In a sense, then, the crew of *Sindri* died protecting us. Though she was not a fighting ship, her crew was as much a part of the Free Republic Navy as any of us, and they gave their lives doing their duty. For that reason, I say, we should not feel guilty at our failure so much as we should feel pride and respect for them."

Tolwyn paused a moment. "For some time now I've been under pressure to give a new name to this ship. Calling it for a Kilrathi hero is not exactly appropriate to our plans for her, after all. There have been plenty of suggestions, some laudable, not a few disparaging or downright obscene." That stirred a ripple of laughter in the audience, despite the solemnity of the occasion. "President Kruger wants us to bear the name *Alamo*, after the heroic struggle for freedom by a dedicated band of patriots. I've resisted him on a point of principle. I don't like my ship being named after a bloody massacre where the defenders lost the fight!"

A few of the crew on the flight deck laughed. Tolwyn raised a hand and went on. "Today, though, I've settled on a name I intend to put forward to the Navy as soon as possible, if all of you approve. It's not normally my habit to run a democracy on my ships, as anyone who knows me will tell you, but in this case I want you all to feel that this ship stands for something." He smiled. "Some of you might not be familiar with the background from which I've taken this name, so bear with me while I explain it to you. In the mythology of the Scandinavian countries back on Terra, dating back to a time before Christianity, it is told that the gods once asked a master smith of the dark elves to make them a collection of wondrous gifts. There was a magic ring that produced copies of itself, a boat that could be folded up into a pocket, a wig of spun gold to replace the golden hair stolen from one of the goddesses by the trickster Loki, and so on. Now Loki became jealous of the craftsman's work, and set out to ruin it. He changed himself into a stinging insect and did his best to keep the dark elf from his work. But he was only partially successful in this. Only one gift was marred, the war hammer intended for the weather god Thor. The handle ended up too short, but the weapon itself was still a powerful one that the Thunder-God used time and again to smite his powerful enemies."

Tolwyn scanned the audience for a moment before continuing. "The name of the craftsman was Sindri. It's the FRLN's custom to name tenders after mythical smiths and craftsmen, and the tender we lost today was named for this mythic Norse character. Like the dark elf, we were plagued by flying insects . . . and they did more than just distract our *Sindri*. So I think it only appropriate that we call our ship after the weapon that Sindri made, marred perhaps but still a powerful force that will smite the enemies of the Landreich wherever we find them.

"Thor's hammer was called 'Mjollnir.' And that is the name I think we should give to this ship, our war hammer. Our thunderbolt." He paused, milking the moment for all the drama he could draw. "Ladies and gentlemen, I give you FRLS *Mjollnir!*"

The pronouncement was greeted with applause and even a few cheers. Bondarevsky smiled despite himself. Under ordinary circumstances such a choice of names wouldn't have been likely to go over well. It was an awkward, archaic name, and drew on esoteric knowledge of ancient mythology. A bureaucrat assigning names from a computer list might have come up with it— that was surely how someone had arrived at something like *Sindri* in the first place—but it wasn't the sort of name to inspire any enthusiasm or win contests among the crew.

Yet Tolwyn's little speech had made it the perfect name for the carrier. Wherever they went, whatever they did, whichever battle honors they won in future encounters, they would always know that the name of their ship commemorated the thirty-two who had given their lives helping to forge a new weapon of war for the Landreich's arsenal.

In a way the choice even honored Viking, the dead pilot, whose ancestors in Earth's remote past had likely worshipped the god of Thunder and told stories of how he'd acquired his great weapon. Bondarevsky thought for a long moment, then allowed himself a brief nod of approval. It was fitting, however you looked at it.

FRLS *Mjollnir* . . . the Hammer of Thor.

Guild VIP Office, Guild Base
Hellhole, Hellhole System
1631 hours (CST), 2671.015

Hellhole had taken a pounding during the Kilrathi attack on the Landreich back in the days preceding the Battle of Earth. The Landreich base there had served as a field headquarters for the president's personal task force, and when the Cats had launched their assault they'd devastated the tiny Landreich colony before they were turned back by the Free Republican Fleet. The harsh conditions on the planet coupled with the complete loss of the original colony had made resettlement a chancy proposition at best, and the Landreich's government had decided against any such attempt.

That had suited Zachary Banfeld just fine. In fact, he had spread around plenty of money among the members of the Council to encourage them to vote down Kruger's request to invest in a new outpost there. Hellhole's strategic position squarely on the border between Landreich and the nearest Cat colony had made it useful to the Republic's war effort. But that same position made it just as valuable to the Guild. Once it was certain the Landreich wouldn't be coming back, Zachary Banfeld's people had moved in to set up a base of their own on the single marginally habitable planet that circled the binary system.

Now, sitting at his desk in the office reserved for his use when he visited the Hellhole base, Banfeld was feeling frustration and worry. *Bonadventure* had brought him back after the abortive fighting at Vaku, and remained in orbit overhead. But though this base was a secret, known only to a few key men in his organization, Banfeld was concerned about the possible fallout from the failed attack.

"Are you sure you can't get *Highwayman* ready any faster?" Banfeld demanded of the man sitting across from him. "The clock is ticking."

"Can't move any faster," Antonio Delgado told him. The commander of the Guild's secret base on Hellhole was a large man with a bristling black beard and swarthy skin. He accorded little respect to anyone, even the leader of the Guild, but he could get away with it. He was one of Banfeld's best base commanders, even if he had joined up with the Guild less than three years back. Before that he'd been a mercenary resistance leader Banfeld's people had dealt with during the Cat occupation of Siva. "Not if you want the cloak working. Three days, minimum."

"Three days," Banfeld repeated, getting to his feet and pacing restlessly across to the window that overlooked the tarmac where a small party of base workers were busy opening up the access ports along the sides and stern of the scoutship *Highwayman*. Banfeld knew Delgado was right about the estimated time to complete the work, but that didn't make him any less anxious.

The battle in the Vaku system had shaken the privateer leader badly. After making his plans so carefully, his strike force had been thoroughly rebuffed, and a quarter of his best pilots had been lost before they'd been able to disengage from the unexpectedly potent supercarrier. Now there was no question of trying again, not with his available resources. Banfeld hadn't become a power in this sector of space by throwing good money—or men—after bad. But the trouble was that there were sure to be people on that carrier who knew about

Bonadventure. That meant his connection to the attack might come to light, and that would threaten his cozy position inside the Landreich.

And by the same token all the original reasons for taking that carrier out of action still remained. If the Landreich gained the upper hand in the arms race against Ukar *dai* Ragark, there was an end to the healthy profits the Guild had enjoyed. Especially if Max Kruger declared war on the Guild in retaliation for their attempt to hijack his pet project.

The only way to deflect the double threat was to get the Landreich embroiled in combat *now*. Kruger wouldn't have time or resources enough to go after the Guild once he had Kilrathi ships knocking on his front door. In fact, he'd need the Guild, with its black market contacts and its pipeline to the arms dealers Kruger relied on back in the Confederation. It was just possible that by the time the dust cleared Max Kruger would owe too much to Banfeld to move against him . . . but only if Ragark struck now, before the Landreich could respond to the news of the attack on the supercarrier at Vaku.

There was only one way to guarantee that. Banfeld would have to reveal what he knew to the Cats. News of a supercarrier fitting out inside the Landreich, a Cat supercarrier at that, would probably be enough to goad even a cautious leader like Ragark into action. And, if not, there was that other tidbit of information, news that there was also an Imperial heir alive and well on that same vessel. That was sure to interest Ragark. And hopefully it would lead him to strike now, while he could still catch the carrier at Vaku and eliminate it with a raid in force.

That should precipitate a very nice little conflict. The confees, Williams and Mancini, might not be too happy to see the fighting start so soon. Y-12 and the Belisarius

Group were trying to control the timetable for events out here very carefully, although Banfeld wasn't entirely sure why. He only knew they were taking the long view.

But the long view was something the Guild could no longer afford. *Highwayman* had to be readied for launch as quickly as possible so that Banfeld could act before the effects of the battle at Vaku overwhelmed everything he had worked his entire life to build.

If *Bonadventure* was the crown jewel of the Guild fleet, *Highwayman* was its best-kept secret. It had taken plenty of bribe money to obtain a surplus stealth generator big enough for a scoutship, but the money had been well-spent. *Highwayman* could slip across the border and back without being spotted by outlying patrols, and that meant that Banfeld could get to Baka Kar and get in touch with his contacts in Ragark's government without exposing himself to any trigger-happy Cats who might not understand the finer points of keeping private channels open between enemy states. Ragark's Economic Minister, Baron Ghraffid *nar* Dhores, had found it highly profitable to cooperate with the Guild from time to time in the past. He would see to it that Ragark learned what he needed to know.

Then rest would follow easily enough . . . and maybe, just maybe, the Guild would see its way through the crisis intact. The alternative was unthinkable.

Commander's Office, Guild Base
Hellhole, Hellhole System
1645 hours (CST)

Antonio Delgado locked the door behind him as he entered the tiny office that was his innermost sanctum at the Hellhole base. He crossed to the bank of communications equipment along the far wall and seated himself at the console. With the ease of long and constant practice he activated a circuit that would alert him if there was any kind of surveillance in progress. He thought Banfeld trusted him—at least as much as the privateer leader trusted anyone—but it was always wise to take precautions in Delgado's line of work.

He switched on the hypercast transmitter and began programming the transmission parameters. He needed a narrow beam directed precisely at the communications station at the jump point from Hellhole back to Landreich. An ordinary broadcast might be picked up by Banfeld's men, and that would not be good for Antonio Delgado. While the computer worked on those instructions he called up the subroutines to encode and scramble the transmission, as added precautions.

At length the computer informed him that the parameters had all been met and the hypercast was ready to begin. He switched on the audio-visual module, leaned close to the microphone, and took a deep breath before he began to speak.

It was important that he inform his employers—his *real* employers, not Zachary Banfeld—of the latest developments on Hellhole. Banfeld hadn't shared his plans with Delgado, but the only possible reasons for readying *Highwayman* for a trip so soon after returning from the ill-fated attack on the Landreich carrier at Vaku were liable to go against the wishes of the Y-12 organization.

Delgado couldn't delay Banfeld more than a few days without raising suspicions, so it was important that he pass on the information as soon as possible. He hoped he was acting in time to be useful to Y-12. Though he was only a small cog in the Belisarius Group, he knew he played an important role in being one of the Confederation's men assigned to keep an eye on Zachary Banfeld.

He began his message.

Terran Confederation Embassy Compound, Newburg
Landreich, Landreich System
1841 hours (CST)

"Damn it! The man's a loose cannon!" Clark Williams slammed his fist down on his desk, making a rare Firekkan vase jump alarmingly. "The stupid bastard wasn't satisfied with screwing up the mission against the carrier. Now he's abandoned us entirely and getting ready to go freelance!"

"You're sure your agent can be trusted?" Mancini asked, sounding calm and cool. "And, more importantly, are you sure you're interpreting the report accurately? This man Delgado didn't give any details as to what Banfeld is planning."

"Delgado's a good man. He's been sending reliable reports ever since we slipped him into the Guild organization." Williams leaned forward in his chair. "As for what Banfeld's up to, there're only two reasons I can think of to prep a stealth-capable scout. Either he's planning to make a run for it before Max Kruger finds out he was behind the carrier attack, or he's planning a run into Cat country. My vote's for the second choice."

"Any reason why? Other than your well-known reliance on logic and rational thought?" Mancini's tone was sarcastic, and Williams forced himself to calm down. The colonel's implied rebuke made him take stock of his behavior. It wasn't wise to let his anger get the better of his judgment, no matter how furious the events of the past few days had left him.

"I know Banfeld," he said, striving for a quiet, controlled voice to match Mancini's own. "He would only run if he had reason to believe that the Guild was going down once and for all, and he's got no reason to believe that the Landreichers know where any of his bases are. So until he has some kind of proof that the Guild is really in danger of immediate reprisals, his immediate response will be to try to strike some kind of new balance that'll keep the operation intact."

"That makes sense," Mancini admitted.

"So odds are he's on his way to Ragark. He'll want to sell the Cats whatever secrets he can provide." Williams sighed. "Not just for money, either, I'm afraid. He's liable to figure that word of the Landreichers refitting that carrier will stir Ragark up and make him attack. That would take the pressure off the Guild if Kruger or the Navy realize that Banfeld was the one who hit at Vaku."

"I'm not sure that would be such a bad idea," Mancini said. "Clearly Richards and Tolwyn were able to get a lot more of their systems on-line before Banfeld could launch his strike. The previous report from Delgado suggested they had salvaged Kilrathi planes backing up their Landreicher craft, and full shields on top of that. Banfeld couldn't hope to threaten them now . . . but maybe a full Kilrathi strike force could turn the trick."

"No, damn it!" Williams exploded again. "No! This isn't the way to handle the situation." He slumped back in his chair. It was all very well for Mancini to be so rational, but the fact remained that the whole scheme to take out the supercarrier before it had a chance to become a real threat to the Belisarius Group's plans

for the Landreich had come unraveled thanks to
Banfeld's failure. "The stupid bastard. First he screws
up the carrier attack, and then he breaks and runs instead
of finishing the job. Now this . . ."

Mancini shook his head. "He didn't screw up anything,
Commissioner. He was just caught by bad intelligence
data, that's all. And once he was confronted by an attack
gone bad and a pair of destroyers threatening his ship,
he did the only thing he could do. He got out of there
while he could. You wouldn't expect Zachary Banfeld
to go down with his ship against hopeless odds, would
you? There'd be no profit at all in playing the hero."

"Was Springweather feeding us bad information?"

The colonel shrugged. "I doubt it. Look, she said they
were having trouble with the shields on the carrier, and
needed the tender. But the information was almost two
weeks old. Time doesn't stand still just so we can plan
military ops, Commissioner. Richards and Tolwyn have
a good team out there, and they're moving faster than
we expected, pure and simple. Shields repaired, more
fighters deployable. Maybe if Banfeld had made it to
Vaku a few days earlier . . ." He trailed off with another
shrug. "In any event, you were telling me why it wouldn't
be wise to let Ragark handle our little problem with
Richards and Tolwyn for us."

"There are plenty of reasons, starting with the fact
that something like that could ruin the whole plan before
it gets off the ground," Williams said harshly. "If he
strikes too soon, out of panic or some misguided notion
of protecting Kilrathi honor or whatever the hell it is
that makes Cats like him tick, we could be right royally
screwed. What if *he* didn't get the carrier, either? Or
what if he did, but lost too many of his own resources
to follow through with an attack on Landreich? A strike
into Landreich space that didn't result in a clear-cut

victory for Ragark—and I'm talking about taking the Landreich system itself, not just grabbing up outlying outposts or winning a couple of minor engagements— an attack that didn't overrun this part of the frontier could trigger Confederation intervention before we have a chance to build the case against the government and launch our coup. Then we'd be back where we were when Blair took out Kilrah with the T-Bomb." He paused. "And don't forget that our pirate friend has another secret to sell. Us."

"Meaning?"

"Meaning that Ragark wouldn't like it at all if he found out we were trying to manipulate him into an attack. If Banfeld told him about Belisarius, and what he knows about what we've been doing the last few months, Ragark might back off entirely. And that would be even worse than letting him go off half-cocked."

"Yeah, I see your point." Mancini nodded. "Ragark's predictable within certain narrow limits, but there's no telling how he might react if any of this other stuff comes out. Okay, we don't want him going to Ragark. How do we stop him? Your man Delgado?"

Williams shook his head. "Not a chance. Banfeld's too canny to be caught by a lone assassin, and he's well-protected. Delgado would turn down an order like that cold, and I'm not sure I'd blame him."

"What, then? We don't have the resources to stop him."

"No, we don't." Williams allowed a cold smile to crease his puffy features. "But the Landreichers do. And they've got plenty of motivation, too, after the attack at Vaku."

"But they don't know . . ."

"That can change. Easily." Williams showed his teeth in an expression that reminded Mancini uncomfortably of a Kilrathi warrior anticipating a killing. "We leak what we know about the Hellhole base to one of our people in Kruger's government. He passes it on to the Navy, and Kruger sends his fleet in to smash Hellhole before Banfeld gets away. We've got a narrow window to make it work, but Delgado will buy us as much time as he can."

"That could work," Mancini said. "Who do we own in the government who could do the job for us?"

"We don't own him, but I think Councilman Galbraith is the man. His son's a captain in the Navy, and they're both ambitious as hell. I'm sure they'd both be pleased if they could be the ones responsible for evening the score for that tender that was lost."

"Not bad . . ." Mancini paused, a wolfish smile lighting up his own face. "Not bad at all, Commissioner. We can also use this to our own advantage, maybe help the plan along a little."

"Oh? Tell me." Williams leaned forward again, intrigued. He'd been improvising his way out of a crisis, but it sounded as if Mancini saw something even better.

"For months we've been doing our best to counter Kruger's claims of Kilrathi raiding by building a case for pirates operating on both sides of the border. Now we've had a demonstrable pirate attack on a unit of the republican fleet, and the people involved—Tolwyn, Richards, Bondarevsky, and so forth—are unimpeachable witnesses. All we need to make the case perfect is a real, live pirate base and a genuine pirate leader, Banfeld. It'll go a long way towards making our whole case for us."

"Very good, Colonel," Williams said with a smile. "Excellent. If we could go a step further and stir up some political opposition to Max Kruger as a result of it all, we might even be able to sidestep the whole mess with the carrier at Vaku. Let them think he's been directing all his energies—and all the Landreich's resources—against the wrong opponents after all."

Mancini gave a nod. "That's one option. As close to bankruptcy as Kruger's government already is, how do you think the Council would react if they found out what he's been investing in? The refit on that supercarrier must be costing a fortune. Their factory ship alone represents a major investment that ought to be earning its keep instead of producing spare parts for a derelict. Not to mention the money Kruger's been spending to bring in surplus ConFleet ships and high-priced outside talent."

"Councilman Galbraith's the man to use, for this part of the operation as well as the other," Williams said slowly. "He's already miffed that Kruger's been bringing in people like Tolwyn and Bondarevsky. Makes his son's career that much less spectacular, and Old Man Galbraith's got political ambitions for his son the would-be naval hero. Probably figures on having Kenny win some spectacular fight and then beat Kruger in an election, with Daddy pulling the strings afterward. Might just work, if Kenny can manage to land the op that takes out Hellhole."

"So . . . we leak what we know to Galbraith and let him ask some hard questions in Council about the carrier and some of the other rearmament policies." Mancini rubbed his jaw. "Do you think the Council will really pull the plug on him? The war party's still strong. Hell, Galbraith's no pacifist. He just wants to squeeze out Max."

"It doesn't really matter what the final vote is," Williams said. "The point is, it'll slow things down all around. Kruger will be facing a political crisis and won't dare throw any more resources at the carrier until there's some kind of decision. And more delays give Ragark more time to get his plans in motion." He paused. "Sounds like our best plan. By God, Mancini, we might pull this off yet. Even if we did damn near lose it all to Zack Banfeld."

Commander's Office, Guild Base
Hellhole, Hellhole System
2330 hours (CST)

The door to the office swung open soundlessly, and the figure silhouetted against the lights out on the tarmac stood for a moment as if unsure of what to do next. After a moment he let the door close behind him and hit the locking stud. Only then did his fingers touch the light plate. When nothing happened he started to curse in Spanish.

"Please, Antonio, such language," Zachary Banfeld said quietly. "There's nothing wrong with the lights. I just overrode the wall plate from here." He tapped a control on Delgado's desk, and the lights came up bright.

Delgado gaped at the laser pistol Banfeld held trained on him with an unwavering aim.

"What—what do you think you're doing?"

Banfeld smiled. "All your precautions, Antonio, and you didn't think that I could monitor your power usage, did you? When I found out you were making a hypercast so soon after our meeting this afternoon, I just had to know who you were sending to." He shook his head. "It took time to get the back traffic downloaded from the comm satellite at the jump point . . . and even longer to crack your codes. But once we had your message to Williams, well . . ." He shrugged, but the barrel of the laser pistol didn't shift at all. "Three days to bring the *Highwayman's* stealth systems back up to standard, eh?

Imagine the shock when the work crew discovered that you had simply tampered with the control mechanisms, and the stealth generators turned out to be fine after all. I can leave tomorrow . . ."

The traitor's eyes flicked toward the comm gear.

"Oh, don't worry, I'm told we can produce an excellent computer simulacrum to keep your friends Williams and Mancini quite happy. You'll continue to make reports as needed." Banfeld paused. "I wish I didn't have to leave so quickly, Antonio. I'm sure a few days with our persuasion specialists will have you eager to spill everything you've given away about Guild activities. But I really do have to be on my way, so I'll have to defer the pleasure of listening to you scream until I get back."

Delgado lunged forward, but Banfeld was ready for him. He fired the laser pistol, aiming for the big mercenary's knee. Delgado screamed once and collapsed.

"That was just a sample. You'll find things will get much worse as time goes on, Antonio. Much, much worse."

• CHAPTER 15

> *"Never permit your enemy to learn your
> advantages, unless doing so can cause him to
> become fearful so that he stumbles during the
> chase."*

from the Ninth Codex
21:05:10

Bridge, Guild Scoutship *Highwayman*
Near Baka Kar, Baka Kar System
1034 hours (CST), 2671.017

"Cloak is holding. All systems nominal."

Zachary Banfeld nodded at the helmsman's report,
his eyes on the tactical plot beside his command chair.
The voyage to Baka Kar had gone smoothly, but Banfeld
was still nagged by worries. How much had Delgado
betrayed of the Guild's secrets? What was going on back
in the Landreich while he made this foray into Kilrathi
space? How would Ragark receive his information?
Everything now balanced on a knife-edge, and he knew
one wrong move could spell disaster.

The trouble was, so many of those possible wrong
moves weren't even his to make. That was what galled

him most, not being in control. That had hardly ever happened to Banfeld before, and he didn't care for the feeling at all.

The scout had managed the three jumps from Hellhole to Baka Kar in less than two standard days, a tribute to the high acceleration *Highwayman* could generate at need. With the stealth generators on, they had slipped past the Kilrathi picket boat at Vordran, where a whole locus of jump points located close together made the system a vital strategic link along the frontier of the Hralgkrak province. Now they were less than two light-minutes out from the provincial capital, still cloaked.

Banfeld was still not sure how to initiate contact with the Kilrathi. He had never sent one of his smugglers to the provincial capital before, never faced the problem of dealing with so much naval traffic. If they were in a trigger-happy mood the Guild ship could be fried by patrolling elements of Ragark's fleet before he could get a message through, once the cloak went down. But he had none of the usual facilities for making contact with his links to the Economic Minister. The usual procedure required initiating contact at a remote outpost, but there wasn't time for that.

He would have to hope the Kilrathi would give him time to talk rather than take *Highwayman* for a spy or the forerunner of an attack. All he had to do was get in touch with Ghraffid *nar* Dhores, and the Baron would do the rest.

"Drop the cloak," he ordered. "Jonas, broadcast the hail. Broad channel . . . we want everyone to know we've got business with the Minister."

"Broad channel," Jonas Hart, manning the communications station, confirmed.

He continued to study the tactical monitor. The traffic

in the system was making him edgy, and he was sure there was something important he just wasn't seeing out there . . .

Certainly there were plenty of Kilrathi ships orbiting the planet. On the way in from the jump point Banfeld had counted four escort carriers and their battle groups, an imposing fleet indeed to be assembled at one point. Assuming Ragark had garrisons posted at other worlds of the province, his fleet was going to be a powerful threat to the Landreich even if the carrier at Vaku was made operational. Perhaps he had worried unnecessarily about the threat to the balance of power, led astray by the paranoia of Williams and Mancini.

On the other hand, that salvaged carrier had turned out to pack quite a punch, and with the support of the rest of Kruger's fleet it could still turn the tide against a Kilrathi task force made up of escort carriers. Banfeld would stick to his original plan.

But there was still something that wasn't quite right about the readings they were getting. He continued to look at the monitor, especially at the symbols that described the main orbital docking complex over Baka Kar.

He stared at the readout for a long time before it hit him. The mass was wrong, completely different from everything in their records on the facilities at Baka Kar. The docking complex was supposed to be large, but these figures were almost twice what they should have been. Banfeld ordered the computer to zoom in on the orbital dock so that he could study it more closely.

It took a long time for the computer imaging system to interpret the sensor data well enough to comply with his request, and that wasn't right either. Something anomalous was out there, something that was distorting *Highwayman's* probes . . .

Banfeld let out an audible gasp as the computer imager finally displayed a picture based on the collected data. Something massive really was over there, docked with the orbital facility. Something that dwarfed the spidery framework of the station. It was the biggest ship Banfeld had ever seen—if it *was* a ship, and that's what the computer was insisting. It measured nearly twenty-two kilometers in length, bristling with hardpoints and radiating an awesome amount of energy even when it lay quiescent alongside the dock.

The Guild leader had only heard rumors about such ships, but now he was sure he was seeing the reality behind those rumors. A Kilrathi dreadnought, one of the vast and powerful warships Prince Thrakhath had ordered for the final solution to the war with Mankind.

And it was here, with Ragark's fleet.

Cold fear washed over Zachary Banfeld. He had wanted to help Ragark even the odds so that the war on the frontier might be prolonged and the Guild profit from the war. But a Kilrathi dreadnought made all the defenses of the Landreichers useless. Even their new supercarrier would be no match for such a powerful ship of war, whether they fully restored it to fighting trim or not.

When the Kilrathi smashed their way across the border, the question of Guild profits would no longer be a factor in his plans. The question would be one of Guild survival.

"Abort the mission," he ordered sharply. "Get us back to the jump point. Best speed. And get the goddamned cloak back up!"

Reception Area, Orbital Station Asharazhal
Orbiting Baka Kar, Baka Kar System
1040 hours (CST)

Ukar *dai* Ragark stood by the broad transplast window
and studied the impressive bulk of the *Vorghath*, or
rather the comparatively tiny part of him visible from
this part of the orbital dock. Ragark had never seen
one of Thrakhath's dreadnoughts, and merely reading
over the specifications had hardly prepared him for the
reality of seeing the huge ship in person.

One such dreadnought could carve out a new Empire.
The apes would never stand against his firepower.

He turned to look at the crowd of ministers and
officers waiting a respectful distance behind him. "Look
at him, my friends," he said expansively, gesturing to
encompass the great ship that lay outside. "Look at him!
Vorghath the Hunter, come to lead us to victory. With
this ship, we shall crush all opposition, and have our
revenge on the apes for the Homeworld."

As if in response to his declaration the boarding tube
door adjacent to the window cycled open, and Dawx
Jhorrad stepped through with an eight of his senior staff
behind him. Jhorrad was a short, thickset *kil*, half his
face hidden by an extensive prosthetic plate that contained
bionics to replace an eye and an ear lost in the first Terran
raid against Kilrah years ago. No one could have mistaken
him for an aristocrat even if he'd born the honorific
between given name and surname that marked a noble's
rank. But despite being a commoner Jhorrad was a
brilliant tactician, and his underlings, even those who
were titled, would follow him to the Underworld and
back at his slightest command.

Ragark envied him his charisma, but he didn't allow
that envy to warp his perceptions. Dawx Jhorrad was

the perfect subordinate. He could never aspire to lead the Empire; he had to pledge his loyalty to someone else, someone of birth and land, and titles. That was why he had come to Ragark after so many eight-days of wandering. Ragark could give him the two things he needed—a purpose, and a chance to keep on fighting the apes he hated so passionately.

"Captain Jhorrad," Ragark said, stepping forward and opening both hands in a gesture of greeting. "It is a pleasure to see you at last."

Jhorrad sank to one knee and bowed his battle-scarred head in submission. "My lord Ragark," he said formally. "Permit me to pledge you my service. I offer you my claws and teeth, to rend your foes. I offer you my mind and spirit, to do your bidding. I offer you my eyes and ears, to seek out your foes. And I offer you my throat, to slash, should ever I be found unworthy."

Ragark showed his teeth. The full Warrior's Oath, right out of the Codices . . . that hadn't been heard in the Empire for years, not after Thrakhath had revealed his irreligious nature to the nobility. Jhorrad did him the ultimate honor, pledging a form of fealty that placed him entirely at his new master's command.

"Rise, Captain," he said sternly, recalling the proper formula. "I accept your pledge of service, your claws and teeth, your mind and spirit, your eyes and ears. May I never require to accept your throat, as long as you serve my *hrai*."

Jhorrad stood. "I thank my Lord."

"You have journeyed for a long time, Captain," Ragark said in a more conversational tone. "Tell me, how is *Vorghath*? When will he be ready for service?"

"Many eight-days, I fear," the commoner said. "The ship was badly damaged when Kilrah was destroyed. We barely escaped the system. Since then we have had no place of refuge to make more than makeshift repairs, and Melek's ships have hounded us." He showed his teeth. "But even wounded, *Vorghath* taught those a lesson in respect, and Melek gave up the hunt some time ago. We need an extensive refit. New stores, a complete retuning of shield generators and fusion plants. Repair of battle damage to the hull. Replacements for crew members killed and wounded, and for those who have expressed a desire to be discharged now that their oath to the Emperor binds them no longer."

Ragark almost responded with an angry remark about Warriors who abandoned their posts before their lords gave them permission, but he grasped the words before they were uttered. He was not the Emperor yet, and until he was acclaimed and seated upon the throne he would have to watch his step, even with commoners like Jhorrad. Especially with Jhorrad, who could smooth over so many possible obstacles that lay between Ragark and the throne.

Before he could say anything at all, a warning siren sounded. Nerrag *jaq* Rhang raised a commlink to his face and spoke urgently. Then he turned to Ragark.

"My Lord, sensors have registered a ship of Terran design decloaking less than two light minutes from orbit. It is broadcasting a signal asking to speak with Ghraffid *nar* Dhores, and identifies the sender as a 'Zachary Banfeld.' "

Ragark turned to face the block of followers nearby. "What is this about, Lord Ghraffid?"

The Economic Minister looked abashed. "Lord, the Terran Banfeld is a renegade ape who works for his own profit. I have found it useful, from time to time, to have dealings with him . . . as a way of gaining access to information about activities on the other side of the frontier."

Ragark studied him for a long moment in silence. "And of course my Economic Minister needs such intelligence from Terran space, to know what the price of raw meat and claw sharpeners is on their side of the frontier," he said, mustering all the sarcasm at his command. "Let me see, how often has this source of yours been mentioned in the frequent talks we've had regarding intelligence operations conducted by your Ministry?" He paused. "You have been dealing with a smuggler, a black marketeer, and the only reason I can think of for that is the desire to make profits of your own. Isn't that right?"

"N-no, my Lord . . . I mean, not simply that . . ."

"Never mind. I will deal with you later." Ragark made a dismissive gesture. "Your smuggler friend has arrived at a very bad time, I'm afraid. He has been in the system, under cloak, for an unknown period of time. Long enough, at least, to register the presence of the *Vorghath* here. This is information we cannot afford to let the apes have too soon." He turned back to Nerrag. "Order that ape ship intercepted and destroyed. We cannot allow him to pass on word of *Vorghath* to his people. And have this *huckster* arrested and held for trial. *Now!*"

"More information, my Lord," Nerrag said, looking up from his commlink. "The ape has cloaked again. Last readings indicated he was heading for the jump point at top speed. Interception will be difficult as long as he remains under cloak . . ."

"I know that!" Ragark snapped. "All right, if you cannot stop the ship, pursue it. Energy readings at the jump point should give a fairly good idea of when and where he goes. Dispatch a task force to follow the ape—the carriers *Hravik* and *Klarran*, and their battle groups. Some time he will have to decloak, and when he does I want him destroyed! And any other apes he comes in contact with, as well. See to it, Nerrag."

Ragark turned away, seething, to hide his look of frustration from the others. Especially Jhorrad, the peasant who must never see his Lord at a loss.

Combat Information Center, FRLS *Independence*
Near Hellhole, Hellhole System
0730 hours (CST), 2671.019

"Wing Commander reports all resistance on the planet has ended, Captain. Bombers are proceeding with planned strikes on the base. The carrier has broken orbit and is withdrawing in the direction of Jump Point Six . . . to Vordran, sir. Cat territory."

Captain John Galbraith leaned forward in his command chair, full of anticipation. "Thank you, Commander Roth." He said formally to his Exec. "Instruct Commander Tolwyn to have his fighters pursue the carrier. I want it stopped."

"Aye aye, sir."

"Navigator, lay in a course to intercept the Guild carrier. Helm, increase to maximum acceleration. Break orbit and get us up to that ship ASAP." He turned towards Roth. "Order the bombers to complete their runs, catch up with us, and rearm. I want them ready in case Tolwyn can't finish off the pirates by himself." Actually, he intended to get a few blows in whether Tolwyn could handle the job or not. It was important that he be able to demonstrate his own vital part in this whole affair, and not let an outlander like Admiral Tolwyn's nephew claim any of the credit.

He leaned back again, feeling satisfied. *Independence* had caught the pirates in the middle of disassembling their base on Hellhole and smashed through their feeble attempts at resistance. Several pirate ships had broken orbit and scattered, and in the absence of orders from Camparelli, who was in his bed today as he had been for the past week, Galbraith had ordered the rest of the battle group to split up and pursue the various fleeing vessels. Now the pirate base was under aerial bombardment and their largest surviving ship, the so-called carrier that had attacked the Goliath Project at Vaku and then escaped from Richards and his men, was running once again. Galbraith would make sure it didn't get away. That would be quite a feather in his cap when *Independence* returned to Landreich.

His father's political faction would gain considerable influence as a result, perhaps even enough to finally topple Max Kruger.

Galbraith wasn't sure where his father had obtained his intelligence information, but it had checked out one hundred percent so far. News that the pirates were operating out of a base on Hellhole had brought loud demands for naval action in the Landreich Council Hall, and the orders for *Independence* and her brand-new battle group to spearhead the attack had come down almost immediately. With the fighter wing brought back up to full strength, a new Marine contingent on board, and a battle group that now consisted of two cruisers, three destroyers, and a pair of stealth scouts, *Independence* had come roaring into the Hellhole system ready for action. The pirates had barely registered them on sensors before Tolwyn's fighters were in among their orbiting ships. The rest of the battle group had split up to pursue the smaller pirate ships attempting to reach several different jump points that lay fairly close to the planet.

Yes, it was a textbook operation, and it could only help bolster his naval career. Perhaps when Kruger lost a vote of confidence in council some changes would be made, the outsiders relegated to their proper place and a proven commander promoted to command the supercarrier when it was finally ready to leave the Vaku system and go into action.

Galbraith smiled, thinking of the possibilities.

Raptor 600, VF-84 "Liberators"
Near Jump Point Six, Hellhole System
0752 hours (CST)

"All right, boys and girls, let's give these bastards an idea of what it is to tangle with the Liberators!" Kevin Tolwyn matched actions to words and broke formation, rolling his heavy fighter sideways and accelerating toward the limping ship that looked even less like a carrier than it had before it had taken a string of hits in the opening round of the fighting planetside.

The converted transport swelled as he plunged closer, a single turret offering Double-A-S fire that went wide of the mark. Tolwyn targeted the engineering section and opened fire with neutron guns and mass drivers, unleashing the full power of the heavy fighter's arsenal in a single consolidated burst. It drained his power supply quickly, but with no sign of enemy fighters around and such a poor showing from the carrier's own gunnery it was a safe enough maneuver.

Energy sparkled and flared as the weapons met the carrier's shielding. At the last possible moment, Tolwyn pulled up to whip past the stern section at full military acceleration. The shields were still holding, so he didn't waste either of his two remaining missiles yet, but he had softened the enemy up for the next fighter, his wingman for the day's ops, Lieutenant Carlos "Venture" Ventura. The second Raptor mimicked Tolwyn's attack, but as Venture skimmed over the engineering section he released two Gladius heat-seeking missiles. The first hit the ship's shielding, but the energy released by its detonation brought the carrier's rear shields down and the second hit armor.

"Now that's the way to let 'em know we're out here!" Ventura whooped.

"Good shooting, Venture," Tolwyn said. "Stormy, Jazzman, you take the next run. Let 'em have it!"

"Skipper?" That was Commander William "Willie Pete" Peterson, the CO of the Hornet squadron, the Stingers of VF-16, which had just joined the wing to replace Babcock's Flying Eyes. *"I'm getting a disturbance at the jump point, but no visual. Could be something cloaked coming through . . ."* He trailed off. *"Holy shit! Multiple disturbances now . . . we've got company coming, skipper, and a hell of a lot of it!"*

"Camelot, Camelot, this is Lancelot," Tolwyn said, switching to the carrier's frequency. "Camelot, did you copy that? We've got ships incoming through the jump point . . ." He stopped as the first targets began registering on his screens. "My God, they're Cats. I'm reading a Cat task force, one carrier . . . no, two carriers now, plus cruisers and destroyers. Repeat, Cat task force with two carriers and supporting combat ships. What are your instructions, Camelot?"

But there was no response from the *Independence*.

Flag Bridge, KIS *Klarran*
Jump Point Six, Hellhole System
0755 hours (CST)

Jumpshock blurred his vision and made it hard for him to concentrate, but Admiral Julgar *nar* Ta'hal forced himself to focus on the flag bridge's tactical monitors.

What he saw caused him to bare his fangs in an instinctive desire to rend and tear.

His task force had pursued the Terran scout for nearly six-eights standard Kilrah hours, but the cloaked ship had led them a merry chase. At times it had been almost exhilarating, like a primal hunt for a cunning and well-camouflaged prey animal, but Julgar had been uncomfortably aware of the serious nature of his orders from Ragark. The initial instructions had been blunt: catch the Terran ship, whatever the cost, and smash it and any other apes it came into contact with. But before jumping from the Baka Kar system more detailed orders had come from Ragark in person. The Governor had been adamant about stopping the human vessel, yet he had also been determined that the Kilrathi ships should not get drawn into a major battle. Until the *Vorghath* was refitted Ragark needed all his combat ships intact, ready to block the expanding Landreich fleet or to carry out the initial moves of the planned invasion of the human frontier worlds. A major clash of ships at this stage would be premature, and Ragark would entertain no tolerance for failure.

So they had followed the humans to Vordran, alerting the picket boat posted there of the cloaked ship's presence in the system. Running at maximum acceleration, they had arrived at the jump point from Vordran to Hellhole just in time to see the last stages of a skirmish between the picket boat, the escort *Wexarragh*, and the human vessel which had been forced to drop its cloak for an instant in order to transfer power to its jump drive. The escort had damaged the Terrans, but they had jumped anyway, switching the cloak back on as they slid into the hyperrealm for the interstellar transit to Hellhole.

The task force had followed close on the enemy ship's

heels. Julgar had almost been able to smell the chance at a kill, knowing the prey was damaged.

But what awaited the Kilrathi task force on the other side of the hyperrealm was not a single badly damaged scout, but a large ship and a swarm of fighters almost on top of the jump point, and more warships identified by the computer as elements of a Landreich carrier battle group further off, out of formation but representing a potent force.

The Imperial ships had the edge in numbers, but they were risking the possibility of a major battle . . . exactly the thing Ragark had warned against. How could Julgar carry out both sets of instructions?

To add to his troubles, that nearest Terran ship was entirely too close to the *Klarran* for comfort. In his zeal for the pursuit Julgar had taken his flagship through the jump point first, rather than sending lighter ships on ahead. That put the *Klarran* in a dangerous position. His speed was minimal after the hyperspace transit, and it would take time to build up a substantial vector. Meanwhile the Terran ship was well within the usual defensive perimeter a battle group's destroyers and cruisers were supposed to maintain. Carriers were not intended to engage in ship to ship duels, but there was a risk here. The rest of the task force would be following, of course, but hyperspace transit arrival points were wildly variable and some of the other ships might not build up a vector that would get them to the scene of the battle for as much as an hour.

Much could happen in an hour.

Julgar flicked his claws in and out nervously, studying the tactical board and trying to get over the lingering effects of jumpshock. The Terran ship was like nothing in the Kilrathi warbook program. The computer was calling it a transport, but energy readings were equivalent to a destroyer or a small cruiser . . . and the long-range imaging scan made it look like some kind of pocket carrier. The fighters around it were old human designs, but time and again even older human fighters had dealt severe blows to Kilrathi fighter squadrons in actions during the decades-long war.

His thoughts finally began to come together, and Julgar turned his seat to face his communications officer. "Establish a blanket jamming field," he said. "I want no contact between the apes here and those on the edge of our sensor range. Lord Ragark does not want the ship we are chasing to communicate with anyone else."

"Yes, Lord Admiral," the officer responded crisply. "We will not be able to damp out tight-beam communications, my Lord. At close range they will still be able to maintain contact. It is possible there will be intermittent contact over the longer range as well, at least between the larger ships."

"Understood. Do your best." He turned to his own console. "Captain, this is Admiral *nar* Ta'hal. Launch all fighters, fastest possible rotation. Crush the enemy ships nearest us as quickly as possible. Especially the scout, if you can locate it. I would suggest it will probably be attempting to rendezvous with the capital ship ahead of us."

"*Yes, Lord Admiral,*" the *Klarran's* captain responded.

"Do not get underway from this position, Captain," he went on. "I do not wish to be drawn into closer action until we have some support from the rest of the task force. Keep the vector low until then. Pass the word to the rest of the task force as well."

"*Yes, my Lord,*" the captain responded.

"And once the fighters have launched, put out a pair of Zartoths. We will be jamming enemy communications, but I want to be able to extend our area of interdiction in case the apes attempt to break off."

Julgar cut the intercom link before the captain could reply. He bared his fangs once again, this time in anticipation. A single overwhelming attack would eliminate the fugitive and anyone he communicated with here. Then the task force could disengage if they needed to . . . or, if the odds looked favorable, they could close with the other apes and defeat them as well, whatever Ragark's orders specified.

It was a glorious day for combat.

Flag Officer's Quarters, FRLS *Independence*
Deep Space, Hellhole System
0759 hours (CST)

Admiral Vincent Camparelli struggled to sit upright in his bed despite the pressure in his chest and the uneven wheeze of his breath. Although ill and confined to his bed, he had been monitoring the tactical board from his bedside computer hookup and the holographic projector that occupied a table by the door. He had watched in satisfaction as the battle group had surprised and scattered the pirates, although he'd been tempted to call back the capital ships Galbraith had scattered in pursuit of the fleeing enemy. In the end, though, he'd decided against that. Galbraith knew what he was doing, and didn't need an old, sick man telling him what to do from his bed.

He had promised himself that this would be the last cruise. No matter how much Max Kruger wanted him to stay in harness, Camparelli knew it was time for the old war-horse to go to pasture.

The admiral had almost dozed off, until a warning

alarm had signaled the appearance of new ships on the board. Awake once more, he had studied the newcomers, his chest tightening as he'd realized who they were.

Cats . . . a small task force built around a pair of carriers. They had erupted almost on top of the fighters and their quarry, the makeshift pirate carrier.

Camparelli reached for the intercom controls at his bedside. *Independence* was heading straight into that mess at maximum acceleration, and without any supporting destroyers or cruisers. The carrier operating alone wouldn't stand a chance against those Cats.

He fumbled with the controls, and swore an ancient oath in the Italian dialect of Romanova, his boyhood home. His fingers weren't obeying the orders from his brain—a fine admiral he made, unable even to command his body any longer, much less his battle group—and a sharp pain was shooting up his left arm and side.

Camparelli persevered and activated the intercom circuit, now gasping for breath. He had to get Galbraith to act . . . or *Independence*, maybe the entire battle group, would be lost.

Combat Information Center, FRLS *Independence*
Deep Space, Hellhole System
0801 hours (CST)

Galbraith stared at the tactical monitor, hardly able to comprehend the new data flowing across the screen— or the Wing Commander's words echoing in his ears. Of all the times the Cats could mount a raid . . .

"Sir? Admiral Camparelli on the line." Roth didn't wait for Galbraith to respond. She switched the intercom on.

The admiral's face looked pale and drawn. "*Captain . . . Captain, you have to get the battle group together quickly. The other ships are too badly dispersed . . . too badly dispersed . . .*" The battle group commander was gasping. "*Get them together . . . have to withdraw . . . Cat force too large for a stand-up fight . . .*" He trailed off, still fighting for breath. "*Can't . . . can't think straight, Captain. Turning over full command . . . to you.*" The screen went as dead as Galbraith's hopes.

He forced himself to act. "Helm, kill our vector. We won't sail into the middle of that without some support from the rest of the battle group." He paused. "Exec, have a medical team lay down to the flag bridge and see to the Admiral. And order all ships to break off operations immediately and form on *Independence* ASAP."

"Aye aye, sir," Roth replied. "Sir . . . what about Tolwyn's flight wing? He was calling for orders. Then everything went dead. Looks like jamming by the Cats. We can't recall him, and we can't even let him know our plans." Something in her tone suggested she wanted to know them herself. "The Cats have started launching fighters, and I don't know if Tolwyn's got enough planes to handle fighters from two Cat escort carriers."

"I know," Galbraith said grimly. "But he's going to have to try. The Flight Wing has to buy us some time, keep those Cats off our backs until we reassemble the battle group and can pull back to the jump point to Landreich." He paused, swallowing. "He's a good man, Tolwyn. He'll know what he has to do."

Raptor 500, VF-84 "Liberators"
Near Jump Point Six, Vaku System
0804 hours (CST)

"It's no good, skipper," Peterson said. *"The jamming's too damned thick around here. I can't raise Camelot."*

Kevin Tolwyn cursed under his breath. If a Hornet fitted out with an elaborate suite of electronics and communications gear couldn't break through the static, none of them could. That left the Liberators on their own, and Kilrathi birds were already beginning to form up around their lead carrier as if organizing for an attack.

Meanwhile he didn't know what to do. If he withdrew to the carrier he risked getting jumped halfway by the Cats . . . or, worse yet, drawing them back to *Independence*, where they could inflict a lot of damage before the Kilrathi capital ships came up and finished her off. But if he stayed out here his fighters, already short on missiles and fuel from the long running battle with the pirates, were likely to be overwhelmed.

Everything depended on what the Kilrathi did.

He turned his attention to his sensor readouts, and gave a low whistle as he took in the changing situation out there. He had forgotten about the pirates.

In the confusion that had followed the appearance of the Cats, the battered pirate carrier had altered course. Strangely, though, it was not running away, not from the Landreich fighters, nor yet from the Cats. It had veered so that its course took it across the line of advance of the oncoming Kilrathi. In the circumstances it was an insane move . . .

Unless they had a reason.

Tolwyn remembered the surge of energy in the jump point that had preceded the appearance of the Cat ships.

Something had come through ahead of them, unseen. A cloaked ship?

Maybe . . . and if it was a cloaked pirate, it may have contacted the carrier on a channel the Landreichers couldn't monitor, a tight-beam laser, for instance.

Which meant there was more going on out here than met the eye . . . maybe a lot more. The Cats had appeared right behind the cloaked whatever-it-was. As if they were chasing it . . .

As if to confirm his line of thought, the first wave of Cat fighters peeled off toward the pirate carrier, opening fire from long range. A sustained bombardment washed over the carrier's forward shields and across her bow in a seemingly random firing pattern. But one of those bolts hit something.

The scout craft shimmered as it materialized, its stealth generators failing. A flurry of fire erupted from the Kilrathi fighters, Vaktoth heavy attack craft fitted with a wide array of powerful beam weapons. The damaged scout ship couldn't stand up long under such an assault, and even the carrier wasn't likely to be much protection under the circumstances.

The pirates had been the enemy just minutes ago, but anyone the Kilrathi wanted to get this badly was someone Kevin Tolwyn wanted to protect—at least until he could find out why.

"All Liberators, all Liberators, this is Lancelot One," he said over the all-squadron tactical channel. At close range the jamming might distort it, but the message would get through. "New orders. Concentrate on the lead Cat squadron. Give them everything you've got . . . and protect the two pirate ships out there. Repeat, the pirates are no longer considered target. Protect them from the Cats. Let's go!"

He advanced his throttle and felt the internal gravity

variance pushing him back into his seat as the Raptor accelerated. If the Cats were chasing that pirate scoutship, then the Landreicher intervention in their little fight was a sure way of getting their attention, just what Galbraith wanted.

Of course, the odds were that very few of the outnumbered Liberators would get out of the battle alive.

Bridge, Guild Scoutship *Highwayman*
Near Jump Point Six, Hellhole System
0808 hours (CST)

Smoke filled the bridge from half a dozen small electrical fires. The automatic firefighting system hadn't cut in, so the bridge crew was battling the blaze with fire extinguishers. Banfeld sat motionless in the command chair. Everything had gone wrong, and on the screen in front of him was the proof.

After dodging everything the Cats could throw at them for two days, *Highwayman* had reached Hellhole, but damaged and with two Kilrathi carriers close on her tail. And the first sight to greet them on arrival was *Bonadventure*, under attack by Landreicher fighters and obviously suffering severe damage to her engineering section. There was no sign of Guild activity near Hellhole itself, but the long-range sensors had picked up scattered ships, Guildsmen and Free Republic Navy, in running fights far removed from planetary orbit. So Delgado's betrayal had led to a government attack . . . and Banfeld's beleaguered scout had jumped out of Kilrathi space right into the middle of this new trouble.

And the old trouble had followed him here. It was disaster, pure and simple.

"Cloak is down, sir," Jonas Hart reported. "No way to get it back on-line. Port and ventral thrusters off-line. Shields are coming back up, but they can't take sustained hits. We've lost most of the ventral armor, and there are at least three compartments open to space. Casualties . . . five killed, including the Chief Engineer and his mate." Hart paused, his head cocked to one side as he listened to another set of reports coming in. "The captain of the *Bonadventure* is on the laser tight-beam. He wants further instructions. He says the Landreich fighters are vectoring in on our position, but they are no longer firing at the carrier and seem to be intending to engage the Cats. He wants to know if he should open fire on them as they close."

"Good God, no, man!" Banfeld said. "If they want to fight the Cats, for God's sake let them! Tell him to get whatever fighters he has left out there to help the Landreichers, and to let them know we'll cooperate!"

"Aye aye, sir," Hart said, sounding dubious.

"And tell him to extend his shields to give us some cover before—"

Another burst of Kilrathi fire slammed through the shields and into *Highwayman*. From the sound of it, the fire must be coming in against the dorsal armor. That was fortunate. The scout couldn't take any more damage to her underside. But it wouldn't be long before they were out of armor plating everywhere.

Banfeld gripped his chair and tried to think. There wasn't much left that he could do. It was up to the Landreichers now. . . .

• CHAPTER 16

> *"Victory must inevitably go to the Warrior
> whose desire for conquest is greater than his
> fear of death."*

from the Third Codex
18:10:05

Raptor 500, VF-84 "Liberators"
Near Jump Point Six, Vaku System
0810 Hours (CST)

*"Repeating, I am under orders to cooperate with you
against the Cats, and am launching fighters now. They
are not hostile to Landreich forces, but will protect
themselves if fired upon . . ."*

"Understood, *Bonadventure*," Kevin Tolwyn replied.
"I agree . . . we'll save our own differences for later."
He paused. "Request that you attempt to get a tight-
beam link open to the *Independence* and bring them
up to speed."

"We'll give it a try," the carrier's captain answered.
"But I don't know how long we can maintain it."

Tolwyn switched off and concentrated on the pair
of Vaktoths that were maneuvering to try and get off

shots at the crippled scoutship. A Raptor was a poor match against one of the newer, more powerful Kilrathi heavies, but Tolwyn went in with all guns blazing and was lucky enough to find the lead Cat pilot distracted by his attack run. His neutron guns pulsed again and again, until they had completely drained his reserve power, but on the last shot the first Vaktoth came apart in whirling debris.

The second Vaktoth did a sharp left roll and came up on Tolwyn's rear, the warning tone in his ear alerting him that the Cat had locked his weapons. Tolwyn reversed thrusters at full military power, a maneuver forbidden by just about every safety regulation in the ConFleet manual and probably most of the Landreich's as well. He could feel the strain on his fighter as it made the drastic vector change, slowing radically with regard to the pursuing Vaktoth. The heavy fighter surged past him, and Tolwyn parted with one of his precious missiles—he only had one more, a Spiculum Image-Recognition missile—while he waited for the energy weapons to recharge.

A moment later his wingman, Ventura, dropped in alongside him with mass drivers and ion guns blazing. In combination with Tolwyn's missiles the sudden attack overwhelmed the Cat's screens, and the second Vaktoth was gone.

At the same moment, though, two Raptor pilots were calling for help, and one of them was cut off abruptly as the second wave of Kilrathi fighters, Dralthi Four medium attack fighters from the closest Kilrathi carrier, arrived on the scene and added their firepower to the battle. It was rapidly degenerating into a free-for-all, where Kilrathi numbers were sure to tell over human discipline and tactical doctrine.

"*Landreich Wing Commander, this is Captain*

Tanaka of the Bonadventure. *Can you respond?"*

"Keep it short, Captain," Tolwyn said, putting his stick hard over to circle back into the thick of the fighting.

"We've contacted your carrier. Your commander wants you to engage the Kilrathi here while he regroups the rest of your ships without interference."

"Roger that," Tolwyn said. He'd figured that would be Galbraith's decision. It was the logical one to make . . . but it left the Liberators flapping in the breeze.

"Look, Navy, you know this battle is hopeless. You know that, don't you?"

"Your point, Captain?" Tolwyn replied through clenched teeth, all too aware of the truth in the man's statement, but unwilling to admit it.

"Bonadventure isn't getting out of here no matter what happens," Tanaka told him. *"The engines were too badly damaged by your last attack. I can make minimum thrust, but there's no way I'm outrunning those Cats."*

"You want an apology? I'm sorry we treated you the way we treat any pirate who shoots up one of our ships."

"Damn it, I'm trying to offer you a way out of this mess!" the pirate captain flared. *"Look, that scoutship's in a bad way, and Zachary Banfield is on board. If you'll have a couple of your fighters tow him clear, and group the rest of your birds around my bow to give me some cover, I think* Bonadventure *can take this fight to the enemy. All the way in to the enemy."*

Tolwyn frowned. "You mean . . ."

"I mean right down their throats," Tanaka said, almost snarling the words. *"I'll ram the closest Cat carrier if I can. They have almost no vector built up over there. They'll be a sitting duck. And the rest of the Cats will have to assist . . . a carrier's too valuable to throw away, even an escort job. In the confusion, your pilots can*

break off and get the hell out of here, back to your battle group. Just take Banfeld with you. The Guild needs him.

"I don't give a damn about what the Guild needs," Tolwyn said. "But we have our own reasons for reeling him in. But I don't think you should try this stunt, Captain. Didn't you just say that a carrier's too valuable for this?"

Tanaka's face on the communications screen creased in a bitter smile. *"As I said, we don't get out of this one way or another. And I never really considered this bucket to be much of a carrier in the first place."*

"All right, Captain," Tolwyn said reluctantly. "It's your choice, I guess. I'll organize my people."

"Understood." Tanaka paused. *"May I ask you one favor? A personal matter?"*

"Sir?"

"I have a wife and two children, on Landreich. Haven't seen them in over a year . . ." Tanaka seemed to gather his resolve. *"Would you see to it that they do not suffer for what I have done? No government confiscations, no dragging them through the courts? They knew very little about my involvement with the Guild, and persecuting them will gain the government nothing."*

Tolwyn swallowed. "I can't promise anything, Captain. I'm not that important. But I'll do everything I can."

"Thank you. Tanaka clear."

Kevin Tolwyn swallowed as he reached for the commlink controls to pass on the new orders to the Wing. Somehow he had never thought of a pirate as leaving a family to mourn him.

Combat Information Center, FRLS *Independence*
Deep Space, Vaku System
0818 hours (CST)

"I'm afraid the Admiral didn't make it, Captain. Sick Bay reports he died at 0813 hours."

Galbraith scowled. "Thank you, Commander. What's the status on the rest of the battle group?"

"All ships have acknowledged orders and broken off their pursuit, sir," Commander Roth responded. "Best estimate is ten minutes before the *Themistocles* is back in supporting range. She's the furthest out."

"And the Flight Wing?"

"Heavily engaged, sir. The pirate carrier reports they are working together on a maneuver to tie up the Cats now. It's steering a course toward the Kilrathi task force, and is coming under increasingly heavy attack. Commander Tolwyn reports that he's lost five Raptors, four Scimitars, and a pair of Hornets so far. Also two of the pirate Broadswords that sortied to support the Wing."

"God . . . almost a third of the fighters we had out there." Galbraith looked away. "Very well, Commander. Keep me apprised. I want to know when the battle group is fully reassembled. Navigator, lay in a course for the jump point to Landreich . . . but execute it only on my mark."

"The jump point, Captain?" Roth asked with a raised eyebrow.

"You heard the order, Commander," Galbraith said, more harshly than he had intended. Roth was like the voice of his conscience, and he couldn't deal with having his decisions second-guessed right now. He was unsure enough without having to justify his decisions.

Galbraith sagged in his chair, the weight of responsibility

all but overwhelming. He had thought to emerge from this day a war hero. Instead he would be remembered as the man who had sacrificed an entire flight wing to prevent the loss of his entire battle group . . . not exactly how he'd pictured the outcome of the day's operations.

Raptor 500, VF-84 "Liberators"
Jump Point Six, Vaku System
0827 hours (CST)

"The bastards just keep on coming," Tolwyn said. "You still with me, Venture?"

"Hanging in there, skipper," his wingman replied. *"But next time you throw a party, I'd just as soon you left me off the guest list, okay?"*

"Next time, I'm leaving the *Cats* off the guest list," Tolwyn replied, taking a shot at a Darket light fighter that swept past his bow.

They had battled their way through increasing resistance, the human fighters forming a protective screen out ahead of the battered pirate carrier as it shaped its course right into the heart of the Kilrathi task force. In a conventional fight the humans would never have been able to penetrate so close to the two Cat escort carriers, but the Kilrathi had been disorganized coming out of their jump so close to the *Bonadventure*, so they hadn't been placed to block the approach with their cruisers or destroyers. These were closing in as fast as possible, but the *Bonadventure* was going to win the race by a slim margin . . . if the Kilrathi fighters could just be held at bay.

It was costing entirely too many of the Liberators to do that job, and Tolwyn could only pray that the sacrifice was worth it. At least the Cats had concentrated on the main threat as soon as they'd perceived it, leaving both the Landreich battle group and the crippled scoutship with its escort of three Hornets alone while the fight raged around the pirate carrier.

Earlier he'd scorned the pirate ship as a clumsy improvisation. Now Tolwyn could feel a grudging respect for the ship and crew. He'd never seen a Navy ship, ConFleet or Landreicher, bear up any better under fire than *Bonadventure*. Her captain would have done ConFleet proud, under different circumstances.

The carrier held on course, aimed straight for the Kilrathi escort carrier ahead.

"Skipper! Skipper! Heads up!" Venture's voice was hoarse with adrenaline. *"Four Dralthis closing fast . . ."*

Tolwyn cursed his own inattention. He'd let himself become distracted, and the Cats had turned up the heat against the beleaguered Landreichers. He cut sharply to port just in time to avoid multiple hits from the incoming Kilrathi medium fighters, all of them swooping down on him with their energy weapons searing the midnight sky of space.

"Mongoose" Callahan in Raptor 506 wasn't so lucky. As the Dralthis flashed past Tolwyn's fighter in tight formation they maintained their fire, battering Callahan's shields.

"Get 'em off me!" Callahan shouted.

Tolwyn tried to fall in behind the enemy formation, but they were too maneuverable. His Raptor wasn't designed for tight turns or fancy maneuvers, and he was just too far out of position to be effective . . .

Broadsword 206, Guild Squadron "Raider-One"
Jump Point Six, Hellhole System
0828 hours (CST)

Winston Drake saw the four Dralthis attacking the
Landreich Raptor, and almost instinctively rolled
sideways to line up a shot on the nearest of them. It
was only after he'd squeezed the trigger to activate a
full-spectrum energy weapon bombardment that the
irony of the situation really hit him.

Less than two hours ago he'd been dogfighting with
the Landreichers, whose vast superiority in numbers
had accounted for nearly half his fellow pilots from
Bonadventure. The onslaught had been so fierce that
Captain Tanaka had hastily ordered a retreat. Otherwise
Drake himself would probably be vapor by now.

Yet with the appearance of the Cats everything had
changed. Now the humans were working together, and
that Raptor pilot out there who might have accounted
for one of Drake's buddies earlier was now an ally to
be saved.

His beam weapons burned through the rear shields
of the Dralthi and bored into her stern. A moment later
there was nothing left of her except an expanding cloud
of debris. Drake let out a whoop and started lining up
his next shot. This sure as hell beat sniping at unarmed
tenders or getting pummeled by overwhelming Landreich
forces.

The Cats realized their danger and broke in three
directions at once. Muttering curses under his breath,
Drake pulled right and increased to full power, trying
to keep the more maneuverable Dralthi in his sights.
He squeezed off several shots, but couldn't maintain a
target lock long enough to have any real effect.

Then the Kilrathi ship he was chasing burst into flame

and shards of hull plating as the pilot he'd rescued joined the party. *"Whoever you are, thanks for saving my bacon back there,"* the Raptor pilot said over the comm channel.

"Glad to help," Drake said, surprised to find he really meant it. "Check your low two. One of them's heading in!"

The Raptor turned slowly onto the new vector, and Drake's Broadsword shot past him, opening fire again. But the Dralthi's forward shields were better than those protecting the stern, and the Cat pilot made no effort to evade the incoming fire. Instead he fired back, soaking up everything Drake had to give him and countering with his own full-powered beams.

Drake gave a cold grin. The Dralthi's energy reserves didn't cycle back to full power as quickly as a Broadsword's did, and his forward shields were weaker. This Cat wanted to trade body blows? That was fine with him. "Goodbye, puss," he said, tightening his grip on the trigger on his stick.

It was only then that he spotted the second Dralthi rising from behind the first one, adding its own hellish energies to the onslaught hammering at his forward shields. He barely had time to register the fact before half-a-dozen alarms went off in his cockpit.

After that, Winston Drake knew no more.

Flag Bridge, KIS *Klarran*
Jump Point Six, Hellhole System
0829 hours (CST)

Admiral Julgar *nar* Ta'hal could feel the cold claws of the God of the Running Death closing around his throat. "Where in the name of all the Gods are the cruisers?" he demanded.

His aide had to grab on to the back of a chair to steady himself as another hit rocked the carrier. "Closing, Lord Admiral. They have already opened fire on that . . . ship. Whatever it is."

"Not enough . . . and not in time. Who would have conceived of the apes being willing to use a ship that size as a suicide vessel?" Julgar clenched one hand. "We were so close! But we cannot even carry out the original mission now. The Terrans have too big a lead. The scoutship will be out of our reach in a few more minutes, and then they will jump." He paused. "And Ragark will have my throat."

On the monitor, they could see the slow but inexorable approach of the ship that looked like a transport, carried fighters like a carrier, but acted now like a deliberate sacrifice on its way to the altar. Bow on and closing, it was plain that it intended to ram, and the Kilrathi carrier's vector was such that it would take a minor miracle to outmaneuver the humans.

As Julgar watched, the cruiser *Dravnor* hammered the Terran ship. Explosions erupted along the vessel's ventral surface, and a few of the *kils* in the flag bridge raised a victory chant. The Terran carrier was coming apart . . .

Too late.

"We have them!" Julgar's aide shouted.

"Wait," was Julgar's low-voiced reply.

Out of the expanding fireball, eights of fragments, each the size of a heavy fighter or larger, were whirling outward. Most retained enough of their original vector to remain on a collision course with the Kilrathi ship.

The chants had not died down when the first of those chunks of twisted metal slammed into the *Klarran*. The kinetic energy from the Terran ship's terminal velocity was enough to overwhelm the shields, and as each subsequent piece hit home *Klarran* shuddered again and again, as if a hand of the God of the Running Death had reached out to shake the carrier like a child's toy.

Bridge, Guild Scoutship *Highwayman*
Deep Space, Hellhole System
0833 hours (CST)

The bridge had been hulled several times, and the air was gone. Banfeld had his helmet on and his suit fully sealed, but it had taken time. He could feel the blood trickling from his ears and nose, and his throat had been burned raw by decompression. It was an effort to breathe. He suspected lung damage, but he wouldn't know for sure unless he reached a doctor.

Outside, an FRLN Hornet had latched on to the scout and taken her under tow, while two others flew escort in tight formation. Somehow the computer and the sensor imaging system were still on-line, though precious little beyond that was working on the bridge. *Highwayman's* power was nearly exhausted, her fusion plant down, her engines and weapons as useless as the failed stealth system. The internal gravitics were out, too, and bodies and wreckage floated weightless in the bridge. He spotted Jonas Hart among them, but he couldn't recognize any of the other dead from where he was.

The ship's hull was twisted and shattered in a dozen places. She would never again fare among the stars, on Guild business or any other.

Banfeld pulled himself back into his seat awkwardly, favoring an arm that was probably broken. He strapped himself down one-handed and stabbed at the controls for the sensor systems.

On the monitor, an image of the *Bonadventure* sprang into focus. Tanaka had done as he'd said, steered her right down the Kilrathi carrier's throat. As Banfeld watched she started coming apart, the pieces left from the multiple explosion ripping into the upper half of the Cat ship.

"My poor, poor Guildsmen," Banfeld croaked. "What have I brought you to?"

The emotions battling inside him proved too much, and he slipped into the black pool of unconsciousness.

Raptor 500, VF-84 "Liberators"
Jump Point Six, Hellhole System
0834 hours (CST)

"That's our cue! Break it off and head for home!" Tolwyn shouted the order as he peeled off, dodging a piece of the wreckage of the Guild ship. Behind him, the lead Kilrathi carrier was trailing atmosphere, a good chunk of her superstructure smashed by repeated hits from the remains of the *Bonadventure*. A massive repair effort would probably get her back in service in a few months, but she was of no use as a fighting ship for now.

Of course, that left a second carrier and an assortment of cruisers, destroyers, escorts, and fighters, but Tolwyn knew he had a few minutes to regroup before the Kilrathi battle lust took over and they organized their pursuit. And meantime the damage to the carrier would certainly keep a few of the Cat ships occupied.

The Liberators had done all they could. Whether or not it would prove to be enough remained to be seen.

Combat Information Center, FRLS *Independence*
Deep Space, Hellhole System
0835 hours (CST)

"The battle group has reformed around us, Captain.
And the Flight Wing has broken off the action. They're
being pursued."

Galbraith looked across at Roth, biting his lip. They
had watched the pirate carrier's last act, and knew the
Kilrathi had taken serious damage to one of their carriers.
But their task force still outnumbered the *Independence*
battle group in fighting ships, and their two carrier wings,
though they'd suffered heavily in the fight with the
Liberators, outnumbered his remaining fighters by a
wide enough margin to make them a serious threat.

And Tolwyn didn't have enough fighters yet to hold
them for long. This time, if they decided to attack the
battle group, there was nothing left to slow them down.

"Order the battle group to retire to the jump point,"
Galbraith said.

"But, Captain . . ." Roth looked stunned.

"Do it!" he snapped.

At that moment, the ship's Tactical Officer spoke up.
"Disturbance in Jump Point Two," he said. "Ship coming
through from Landreich . . . now."

Out in space, a vessel took form as it dropped out of
the hyperrealm. Galbraith was almost afraid to check
the tactical readouts. The ship's IFF beacon, hypercasting
an exclusive ID signature, registered on the monitor
almost immediately.

"That's *Arbroath*!" Commander Roth exclaimed,
reading the information from her own board.

Arbroath—previously the TCS *Saipan*, a sister ship
of *Independence* only recent acquired by one of Kruger's
purchasing agents. Galbraith remembered his father's

acid comments about Max Kruger's latest toy. She had been refitting in Landreich orbit when *Independence* had left, nearly ready for her space trials but far from prepared to go into combat. What was she doing here?

"Incoming message, sir," the Communications Officer announced.

The comm screen lit up to reveal the craggy features of Max Kruger. "*Independence, what the hell's going on out here? I came to see what you found at the pirate base, and I'm reading Cat ships on my long-range sensors. What's the situation?*"

"Mr. President," Galbraith said, leaning forward. "Mr. President, you have to withdraw immediately. Our Flight Wing's been cut up by Kilrathi fighters, and their task force outnumbers us heavily. I was preparing to withdraw to cover the capitol when you jumped in."

Kruger looked angry. "*Withdraw? What do you mean withdraw? My sensors tell me one of those two carriers is damaged. And their own fighters must have taken some losses by this time.*"

"Yes, sir, but not enough—"

"*Listen, son, if they've taken any kind of losses at all they're not likely to want to hang around now that we have two undamaged carriers and the prospect of fresh planes coming into the battle. Where's Camparelli? He'll understand what we need . . .*"

"He's dead, sir," Galbraith said. "He—"

"*Then by the power vested in me as Commander-in-Chief, blah-blah-blah, I hereby take command of this task force. Have your battle group reverse course and head for those Cats, Captain!*"

"But, sir . . . I know you don't have a full flight wing on board. You can't! Not unless you put it aboard in the last couple of days . . ."

"*Nope. Not a one.*" Kruger gave him a wolfish smile.

*"But, of course, the Cats don't know that. Now give
those orders, Captain, or I'll have you relieved of
command!"* The screen went dead, leaving Galbraith
to stare at the blank monitor.

A feeling of relief swept over him despite the desperate
situation they were sailing into. At least Kruger would
bear the responsibility for whatever happened, win or
lose.

Command Bridge, KIS *Hravik*
Jump Point Six, Hellhole System
0838 hours (CST)

"Terran reinforcements!" Captain Ghadhark *nar*
Volles snarled. "Another carrier . . . same class as the
first."

"Yes, my Lord," his Executive Officer said.

"Any sign of supporting ships for the new arrival?"

"No, my Lord. But the jump point is at the limit of
our current sensor range. More vessels may be coming
through, and we simply are not picking up the disturbance
they would generate."

Ghadhark glanced at a monitor that showed the
battered *Klarran*, with one of the destroyers drifting
alongside and a swarm of small craft closing in to try
to evacuate wounded and put over damage control
parties. The admiral had gone off hypercast soon after
the ape ship had been destroyed and the rain of
fragments had started slamming into *Klarran*, and it
was certain that the flag captain was dead. That left
Ghadhark senior officer. The next moves were his to
make.

Ahead, the Terran fighters were withdrawing in
disorder, pursued by Kilrathi squadrons who still

outnumbered them by several eights. But the human battle group was changing vector, and the computer projections now put their course as heading straight toward the task force. The second carrier seemed alone, but it could be just the first of a whole wave of reinforcements . . .

The apes had already crippled one Kilrathi ship today, and that would drive Ragark into a rage. More losses would only compound the disaster . . . and could not be laid at the admiral's door, as the damage to *Klarran* could.

And by now the apes could have received the information the scoutship had carried and spread it too far for the task force to be sure of stopping it from getting back to their capitol, Landreich. That part of the mission was a total write-off. Not that it would do the apes any good to know that Ragark had a dreadnought in orbit over Baka Kar. There was little enough they could do with that information.

At this point, the best option was to withdraw. Even with the dreadnought, Ragark would still need all the carriers he could muster for the coming campaign. The dreadnought could overpower whole fleets of smaller ape ships, but only carriers could project Imperial force against several different targets at the same time. Ragark might rage at the decision to pull back, but additional losses would be by far the worse. Not just for the Empire, but for Ghadhark's throat.

"Order the fighters to return," he said at last, knowing he had made the right decision. "And instruct the other ships to prepare for the return jump to Vordran."

Operations Planning Center, FRLS *Independence*
Near Jump Point Two, Hellhole System
1243 hours (CST)

"I'm afraid we've lost close to half our fighters," Kevin
Tolwyn said grimly. "And a lot of the planes that came
back are in a bad way. We couldn't intercept a determined
squadron of sparrows and be sure of winning the fight."

He sat beside Captain Galbraith at the big triangular
table, looking across at Max Kruger and the captain of
the *Arbroath*. A handful of other senior officers were
present as well to bring Kruger up to date on the day's
fighting.

"You did a good job, Commander," Kruger said. "It
must've been a tough call to make, joining forces with
the pirate who was probably the guy who tried to take
out your uncle. But you did the right thing. It was the
pirate carrier that turned the tide, but they wouldn't
have gotten through without your fighters for escort.
Congratulations are in order, Captain Tolwyn, for a job
well done."

It took Tolwyn a long moment before he realized he'd
just been promoted. Kruger's off-hand manner made
it seem like something of no great importance.

Commander Hiro Watanabe, *Independence*'s Chief
Engineer, stirred in his seat nearby. "If you hadn't arrived
when you did, Mr. President, I'm afraid things wouldn't
have turned out this well."

Kruger glanced at Galbraith with a look Tolwyn couldn't
quite place. Anger? Or contempt? "I wish I could say
it was all part of my grand plan," he said, flashing a
smile in Watanabe's direction. "But the fact is I wanted
a first-hand look at this pirate base, so I ordered *Arbroath*
out of spacedock for early spacing trials. She has a
skeleton crew and less than two full squadrons of planes

on board—most of those noncombatant types. Not much of a reinforcement. But of course the information that brought us here in the first place didn't say anything about us needing reinforcements, did they?"

Galbraith flushed. "The data on the pirate base was completely accurate, sir," he said stiffly. "I don't know my father's source, but it was right on the money. How could we have predicted a Cat attack? For a while there it was starting to look like our problems really were with pirates, and not Ragark's crew."

"Well, today puts that notion right out the airlock, doesn't it, Captain?" Kruger shrugged. "These pirates have been a complicating factor, I'll admit, but we've had plenty of proof of Cat activity for a long time. This gives us more. Maybe after today that fat-assed bastard Williams will listen to us. You have gun camera footage, Captain Tolwyn?"

He nodded. "Plenty of it, Mr. President. But I really doubt there's much point in taking it to Williams. You know he'll just accuse us of faking it, like he did last time."

"Suppose you leave the politics to me, son," Kruger said. "Since that's about all I'm allowed to do any more." He paused. "What about Banfeld?"

Commander Roth answered him. "The scoutship wasn't worth keeping even for spare parts, but about half her crew survived. Including Mr. Banfeld. He's in Sick Bay now undergoing treatment for decompression sickness. The Doc thinks he'll be able to start singing in a day or two."

"Zachary Banfeld," Kruger mused. "You know, I helped set him up with his Guild, way back in the beginning. Sounded like a damned good idea, letting the merchants provide their own protection. I didn't even mind it much when he branched out into mercenary and privateering work. It was all directed against the Cats anyway. But now . . . damn it all, he could have been part of the team even yet. Instead, he turned on us. I'm getting heartily sick of having the people I've trusted turn on me." He looked at Galbraith. "Next time you see your father, Captain, you tell him from me that his political party's done more to undermine our chances of stopping Ragark and his crew than the pirates or even the Cats themselves!"

"Sir?" Galbraith made a show of looking innocent. Tolwyn didn't believe it.

"Yesterday he revealed the details of the entire Goliath project to a closed session of the Council," Kruger said. "His same unimpeachable sources at work, no doubt. At least he didn't bring it up in front of the holo-cameras. If it went public, the Cats would know about it and any hope we had left of surprising them would be over. But he's done well enough without letting the public get hold of it, damn him."

"What is it, Mr. President?" Tolwyn asked. "What's going on?"

"I'm accused of wasting Landreich resources and funds on a hopeless project, and it looks as if he's finally going to get that vote of no confidence he's been wanting for all this time. Before the month is out, odds are I'll be out of office." Kruger gave Tolwyn a wan smile. "You got any place for an aging navy man in your flight wing, son? I might be needing a job pretty soon."

The words were bantering, but behind the old man's eyes Tolwyn could see the pain of a man who was watching his whole life's work crumbling around him.

Audience Hall, Brajakh Kar
Baka Kar, Baka Kar System
1228 hours (CST), 2671.024

The body of Ghadhark *nar* Volles lay sprawled on
the rug in front of the raised dais that held the Governor's
throne. Ukar *dai* Ragark looked down from his seat
with a sneer.

"The rewards for *interpreting* orders without winning
a victory," he announced, nodding to the bodyguard
who had plunged his knife into the captain's back on
Ragark's signal. "Have the prey removed. We will clean
the carpeting later."

"Yes, my Lord," the guard responded, signing for two
of his men to help him with the corpse. They gathered
up the body and backed away hastily, as if thankful to
be out of Ragark's reach for the moment.

He bared his fangs. It was a good idea to be afraid
of Ukar *dai* Ragark today. The news of the damage to
the *Klarran* and the failure of the pursuit mission had
left him ready to lash out at anyone, everyone, who
had the misfortune to attract his ire. The crowd of
nobles, officers and ministers packed into the Audience
Hall, stirred restlessly under his glare.

Ragark wished he could vent some of his rage on the
unfortunate Ghraffid *nar* Dhores, but the Economics
Minister had expired while being questioned regarding
his smuggling contacts with the humans. The interrogator
assigned to the case was also dead, for allowing his
subject too easy a death.

He beckoned to Dawx Jhorrad. "Well, Captain, it
seems we have lost the advantage of surprise," he said,
forcing himself to quell the rage and speak coolly. "The
Terrans must surely know about *Vorghath* by now."

"Does that matter, my Lord?" the commoner asked,

his face hard to read behind the metal-and-plastic prosthetic mask that obscured half his face. "What, exactly, can the apes do about a dreadnought? Even before he reached your docks, he could have fought their entire Landreich fleet to a standstill. Give us another three eight-days to complete resupply and refitting, and *Vorghath* will defeat anything they send against him. Nothing will stop you from orbiting Landreich and forcing their capitulation."

"True enough, I suppose," Ragark admitted. "Still . . . the apes are dangerous. Inventive. I think we must do something to distract their attention from *Vorghath* for the time being. Bring pressure to bear on them so they don't entertain any thoughts of attacking the dreadnought while he remains in dry-dock."

"They couldn't get past the jump point garrison!" That was Akhjer *nar* Val. If that skeptic was now so confident, perhaps Ragark's cause really was prospering despite the setbacks they had suffered. "How could Terran ships even get into position to threaten the orbital dock, or *Vorghath*?"

Ragark looked at him. "How did the Terrans destroy Kilrah, with the whole fleet preparing there? How did they get within two light minutes of the orbital dock? Cloaked ships could penetrate our defenses."

"They have no cloaked ships larger than scouts," someone protested. "Certainly no capital ships that could evade detection."

"None that we know of," Ragark corrected. "And the Temblor Bomb was delivered by a mere fighter. No, we must not take chances. We know the strength of Kruger's fleet. We must send a strong enough raiding force against a key world, one that will guarantee that they will have to commit their full force to defending against us. In the meantime, we maintain a strong garrison here . . . just to be sure. If we stalk the prey correctly, they will never have a chance to strike at *Vorghath* before he is ready to sail again. And once we reach that point, the two strike fleets can converge on Landreich and end this farce once and for all."

"It sounds like an excellent plan, my Lord," Jhorrad said. His good eye was shining with anticipation. "When will the strike force depart?"

"We will take time to put the operation together," Ragark replied. "And to guard the system here in case Kruger attempts an immediate sortie, though I think that is unlikely. Say two eight-days to assemble our forces. After that . . . we strike!"

"I wish I was coming with you, my Lord," Jhorrad told him.

"Your part will come soon enough," Ragark assured him. "And your name will be remembered long after high-born fools like Thrakhath and that scum Ghadhark have been forgotten."

• CHAPTER 17

> *"The true leader offers his Warriors in sacrifice only when there is no alternative; the true Warrior offers himself in sacrifice in the knowledge that only thus will the battle be won."*
>
> from the Seventh Codex
> 12:16:07

Shuttle *Mjollnir Echo*
Orbiting Nargrast, Vaku System
1622 hours (CST), 2671.033

The Kilrathi-made shuttle hung in space, dwarfed alongside the bulk of the carrier now called *Mjollnir*. From the cockpit, Lieutenant Aengus Harper and his Wing Commander, Captain Bondarevsky, studied the repairs to the outside of the port side flight deck, recording everything on video and computer-imaged still pictures. It was painstaking work, but an essential part of the refit, making sure there were no obvious weak spots in the refurbished hull. So Bondarevsky had assured Harper several times now, though Harper suspected his commanding officer was growing as weary of this "essential duty" as he was. Still, as the wing commander had pointed out earlier, it was better to invest the time and effort now that to discover they'd overlooked something crucial when an unlucky hit opened up the hull in the middle of a battle.

Harper quite frankly couldn't see any spot that *didn't* look weak. The hurry-up repair job on the port side flight deck had definitely stressed speed over all else, and the haste showed in rough patches and crude welding jobs. He hoped the computer's structural analysis would belie the look of the work, and yield results within acceptable limits.

"Section one-twenty-five," Bondarevsky said, sounding tired. He pressed a button on the co-pilot's console. "Recorded. That's the last of them, Lieutenant."

"Thank God and all the Saints for that, sir," Harper said with a grin. "Shall I be taking her back to the barn, then?"

"Take the scenic route," Bondarevsky said. "I want to get a better look at the old girl . . . a wider view, something with fewer rivets and weld marks."

"Aye, sir, that would be a big improvement." His hands danced over the shuttle controls. "Do you think the work will pass the inspection?"

Bondarevsky let out a sigh. "God, I hope so." He paused. "Yeah, I'm pretty sure it will. At least it'll do for routine ops for a while, until we have time to do a better job on her. Richards told me this morning that it's likely we'll still be overhauling her six months from now . . . unless Ragark tries something sooner."

"Six more months of this, sir?" Harper made a face. "I think I'd rather have Ragark charging across the border with guns blazing."

"Be careful what you wish for," Bondarevsky told him. "Fact is, we need all the refit time we can get. I never thought we'd get this far, Aengus, but we still have a long way to go before this old lady can stand toe-to-toe with hostiles in a real fight."

As the shuttle lifted slowly away from the carrier's battle-scarred hull, Harper remained silent, mulling over the wing commander's words. After a truly Herculean effort by the entire crew, *Mjollnir* was more or less operational. She had powered up her maneuvering drives a few days earlier and lifted clear of her long elliptical orbit around the brown dwarf, exchanging it for a high planetary orbit over Nargrast. The rest of the battle group occupied various similar orbits, spread out now to cover possible approach vectors and give the carrier warning in case of further unfriendly visits to the system. Both flight decks and all of the remaining planes were available now, and Bondarevsky had been holding daily training exercises in simulators and out in space to familiarize the pilots assigned to the Kilrathi squadrons with their planes, and to get the entire Black Cats wing used to working together.

That had meant more than just exercising the fighter squadrons, too. The support craft—electronic warfare birds, resupply boats, command and control planes—had all been put through their paces. In some respects the Kilrathi had a superior system to the Confederation and Landreich navies, using such auxiliary craft very effectively in conjunction with fighters and bombers. Bondarevsky had decided early on to adapt the same techniques to the ex-Kilrathi carrier's operations, to bridge a gap in technologies that reflected the difference in doctrine. The supercarrier itself had fewer onboard systems adapted to the roles filled by those special planes, and Bondarevsky had quickly decided it was easier to get used to operating like Kilrathi pilots rather than attempting to upgrade the onboard support systems to carry out these same tasks. So fighters and bombers were often re-armed and refueled on the fly instead of coming back aboard for servicing, and lightly armed recon planes performed the scouting duties of a human light fighter squadron. The Primary Flight Control center aboard the carrier extended its reach by handing off coordination duties to the Command/Control birds.

It all took a lot of getting used to, and Harper had heard plenty of grumbling and cursing from the rest of the wing. But slowly they were getting accustomed to Bondarevsky's demands, and starting to show pride in their roles.

Harper wondered about the Admiral's estimate of needing another six months to finish the refit. Graham was still working on the jump generators, the last major ship's system that hadn't been tested under field conditions. But there were fewer problems there than the engineering crew had first feared, and the work was going quickly. After the jump drive was pronounced ready, *Mjollnir* would probably be as ready as she ever would be. There would be plenty of minor things to take care of, to make the ship more efficient and more comfortable, but already she had engines, sensors, guns, and a working flight deck. That, to Harper's way of thinking, qualified her as a fighting ship.

They had pulled far enough away by now to be able to view the entire carrier. From this distance the individual damage didn't show much, except for the scar on her superstructure where the original Maneuvering Bridge had been patched without being restored. The unearthly lines of the Kilrathi-built supercarrier never failed to make Harper just the least bit uneasy. There was something about a Kilrathi ship that summoned up an instinctive desire to fight or flee. Even the giant supercarrier was all knife-blades and sharp angles, a deadly sword to be wielded in battle.

"Very nice, Mr. Harper," Bondarevsky commented. "From out here you can almost picture her as a warship, and not a collection of repairs waiting to fall apart."

Harper frowned. Of late Bondarevsky had been sounding more pessimistic about the whole refit project. He worked hard, driving himself even more unrelentingly than he drove his subordinates, but he had been badly shaken by the encounter with the pirates. Sometimes it seemed as if he blamed himself for the loss of *Sindri*, and was frustrated by the continual problems that cropped up to remind them all of how big a job the refit process really was.

"Beggin' your pardon, sir," Harper said quietly. "I know 'tis not my place to say so, but I think you should lay off the cracks about the ship."

Bondarevsky looked at him with a puzzled frown. "What's that supposed to mean, Lieutenant?" he asked.

"A lot of the crew has started to take some real pride in *Mjollnir*, sir. She may look like hell and be held together by spit and good intentions, but she's *ours*. Like the Landreich itself. We're no Terran Confederation out here on the frontier. We can't afford the best ships or the best crews, so we make do with what we have. And we're proud when we can achieve something good by the sweat of our brows and the skill of our hands. 'Tis bad for morale to hear *Mjollnir* being put down as second rate, sir."

Bondarevsky shook his head, then smiled suddenly. "Sometimes, Mr. Harper, you really do make me think," he said. "Okay, you win. From here on out she's the best ship in the fleet, bar none." He paused. "But I hope you won't mind if I try not to sneeze too hard. I'm still afraid of what might happen."

Harper grinned. "Aye, the Cats could take us out of action for good with one strong dose of the flu."

"Take us home, Lieutenant," Bondarevsky ordered. "Before you have me convinced that old lady is actually as good as you seem to think she is."

The return to the port side flight deck took longer than they had planned, thanks to an unexpected new arrival. A courier shuttle, light, fast, and fitted with jump drives, had arrived while they were conducting their survey, and was on final approach when Harper contacted Boss Marchand for landing clearance. They held clear of the flight deck until Marchand came on the line to let them know it was safe.

The shuttle settled onto the deck just aft of the courier. As Harper and Bondarevsky exited, the hatch on the top of the courier opened up and a suited figure clambered down the ladder on the port side. When he undogged his helmet and lifted it clear of his head, Harper saw the new arrival was Kevin Tolwyn.

Bondarevsky advanced, hand extended. "Kevin! What are you doing here? And why the flying coffin?" Courier shuttles were notoriously cramped and uncomfortable, with just enough room for a pilot—and a passenger if they were very friendly—with a cockpit and a tiny cabin mounted in front of nothing but fuel tanks and engines.

Taking the proffered hand, Tolwyn shrugged. "Old Max sent me. I'm his new fair-haired boy these days, and he wanted me to bring you guys the latest news."

Bondarevsky stepped back. "Captain's bars, is it? You're not bucking for my job again, are you?"

"Not me," Tolwyn told him. "We had a little dust-up with some Cats a few days back, and Max thought I had earned a promotion. He even gave me a case of beer after we got back to Landreich!" The younger man paused. "Look, Jason, I've got dispatches and orders for Admiral Richards. We've got troubles, and I'm afraid *Karga* is in for a rough time."

"She's *Mjollnir*, now," Bondarevsky said absently. "What kind of troubles, and how rough a time?"

Tolwyn dropped his voice, but Harper could still hear. "The Cats have a dreadnought," he said. "Under repair at Baka Kar. And our intell says they're getting ready to sortie against Ilios with a carrier task force."

"A dreadnought?" Bondarevsky's face went pale. "If that thing comes calling, we might as well just start the evacuation now . . ."

"There's more," Tolwyn said. "A lot more. But the big thing is your orders. Kruger wants you guys to take the carrier in and try to kill the dreadnought. And soon."

Bondarevsky's bionic hand clenched into a fist, then went into the worst set of spasms Harper had seen in weeks. "God *damn* it!" he said sharply. After a long moment he regained control of the appendage, but his scowl was black. He lowered his voice. "Is he crazy? This heap of junk is supposed to take on a dreadnought?"

Tolwyn nodded. "I'm afraid so. I have the orders here. Too sensitive to hypercast." He looked Bondarevsky in the eye. "I have to report to Admiral Richards. But I think you'd better come too . . . and my uncle. You'll all need to hear this."

Bondarevsky looked back over his shoulder at Harper. "Finish the post-flight, Lieutenant," he said. It was almost a growl. "I'll be with the Admiral."

He and Tolwyn walked off before Harper had a chance to respond. The lieutenant watched them, trying not to betray his whirling emotions. A little while ago he'd been hoping for action. Now, it seemed, they would get it. But from the sound of it, *Mjollnir's* first real combat op was likely to be her last as well.

Flag Officer's Ready Room, FRLS *Mjollnir*
Orbiting Nargrast, Vaku System
1715 hours (CST)

The holo-image showed a man in a sick bay bed, breathing with considerable difficulty and speaking in a ragged, throaty voice. Zachary Banfeld didn't look much like a ruthless pilot, Bondarevsky thought. More like the frightened survivor of a disaster.

Apparently that's just what he was.

"Will you repeat that last statement, please?" The voice off-camera belonged to Max Kruger. "*How* big was this ship?"

"Best estimate was twenty-two kilometers long," Banfeld said. "Mass was right off the scale. It was huge, Kruger! Huge! And it must have had thirty heavy energy batteries. Turrets everywhere!"

"A dreadnought." It was strange to have Kevin Tolwyn's voice interjecting the comment on the recording, while he sat beside Bondarevsky and stared down at the table in silence.

"That's enough," Admiral Richards said, shutting off the recording and bringing the lights back up. He looked around the ready room. Aside from Bondarevsky and Kevin, Admiral Tolwyn was the only other one present. Richards had even dismissed Lieutenant Cartwright, his flag lieutenant. "It must be the *Vorghath*. We kept hearing rumors of a dreadnought that had escaped from the destruction of Kilrah, but nobody could track down anything solid. Her captain refused to acknowledge Melek as Thrakhath's successor, apparently, and he set off in search of someone he could sign on with."

"Ragark," Admiral Tolwyn said.

"Ragark," Richards echoed. "With that thing in his

arsenal, there'll be no stopping him. Not in the Landreich, and not in the Confederation. I suppose if we assembled most of ConFleet in one place we could fight *Vorghath* to a standstill, but the rest of Ragark's fleet will be able to do pretty much as he damn well pleases in the meantime."

"The President thinks the same," Kevin said. "He says the only way to stop it is to hit it while it's still at spacedock."

"We don't even know how long that will be," his uncle said gloomily.

"Banfeld said that it looked pretty badly beat up. His estimate was for several weeks of repairs." The younger Tolwyn looked away. "But there wasn't any reliable data left in the scoutship's computers to back up what he said. Hell, the whole story could be a fake. But I doubt it. He sounded sincere to me. And frightened. After all, if that monster sorties, it's the end of the Guild as well as the Landreich."

"Even if the estimate he made was accurate, it could still have enough firepower to swat the whole Landreich fleet," Richards said. "There's no way of telling what we're up against, and damned little chance of getting any additional intelligence."

"President Kruger went so far as to approach Clark Williams again," Kevin said. "He went armed with our footage of the battle, and Banfeld's recorded statement. He figured the ConFleet was about the only hope left to take the dreadnought out while it was still relatively defenseless."

"And no doubt he got thrown out on his ear," the elder Tolwyn growled. "It was stupid to waste the time."

"That's about the size of it," his nephew agreed. "Williams accused us of faking the data and the statement both. Said Banfeld was a pirate and a renegade who just wanted to embroil the frontier in a major war, and that was that. ConFleet won't help."

"So instead he expects us to take a hand?" Richards sounded as incredulous as Bondarevsky had been ... and almost as angry. "We've done wonders, but we're not combat-ready. Even with the whole damned Landreich fleet backing us up, Ragark would have us for breakfast before we got anywhere near Baka Kar."

Kevin Tolwyn flushed. "That's the problem, Admiral. The Landreich fleet can't attack Baka Kar. We've intercepted coded hypercast signals from Ragark's fleet calling in additional units for a strike on Ilios. We can't ignore it. If the fleet isn't there to meet them, they could smash the colony and then go straight to Landreich. That would beat us just as surely as having the dreadnought sortie."

Richards frowned. "If that signal was intercepted, it was because Ragark wanted us to hear it," he said. "He's too good to entrust that much detail to a code unless he knows for sure we can't break it. In fact, odds are he'd've sent it by courier if he didn't want us to pick it up."

"That tells us he wants Kruger on the horns of this exact dilemma," Admiral Tolwyn said thoughtfully. "Which implies that he's worried about an attack before the dreadnought's ready. Don't you think so, Vance?"

Richards frowned. "I suppose so. He'll know Kruger's reputation. Old Max is just crazy enough to launch an all-out attack to try to cripple the dreadnought. Therefore, threaten a target Max can't ignore. He doesn't have the forces to do both ..."

"And *Vorghath* escapes attack until her refit is finished," the elder Tolwyn finished. "It's elegant, you have to give the Cat bastard that much."

"*Karga ... Mjollnir* is the President's ace in the hole,"

Kevin said. "He figures the fleet can give a good account of itself at Ilios. Without you, or your battle group."

"We'd never get past the jump point," Richards said. "You can bet he'll have more than just *Vorghath* guarding his capitol. So we'd have to slog our way through all their defenses . . . and by the time we did reach the orbital dock, *if* we reached it, we'd be badly damaged and they'd be fully on the alert. Same thing with a fighter sortie, for that matter, eh, Jason?"

"Yeah . . ." Bondarevsky trailed off as an idea struck him. "Admiral, there's one way we might get in close enough to take them by surprise."

"Not your Strakhas," Richards said, holding up a hand. "I know Blair managed to get in close enough to launch the T-Bomb in a cloaked Excalibur fighter, but he lost pretty near his whole damned squadron getting there. And we don't have a bomb big enough to do more that scratch the hull of a dreadnought."

"No, sir," Bondarevsky agreed with a nod of his head. "No, we can't hit them with one squadron of fighters. But we could get *Mjollnir* close enough to do the trick . . ."

Admiral Tolwyn slapped the table with one hand. "By God, Jason, you're right! We're the one ship in human space that could pull it off!"

Richards looked from one to the other. "You want to impersonate a Kilrathi ship . . . ?"

"Exactly," the other admiral replied. "Look, we're in a Cat carrier with heavy damage. They're used to Cats coming in and joining up . . . *Vorghath's* not the only new recruit to sign on with Ragark's fleet, after all. So we sail past their pickets and ask ever so nicely for a berth at the spacedock to get some much-needed repairs."

"Lord knows that's believable enough," Bondarevsky

commented wryly. He was thinking of his conversation with Harper back in the shuttle. Their very weakness could sell their story to the Kilrathi.

"We could even use the rest of the battle group for verisimilitude," Tolwyn went on, an excited light dawning in his eyes. "They play the part of human ships in hot pursuit. So there's a fight near the jump point, all right, that draws other Cat patrols away from Baka Kar. That lets us get in nice and close without being engaged. Then . . . we strike. We may not have as many weapons as they do, but I dare say Mr. Deniken could cause some damage with his guns. And we sortie the whole flight wing, for cover, and to add to the attack."

"Our Kilrathi fighters will work to our advantage there, too," Bondarevsky added. "Especially the Strakhas. The Black Cats will tie their defenses in knots."

Richards raised a hand. "The enthusiasm is commendable, gentlemen," he said. "But there's plenty you haven't covered. Such as how we pass ourselves off as Cats . . ."

"Computer simulacrums," Tolwyn interjected. "With a claim of comm damage, they'll be convincing enough."

"*And* there's the matter of codes and ciphers," Richards went on as if his fellow admiral hadn't spoken. "They're no doubt buried in the material we extracted from the computer during the refit, but we'd have to do a lot of digging . . . and they still might not be enough." He paused. "And the big one, people. Good as your plan sounds, it's almost certainly a one-way mission. *Mjollnir* might get off a few good hits, might even damage the dreadnought and the spacedock thoroughly enough to remove the threat, but with the whole system stirred up against us I seriously doubt our ability to get out of there again."

Admiral Tolwyn fixed him with a fiery eye. "Vance . . . this is the big one. What we put this ship back into operation for in the first place. Look—thanks to the conspirators back home Ragark's had a free hand to move against the Landreich. No doubt they figured he'd win a handy victory, but then when ConFleet mobilized at last they could contain him. Go in with T-Bombs or whatever it took and neutralize his little empire. But they screwed up, Vance. None of them could have been expecting a dreadnought. Ragark will roll right over the Landreich and just keep on going, as far as he wants. Remember the Battle of Earth? All those cities going up in flames? If the *Vorghath* orbits and turns her guns on Earth, there won't be anything left. Ragark will do what Thrakhath always wanted . . . blast Mankind back into the Stone Age on every planet we've settled, and keep a few survivors around for sport or slaves." He leaned forward in his chair. "Jason's scheme is the one chance we have of getting in there and neutralizing that monster before it gets loose and brings down everything. If it means we don't come back . . . well, all of us have been there before."

Richards looked at Bondarevsky. "I imagine you agree with him, Jason," he said quietly.

"Yes, sir," Bondarevsky replied. "I don't see how we can ignore the threat. And I don't see any other way to deal with it."

Kevin Tolwyn spoke up again. "Whatever you do, you'll have to do it fast," he said. "That's the rest of the bad news. Somehow the Council's gotten hold of details of the refit here. Some of the political types are demanding the whole Goliath Project be called off right away. They'll strip away the battle group, order the carrier scrapped, and relieve or reassign the whole crew. And probably stage a vote of no confidence that'll kick Kruger right out of office."

"With a dreadnought staring down their throats?" Richards demanded.

"The President hasn't shared that particular bit of intelligence, sir," Captain Tolwyn replied. "He says it would only cause needless panic, under the circumstances."

"That's Old Max, all right," Richards said grimly. "Willing to scuttle everything he's done just to stand on a principle. How long?"

"The vote will be in a few days. It depends on whether the President can manage to stall them with parliamentary tactics."

"I doubt that Max Kruger would know a parliamentary tactic if it pulled a laser pistol on him," Richards said. "So we have to get moving before somebody notices what we're up to, is that it?"

"Yes, sir," the younger Tolwyn said.

"I hope all of you know just how little I like this," the battle group commander told them. "Okay. We're out of options and out of maneuvering room. I'll draft the orders to get underway as soon as we can take care of all the noncombatant ships and personnel."

"We could escort them as far as Oecumene," Admiral Tolwyn suggested. "There's a small fleet detachment there that could look after the *Carnegie* and the *City of Cashel*. That way we wouldn't have to detach any of our combat ships for escort duty."

"Good thought, Geoff," Richards said. "God . . . there's a thousand things to do, and no time to do them." He looked at the younger Tolwyn. "I imagine you'll want to get back to Landreich before *Independence* spaces."

"Yes, sir." Kevin paused. "I'd rather go with you, but I have my own Flight Wing to consider. They're drafting every spare plane that can fly to rebuild from the losses we suffered at Hellhole. And we're competing with *Arbroath*, too, for birds and pilots. I have to be there."

"You always did know where your duty was, Kevin," Bondarevsky said, rising as the younger man did and taking his hand. "We've had to say good-bye a good many times not knowing if one or both of us was going to buy the farm out there. This time . . . well, who knows. Take care of yourself."

"You, too, Jason," he replied. He turned and gave Richards a salute. "Sir, I don't think luck's of much use where you're headed, but good luck to you anyway."

Richards shook his hand. "And to you. Watch that ass Galbraith."

Kevin's uncle stepped up to him last of all. "I brought you out here because I was afraid for your safety back on Earth," he said. "Now both of us are back in the front lines again. I'm sorry, Kevin."

"Don't be, sir," the younger man said. "This is the job I chose. And you know I'm pretty damned hard to get rid of. Just make sure you're as hard to kill off, when you hit Baka Kar."

The admiral looked old as he faced his nephew. "You've done the family proud, Kevin. Always remember that." Then, after the briefest of embraces, he stepped back. "Now get back on that courier and go tell Max Kruger we'll make his suicide run for him. But if I get back from Baka Kar alive I expect to see every can of beer on Landreich waiting for me!"

Kevin saluted again and left. As the door slid shut behind him, Richards spoke again. "All right, gentlemen, it looks as if we have some planning to do. Let's break it down into a few main headings. There's the jump drive . . ."

Flight Deck, FRLS *Mjollnir*
Near Jump Point One, Oecumene System
1315 hours (CST), 2371.036

"What do you mean, I don't have a spot? For God's sake, woman, I'm a civilian! And I'm not riding this tub into a war zone!"

Bondarevsky strode purposefully across the open flight deck toward the source of the shouts and abusive language. As he'd expected, he discovered Armando Diaz at the center of it all, engaged in a heated argument with Sparks. The woman looked uncomfortable, standing by the ramp up to the shuttle with a computer clipboard in her hand and a harried expression on her face. Sparks was used to dealing with small craft repairs and resupply, where her charges didn't talk back or make demands. But Bondarevsky had press-ganged her into this detail because every department on the ship was so short-handed.

"What's the problem here, Lieutenant?" he said loudly as he strode up behind Diaz.

The salvage expert turned. "The problem, Bondarevsky, is that I haven't been given a seat of any of the outgoing shuttles. This *is* the final evacuation flight to the *City of Cashel*, is it not?"

He nodded. "It is, Major," he said, slightly emphasizing the courtesy rank to remind Diaz of his status. "I'm afraid there must have been a mistake made somewhere—"

"There certainly has been!" Diaz interjected.

"A breakdown in communications," Bondarevsky went on. "Apparently you weren't informed that the Admiral had requested you to stay on with the other computer experts from your team."

"What? I'll do no such thing! I'm—"

"You're a major in the Landreich Armed Forces, sir,

and thus under military discipline. And your services as a computer expert are very much in need right now. We have a great deal of information to extract from the Kilrathi computer records, and only a limited number of people to take care of the problem."

"Now see here, Bondarevsky—"

"That's Captain Bondarevsky, Major," he said quietly. "Look, I'm not happy about the situation either. But you answer to Admiral Richards. You have a complaint, you take it to him. In the meantime, get off my flight deck and stop holding up people who have a legitimate reason for leaving the ship. Or shall I ask Colonel Bhaktadil to have some of his marines escort you to your quarters? Or to see the admiral?"

Diaz opened his mouth, then caught the look in Bondarevsky's eyes and closed it again. He turned and stalked away without another word.

"Thanks, skipper," Sparks said. "I'm afraid I didn't handle him very well."

"Don't worry about it," he told her. "Lieutenant Cartwright was supposed to handle it, but he got sidetracked by half-a-dozen other jobs. Not that Richards is likely to forgive him any time soon."

"I've seen a lot of confusion in my day, skipper, but I think this takes the prize."

"Yeah. How's it going otherwise?"

"This is the last batch," she told him. "The only other problem . . . well, I'm not even sure it *is* a problem, sir. But most of the Cats didn't show up for their shuttle. What should I do about it?"

He smiled faintly. "This time I'm the one to blame for not keeping you informed, Sparks," he admitted. "I just got out of a meeting with Murragh and the Admiral. Most of the Cats want to stay with us."

"That's crazy," she said flatly.

"That's what I said. But Murragh convinced the Admiral it's the best hope we have of getting past Ragark's pickets. And I'm afraid he might be right."

He didn't tell her about the fierce argument that had raged in the Admiral's ready room for the better part of two hours. Murragh had been given instructions to transfer with all of his people across to the *City of Cashel* along with the rest of the noncombatants on board— excepting the handful who, like Diaz, were needed to help them prepare for the raid on Baka Kar. But the Kilrathi prince had managed to learn the reason for the transfer order, and he had appealed directly to Richards for permission to stay on board.

"My cadre still know the systems better than most of your men, Admiral," he had said. "And it might be a very good idea to have a few genuine *kili* on board in case your simulacrums are not effective." His shrug had been thoroughly human, as eloquent as a Frenchman's might have been. "You cannot tell, can you? What you might encounter? I would say it was a bad time to throw away your assets."

"It isn't your fight, Murragh," Richards had told him coldly. "And anyway, we're talking about a suicide mission. This is no place to risk the rightful prince of the Empire. Not when it is likely we'll be destroyed out there."

"Unless you think you can persuade your people not to fight?" That had been Tolwyn, who had been summoned to the meeting in haste once Richards and Bondarevsky had learned what the Kilrathi prince wanted.

"That, I fear, is unlikely," Murragh said. "I am the legitimate heir to the throne, closest survivor to the old Emperor's bloodline. But that is *all* I am. *Hraijhak* . . . the closest equivalent I have seen in any of your books was in something Graham lent me, a book on Celtic history. I am . . . *tanist*, the most likely heir. But until I have been seated upon the Imperial Throne and received the fealty of the major clan leaders, I have no authority. And if it really is Dawx Jhorrad who commands *Vorghath*, you can be sure that he, at least, will not renounce whatever oath he has sworn to Ragark simply because I may have the better claim. Especially as Ragark is quite evidently a powerful warlord now while I . . . have but a small following."

"All the more reason to keep you out of harm's way, then," Richards had said.

"No, Admiral, it is quite otherwise. If I am ever to claim my place in the Empire, I must first prove myself against Ragark and the other would-be usurpers. As I have no following of my own, I must find my allies where I can. My people respect warriors who will go into battle against their enemies, Admiral. Let me go into this one with you. I promise that my people will be able to assist you."

Richards had yielded at last, grumbling, just as he had when the original orders had come from Kruger. So Murragh and nearly a hundred Kilrathi would be on board as part of the crew when the *Mjollnir* went into action. Only those whose commitment to the Prince's cause was doubtful were being shuttled across to the transport as the battle group prepared to leave Oecumene.

At least the jump engines had worked. That had been the last remaining worry as they broke orbit and began the voyage outward from Vaku. Once again Graham had proven his worth as Chief Engineer. *Mjollnir* was ready for action . . . or at least as ready as she ever would be.

Watching the confusion on the flight deck as the last of the nonessential personnel made ready to leave, Bondarevsky could only hope they were ready enough.

Carrier Space Traffic Control Center,
FRLS *Independence*
Orbiting Landreich, Landreich System
1515 hours (CST)

The communications monitor in one corner of CSTCC
had been tuned to a commercial news and information
holo-vid channel broadcast from the capitol. Almost
everyone in the compartment, from Kevin Tolwyn down
to the junior spacer assigned to sweep up and keep
coffee cups filled, spent at least as much time watching
that monitor as they did doing their real jobs.

"What do you think, Tolwyn?" the Space Officer,
Howard Reed, asked around a mugful of coffee. "Will
Old Max pull it off? You're his new fair-haired boy, after
all."

"I don't know, Boss," Tolwyn replied, shaking his head.
"I just don't know if he can manage another miracle
this time."

On the monitor, they could see the Council of
Delegates waiting in the Council Hall. There was a
restive air about them, and the commentator was filling
time with a lengthy explanation of the procedures for
a vote of no confidence under Landreich's constitution.

Tolwyn had barely returned from Vaku when the
announcement had gone out. Galbraith's faction had
moved to call a fresh session of the Council, and foremost
on the agenda was a move to censure Kruger for his
reckless handling of defense funds. That could only
mean that Galbraith had decided to reveal the details
he had somehow learned of the Goliath Project, which
meant that the secret of the *Mjollnir* would soon come
out for all to hear . . . including the Kilrathi.

Knowing that Richards and the others had been
discussing a plan involving pretending to be a Kilrathi

carrier, Tolwyn was worried. So far the newsmen were still in the dark, since Galbraith clearly wanted to reveal the Goliath Project in the most dramatic fashion possible. But once this session got under way, there would be no stopping the truth from coming out.

And *Mjollnir* would end up sailing right into disaster, unless they heard the news and turned back. Tolwyn doubted they'd have a chance. By his calculations, based on the schedule he'd received in last contact between the carrier and his courier shuttle heading for home, they would just be getting ready to make the hyperjump from Oecumene to Hellhole, and then on to Baka Kar. Tolwyn doubted they'd be watching LN&IC news, and it was unlikely that anything would be going out on official channels. Not unless Kruger decided to call them off now that he knew he wouldn't escape his political enemies . . . and that didn't sound one bit like Old Max.

So *Mjollnir* was heading straight into trouble, and the Landreich fleet had been held back by a direct Presidential order on the eve of spacing for Ilios. The entire strategy was coming apart, and all because Max Kruger's government was falling apart around them.

No one knew why the President had held back the fleet. Some thought he might try to use it to stage a coup of sorts and retake his own government, but with Galbraith the senior captain it seemed unlikely he'd get much support for such a move. Whatever game he was playing, it involved holding his cards close. He hadn't even made it on time to the Council session. Hence the restless Delegates and the chattering news commentators.

"Shuttle coming in from planetside, Boss," one of the technicians announced. "From the Navy Compound at Lutz Mannheim. All IFF codes approved."

"Clear them," Boss Reed ordered, setting down his

coffee. "Must be that last load of maintenance stores Watanabe was complaining about."

The shuttle came in faster than Tolwyn liked, flaring out to stoop low over the flight deck and come in for a slap-dash landing. The duty LSO winced and scrawled some comments on his computer board, the frown on his face and the way he underlined some of the words with an angry flourish making it clear to Tolwyn that he planned to dress down that pilot thoroughly later . . . if there was anything left after Boss Reed got through with him.

Through the transplast window overlooking the flight deck, Tolwyn could see technicians swarming in to secure the craft, but everything stopped when the hatch opened and the ramp unfolded down to the deck.

Standing there at the top of the ramp, dressed in a flight suit and holding a pressure helmet under one arm, was President Max Kruger.

Tolwyn left the CSTCC at a dead run.

It took only a minute or so to reach the flight deck, and Kruger had just stepped clear of the ramp. His craggy face broke into a smile as he caught sight of Tolwyn rushing breathless across the wide expanse of the deck. "Ah, Captain, I'm glad you were on duty," he said genially. "Is the flight deck security monitor recording?"

Taken aback, Tolwyn could only give a quick nod.

"Good," Kruger said. He pulled out a folded paper from inside his flight suit, checked his wrist computer briefly, and opened the paper up. "It is now fifteen nineteen hours Confederation Standard Time," he said. He started to read, the words so fast he was almost gabbling them in his haste. "To Maximillian Kruger, Commander-in-Chief, armed forces of the Free Republic of the Landreich, Sir: You are hereby requested and required to take up the charge and command of Admiral, Task Force Ilios, with your flag in the FRLS *Independence* or such other vessel as you shall see fit to choose, and with said Task Force proceed on operations out-system at your discretion. Nor you, nor any of you shall fail at your peril. Signed this thirty-sixth standard day, A. D. 2671, Maximillian Kruger, President and Commander-in-Chief." He dropped the paper and met Tolwyn's eyes. "I have now read myself in and taken command of this Task Force, Captain."

Incredulous, Tolwyn nodded. "Yes, sir, you have."

"Very well then. Please inform the Commanding Officer that the new Admiral is aboard and has ordered radio silence except for essential intership communications— no contact with the planet by any ship. The Task Force will get under way immediately." He smiled again. "I would appreciate it if you would pass on those orders *before* you inform Captain Galbraith of the *name* of his new CO."

"What's this all about, sir?" Tolwyn asked.

Kruger's smile turned predatory. "Danny Galbraith wants to use parliamentary tactics to get me? Well, I know a few of those myself, whatever my detractors might think. I helped write the damned Constitution! *'No session of the Council of Delegates may be convened . . .'*"

" '. . . *without the President or his appointed representative present to take charge of the meeting,*' " Tolwyn finished the quote. "You mean . . . ?"

"Right now, a whole roomful of politicians is waiting for me to show up. And I'm not going to be around."

"There are safeguards . . ."

"I know. I wrote those, too. They have a whole lot of nonsense to go through, formally establishing my absence from the capitol, waiting to see if they can locate me or my designated Speaker, declaring me formally in contempt, appointing a Speaker-Designate . . . it'll take them a week to get back to the business at hand, Captain. And meanwhile we're going Cat-hunting at Ilios. The crisis will be over inside of that week. If we win, it won't matter if they vote me out. And if we lose, either at Ilios or at Baka Kar, then it won't matter one damned bit who's President when we all go under." He straightened his shoulders. "Now pass on my orders, Captain Tolwyn, and let's get this show on the road."

- **CHAPTER 18**

> *"Vigilance is the Warrior's salvation; inattention the Warrior's most dangerous foe."*
>
> from the First Codex
> 12:16:03

Command Bridge, KIS *Wexarragh*
Near Jump Point Nine, Vordran System
2322 hours (CST), 2671.041

Captain Nrallos *lan* Vharr lounged in his command seat, letting his bridge officers perform their jobs without interference. The duty here was routine after nearly eight eight-days on this station. *Wexarragh* was nearly due to rotate home to Baka Kar, and Vharr for one didn't believe that day could come too soon. He was heartily sick of picket duty in this worthless frontier system.

The Vordran system was something of an anomaly, a seemingly ordinary red dwarf star system which supported an incredible number of strategically valuable jump points. Nearly thirty had been surveyed by Imperial astrogators, but many more were believed to be present. No doubt the humans knew of others.

Balancing the number of jump points was the scarcity of worthwhile real estate, though. A single loosely defined asteroid belt circled the star at a distance of just over one AU, and even the mineral content of the orbiting chunks of rock was too low to make it worth exploiting the system. Early in the war the Landreichers had established an asteroid base, which the Kilrathi had promptly blown up and replaced with one of their own. After it, in turn, had been destroyed by raiders from the Landreich both sides had decided the place just wasn't worth a full-scale presence. After the destruction of the Landreich installation on Hellhole the Landreichers had stopped even trying to maintain ships in the system, since there was only one jump point leading into human-controlled space anyway and the Landreich's posture had always been primarily defensive. But there were plenty of jump points leading in to the Empire, so Governor Ragark had ordered a constant presence be maintained.

At one time this would have entailed the presence of an entire carrier battle group, perhaps a task force, but Ragark had been steadily pulling back most of his capital ships to Baka Kar to build up his strike fleet or to detach on garrison duty elsewhere in the province. Ever since Kilrah had been destroyed, Kilrathi star systems had started declaring their independence as the clans pulled their separate ways, deprived of the unifying force of Emperor and Homeworld.

Vharr understood the need for ships elsewhere in the province, but he sometimes wished there was still more than a single picket ship posted in the system now. The new strategic thinking seemed to be that all they really needed out here was a tripwire, a ship that could report if the Landreichers entered the system so that defensive forces could be mustered at Baka Kar to stop them. Under that theory, the picket vessel could be considered expendable once it had got off its warning by hypercast. Why waste additional ships when one could do the job?

All well and good . . . except when you were the expendable ship in question. And it could get boring, endlessly watching the same extent of space for eight-days on end, without another ship or crew to provide relief from the tedium. The only excitement they'd seen on this tour had been the encounter with the cloaked human ship that had escaped through the jump point after *Wexarragh* had damaged him, and that had filled less than twenty minutes all told.

"Disturbance in the jump point," the Sensor Officer reported suddenly.

"Specifics," Vharr rasped, turning to face him.

"It appears to be a single point-source, Lord Captain. Displacement in excess of one hundred thousand tons."

"Carrier-equivalent. I did not think the human Landreichers had a ship that large." Vharr swiveled his chair to face forward. "Helm Officer, get us under way. Build a vector outward from the jump point until we see what we're up against. I have no desire to be engaged by something while we're at a standstill. Communications Officer, send a hypercast. 'Unknown ship is emerging from Jump Point Nine' . . ."

"There he is!" the Weapons Officer announced.

The ship emerged suddenly from the hyperrealm, large and angular. It had come out of jump within a hundred kilometers of the *Wexarragh*, and the sensors and computer imagery systems were already beginning to process the data.

"IFF transponder reads him as the *Karga*, Lord Captain," the Communications Officer reported. "Imperial carrier of the *Bhantkara* Class. Computer lists it as missing in action since early last year, operating against Landreich under Admiral Cakg *dai* Nokhtak and Captain *nar* Hravval."

"An Imperial carrier?" Vharr studied the computer image forming on his monitor. It certainly looked like an Imperial carrier, at that, one of the new breed of supercarriers created by the Ministry of Attack following the Battle of Earth. Not so big as Thrakhath's fleet carriers, with two flight decks rather than three, but powerful ships with plenty of fighters. Could he really have survived all this time behind enemy lines? It seemed almost beyond belief.

The images showed signs of extensive damage, crudely repaired. Vharr leaned forward, studying the monitor intensely. It would make a story for the Codices, he thought, to hear how the carrier had survived on its own for so long . . .

"Incoming message, Lord Captain." The Communications Officer announced.

"On my screen."

A plain-faced *kil* wearing the rank tabs of a *Trathkhar* of Communications appeared on the screen. "This is the carrier *Karga*. Admiral *dai* Nokhtak commanding." The signal broke up for a moment, then returned. "We have evaded a force of ape ships which had been following us for several eight-days. Request clearance through to Baka Kar so we can make repairs and report to the Imperial Governor for new orders."

"*Lan* Vharr, escort destroyer *Wexarragh*. Your authentication codes, if you please. And I would like to speak to your commanding officer."

Combat Information Center, FRLS *Mjollnir*
Jump Point Nine, Vordran System
2327 hours (CST)

"Well, you heard the *kil*," Admiral Geoff Tolwyn said.
"Give him his authentication codes."

Jhavvid Dahl, the Kilrathi communications specialist,
turned in his chair to look at Tolwyn. "These codes are
a year old. We can only hope they have them on file."

"Just do it," Tolwyn snapped. He turned to face the
monitor beside the *kil*. "Prince Murragh, are you ready?"

The Kilrathi prince gave him a grasped-claw gesture
in response. Murragh was on the carrier's flag bridge,
surrounded by other Kilrathi officers and enlisted ratings
from amongst his castaway group. Dahl had assured
them that he could use the ship's computers to morph
Murragh's features into those of his uncle, drawn from
the communications files, in a real-time program that
would allow Murragh to provide the interactive
movements and the phrasing of his uncle far more
effectively than a pre-programmed simulacrum. With
luck, what the picket ship's captain would see would
be a convincing imitation of a bridge full of Kilrathi.

Tolwyn hoped it would work. If the picket ship got
off a warning, they would never penetrate to Baka Kar
to take out the dreadnought. Everything was riding on
this ploy, and Geoff Tolwyn carried the whole weight
of responsibility for the operation squarely on his
shoulders. Admiral Richards had transferred his flag
to the *Xenophon* at Hellhole to take command of the
Terran-made warships of the battle group, leaving
Tolwyn to handle the approach to Baka Kar entirely
on his own.

The last time he'd held command had been the
Behemoth mission. Memories of the battle passed

through his thoughts from time to time, reminding him of just how much was riding on his performance as a commanding officer.

Right now, though, it was Murragh's performance as an actor that counted most.

"This is Cakg *dai* Nokhtak," Murragh intoned solemnly. It was strange to see his familiar face and figure on the intercom screen, but beside it, on the intership monitor, the computer-altered image of his uncle, shorter, stockier, with touches of silver around his blunt-faced muzzle. "It is good to see another Kilrathi face again after all this time, Captain. We have been cut off for many eight-days . . . over a Kilrah-year, in fact."

The captain of the escort was looking unsure of himself. "Your authentication codes are not current . . ."

"Didn't I just say we've been out of touch!" Murragh roared, flexing his claws in evident agitation. "*Karga* was badly damaged in battle with the apes. All his battle group destroyed! We have been stranded in a system in ape space, our engines useless, since then. Only recently were we able to effect repairs! Of course our codes are invalid. Check your records for the period when we left on our mission! And be quick about it!"

Tolwyn had to smile. Murragh hadn't actually uttered a single untruth. He had simply omitted a few crucial things. And he was doing a credible impersonation of an irritable and irritated aristocrat about to have a junior's head, quite possibly literally. In the Imperial fleet, junior officers did not offend a senior officer's sense of honor and live to tell the tale.

But the look on the picket ship captain's face bothered Tolwyn. *He isn't buying the story*, he thought grimly. *And he's already sent out a message alerting them that something's on the way. If we don't get him to pass us through, we're finished . . .*

Command Bridge, KIS *Wexarragh*
Jump Point Nine, Vordran System
2329 hours (CST)

Vharr's claws flexed nervously. The admiral's anger
was enough to make him cringe. But there was something
that nagged at him, something not quite right.

He studied the monitor more closely. *There* . . . that
was what was bothering him. An almost unnoticeable
distortion in the video image. It seemed to be localized
right around the admiral. If it had been a systems
problem, surely it would have disrupted the whole
screen . . .

A trick of some kind? Or just a communications
glitch? Vharr didn't like the choices he was being
offered. A wrong choice either way could lead to the
utter disgrace of the Vharr *hrai*, not to mention his
own execution.

"Lord Admiral," he said cautiously, thinking fast. "I
am required to send over a shuttle. To verify . . . and
to assist." He turned away from the monitor, gesturing
to his Executive Officer. With the transmission briefly
muted, he gave his orders. "Send a detachment of assault
troops on the shuttle. The admiral is to be given all
due deference . . . but we must verify his story. I don't
like the smell of it."

A squad of troops would be useless against what could
be aboard that carrier, but they, like the ship himself,
were a tripwire. If there was trouble, they would alert
him to it, and he could alert Baka Kar . . . before he
died in turn.

Combat Information Center, FRLS *Mjollnir*
Jump Point Nine, Vordran System
2330 hours (CST)

"He is within his rights," Dahl said. "And if he truly does have orders to inspect passing ships, he would not yield even to an admiral. It would cost his honor to do so."

"Yeah," Tolwyn said. "And we just look more suspicious if we try to argue it. Okay, Murragh, give him the go-ahead. And get me Bhaktadil and Bondarevsky on the intercom circuit. Time for Operation Welcome Wagon."

Starboard Flight Deck, FRLS *Mjollnir*
Jump Point Nine, Vordran System
2345 hours (CST)

Bondarevsky crouched behind a bank of instruments, uncomfortable in full space armor. With his helmet set to infra-red imaging to compensate for the dim lighting of the flight deck, he was starting to get a headache. And the waiting was starting to get to him. He wondered how the marines could bear it. This was nothing like being in the cockpit of a fighter on the way into battle . . . or even holding down the command chair on the bridge. There you had enough to do to keep you from having to think about what was coming. All he could do now was hunker down and try to keep from worrying.

The Kilrathi shuttle passed slowly through the airlock force field and stooped in for a landing on the flight deck. It was an older design than those used aboard the *Mjollnir*, somewhat smaller but standing high on landing gear that gave plenty of clearance for the loading ramp that opened from its belly. The design allowed for savings in space aboard cramped ships like the escort, where the ventral ramp would open up into an airlock through the outer hull of the escort when the shuttle was secured to its piggyback position aft of the bridge.

Bondarevsky could almost feel the intensity of the emotion on the flight deck now. He wondered what they were thinking aboard the shuttle. With no Kilrathi in sight to greet them, they were probably getting edgy.

He gave a hand signal that he knew Sparks could see from the windows of Primary Flight Control overlooking the flight deck. They had planned for the contingency of boarders, and the sequence had been rehearsed, but Bondarevsky's heart still beat a little faster, knowing that this time it was for real.

If all was going according to plan, the carrier was now broadcasting on the same frequency they'd picked up from the shuttle on its way across, a panicky broadcast as if from the CSTCC claiming the shuttle was in trouble on final approach. There was a localized jamming field here on the flight deck, though, to keep the Cats from realizing they were featuring in an imaginative drama playing for the benefit of their suspicious friends. The Kilrathi communications expert, Dahl, would be playing his role to the hilt. The tough old peasant had seemed to enjoy the notion of putting one over on the aristocracy when he'd helped them hatch the scheme during a council of war at Oecumene.

The ventral ramp opened slowly, and a pair of Kilrathi in armor came cautiously down. After a moment they were joined by more. It looked as if there was entire squad of assault troops there, plus a single Cat in the cockpit of the shuttle. With the troopers beginning to fan out, and no more in evidence, Bondarevsky gave a second hand-signal for Sparks.

In an instant, the silent, darkened environment of the flight deck changed dramatically. The lights came up to full intensity, a siren began hooting an urgent warning, and the artificial gravity cut off.

Then the airlock force field cut off, and a wind like a sudden, unexpected tornado swept through the long, tunnel-like flight deck.

The Kilrathi troops, armored and trained for work in space, were in no actual danger from any of it, but the sudden combination of distractions was enough to confuse them for a few crucial seconds. Unable to see clearly, and instinctively clutching to save themselves as they were blown free from the deck in sudden zero-g by a torrent of escaping air that threatened to carry them into the vacuum of space, none of them was in any position to think of anything beyond the immediate crisis. Even the pilot in the shuttle was caught by surprise, rushing to help his friends.

Colonel Bhaktadil's marines, on the other hand, were braced and ready.

They had been posted in the shadowy corners of the flight deck, wearing full space armor and magnetic clamps that secured them into position. Like Bondarevsky, they had set their helmet vision aids to infrared, so the sudden change in lighting didn't bother them. And, most importantly, they knew what was coming. Neither the rush of air nor the loud blare of the siren disoriented them for an instant. Instead they opened fire with low-power lasers, and sixteen Kilrathi troopers were cut down almost as one. A sniper took out the pilot as he hesitated for an instant at the top of the ramp. It was over almost before it had started, and Sparks cut off the distractions and restored atmosphere and gravity a few seconds later.

Bodies hit the deck with loud thumps. Most of the Cats were only wounded, but suddenly being slammed against a metal deck did nothing to improve their already grim condition.

Bhaktadil and his marines swarmed out into the open, moving in to disarm and secure the survivors.

The unfriendly visitors had been secured. Now they had to take the next step . . . and the clock was ticking.

Bondarevsky moved to the nearest intercom terminal and signaled CIC. Tolwyn's face appeared on the small monitor screen with barely a pause. "The shuttle is secure, Admiral," he reported.

"Good. Have the Colonel get his platoon aboard." Tolwyn paused. "That escort's the same class as the one that went down on Vaku. Some of your people went over that ship while you were pulling the castaways out."

"Yes, sir. I was one of them."

"I want a couple of people who know the layout of a Kilrathi escort with the marines. Time is crucial. If someone can save them a few minutes by knowing the layout, it could spell the difference between success and failure." Tolwyn seemed to hesitate. "It's a volunteer mission . . ."

"I'll go," Bondarevsky told him. "And I'll see who else I can round up."

He cut the intercom and strode across the flight deck, shouting as he walked. "Harper! Somebody get me Harper!"

A small knot of flight wing personnel were helping the marines load up on the shuttle. Harper was among them, swapping low-velocity projectile weapons for marine lasers. In the open flight deck, in ambush, lasers had been the best weapons to use, but if the marines were going to fight a boarding action in the smaller confines of a Kilrathi escort, they'd want weapons less likely to cause accidental structural or equipment damage. Using magnetic pulses to fire small projectiles at variable initial velocities, the Marscorp MPR-27 was the best possible weapon for the job. Bondarevsky joined Harper, explaining the situation. The aide nodded cheerfully. "I'm with you, sir," he said.

"Me, too." That was Alexandra Travis. He hadn't even seen her there, passing out webgear hung with grenades and extra magazines. He remembered that she had been one of the party surveying the downed Cat ship on Nargrast, but he shook his head.

"Harper and I can handle it, Amazon," he said, using the nickname she'd picked up after the fight with the pirates.

"You said it was a volunteer mission," she said stubbornly. "I'm volunteering." She lowered her voice. "Look, Captain, you might need an extra person who knows that layout . . ."

There wasn't time for arguments. "Fine. Gear up and get aboard. Harper, leave off this detail and give Boss Marchand my compliments. She can deploy the symphony now."

Harper grinned and hurried off to carry his message. The frantic preparations went on.

Captured Kilrathi Shuttle
Near Jump Point Nine, Vordran System
2356 hours (CST)

The shuttle made contact with the Kilrathi escort with only the gentlest of bumps, and Bondarevsky momentarily forget his apprehension as he silently praised the skill of the Cat pilot, Jorkad *lan* Mraal. Stiff and pompous he may have been, but he was also one hell of a good flier.

They had needed a Cat to be visible in the shuttle's cockpit, and Jorkad had volunteered for the job. Though he wasn't part of the Cadre, he was fanatically loyal to Prince Murragh, and had developed a genuine liking for many of the humans in the flight wing. Bondarevsky had been faintly concerned at what might happen if his new-found allegiance was tested too hard, but so far he'd done an admirable job.

The operation was moving into the final phase now. The broadcasts from *Mjollnir* had shifted to reporting that all was well with the shuttle, except for a minor problem with the computer and communications systems. Jorkad had bolstered the story by using a searchlight semaphore code to communicate with the escort on the way across, the same technique Graham had used when they'd first encountered him at Vaku. An obviously Kilrathi pilot, flashing a well-known emergency semaphore code from the cockpit of the shuttle, should have been reassuring to the captain of the picket boat. At least they had allowed the shuttle to dock, and no further messages had been hypercast regarding the carrier.

They wanted only one additional message to be sent from the picket boat, and that would have to be one of their own composition, since they hadn't been able to keep the suspicious captain from investigating. Now the trick was to capture the escort with its communications codes intact, so that they could transmit the word to Baka Kar that the carrier was a friend. In the meantime, nothing further could be allowed to go out.

Bondarevsky checked his wrist computer's timepiece. In another thirty seconds . . .

When the countdown hit zero, he nodded to Colonel Bhaktadil. "They should be starting," he said.

While the shuttle had made its way across the gap

between the two vessels, a second plane had lifted from the far side of the *Mjollnir*. A Zartoth EW craft had remained loitering in the shadow of the carrier. Now it would be accelerating toward the escort, looking like a Vaktoth fighter out on routine patrol. But it would be starting the "symphony" they had planned, a full-spectrum jamming effort to block all possible communications from the escort.

Right about now the captain and crew would know their suspicions had been right after all . . .

Bhaktadil strode to the head of the loading ramp, kicking the pedal that operated the ventral door. As it slid open he calmly pulled a grenade from his webgear and dropped it through the gap. Five seconds later it exploded in a blinding flash of light and a deafening clap of noise. The flash-bang wasn't designed to do damage, only to distract and disorient.

The marines poured down the ramp, guns at the ready. A few shots echoed from below as they took care of their stunned targets. After a moment Gunnery Sergeant Martin called up that the docking area was secured. Bhaktadil led Bondarevsky, Harper, and Travis down to join his men.

The small docking compartment was crowded. Thirty-six marines, their colonel, and the three Navy officers made a fair-sized party to be crowded in this one fairly small chamber. At Bhaktadil's signal one of the marines hot-wired the door. It slid open, and a pair of his men rolled through the opening with their MPRs blazing away on full auto. The others followed after the two on point announced the corridor clear.

It proceeded like that for the first few minutes, with the marines leapfrogging their way forward, trying to get to the bridge. But they ran into a stiff pocket of resistance in the warren of control rooms under the main bridge, where ten or twelve Kilrathi with small arms contested their approach from cover. The marines bogged down, unable to clear the Cats from the strong position without risking unacceptable casualties.

Bhaktadil dropped to a crouch beside Bondarevsky and Travis. "Any suggestions?" he asked coolly.

The two Navy officers exchanged looks. "Seems to me I remember some kind of an access tunnel running from somewhere around here to the rear of the bridge," Travis said, frowning.

Bondarevsky nodded. "You're right. I remember it too." He called up a tiny schematic on the screen of his wrist computer. "There . . . behind that bank of instruments." He pointed.

"Loomis! You take Bravo Squad. Follow these two." Bhaktadil jerked a thumb at Bondarevsky and Travis.

They found the entrance to the hatch easily enough, pulled off the access plate, and started in. The tunnel ran upward at a sixty degree angle, with rungs planted inside at intervals just slightly too far apart to be entirely comfortable for human hands and feet. It would have been cramped for Kilrathi technicians, but it was reasonably wide and open for the Landreich party.

Travis insisted on leading the way, with her own wrist computer displaying the route. There were several tricky branching before the tunnel reached the bridge. Bondarevsky would have preferred to lead, but as a senior officer it was foolish for him to take the lead in something like this . . . as foolish as Max Kruger personally leading every foray by the Landreich's fleet.

They had nearly reached the top when they realized they were in trouble.

Up ahead, a clang of metal on metal and a sudden gleam of bright light alerted them to the fact that the Cats had opened up an access plate. Bulky figures clambered into the tube, then stopped, obviously taken by surprise by the sight of the human marines climbing toward them. Evidently someone had hit upon the same idea as Bhaktadil, of using the alternate route as a way of outflanking their enemies.

There was a pause when nothing happened. Then the lead Kilrathi opened fire. Mag-pulse projectiles whined through the tunnel, ricocheting as they hit the bulkhead. The first burst sent Alexandra Travis tumbling back against the marine just behind her, both of them crying out.

The only thing that saved the Landreicher party was the heavy build of the typical Kilrathi. Lieutenant Loomis, third in line, was able to get off a clear shot past the two sprawled figures, and her fire brought the first Cat down. The one behind him, hampered by the massive figure of his comrade, went down as well. If there were other Kilrathi at the entry, they backed off fast.

Loomis squeezed past Travis and the marine and pulled out a flash-bang. She signaled to two of her troopers to join her, then flipped it past the two Cat casualties, through the hatch. Somehow she managed to get past the bodies and start pumping full-auto fire through the hatchway.

Command Bridge, KIS *Wexarragh*
Near Jump Point Nine, Vordran System
0010 hours (CST), 2671.042

Vharr surged from his chair as the grenade clattered on the deckplates, snarling a Kilrathi battle-challenge. The blinding light and the overwhelming shock pulse as it detonated seemed to sear directly into his brain, and for long moments he couldn't see, or hear, or think.

Then mag-pulse weapons shrilled and chattered, and more by instinct than by coherent reasoning he hurled himself behind the protective bulk of his command chair.

Most of the others on the bridge weren't so lucky. The party that had reeled back from their attempt to use the tunnel as an alternate attack route were caught completely in the open. Most of them went down in clawing, screaming red agony. The Executive Officer got off a single wild shot with his sidearm before he fell.

Summoning all his willpower, Vharr threw off the effects of the stun grenade and hurled himself across the bridge at the computer station, one massive hand upraised to initiate the sequence that would wipe the computer codes clear.

A human—a human *female*, at that—intercepted him, planting the muzzle of her sidearm squarely in his chest. "My name is Lieutenant Katherine Loomis, Free Republic Marine Corps," she said in flawless Kilrathi. "And you, sir, are my prisoner."

Access Tunnel, Deck Two, KIS *Wexarragh*
Near Jump Point Nine, Vordran System
0013 hours (CST)

Bondarevsky didn't pay attention to the firefight. He crawled to where the two human casualties lay, turning them over. The marine was clearly dead, a full burst of mag-pulse projectiles making a nice target grouping right over his heart. But Travis was still breathing, and moaned as he pulled her to one side so that the rest of the marines could work their way past.

Her armor hadn't been able to stop the bullets from

such short range, and he could see where it had given way along her left side. Bondarevsky pulled off her helmet, checking the pulse at her throat, then unsnapped the chest plate and worked it free. The t-shirt she wore under the armor was wet with blood. He unhooked the first aid kit from his web gear and opened it up, then drew his knife.

Her eyes focused on the blade, and she managed a faint smile. "C'mon, it can't be *that* bad," she said, wincing. "I mean, you don't have to go through this 'put her our of her misery' routine . . ."

"Stay still," he ordered. "I have to stop that bleeding."

He used the knife to cut open her shirt. The blood was still flowing freely from multiple lacerations on her side. A few centimeters over and she would have been dead.

Bondarevsky used the t-shirt to clean the wound as well as he could. Then he began to apply a healstrip which would trigger clotting of the blood leaking out from the multiple wounds. Pulling her artificial blood pack from her belt, which was coded to match her type, he squeezed the bag. An energy cell inside the bag ruptured, mixing the dried blood with a frozen saline solution and heating it to body temperature. Wrapping the bag to her forearm, he took the needle attached to the side of the bag and slipped it into a wrist vein, then lashed the bag in place.

It was touchy work, and he was afraid his artificial hand might go back into spasms again if he tried to do anything too delicate.

He was so wrapped up in the job that he didn't notice where his other hand rested as he tried to steady himself. Travis flashed a painful grin. "Most guys at least give me dinner and a holo-vid before they try something like that," she said.

Bondarevsky pulled his good hand away from her bare breast, flushing. "Sorry," he muttered.

"Don't worry about it," she told him. "All in a good cause. Just remember about the dinner if we get back to Landreich, okay?"

"It's a date," he said, adjusting the healstrip one last time. "Can you handle the armor again?"

She nodded. "Yeah. But I won't be doing any dancing for a while." He helped her back into the chest and back pieces of her space armor, uncomfortably aware of her bare skin now. When it was sealed up, he gathered up her helmet and pointed to the top of the ramp.

"The firing's stopped. Let's see what's going on."

She gave a nod, and allowed him to help her up the incline.

Combat Information Center, FRLS *Mjollnir*
Deep Space, Vordran System
0315 hours (CST)

Vectors matched and flying in close formation, *Mjollnir* and the captured picket boat shaped their course for Jump Point Three, the route that led straight to the Imperial provincial capitol at Baka Kar. Tolwyn should have been in his quarters, at least pretending to sleep now that they had passed the first obstacle, but he was too wrapped up in considerations of what the new day would bring to even consider retiring to his bunk.

The captured escort had been relatively easy to pacify once the bridge had been secured. The crew of one hundred thirty-two had been ferried across in stages, and were now secured in a locked cargo hold aft of the port hangar deck. Casualties had been fairly light, with two marines killed, three wounded, plus one of

Bondarevsky's officers. And, most importantly, they had captured the computer files intact, and extracted the communications codes and protocols they needed without difficulty. Dahl had put together a soothing message from the picket boat to the Cats at Baka Kar, declaring that the carrier they had encountered was friendly and headed in to the capitol to refit after their long ordeal in space. Encoded with the picket ship's burst signal encryption tag, the transmission would read as a completely genuine message from Vharr.

Tolwyn checked a status display. The last shuttle load of crew and passengers for the escort was on the way over. He had decided to put a prize crew aboard, a mix of trustworthy Cats from Murragh's party and human crewmen. They would keep the picket boat on station for the time being, with orders to run if anything came after them looking for trouble. It gave him a way of keeping watch over his rear as he went through to Baka Kar . . . and a place to offload his few remaining noncombatants. Armando Diaz was probably glad to be off the carrier as it spaced into battle. He and his two top computer experts, Voorhies and Mayhew, had done wonders extracting the authentication codes and transponder signals from the old computer records, and their work on the simulacrum of Admiral *dai* Nokhtak had been about as good as anyone could have produced on either side of the frontier. But there wasn't much more they could do at this stage of the game, so they were aboard the escort, clear of *Mjollnir*'s upcoming fight. But many of the crew detailed to the picket ship had been reluctant to go. Even though they knew the odds against them, their morale was high. Even the casualties from the firefight had refused the chance to go.

Murragh and the other Kilrathi were just as adamant,

too. Tolwyn was beginning to get a renewed faith in the loyalty and support of a good crew. The Belisarius Group had shaken that faith once, but *Mjollnir's* officers and spacers proved that not everyone was tainted with that kind of corruption.

"Sir, multiple disturbances in Jump Point Nine," Kittani reported. After a moment, the Exec went on. "First trace is the *Xenophon*. It's the battle group."

He nodded. "Right on schedule. Pass on an update of our situation to Admiral Richards, with my compliments, Lieutenant Vivaldi."

"Aye aye, sir," the Communications Officer responded.

"What's our status, Exec?" he asked.

"Four hours to Jump Point Two," Kittani responded. "All systems are nominal. Mr. Deniken reports that he's come up with a solution to that gunnery problem you posed him yesterday, and he should have it in operation by the time we reach Baka Kar. And the Wing Commander passed the word that he's got two Zartoths and a Kofar ready to launch. He recommends you delay dropping them until we're ready for the jump."

"Very good." He stood slowly, stretching weary limbs. Suddenly he felt that he might, after all, be able to sleep for a little while. Everything was running smoothly . . . and if he didn't rest now, while he could, he'd certainly have no opportunities later. Once they hit Baka Kar, rest would be impossible for any of them. "Call me when we are ready to make the jump. You have the bridge, Mr. Kittani."

The Turk nodded solemnly. "I have the bridge, sir," he said formally, taking the command chair.

Geoff Tolwyn left CIC, striding with his back ramrod-straight. They might be about to engage in their last battle, but he was damned if he was going to show the least sign of strain or worry.

Right now, he had everything he could want—a good ship, a good crew, and the prospect of striking a blow for freedom.

For Geoff Tolwyn, that was enough and all else, all the other things were at last, for this moment, forgotten. Things were again as they once were.

• CHAPTER 19

> "Consider the story of Karga the Hero, which
> tells of the rewards of honor and duty. Consider
> the story of Vorghath the Hunter, and reflect on
> the perils of complacence."

> from the Seventh Codex
> 04:17:09

Flag Bridge, KIS *Dubav*
Deep Space, Gorkhos System
0410 hours (CST), 2671.042

"A message, Lord Admiral. Passed on by Fleet
Command."

Ukar *dai* Ragark turned to face the speaker. "What
is it, Communications Officer?" he asked, glowering.
He was beginning to feel frustrated and impatient at
the annoying problems that had cropped up over and
over since the task force had departed from Baka Kar.

They had made a round-about voyage of it, traveling
by way of Dharkyll, Khrovat, and Preesg to pick up
additional ships for the strike group, including the escort
carrier *Larq*, which replaced *Klarran* in his tactical
dispositions. The idea had been to move slowly enough

to let the Landreichers know they were coming, yet quickly enough to hit Ilios ahead of any possible response, but in practice it hadn't worked that way. First there had been the delay in assembling the reinforcements, including *Larq*, at Khrovat, where the ships had recently been involved in the suppression of a rebellion. They had reported resistance completely ended on the colony, when it fact they had still been in the last stages of putting it down when the task force jumped in. He would have left them to their work and gone on, but Ragark had found that the falsely optimistic reports weren't the only thing wrong at Khrovat. He suspected the System Administrator of entertaining notions of making his own bid for power within the province and using the rebellion as an excuse to retain those ships under his own command, so Ragark had been forced to intervene directly and clean out the corrupt administration before carrying on. It would not have been wise to take the fleet onward leaving a nest of traitors behind him.

Then the *Hravik* had developed jump drive problems at Preesg, which necessitated hasty repairs. Over an eight-day behind schedule, they had finally arrived at the designated staging area here at Gorkhos. Ragark had decided to hold back for a few hours longer, though, and send a scout ship ahead through the jump point to Ilios. Even if the Landreich had mustered a fleet to meet him, he calculated that he had the strength to defeat it, but Ukar *dai* Ragark was not the *kil* to leave things to chance. He wanted to know his opposition, rather than allow himself to be taken by surprise as Thrakhath, curse his name, had been time and again in battle against these unpredictable humans.

But the petty frustrations had been building, and he was feeling less than patient.

"Lord Admiral, a report from Vordran. The picket there. Captain *Ian* Vharr has reported the arrival of the carrier *Karga*, believed lost over a year ago. It apparently was damaged and had to make repairs deep behind the human frontier, and is now on the way to Baka Kar for a more thorough refit at the docks." The Flag Communications Officer gave him a triumphant upraised fist. "Yet another addition to our strength, Lord Admiral! *Karga* is one of the newer supercarriers . . ."

Ragark raised a hand and made a slashing motion, cutting off the report. *Karga* . . . he seemed to remember the name. Yes, a carrier . . . he had used Baka Kar as a staging area for a raid by a small battle group. One of Thrakhath's worthless sideshow campaigns, intended to exact vengeance for the Landreich leader's support of the Terrans in the Battle of Earth. The entire battle group had disappeared across the border, never heard from again.

That wasn't quite right. There had been one contact, he remembered. One final message . . .

The admiral in command had announced that he was sacrificing the carrier for the glory of the Empire! That was it . . . that was why he remembered the whole affair so well. The hypercast had been distorted by static, but he could still remember listening and saying a death-chant over the loss of so many brave Warriors. So how could *Karga* still be alive today? No admiral would dare withdraw a self-destruct command at the risk of honor and *hrai*. Could it be a trick of some kind? But the captain of the picket ship had apparently been satisfied that it really was *Karga*.

Ragark remembered something else, something that made him bare his teeth. The admiral commanding the *Karga* battle group had been Cakg *dai* Nokhtak. A cousin of Thrakhath's . . . a member of the Imperial House.

A possible claimant to the throne . . . certainly a tanist with better credentials than Ragark's own. What if he *had* avoided the destruction of his ship, and survived until now? Would Cakg *dai* Nokhtak be content to join Ragark . . . or would he seek to replace him? Imperial blood would have a strong lure for many of his followers, possibly even Dawx Jhorrad. Especially if it was backed by a carrier and a story of heroism in the war.

He had been held back by the possibly disloyalty of the Administrator at Khrovat. This could be far more dangerous. He could return to Baka Kar to find his entire position undermined . . .

Ragark leapt to decision. "Transmit new orders to the task force," he said. "We will move to the jump point to Vordran and investigate this story in more detail. The move on Ilios is postponed. See that all captains are aware of the change of plan. We get under way immediately!"

If *Karga* was a friend, he could afford the delay. After all, his move on Ilios had been designed to draw the humans away from threatening the repairs to *Vorghath*, and he was sure he had already accomplished that through the threat he had posed.

But if *Karga* was an enemy, his four carriers, combined with the two at Baka Kar, would crush him.

Operations Planning Center, FRLS *Independence*
Orbiting Ilios, Ilios System
0845 hours (CST)

The single figure sitting at the big triangular table in OPC looked very much alone when Kevin Tolwyn entered the compartment. Max Kruger was hunched over his computer terminal, calling up holographic charts of possible battle plans for the defense of Ilios, but the dejected set of his shoulders told a different story altogether.

"Sir," Tolwyn said, "patrols have destroyed a Cat scout ship near the jump point to Gorkhos. And our long-range communications monitors have picked up traffic from the same direction. It sounded like an abort order, recalling the Cat fleet to form on their flagship and prepare to jump outsystem."

Kruger raised red-shot, weary eyes. "When?"

"That's the thing, sir. The signals are several hours old now. It took that long to get them correlated and descrambled. If they were jumping to attack us here, they should have started coming through the jump point long since."

Kruger didn't answer him. The President shut off the holo-projector, but sat staring at the center of the table as if it was still displaying an image.

After a long moment of silence, Tolwyn spoke again. "Mr. President . . ."

The older man raised a hand in a dismissive gesture. "By now, I doubt that," he said. They had monitored word from the Landreich that Galbraith had rammed through a response to Kruger's tactics in record time. As they spoke, the Council would be meeting to consider the Opposition's call for a vote of no confidence. There had even been a rumor they were considering a vote to impeach Kruger for his abandonment of the capitol.

"Sir," Tolwyn insisted. "Nothing official's happened yet. Even Captain Galbraith can't act against your orders until he receives an official message from Landreich."

"So? What would the point be, Captain? Whatever I do now, they'll nullify it."

"The only reason I can think of Ragark to back down from the plan to attack here is if he had some kind of information about a threat to Baka Kar. If *Mjollnir* was keeping to schedule, she'd be going in today. And if that's what Ragark's reacting to . . ."

"Then he's got too big a head start for us to make much difference, Captain," Kruger said. "It looks like Richards and Geoff were right. Even if they take out the dreadnought, they'll never get away. Not if Ragark can seal off their escape." He leaned back in his chair, nothing at all like the excitable, enthusiastic madman who had become such a mythic figure in this part of space. Now he was just an old, done man, with nothing left to hold on to. "No, Captain, I suppose I should just save everyone the trouble. Let Galbraith take the fleet back to Landreich and get it all over with."

"Damn it, sir, you can't just write them off!" Tolwyn exploded. "You have no way of knowing what the tactical situation will be out there . . . but if Ragark does get back to Baka Kar, and *Mjollnir* has to face his combined forces alone, it will be a goddamned suicide mission."

Kruger's frown deepened. "We could end up spacing right into Ragark's hands, Tolwyn. We could lose the whole damned fleet . . ."

"When has that ever stopped you before?" he demanded. "You were willing to rush that Cat squadron at Hellhole with two empty carriers and nothing but pure bluff to get you through, and if that wasn't risking the fleet I don't know what the hell was!" Tolwyn was pacing back and forth in front of the President, talking with his hands and body as much as his words. "Anyway, once Galbraith gets in power there won't be much of a fleet anyway. He'll pay off most of the carriers and draw down the rest of the armed forces. Or the Cats will roll right over everything and the whole fleet will be useless against them. What have you got to lose?"

"A lot of good men and women, Captain," Kruger said wearily.

"You've sacrificed people before," Tolwyn said brutally. "Soldiers and spacers . . . that's what we're for, you know. To die, if we have to, to protect the Republic."

"What right do I have now?" Kruger asked. "Damn it, Tolwyn, the Republic's in the process of disowning me! It may not be official yet, but you know that by the time the last gavel falls today I won't have the authority to fire a salute, much less launch a battle."

"Just because you've been disowned by your people, Mr. President, is no reason for *you* to disown *them*." Tolwyn stopped and leaned over the corner of the table, looking down at Kruger. "Your whole life has been about helping the Landreichers when they were being handed a raw deal by some outsider. You gave up your ConFleet career and risked your life and the lives of *San Jacinto*'s crew to defend Landreich from the Cats. You've done the same thing a hell of a lot of times since then, too. Why? Because you were President? You weren't when you were commanding *San Jacinto* and you told Vance Richards what he could do with his withdrawal orders!"

Kruger fixed Tolwyn with a stare, and there was silence in the OPC, a silence that dragged out uncomfortably long. Finally, he stirred in his seat. "You know, Captain Tolwyn, you're turning into a remarkably fine replacement for Jason Bondarevsky. He always liked to play the role of my conscience, too, you know."

"If I'm doing a good job of filling his shoes, I'm glad of it," Tolwyn said.

Kruger snorted. "Wonderful." He stood up slowly. "All right, Captain Tolwyn, we'll try this your way. Maybe we'll bail Vance and them out of a mess . . . or maybe we'll just go down fighting. Either way, at least Max

Kruger will go out with a bang, instead of a whimper, and be damned to the politicians who think they can put me out to pasture!"

Flag Bridge, KIS *Dubav*
Near Jump Point Sixteen, Vordran System
0918 hours (CST)

"No sign of the picket vessel, my Lord. Or anything else. Not even a debris field."

Ragark resisted the urge to snarl a reply to the image of the ship's captain on his monitor screen, forcing his voice to remain flat and calm. "Very well, shape course for the jump point to Baka Kar. Maximum acceleration."

"My Lord!" That was the Flag Sensor officer. "Picking up an emissions signature that corresponds to the *Karga*. Near the edge of the asteroid belt . . ."

"You heard that, Val?" Ragark demanded.

Akhjer *nar* Val gave him a grasping gesture of understanding and assent. "We have it here," he said.

"Then order the fleet to pursue, by the Gods!"

Ragark cut the intercom link, raging inwardly at the seeming inability of his subordinates to do anything competently. When they had first jumped into the Vordran system they had picked up a sensor image from something that should have been the picket boat, but after a burst of encrypted comm traffic the ship had vanished, apparently into the jump point to Hellhole.

Now they were registering the carrier . . . where nothing had been before. Lurking near the edge of the asteroid belt, with transponders shut down, they might have escaped detection. But what kind of game was this *dat* Nokhtak playing?

Zartoth 905, VAQ-662 "Shrill Cats"
Asteroid Belt, Vordran System
0920 hours (CST)

Lieutenant Mbenge smiled inside his flight helmet. By now Ragark's crew should have picked up the signal he was sending, and he wished he could have been there to see the reaction when all those Cats discovered what looked like a carrier appearing from out of nowhere.

They'd be even more surprised when his wingmate, Lieutenant Cynthia Hill, started up her part of the day's fun and games. Bondarevsky had detached the two Zartoth EW planes, plus a Kofar resupply bird to support them in the absence of the carrier, specifically for a situation like this one. Each of the Zartoths could put out signals that mimicked a ship's transponder code and energy readings. The discrepancies of size and mass would be hard to spot as long as the planes remained near the fringe of the asteroid belt, and since they could turn their signals on and off at will they could do a fine job of keeping the Cats occupied, searching in vain for a ship that wasn't there.

With luck, that could buy them some time at Baka Kar, and keep Ragark from setting up an ambush at one of the jump points. Then, hopefully, they'd be able to keep a low profile until the danger passed and someone sent ships from the Free Republic to retrieve them. From everything he'd heard, the carrier might not be coming back from Baka Kar.

He checked the countdown clock beside his sensor screen, and flicked off the switch that controlled his transmission. Let Ragark chew on *that*, for a while . . .

Combat Information Center, FRLS *Mjollnir*
Approaching Baka Kar, Baka Kar System
1118 hours (CST)

"Another cruiser, sir. Routine challenge and reply."

Tolwyn nodded at Lieutenant Mario Vivaldi's report. That was the fourth warship they had encountered since making the jump from Vordran, and so far each one had sailed blithely past with no more than a casual exchange of greetings over the commlink. Richards had been right. If they had tried to come in as attackers, they would never have penetrated this far. There were plenty of fighting ships in the system, though it was clear from long-range scans that the bulk of Ragark's forces were elsewhere, presumably engaged with the Landreich fleet at Ilios—if Kruger's intelligence information had been accurate.

But the deception was working beautifully. The transponder continued to send out the old ID signature which the Kilrathi picked up as friendly. And apparently the ruse with the picket boat had worked according to plan. There was no sign that anyone in space around Baka Kar was the least bit suspicious of *Karga*.

That would all change soon, though, he reminded himself grimly. As soon as the pretense was dropped and they attacked the dreadnought, every Cat in the system would come after them, and the odds were still formidable. With luck they could render the dreadnought useless . . . but it would still take a minor miracle to win clear afterwards.

Tolwyn pushed the dour thought from his mind. He had already crossed his Rubicon. Now he had to hope that all the elements of the strategy he, Richards, and Bondarevsky had mapped out together would come together as planned. And he had to make sure that Geoff Tolwyn, at least, played out his part.

The sensor technician spoke up. "Ships appearing on long-range scanners out of the jump point, sir. Two . . . now three. Lead ship IFF reads as *Xenophon* . . ,"

"Right. Let the Cats get a good look, people."

"Comm activity from the station is increasing," Vivaldi reported.

"Vector changes on three cruisers . . . four . . . destroyers now changing vectors as well . . ." the sensor tech spoke fast to keep up with the changing conditions. "Hell, it looks like every capital ship in the system's changing course for the jump point, skipper."

"That's what we've been waiting for," Tolwyn said. He touched a stud on his intercom panel. "Flight, from CIC."

"Bondarevsky here." Tolwyn was surprised to see the Wing Commander in a full flight suit. The plan hadn't called for Bondarevsky to be strapping on a fighter today. But it was his business to run the Flight Wing any way he saw fit. Tolwyn trusted him . . . and trust was a commodity Geoff Tolwyn rarely extended any more.

"Captain," he said formally. "I make us forty-five minutes from target. The diversionary attack has commenced at the jump point. Get your people ready." He paused. "And . . . good luck, Jason."

Flight Wing Briefing Room, FRLS *Mjollnir*
Approaching Baka Kar, Baka Kar System
1140 hours (CST)

Bondarevsky shut off the intercom and turned back to the assembled squadron commanders. "It's time," he said quietly. "You have your orders . . . but you also have your wits. Use them out there today. Now assemble your squadrons!"

"Black Cats!" Etienne Montclair shouted, smiling like a wolf on the scent of prey. Some of the others took up the call as they rose and headed for the door.

A good team, Bondarevsky thought as he watched them go. Maybe not as good as *Tarawa*'s old outfit, but a damned good team. Would any of them make it out alive? The odds were against it.

He saw Sparks and Harper leaning against the far wall, talking, and started toward them, but he never made it there. Alexandra Travis appeared at the door, her usual easy grace replaced by a stiff, awkward gait as she favored her injured side. He moved to meet her.

"What the devil are you doing out of sick bay?" he demanded. "Doctor Manning told me you'd be out of it for at least a week."

She nodded. Pale from her ordeal the day before, her wan complexion offset the dark helmet of her short-cut hair. "I . . . just wanted to come down and see you off," she said, her voice strained. Pain, or emotion? He wasn't sure. "Sorry I have to sit out this dance."

"Don't worry about it," he said. "I didn't want to have to ride out the whole battle in the command plane anyway." His original assignment for the attack had been to the Gratha Command and Control craft that would be coordinating the carrier's Alpha Strike. But with one of his best Strakha pilots wounded, he had changed his mind. He'd fly one of the stealth fighters today, taking personal charge of the squadron in place of Travis.

He would have been happy that the woman wasn't going into battle today, if the position of the carrier itself hadn't been so hopeless. Bondarevsky had been struck by her resemblance to Svetlana—not so much in face or feature as in the way she carried herself, the way her mind worked so closely attuned to his own—but it wasn't until she was wounded aboard the picket ship that he realized how much he'd come to care for her these past few months. It would have been almost too much to bear if she'd gone out there in a fighter like Svetlana, and never come back.

Her eyes met his. "Take care of yourself out there, Jason," she said quietly. It was the first time she'd ever used his given name. "Don't forget, you owe me a date when we get back to Landreich."

His eyes strayed to the swell of her breasts under the khaki uniform she wore, then back to her mocking eyes. "I'll be there," he said. He would have taken her in his arms, but he was conscious of other eyes on the two of them.

"I'll be there," he repeated, and turned to leave the briefing room. It was time for battle.

Flight Wing Briefing Room, FRLS *Mjollnir*
Approaching Baka Kar, Baka Kar System
1141 hours (CST)

"My thanks to you, darlin' of the flight deck, for making sure my wee bird can fly today," Aengus Harper was saying. A last-minute fault had threatened to ground his Strakha and keep him out of the action today, but Sparks had taken personal charge of the techies who had traced the glitch down and corrected it in time for him to go back on the roster.

If Harper was going to die on a suicide mission, he intended to do it in the cockpit of a fighter, not sidelined as he'd been all these years.

Sparks didn't answer. He followed her gaze to where Bondarevsky and Travis were talking, then looked at the tech officer again. "Does he not know, then, that you love him, lass?" he asked.

She met his eyes and flushed. "What makes you say that?" she demanded.

"I've seen the look a time or two before, lass," he said. "Even put it in a few ladies' eyes, from time to time. You'll not be denyin' that you're in love with him, will you now? And for a long time, I'd say."

She nodded reluctantly. "A long time. But he was in love with another pilot back then, until he lost her on the Kilrah raid. After that . . . well, he was just getting over her, and I was just a techie petty officer besides."

"And later?"

"We almost . . . got together once," she told him. "But the timing was still wrong. He made it a rule not to fraternize with the junior officers once he became captain of a carrier . . . and just when I thought he wasn't going to be my ship's captain any more, we drew another assignment together." She looked away. "After that, I decided I didn't want to trade the friendship I knew we had for a romance I wasn't sure we could ever manage. Now . . . it looks like I've lost him again. To another pilot, too."

"You should tell him how you feel, lass."

She shook her head. "Not much point in it now, Aengus. The last thing he needs is to have something like *that* laid on him now. And everyone says we won't be coming back from this one. So I lose him one way or another . . . better I don't cause him any more grief."

"You're one in a million, Janet McCullough," Harper told her. "And if you weren't head-over-heels for that one over there I might be trying to court you myself."

"Save it, flyboy," she told him. "Or did you forget you've got a launch coming up?"

Strakha 800, VF-401 "Shadow Cats"
Approaching Baka Kar, Baka Kar System
1148 hours (CST)

"Eight-zero-zero, good shot," Bondarevsky said. He pushed the fighter's throttle forward and felt the gravitic differential pushing him back into his seat as the Strakha accelerated. "Good shot!"

"Roger, eight-zero-zero," Boss Marchand replied.

He checked the status of his cloak and nodded inside his flight helmet. No one he'd ever heard of had ever tried launching a stealth fighter with the cloak on, but it had gone off without a hitch. The deployment plan called for the Strakhas to get off of the flight deck early, with cloaks up to hide the launch from prying eyes. It would make the operations cycle easier once the full Alpha Strike went forward later . . . and it guaranteed that the Strakhas would be in position for a very special mission before the Cats suspected anything was amiss.

One by one the rest of the squadron joined him, though his sensors continued to show surrounding space empty save for the carrier herself. When all eight of the cloaked fighters were assembled, Bondarevsky switched on his commlink once again. "Asgard, Asgard, this is Loki. Launch completed. Proceeding to designated target." In honor of the carrier's name—and perhaps in memory of Viking Jensson as well, the codenames for the various elements of the strike mission were drawn from Norse mythology. Asgard, the home of the gods, was the carrier, while the cloaked Strakhas operated under the name of the trickster god, Loki.

"Loki, Asgard, copy," came the reply from Lieutenant Vivaldi. *"Make sure you sting the bastards a couple of times for me!"*

The Strakhas, unseen, undetected, raced inward toward Baka Kar.

Combat Information Center, FRLS *Mjollnir*
Entering Baka Kar Orbit, Baka Kar System
1208 hours (CST)

"My God, what a monster," someone breathed, and Geoff Tolwyn agreed. He had once thought *Behemoth* was a truly impressive piece of machinery, but the huge bulk of the Kilrathi dreadnought was something unimaginably larger and more terrible. The huge space station and repair dock alongside was larger, but not by much . . . and space stations didn't generally fly under their own power.

Or carry sufficient weapons to wipe out a fleet or lay waste a planet.

Still unchallenged, the carrier was on final approach. Dahl and Murragh were busy talking to the station controllers, requesting final approach clearance, ostensibly so they could dock with the station and arrange resupply and repairs for *Karga*. He had been concerned about allowing the Kilrathi to play too big a role in the operation, in case one of them harbored more loyalty to his race than to his Prince, but the encounter with the picket boat had proved he could count on Murragh and the others. Tolwyn could safely ignore that entire facet of the attack. It was in good hands. At any rate, most of the attention at the station was bound to be focused on the distant skirmishing around the jump point, where *Xenophon*, *Durendal*, and *Caliburn* were playing tag with the ever-increasing force of Kilrathi ships closing in on them from all parts of the system.

Richards was playing it canny out there, avoiding combat. The three Landreich ships could dodge away from almost anything their size or larger, altering vectors in plenty of time to avoid coming into range of a Cat ship's guns. It would take a carrier with fast-striking planes to bring them to battle, and so far the only carrier they'd detected in motion was still close to an hour from the scene of the fighting. A second carrier was reported near the station, but its power readings indicated that it had suffered some heavy damage— probably the one Kevin Tolwyn had reported as taken out of action by the pirates at Hellhole.

"We have clearance," Vivaldi announced. "Port side approach."

"Very good," Tolwyn said. "Just where we hoped. Mr. Clancy, I'll thank you to steer for the port side of the station. And make sure you take us in close across the bow of that beast."

"You want centimeters or millimeters, Admiral?" Clancy asked. "Or would you prefer microns?"

"Just bring us across her bow, and I'll be happy. Mr. Deniken, are you ready?"

"All guns standing by," the Tactics and Gunnery Officer confirmed. "Ready for your order."

"A little longer, if you please." He touched an intercom stud. "Mr. Graham? Status?"

"All systems nominal, sir," Graham reported. "Shields cycling at nine-six-five. The drives are looking good. Damage control parties are ready." He paused. "Would this be a good time to wish I was still back on good old Nargrast, freezing my butt off with Murragh and the rest?"

"Luck of the draw, Mr. Graham," Tolwyn told him. "Flight Deck, prepare for launch operations on my signal. All stations, preparatory." Tolwyn waited a long moment, savoring the feeling of command. "Mr. Vivaldi, you may hoist our colors, if you please."

"Aye aye, sir." In the days of sailing ships on Earth, a warship trying for the kind of surprise *Mjollnir* sought today might sail into combat range flying the flag of another nation, a legitimate *ruse de guerre*. But before the first broadside, the false colors would be hauled down and the real national flag hoisted. *Mjollnir* was doing the same thing electronically. Her transponder had broadcast the Identification Friend or Foe signal for the *Karga*, but now Vivaldi switched that transponder signal off and brought up *Mjollnir*'s new code, identifying her as a ship of the Landreich.

The waiting was over. The battle was beginning . . .

"Now!" Tolwyn said. "Execute Ragnarok . . . Now!"

Strakha 800, VF-401 "Shadow Cats"
Near Orbital Dock Asharazhal, Baka Kar System
1216 hours (CST)

"Ragnarok, Ragnarok, Ragnarok. I say again, Ragnarok!"
The Norse battle between the gods and the giants, a fitting code-word for the order to start the attack, thundered in Bondarevsky's ears. He activated his commlink. "That's the signal, Shadow Cats!" he said. "Attack designated targets at will."

His hand reached out to drop the cloak that screened his Strakha from detection. The heavy fighter slowly emerged from its hiding-place in a bent portion of space, hanging bare meters above the hull of the dreadnought. As the Strakha's targeting sensors registered a lock, Jason Bondarevsky opened fire at point-blank range.

They had adapted this portion of the battle plan from the attack Banfeld's pirates had launched against the carrier at Vaku. But they had two advantages the pirates had lacked. Their stealth technology allowed the Shadow Cats to place themselves in close to the target before the attack . . . and the shield emitter arrays of the orbital dock and the massive dreadnought were far better targets than those found on a carrier.

The eight Strakhas had stationed themselves directly adjacent to eight different emitter batteries, six on the dreadnought, two more on the station. Hidden, they had reduced speed to close to zero, using thrusters to keep station against microgravitic influences but otherwise simply matching orbits perfectly with the Kilrathi station and its monstrous consort. Normally fighters tried to operate using high speeds and rapid vector changes, using their maneuverability to protect them from the dangers of Double-A-S. But that limited the time available to achieve a target lock and fire.

Today, though, the situation was different. The Strakhas decloaked and opened fire, pouring sustained energy blasts directly into the crucial emitters at point-blank range before the Kilrathi even knew there were enemies in a position to fire. Neither the station nor the dreadnought had been maintaining shields at combat strength. They were set at low power levels to screen out minor radiation or random chunks of space debris. So the sudden, overwhelming attack quickly punched through the protective screens and smashed into the arrays. In seconds there were huge gaps left in the Kilrathi shielding that would take long minutes to circumvent by reworking their power grid.

In the meantime, station and dreadnought lay wide open to attack.

As he continued to fire into the emitters, Bondarevsky saw *Mjollnir* making a slow, ponderous turn right across the bows of the dreadnought, where the shields were failing fast. Fighters and bombers were streaming from the two launch bays as fast as Boss Marchand could cycle them out, led by the Raptors of Etienne Montclair's Crazy Eights and the powerful Vaktoths in Commander Lin Dan-Giang's Black Lion squadron.

Then the carrier opened fire with her main guns.

Though not intended to engage in close space combat, the carrier had been well-equipped with batteries to ensure the destruction of any smaller fighting ship that managed to slip through her guard. They had only been able to get six of the eight massive laser turrets back in service during the refit, but Tolwyn had angled the ship so that four of those six turrets had firing arcs. They all opened up at once, and a moment later numerous smaller beams contributed to the massive assault. That had been the project Deniken had been wrapped up in since leaving Vaku. He had adapted the computer program that handled the largely automated point defense lasers, which were supposed to knock down incoming missiles or fighters that closed too near. Now they were slaved to the main guns, and if their individual power output wasn't much against the heavy armor that protected the dreadnought, together they increased the already furious energy that washed over the enemy ship's bow.

Armor sloughed off under the intense bombardment, but of course the dreadnought had plenty of armor to spare. Now it was a race between the *Mjollnir*'s ability to pour out sustained energy fire, the dreadnought's staying power, and the Kilrathi crew's response time as they tried to man battle stations and bring the leviathan into the fight.

No one expected them to just sit there and take it for very long.

Command Bridge, KIS *Vorghath*
Docked, Orbital Station Asharazhal, Baka Kar
System
1221 hours (CST)

Dawx Jhorrad emerged from the elevator to find the cavernous bridge of the *Vorghath* in the grip of confusion and near-panic. Striding purposefully toward his command station, he cuffed two enlisted ratings in passing and bared his fangs at an engineering officer who seemed completely out of his depth in the face of the crisis.

"Report!" he snapped, dropping into the command chair and turning the baleful glare of his mismatched eyes, one real, one bionic, on his first officer.

"*Karga* has launched an attack," Khrell *nar* Dhollas announced without any of the honorifics that were usually addressed to a commanding officer receiving a report. He had always resented the fate that had placed him, a Baron of the Empire, under the command of a commoner, and his contempt showed even when he was performing ship's business. But he was a skilled officer, and Jhorrad allowed him a measure of freedom. Neither of them could change who or what they were. "Just before firing, he changed his transponder configuration and signal. The identification is for a Landreich warship."

"Apes!" Jhorrad spat.

"A squadron of Strakhas was also involved in the initial attack, decloaking and opening fire on our emitter banks. Shields are down across the bow as far back as bulkhead one-twelve. Additional fighters are launching."

"Our response?"

"As yet, we have not been able to return fire," Dhollas said. "Generators were off-line and the crew was unprepared." That sounded like an accusation. It was true that he hadn't allowed the first officer to take the ship to alert status when the three ape ships had appeared at the jump point. At the time, there had seemed to be no particular reason for alarm. Two destroyers and a cruiser offered little threat. They would not have been able to penetrate the defensive perimeter, and even if they had tried there would have been plenty of time for *Vorghath* to go on alert status.

Now they were paying for his complacency . . . but there was no need for Dhollas to point out the fact so blatantly. He made a slashing motion, calling the Exec to silence. "Excuses and blame will not serve here," he said harshly. "Only results. All crew to combat stations, and bring the generators on-line. Reroute shields to cover the gap. Weapons turrets to acquire target and open fire. And cast us off from the station. I will not have *Vorghath* caught like a *traggil* in a trap!"

"As you command," Dhollas said stiffly. He turned, shouting orders.

The mighty dreadnought lurched as the carrier fired again and damaged one of the mooring tractors. Jhorrad's claws flexed instinctively.

He would swat this impudent ape who had dared to attack his ship . . .

Combat Information Center, FRLS *Mjollnir*
Near Orbital Station Asharazhal, Baka Kar System
1223 hours (CST)

"He's powering up his engines. Looks like he's getting ready to cast off."

Tolwyn nodded. He'd seen the sensor data flowing across his monitor even before the sensor operator reported *Vorghath's* changed status. He had known they wouldn't have much time before the dreadnought moved into action. The key now was to maximize their own firepower while denying their giant foe the chance to trade them shot for shot.

"Mr. Clancy. Assume position alongside the station. Commander Deniken, shift point-defense to standard operation. The station will be launching missiles once they realize we're vulnerable."

The carrier changed course slightly as Clancy altered her vector. *Mjollnir* was sliding smoothly behind the protective bulk of the station, allowing it to come between her and the dreadnought. It masked the carrier's fire, too, but that wouldn't be the case for long.

The section of the station they were hiding behind was the part the Strakhas had attacked. The shields had failed there, and the orbital dock was only lightly armored.

Tolwyn was assuming that the Cats would be reluctant to fire on their own station, at least for the moment. But he had no such qualms.

Strakha 800, VF-401 "Shadow Cats"
Near Orbital Station Asharazhal, Baka Kar System
1224 hours (CST)

Bondarevsky dropped his cloak once again and opened fire. The battle had developed a strange sort of rhythm, decloak, attack, cloak, move, decloak . . . a seemingly endless cycle of hit and run moves. The entire Strakha squadron was now concentrating their attentions on the dreadnought, leaving the station for other members of the Wing. Working in two teams of four according to a carefully prepared plan, the stealth fighters had switched from hitting the dreadnought's shield projectors to attacks on turrets with a bow firing arc. Each of those massive turrets was easily five times the size of a Strakha and mounted a whole battery of energy weapons far more powerful than anything the fighter mounted, but they couldn't hit what they couldn't lock on to, and the almost random movements of the fighters back and forth across the ship's hull, hidden by the cloaking devices, meant they couldn't even begin to track their attackers. Like tiny stinging insects, the Strakhas could only mount pinprick attacks, but each time they hit an unshielded turret they caused a little more damage. The turrets had weaker armor than the main hull, so the damage mounted up fast.

He was beginning the re-cloaking sequence once again when Harper let out a whoop. *"That's done for the bastards!"* the Taran shouted.

The turret below him erupted in flame as one of Harper's missiles struck and penetrated. Further down the curve of the hull a second turret went up, too.

Even insect stings could kill.

• CHAPTER 20

"The gods expect that every kil *shall perform his duty."*

from the Tenth Codex
17:14:33

Raptor 401, VF-88 "Crazy Eights"
Near Orbital Station Asharazhal, Baka Kar System
1227 hours (CST)

"Thor One, this is Odin One," Doomsday said. "We're starting our run. Follow us in."

"Roger that," Lieutenant Commander Stefan Razin replied tersely. Razin commanded VA-702, the Black Pumas, *Mjollnir's* single squadron of Paktahn-class bombers. Their codename for the day's battle was appropriate to their role. Like Thor, the thunder god, they would hammer the orbital station into submission.

Montclair lined up his fighter and started his run. "Make your run count," he ordered his squadron. They spread out in a loose line, diving straight toward the orbital station's main launch bay.

Fighters rose from the depths of the station, Dralthis, Darkets, even an eight-ship squadron of old-style Jalthi heavy fighters that were the same vintage as Doomsday's Raptor. Montclair grinned and opened fire, pouring on the energy weapons fast enough to deplete his reserves in a matter of seconds. The station launch bay was bigger than a carrier's flight deck, and more fighters could launch simultaneously from it, but they were still constricted as they passed through the airlock force field . . . and the change from atmosphere to vacuum, artificial gravity to zero-g, caused even experienced pilots a moment's loss of control as they made the transition. The Raptors were taking good advantage of that, knocking down enemy fighters almost as fast as they could clear the gaping maw.

A few made it out, though, and streaked up to meet the Raptors with guns blazing. "Break! Break! Break!" Montclair chanted, peeling off to go after a Jalthi. The rest of the Raptors broke formation to pursue individual targets as well, their initial job of covering the approach of the bomber squadron done.

Montclair slid under the Jalthi and did a fast reverse, coming up on his opponent's six and opening fire at close range with a pair of heat seekers and his gatling mass driver. The Jalthi's stern came apart, and then the Kilrathi fighter erupted in a fireball. Doomsday plunged straight through the inferno, already starting to alter course in search of fresh prey. Below, he spotted the Paktahns streaming past in a line, each bomber pulling up at the last possible second and dumping a full load of ordnance straight into the opening of the launch bay. They probably couldn't hope to do a thorough job of destroying such a large target, but the Kilrathi fighters still trying to launch there would be sitting ducks, and the damage those missiles did would be enough to keep the station's contingents of fighters from being a problem for the duration of the day's battle.

A Dralthi maneuvered toward him, trying to work around to the rear of the Raptor. "No way, kitty," Montclair said, pulling his control stick hard over. His fighter rolled and spun, seeking the new target.

Hornet 101, VF-12 "Flying Eyes"
Low Planetary Orbit, Baka Kar, Baka Kar System
1230 hours (CST)

"Here they come!" Babe Babcock called. "Drifter, you cover my tail!"

"With pleasure," Lieutenant Commander David "Drifter" Conway responded.

Babcock's Flying Eyes had drawn the assignment of covering the embattled *Mjollnir* from any attacks that might originate planetside. Sweeping low, they had spotted a tight knot of targets climbing fast from a base on the northern coast of the largest equatorial continent. Evidently they were the only Cats on the ball today. They were the first on the scene, and Babcock intended to punish them for their efficiency.

"Stay close," she said. The Hornets swept forward in a tight formation, swooping down into the upper fringes of the atmosphere at a speed high enough to cause the shields to flare red from the energy they were absorbing. The targets were rising fast . . .

They erupted into view, two full squadrons of Darket light fighters. Their formation was loose; it looked to Babcock as if each pilot was pushing his craft hard to be the first to reach the battle. Instead, she told herself with a smile, the battle had found them.

"Concentrate your fire!" she ordered. Babcock keyed her comm console to identify her own target to the rest of the squadron, then lined up her shot and opened up. An instant later all ten of her squadron-mates were adding their firepower to her own.

It was risky business, ignoring fifteen fighters to focus on one, and the Cats replied to the Hornets' attack with their own fire. But their coordination was poor, so each Hornet took individual hits that were easily absorbed by shields, while the full power of eleven paired Hornet lasers tore into a single target, ripping through shields and armor and destroying the ship in a moment.

Babcock switched her target and fired again, with the same effect. Then the two groups of fighters flashed past each other.

"Break and attack at will!" she called, cutting the targeting transmission. "Drifter, follow me in!"

But Drifter Conway had picked up a pair of Darkets on his own tail. He tried to reverse course, but the two Kilrathi ships cut loose on him as he turned, and he lost control of his plane. A moment later it exploded.

Babcock bit back an oath and nailed the nearest Darket with a missile. Part of her wanted to mourn the loss of another of her Flying Eyes, but this wasn't the time or place. You pushed the feelings aside and concentrated on the job at hand. The job of killing Cats.

The job went on. Her sensors were picking up a fresh wave of planes rising to intercept them, and they already had plenty off foes to deal with as it was . . .

Vaktoth 505, VF-489 "Black Leopards"
High Planetary Orbit, Baka Kar, Baka Kar system
1234 hours (CST)

Laser and missile fire probed outwards from the Kilrathi cruiser, making Lieutenant Commander Ileana Constantine twist and juke her heavy fighter from side to side to avoid the sustained Double-A-S. Around her, four full squadrons of fighters from *Mjollnir* did the same.

Not all the pilots were as skillful—or as lucky—as she was. Up ahead one of the human Darkets was caught in an energy discharge that consumed the entire craft in an instant, like a moth in a flame, and a pair of Dralthi Fours had already been taken out by defensive missiles. But the attackers plunged ahead, trying to get in close enough to cause the cruiser some serious damage.

Planning for the battle today had posed some serious logistical problems for the Wing Commander. Once surprise was lost, *Mjollnir* would become the target of increasing numbers of Cat fighters and bombers, no matter how effectively they managed to block the early response to their raid. Flying the *Mjollnir's* Kilrathi-built planes too close to the scene of the action was a sure recipe for disaster. In the heat of battle, a pilot, or a point defense emplacement, was apt to focus on the type of craft that came into range without necessarily checking an IFF beacon to decide whose side it might be on. Yet Bondarevsky hadn't been in any position to sacrifice more than half his available birds from the action.

Thus, the dispositions for the various *Mjollnir* squadrons. Only the bombers, with a tightly defined mission only they could effectively execute, and Bondarevsky's stealth fighters playing a game of harassment in close to the dreadnought, were to be employed in the immediate vicinity of the carrier. Hornets, Raptors, and Rapiers would be used for the crucial tasks of protecting *Mjollnir* and interdicting various possible sources of trouble. The rest of the fighters, the Kilrathi-built planes, had a different mission . . . to strike any capitol ships that hadn't been drawn away from the planet by the threat that had erupted near the jump point, the three ships of the battle group under Admiral Richards.

When the outlines for the mission had been mapped out no one had known how many targets they might have to face. As it turned out, there were three Kilrathi capital ships still in high planetary orbit over Baka Kar. One was the carrier that was reading as seriously damaged and unable to effectively power up. The other two were cruisers.

The four fighter squadrons—one of Darkets, two of Dralthi Fours, and the Vaktoths of the Black Leopards—had received orders to concentrate on the closest cruiser in hopes of neutralizing it before it could intervene in the fighting around the station.

But killing a cruiser was no easy task. As the range dropped, another Darket was caught. This time the cruiser only grazed the starboard side of the craft, but it vaporized one wing and the engine mounted there. The craft went into a spin, until the pilot managed to use maneuvering thrusters to stabilize the little fighter. But he had to drop out of the formation and head for home. It was no use fighting a battle when your whole attention had to be taken up trying to keep to a steady vector.

"By the numbers, boys and girls," Commander Charles Robertson, CO of the Leopards and acting commander of the entire strike element, sounded ready to handle anything, even a cruiser spitting coherent energy in every direction. *"Let's take it to them!"*

The Darkets peeled off, circling left, trying to get around toward the stern of the cruiser where there were fewer turrets that could fire on the fragile craft. Robertson's Strakha, the odd man out of the heavy fighter squadron, took position at the head of a loose cone of Vaktoths and Dralthi Fours and dived straight in, with all beam weapons firing.

The volume of Double-A-S increased as they stooped down on their intended victim, and another fighter, one of the Dralthi Fours, exploded close by Constantine's Vaktoth. Robertson skimmed low right over the cruiser's hull, dumping a full load of missiles into her shields and then pulling up.

A point-defense battery tracked his craft, a gatling mass driver that used magnetic fields to accelerate tiny slivers of metal to fantastic velocities. A stream of the deadly projectiles intersected with the Strakha.

Robertson's voice was loud in her ears. *"I'm hit! I'm hit! Tell Mary—"*

Then there was silence. Ileana Constantine was the new commander of the Black Leopards.

Strakha 800, VF-401 "Shadow Cats"
Near Orbital Station Asharazhal, Baka Kar System
1238 hours (CST)

"There's just too damned many of them, Bear. We can't cover everybody . . . I don't have any reserves to send!"

"Stay icy, Bifrost," Bondarevsky responded. The code name identified the Command and Control element of the wing, one of the Grathas. "We knew we wouldn't have it all our own way."

He was paying the price, now, for the decision to take over the Shadow Cats in place of the wounded Travis. The Gratha that *Mjollnir* had deployed to help coordinate the fighter battle had been his designated place, but instead it was Commander Tomas Alvarez, the Deputy

Wing Commander, who had the duty. But Alvarez was finding it difficult to cope with the overwhelming responsibility of trying to manage the far-flung engagement, especially now that the Landreichers were starting to run into increasingly heavy resistance. Commander Babcock was engaged with three times her numbers in low planetary orbit, and had lost three of her fighters in a matter of minutes. And the assault on the cruiser had penetrated her shields, knocking out her maneuver bridge, but at the cost of the detachment CO and several other birds . . . and the cruiser was still coming, controlled now from her CIC section, no doubt. The Paktahns had finished their strike and were withdrawing to rendezvous with one of the Kofars to rearm, with Montclair taking his Raptors and the squadron of medium Rapiers down to support Babcock. But that left no more reserves. The Wing was stretched to the limit.

Bondarevsky fought the temptation to lead the Strakhas out to support the other squadrons. The two intense battles were too far away . . . and the primary mission was still to cripple the dreadnought. He couldn't allow himself to be drawn into a sideshow, no matter how bad things might be getting out there.

And he couldn't do two jobs at once. He could be either a Wing Commander or a squadron CO, and he'd made that choice when he strapped on the Strakha.

"You have the big picture up there, Bifrost. Not me. I trust you to do the best you can. Loki One, clear."

He cut the channel and focused on the nearest gun turret. The Strakhas continued their intricate dance, but one short now since Lieutenant Kendricks had come out of cloak just as a point defense battery had opened fire. It wasn't as bad as with some of the other squadrons, not yet, but Bondarevsky knew that attrition was going to take its toll on all of them soon enough.

The monster Kilrathi warship had cast loose from its moorings now, but it was having trouble maneuvering clear of the station on thrusters alone, and didn't dare cut in the main engines so close. Meantime Tolwyn was performing brilliantly in *Mjollnir*. He had fired through the intervening barrier of one of the station's docking arms, and as the structure had come apart more and more of his shots had dug into the *Vorghath*'s armor. By that time the Strakha hit and run raids on the turret emplacements had begun to leave gaps in the dreadnought's forward field of fire, so Tolwyn had shifted his tactics and brought the carrier back into the open. Against the bulk of *Vorghath* even the supercarrier looked tiny, and the difference in maneuverability and precision of control was immediately plain. Tolwyn took the carrier in to point blank range again, maneuvering *Mjollnir* like she was a destroyer rather than a carrier, and the damage to her massive opponent began to tell.

He could see *Mjollnir*'s point-defense batteries firing at the dreadnought again, too, and knew Tolwyn was pressing home the attack with everything he had. Bondarevsky's sensors showed that one of the Cat cruisers, the one the fighters were having so much trouble with, was coming up fast. Once she got into the action *Mjollnir* would be in serious trouble. She was still held together mostly by patches and prayers, with much of her armor gone, and a sustained battle with a cruiser could only end one way.

Tolwyn had to deal with the dreadnought before *Mjollnir* had to fight for her very life . . .

Combat Information Center, FRLS *Mjollnir*
Near Orbital Station Asharazhal, Baka Kar System
1238 hours (CST)

"Her armor's finally going!"

Tolwyn almost joined in the cheer that followed the Exec's hoarse cry. Kittani, his voice all but gone from barking orders, pointed to the main viewscreen with a savage jabbing of his fingers. The beams were indeed penetrating the dreadnought's thick belts of armor at last, especially in the area immediately abaft the gaping missile tubes that Tolwyn had singled out for special attention from Deniken's guns.

"Back us off, Mr. Clancy," he ordered. "If we've got this right, this isn't going to be a real healthy neighborhood in about another thirty seconds . . ."

The helmsman played his controls like a musical instrument, and the carrier backed away, gathering speed and turning slowly to accelerate clear. Tolwyn had remembered a briefing on the Kilrathi dreadnoughts that noted the missile tube in the bow, designed for the massive planetary bombardment missiles the Cats used to lay waste to entire cities. And behind the tubes were the magazines, stocking scores of the huge warheads . . .

The bow of the dreadnought erupted in a fireball, hurtling debris outward like the discharge of a mighty cannon. *Mjollnir's* shields held against the battering impact of armor and hullmetal, but the indicators on Tolwyn's status board went red as Graham shunted extra power into the grid to compensate for the sudden unleashing of massive quantities of kinetic energy that threatened to overwhelm the whole system.

Even that blast wasn't enough to destroy the *Vorghath*. With her whole front end open to space, spilling atmosphere through a titanic hole framed by twisted structural members and blacked hull plating, the dreadnought still rode on its maneuvering thrusters, trying to come about to give the undamaged midships turrets a crack at the gadfly that had stung her so badly. But though the ship was still capable of moving and fighting, it was clear to Tolwyn that the damage she'd just suffered had been devastating. Secondary explosions were rippling down her side, and the power readings tracked by *Mjollnir's* sensors had begun to fluctuate wildly. Even the Kilrathi redundant design philosophy couldn't build in enough alternate circuits and backups to compensate for such massive damage.

Vorghath would live, but crippled. And with the damage the orbital dock had suffered in the battle it would be a long time before the Cats could manage to restore their dreadnought to anything approaching fighting trim. It would be a job that would make the heroic efforts they'd put in to refitting *Mjollnir* pale by comparison.

The balance of power was restored. Ragark no longer had his superweapon, and without the orbital dock in working order he'd have trouble keeping the rest of his fleet combat-ready, too. That would give the Landreich breathing space, at least. And the delay would ruin the Belisarius Group's timetable for precipitating a frontier crisis that could give them their excuse for grabbing power in the Confederation.

Now there remained but one thing to attempt . . . escape. *Mjollnir* had done her job as best she could. Now she had to win free of Baka Kar, against overwhelming forces of capital ships who were fully alerted to her presence now and no doubt eager to exact vengeance for the daring raid that had penetrated their defenses.

"Maximum acceleration, Mr. Clancy. Course to the outbound jump point. Mr. Kittani, have the Flight Wing recalled immediately. Fighters to take station and screen us from pursuit."

"Aye aye, sir," both men responded.

Mjollnir surged forward at flank speed, but two Kilrathi cruisers were in pursuit, and both of them were fast enough to overtake her sooner or later.

Two Commonwealth cruisers had nearly destroyed the carrier at Vaku, and then the *Karga* had been in reasonably good shape. This time, a few good hits could take her out of action, and there was nothing Geoff Tolwyn could do to save her if the Cats pressed home their attack. The only hope was Bondarevsky's fighters, but the fighting around the station had already cut deep into the Wings resources of planes and pilots.

Tolwyn was running out of options, and *Mjollnir* was running out of time.

Strakha 800, VF-401 "Shadow Cats"
Deep Space, Baka Kar System
1255 hours (CST)

The Strakha nestled in tight against the Kofar resupply shuttle, and for a moment Bondarevsky could relax and take his hands off the controls. As fuel transferred from the Kofar's huge reserve tank, robot arms swung into position opposite each of the fighter's hardpoints with missile reloads. Slowly, carefully, they fitted the missiles into position. As each one snapped into place an amber light glowed on Bondarevsky's weapons control panel, and the onboard computer updated its visual display of his ordnance load.

It seemed an eternity before the last new missile was in place and the fuel tanks registered full again, but in fact it took only a few minutes. Bondarevsky's was the last of the Strakhas to be re-armed and refueled. The others were already back in formation, covering the withdrawal of the carrier as the two Kilrathi cruisers strained to bring themselves into range to attack.

For the moment it was a stern chase situation, and though the cruisers were faster and more maneuverable the sheer vastness of interplanetary space made it possible for Tolwyn to keep a few steps ahead, shifting his vector at random intervals and forcing the two enemy captains to play guessing games as to the carrier's intentions. But *Mjollnir* couldn't keep it up indefinitely. Soon, now, Tolwyn would have to begin decelerating in order to reach the jump point moving at a relatively low velocity when he engaged his jump drives. A vessel trying to jump while moving at high speeds risked overshooting its destination, or, worse, unbalancing the jump field and ending up breaking apart. Kruger had pulled it off at the Battle of Earth, but still lost several ships doing it. Chief Engineer Graham had already warned Tolwyn that the delicate balance of the carrier's rebuilt drives couldn't sustain any kind of high-speed jump attempt. So *Mjollnir* would have to approach the jump point losing velocity steadily, and that would give the Cats the opportunity they needed to use their greater mobility against the retreating ship.

If the rest of the battle group could join them in time, they might be able to run interference against the Kilrathi pursuit. But *Durendal* had suffered heavy damage already, and there were several Kilrathi ships trying to come to grips with each of the three Landreichers. The odds would actually get worse as the human ships closed ranks. And they still had close to three hours to go before they reached the jump point. A lot could happen in three hours.

The only other choice Bondarevsky could come up with was one last throw of the dice. Another concerted attack on those closing cruisers with all the fighters remaining in the wing. It would mean more deaths among the Black Cats . . . but if it could save nearly five thousand aboard the carrier, then the trade-off would be only fair.

"All systems nominal," he said aloud. "Ready to detach. Thanks for the drink and the handout."

"All part of the service, friend," a familiar voice replied. Sparks sounded tired, but still game. *"Don't go using all your new toys up at once, you hear?"*

"What are you doing on that Kofar, Sparks?" he demanded.

"It was my turn on the rotation," she told him.

"Yeah. Right. Aren't you the one who draws up the rotation schedule in the first place?"

She didn't reply right away. *"I just figured you shouldn't be the only one who gets to go outside and see the universe, that's all. You got a problem with that, flyboy?"*

"Just make sure you get back in before the fireworks start, Sparks. I wouldn't want you to get caught in the crossfire."

"Thanks," she said. *"And . . . you be careful, too. Come home safe. Not like last time."*

He flexed his bionic hand, thinking of *Coventry*. He'd been so caught up in the action today he'd barely noticed the wounded arm, or pictured that horrible day when Tolwyn's *Behemoth* project had come apart. If he survived today, would the memories of the pilots he lost here at Baka Kar haunt him? Or had he gotten past all that, taking up the Landreich's struggle?

"Separation in ten . . . five seconds . . . three, two, one . . ." He released the clamps that held his fighter to the Kofar and dropped away under minimal thrust. Below and ahead of him, the rest of the flight wing was forming up. "This is Loki One," he said. "All planes form on me. We're going hunting . . . one last time."

Flag Bridge, KIS *Dubav*
Deep Space, Vordran System
1308 hours (CST)

"Decoys!" Ragark slashed the thick padding of his
chair arm with outstretched claws, overcome by savage
fury. "All this time we have been chasing decoys! While
anything could have been happening behind our backs,
at Baka Kar!"

The flag bridge's crew quavered under his angry glare.
For nearly four hours the Kilrathi task force had been
tracking signals that seemed to emanate from the carrier
they had come in search of. They might have searched
for hours longer, if a lucky fighter patrol hadn't picked
up the electronic warfare craft at close range and moved
in for the kill. Thereafter a second signal source had
been spotted, and this time, knowing what to look for,
the computer analysts had identified the trace as coming
from another Zartoth.

But Ragark had lost four hours chasing shadows, and
time was the one thing he didn't have to make up.

"Set course for the jump point to Baka Kar," he
ordered. "Best possible speed. Now!"

Combat Information Center, FRLS *Mjollnir*
Deep Space, Baka Kar System
1345 hours

"*Roll out! Roll out! I'll take him!*"
"*Where the hell are you, Doomsday? You gotta get
this bastard off my tail!*"
"*Bombers, start your run. We'll hold these guys off
as long as we can . . .*"

Tolwyn listened to the commlink chatter, wishing there

was something more he could do, knowing the pilots of the Black Cats were out there risking their lives to defend the carrier. Bondarevsky had thrown his fighters into the attack three times now, but the cruisers kept coming. And now they'd acquired a fighter escort, more of the aerospace defense force scrambled from the planet's surface. One of the two cruisers had taken a serious hit to its maneuver drives, and was beginning to fall behind now. But the other had closed the range relentlessly. It had already started taking shots at *Mjollnir*, and the shields were weakening in several sections.

"*You take the Darket, Lefty. I'm on this Dralthi.*"

"*Scratch another one. Hey, Babe, this is better than simulator target practice. They just keep right on coming!*"

"*Shut up and watch your six, Lefty. I'm—shit! Shit! Where the hell did he—*"

"*God damn. They got Babe!*"

Tolwyn closed his eyes. He remembered Babcock from the first days of Goliath. Competent, professional, a little edgy around the brass, maybe, but she should have had a promising career ahead of her. One day she might have commanded a carrier, even a battle group, herself.

Now she was gone.

"*Cossack, make it look good,*" Bondarevsky's voice came over the commlink clearly. He sounded tense, but in control. "*I want every one of those bombs to count. We're all down to our last loads, and these Cats are in too close to let us rearm on the fly again.*"

"*Understood,*" Commander Razin replied. "*Pumas, follow me in!*"

Tolwyn looked at the tactical screen. Bondarevsky was making a last big push on the remaining cruiser, using the bulk of his fighters to engage the Kilrathi fighter screen and sending in the Paktahn bombers unescorted. It was a damned risky move, but if it worked . . .

The cruiser opened fire on *Mjollnir* again. An alarm shrilled, and Kittani's hoarse voice rasped as he tried to shout a warning. "Hull breach! Hull breach! Aft superstructure! Get me damage control parties to decks three through seven to seal off those compartments! Mr. Graham, shields are down over the aft superstructure!"

"I'm on it! Give me ten minutes!"

"We don't *have* ten minutes, Mr. Graham," the Turk barked. "Make it five! And pray to Allah that won't be too long!"

Strakha 800, VF-401 "Shadow Cats"
Deep Space, Baka Kar System
1349 hours (CST)

A laser cut through space scant meters away from Bondarevsky's fighter, far too close for comfort. The cruiser's attack was directed at the carrier now, trying to exploit the advantage from that last hit. But this beam caught one of the other Strakhas in the squadron. It shimmered into visibility as it came apart.

Bondarevsky gritted his teeth and pushed his throttle forward.

The Paktahn bombers were releasing their loads in one massive, rippling salvo, trying to overload the cruiser's point defenses. Racing past them, Bondarevsky decloaked his Strakha as the point defense lasers opened up against the inrushing torpedoes. The rest of the surviving Strakhas appeared almost as one alongside, and opened fire at close range with their meson guns.

The computer controlled point defense was already

committed to dealing with the threat posed by the torpedoes, and couldn't reassess targeting priorities in time to stop the devastating attack. Concentrated energy poured down on the cruiser's raised superstructure. Suddenly, incredibly, the shields went down, and the meson beams broke through armor to penetrate the hull in five places.

Aengus Harper bellowed the chorus to "Rising of the Moon" as he launched all his remaining missiles at the battered cruiser. Then the Strakhas were past her. As they turned, the cruiser's superstructure exploded, and the ship seemed to stagger in space from the fury of the blast.

"Disengage!" Bondarevsky shouted. "Disengage!"

Combat Information Center, FRLS *Mjollnir*
Deep Space, Baka Kar System
1351 hours (CST)

A cheer went around CIC as the Flight Wing's attack struck home and the power readings from the last pursuing cruiser dropped to near zero in a matter of seconds. Tolwyn felt like joining in. *Mjollnir* would still have to run the gauntlet to reach the jump point, but none of the other Cat ships was placed to give them the same amount of trouble as that cruiser.

A smile was just beginning to form on his lips as he started to phrase a congratulatory message for Bondarevsky, but it was cut short by a cry from the sensor technician.

"Disturbance in the jump point. Multiple targets coming through . . ."

Kittani leaned over the technician's chair to read the incoming data. "Multiple readings. I count four escort carriers . . . ten cruisers . . . twenty-six destroyers . . . configuration is Kilrathi. IFF beacons are Kilrathi . . . It's Ragark's fleet." He paused. "I guess Allah wasn't listening to prayers, today."

Bridge, FRLS *Xenophon*
Jump Point Three, Baka Kar System
1404 hours (CST)

"Multiple contacts! They're coming out all around us!"

Admiral Vance Richards gripped the arms of the seat he had appropriated from a junior communications officer and leaned forward to squint at the tactical monitor over the shoulder of Captain Forbes. *Xenophon* had never been intended as a flagship, and lacked a flag bridge where he and his staff could have monitored bridge operations and directed the battle group at the same time.

But even at his awkward angle he could read the displays well enough to recognize those newcomers as Kilrathi.

The three Landreich ships had evaded their pursuers for perhaps the hundredth time since the start of their strange engagement, half battle, half dance. Only Bikina's *Durendal* had come close enough to take hits, and the wiry little mercenary had shrugged off the pounding she'd taken as "a little dent in the finish." They had offered to join Tolwyn and *Mjollnir*, but the carrier captain had decided that would only draw more unwanted attention his way. So they'd formed up near the jump point, ready to start their whole evasive maneuvering all over again if the Cats made another try at them in the hours left before *Mjollnir* joined them and they could try to duck out through the hyperrealm.

But instead, in an instant, everything had gone wrong.

"Carriers are launching fighters," someone reported. "They must have been prepped and ready to fly the instant they got over their jumpshock."

Forbes looked at the Admiral. "There's not too damn much we can do, sir," he said, sounding apologetic.

Richards nodded. Caught at very nearly a dead stop, with Kilrathi ships all around them, they'd never win free. *Durendal* was a goner, too, no doubt about that. Her damage had included a couple of hits to her maneuver drive, and she would be hard-pressed to make good an escape. Collins in *Caliburn* might have a chance. She was the furthest out from the jump point, and if she acted fast she might be able to accelerate quickly enough to get clear while the enemy was concentrating on *Xenophon*. But of course the Cats could bottle the Landreichers up in the system as long as they maintained their position. Neither *Mjollnir* nor *Caliburn* was likely to escape in the end. There weren't even many jump points leading out for them to choose from. This one led to Vordran. The other two led deep into the Hralgkrak province, behind enemy lines.

"Give them the best show you can, Captain," he said at length. "I want Ragark to pay for his entertainment."

Flag Bridge, KIS *Dubav*
Jump Point Three, Baka Kar System
1407 hours (CST)

"Concentrate on the cruiser," Ukar *dai* Ragark ordered. "The destroyer isn't important."

"Yes, Lord Admiral," the leader of the assault flight responded. The comm channel went dark.

"General Order to the Task Force," Ragark went on. "All ships to remain immobile around the jump point until further orders are received."

"Yes, Lord Admiral."

It was usually poor tactics to let an opponent get an advantage in velocity, but in this case keeping the fleet in position was the best possible option. The apes would have to slow down as they approached the jump point, and when they did they would be sailing right into the guns of his task force. In the time it took them to get past, the human ships would be pounded into space dust.

The humans would pay for raiding Ukar *dai* Ragark's world this day.

Combat Information Center, FRLS *Mjollnir*
Deep Space, Baka Kar System
1412 hours (CST)

There was dead silence in CIC as they watched *Xenophon's* last fight, helpless to intervene, helpless to do anything but watch as Ragark's fighters swept in and hammered the light cruiser. They had thrown up a heavy jamming field around her, too, so they couldn't even raise Forbes or Richards to speak to the men one last time.

It came to an end far more quickly than Bondarevsky's fight with the two Kilrathi cruisers had. One moment *Xenophon* was still alive, lashing out at any craft impudent enough to approach too close. The next minute . . . nothing. The ship was just gone.

And with it, one of Tolwyn's best friends. Admiral Vance Richards had been a good man, for all his faults, and Tolwyn would always remember him as a man of principle and honor. He had a flash memory of before the war, when they were both newly minted young gentlemen and together they had gone on their first mission.

"God's speed, Vance," he whispered.

He frowned at the tactical display. Ragark had left them with no real options at all. They could run, and be pursued, and sooner or later the *Mjollnir* would be cornered and destroyed. Or they could try to get through Ragark's lines to jump out, but the punishment they would take would be far too much for *Mjollnir* to handle.

Or they could just go down fighting, and take as many of Ragark's ships with them as they could.

Tolwyn straightened in his chair. There was really only one choice he could make.

Combat Information Center, FRLS *Mjollnir*
Deep Space, Baka Kar System
1527 hours (CST)

The door to CIC slid open soundlessly, and Bondarevsky stepped into the dim-lit command center, every step weighed down by fatigue. It had been a long day . . . and it wasn't over yet.

Tolwyn looked up as he came in. "Good job out there, Jason. A damned good job. Your people did us proud today."

"Thank you, sir. I wish we could have done . . . more." He knew there was no way the flight wing could have helped Richards and the *Xenophon*, but that didn't make it any easier to accept the old spymaster's death.

Now there was nothing more the flight wing could do, at all. Tolwyn had announced his intention of taking on Ragark's fleet head-on, and Bondarevsky had been ready to lead his fighters out yet again to the attack. But as Tolwyn pointed out there was still an outside chance they might reach the jump point, and if so they couldn't very well stop and take on planes before they made good their escape. The only fighters on board capable of jump were the four surviving Vaktoths, hardly enough to challenge the flight wings of four escort carriers.

So Bondarevsky's pilots would have to ride out the last action aboard *Mjollnir*, passengers for a change. It was probably just as well, at that. The port side flight deck had been put out of action when a returning bomber had lost control at the last minute on final approach. The damage there wasn't quite as bad as what they'd found when they'd first surveyed her, but *Mjollnir's* launch and retrieval cycle would be severely hampered until they could get a chance to make fresh repairs.

Bondarevsky almost laughed out loud. It was a fine time to be thinking about future repair jobs. If there was anything left to salvage, the Cats would get it.

"Any word on the others, sir?" he asked quietly.

"*Durendal* went down fighting," Tolwyn told him. "Collins slipped away, but she's got a pair of destroyers chasing her. How long she can hold out . . . that's anybody's guess."

"Then—"

His next comment was cut off by a call from the sensor station. "More disturbances in the jump point, sir. Multiple targets again . . . My God, sir, they're ours! Landreich ships!"

Kittani was reading off the information from incoming transponder beacons. "That's *Independence* . . . *Magna Carta* . . . *Arbroath*. The whole carrier fleet! *Themistocles* . . ."

"They're right in the middle of the Cat fleet," Clancy said in hushed tones. "I hope to God they can get clear."

"Look at the vectors, Mr. Clancy," Tolwyn said. "They came through the jump point under power. By the time the Cats react they'll be at the edge of weapon's range . . ."

Bondarevsky met his eyes. "My God, it's Kruger. It's got to be Kruger."

Bridge, FRLS *Independence*
Jump Point Three, Baka Kar System
1530 hours (CST)

Max Kruger had the command chair, and it felt good. He'd been forced to relieve Galbraith of duty after the politician's son had tried to resist the order to get under way for Vordran, and it seemed safest to take command himself rather than entrust it to any of Galbraith's officers. Actually, most of them seemed happy to follow his lead, especially Commander Roth.

They had reached the Vordran belt in time to discover two of *Mjollnir's* planes, a Zartoth and a Kofar. Cynthia Hall, the Zartoth pilot, had reported another electronic warfare plane had been destroyed by a Kilrathi patrol, and the Cats had gone through the jump point. Ragark had taken a lead of over an hour, but thanks to the delaying tactics the two pilots had executed so successfully it hadn't been closer to six hours.

Kruger studied the tactical board and nodded his satisfaction. Their initial velocity hadn't been all that high. They had only gone about ten percent over the margins specified in most of the safety handbooks. But it had been enough to allow them to pass through the

Kilrathi ships stationed around the jump point, despite
the disorientation of jumpshock, before the Cats could
react and open fire. Kruger hadn't known what to expect
on this side of the hyperrealm, but he'd tried to be
prepared for every contingency. It had paid off.

His intercom lit up to reveal Kevin Tolwyn's face,
still bleary-eyed from jumpshock. "Place is lousy with
Cats, Mr. President. You want us to launch and see
what we can do with 'em?"

Kruger shook his head. "Not at the moment, Captain,"
he said. "I think Ragark won't be sticking around long
enough for a battle."

Flag Bridge, KIS *Dubav*
Deep Space, Baka Kar System
1534 hours (CST)

"Vraxar!" Ragark cursed. The apes had outmaneuvered
him. His revenge would have to be postponed.

The position had been perfect for interdicting the
escape of the two surviving Landreich ships, and after
hearing reports from Dawx Jhorrad and the commander
of the orbital station Ragark had been more determined
than ever to obtain vengeance from the hairless freaks
who had attacked his stronghold. *Vorghath* was crippled,
unable to maintain shields, his whole front end twisted
and gaping wide like the toothless mouth of a worthless
old *kil*. And the station . . . the launch bays would be
out of service for many eight-days, and half the repair
facilities were destroyed or badly damaged. In one raid
the humans had set back his program by a year or more.

But now he wouldn't even have the satisfaction of
vengeance. Not with the human fleet between him and
Baka Kar. If he remained here to maintain the trap,

they could attack the capital with impunity, and if one shipload had done as much damage as that captured supercarrier had managed, what could an entire task force do? Dividing his forces to try to maintain the blockade of the jump point while also attempting to save Baka Kar would only expose his fleet to the possibility of defeat in detail.

Or he could pursue the new arrivals, giving up the blockade entirely. And the humans would escape. Once the Kilrathi were committed to the pursuit, it would be easy enough for the apes to win back and jump to Vordran once more.

Anger burned in his stomach, pure, raw hatred. It redoubled as the Communications Officer announced, "The human leader wishes to discuss the tactical situation, Lord Admiral."

The ape knew the dilemma Ragark faced. There was no point in pursuing the charade any longer.

But Ukar *dai* Ragark would not forget this day.

• EPILOGUE

> *"Rejoice in the victory of today, but prepare for the conflict of tomorrow, for life is an eternal struggle."*

from the Third Codex
03:18:10

Starboard Flight Deck, KIS *Mjollnir*
Orbiting Landreich, Landreich System
1725 hours (TST), 2671.056

The Presidential shuttle *San Jacinto* lay on the flight deck, side door open and ramp deployed, ready to leave the ship. Bondarevsky watched Kruger standing at the top, and recalled a similar scene the day he had come to *Independence* to see them off at the very start of the Goliath Project. But there were many differences, too. *Mjollnir's* flight deck betrayed its alien origins in the shapes, the structures, the shadows formed by a design and construction no human hand had been involved with, and all the refitting and adaptation in the galaxy would never change that basic nonhuman flavor. The strange shapes of two Strakhas and a Paktahn bomber loomed behind the shuttle, more reminders of *Mjollnir's* unique origin.

And there was the battle damage. *Mjollnir* had limped home from Baka Kar almost as battered as she had been when they first found her at Vaku. Shield failures had been regular all the way home, and Donald Graham had pronounced the jump drives dead on arrival after the final transition through the hyperrealm from Hellhole to Landreich. The port side flight deck was shut down after the explosion of one of the Vaktoths during recovery operations. Four decks of the superstructure were open to space thanks to laser hits during the battle with the *Vorghath*, and as many as five hundred crewmen had died.

Baka Kar had been a victory, but a costly one, and they had all the refit work to do over again before *Mjollnir* could space again. There were some battle scars here in the starboard flight deck, too, to remind Kruger and the assembled officers and crew of what the carrier had given, and what she might be called upon to give again.

Even the vast expanse of the flight deck couldn't hold all of the carrier's crew, but every department was represented by blocks of officers and enlisted men, drawn up neatly in ranks to greet the Presidential shuttle. They were cheering wildly, greeting the man who had saved them when everything had seemed the darkest. And Kruger accepted their accolades, standing, smiling, basking in the glory his last great charge into battle had earned him.

Bondarevsky stood in front of a group of pilots, sadly thinned out after the day of battle at Baka Kar. But Doomsday was there, and Aengus Harper. Alexandra Travis, too, back on duty after being discharged from Sick Bay with her wounds mostly healed.

Others were there in spirit, though no longer in body—Darlene Babcock, Charles Robertson, Drifter Conway, even Viking Jensson, along with far too many others. Bondarevsky had ordered plaques with the names of each squadron's dead posted in their respective ready rooms, to keep alive the memories of the heroes who had served *Mjollnir* well.

He glanced around the flight deck, taking note of the others who were waiting to hear Kruger speak. Donald Scott Graham, with Prince Murragh beside him, living proof that man and *kil* could work together for the common good. Bhaktadil with his marines, his turban and his oversized kukri knife strange against the blue and gray of his full-dress uniform. Deniken, promoted to full Commander for his expertise in handling the carrier's gunnery in the fight with the dreadnought, stood between the irrepressible Lieutenant Clancy and the darkly handsome Communications Officer, Vivaldi, with Kittani close by looking more like an assassin than an Executive Officer. And so many others, who had started out as strangers but become shipmates united by shared danger and the brotherhood of a successful fight against seemingly hopeless odds.

And before them all, Admiral Geoff Tolwyn. The man looked ten years younger than he had when they had met at Moonbase Tycho. Somewhere in the midst of that desperate fight at Baka Kar the tough old admiral had found himself again. Two nights earlier, he and Bondarevsky had gone out drinking together in a Newburg nightclub, and Tolwyn had revealed that he was resigning his commission with the Landreich to return to Earth to accept a posting as commander of the Strategic Readiness Agency.

"You see, my coming out here wasn't just a whim," he announced, "there was something else afoot. Call this a bit of a fact finding mission, an upfront look. With the SRA I now have the data I need to block what others are planning to do."

So Landreich would be losing Tolwyn's services. He had tried to talk Bondarevsky into joining him on his crusade, but *Mjollnir*'s Wing Commander had declined the offer. Bondarevsky had found a home here, a group of people he could work with, a cause worth fighting for, a ship he was starting to think of as his new home. He gave Alexandra Travis a sidelong glance. Perhaps even a woman he could love . . .

He wondered what Vance Richards would say, if he had lived to see Bondarevsky become a convert to the Landreich. Perhaps in some Valhalla the old admiral was looking down at *Mjollnir* today, proud of what he'd helped to set in motion. Proud of what he'd died supporting.

Kruger raised both hands, signaling for silence, and the cheering died away gradually. A throat mike and amplifier projected his words so every man, woman, and *kil* on the flight deck could hear him plainly. No doubt most of the rest of the crew was watching him on video monitors throughout the ship.

"When I decided to try to find and refit this heap of spare parts, people said I was crazy," Kruger began. "And maybe I was, at that. But you people set out to work miracles, and miracles happened! The first miracle was when you got this old girl up and running again. The second miracle was when you took on the *Vorghath*." He paused. "The press on Landreich is calling *Mjollnir* 'the ship that refused to die,' and I for one think that's as fine a title as any fighting ship can bear. Maybe it's true what spacers say, that each ship has a life of its own. *Something* kept the self-destruct system from blowing this proud warrior up after the battle of Vaku over a year ago. *Something* preserved her from harm until you arrived to put her in order once again. And *something* helped you hold together despite everything the enemy could throw at you!"

Kruger still had the touch, Bondarevsky thought. Rough-hewn, gruff, impatient, he could still hold a crowd of spacers in his hand, and lead them on a jump to hell and back at his slightest word. Murragh, the Kilrathi prince, had the same natural, easy authority, but Max Kruger was still the best there was.

The fleet had arrived to find the news of their victory had preceded them, thanks to hypercasts sent out as they waited in the Hellhole system for a week to see if Ragark was going to try to reopen the conflict. By the time they'd made orbit the Council of Delegates had met to withdraw their censure of the President and strike down the short-lived government formed by Councilman Galbraith after the no-confidence vote that had stripped Kruger of his office. Daniel Webster Galbraith had made a public apology to Kruger and personally turned over the gavel so that the President could once again formally convene the Council.

Up on top of the shuttle's ramp, Kruger was still speaking. "Now there's a new threat to this ship that refuses to die, but I have no doubt that you'll weather it the same as you've done all the others." He produced a paper from his pocket. "I received this yesterday, faxed from the Terran Confederation Embassy Compound. It was sent by the Confederation Peace Commissioner, Williams . . . an ultimatum, if you please. The Landreich government is advised that it has 'flagrantly and deliberately violated the terms of the Treaty of Ko-Bar Yagar.' We are directed to immediately arrest and turn over to the Commissioner President Maximillan Kruger. So it looks like I'm on the wanted list again!"

There was laughter, but Bondarevsky didn't share in it. He'd found it hard to believe Admiral Tolwyn's tales of conspiracies and the like, but here was evidence that some within the Confederation—not satisfied with forcing the Landreich into a desperate showdown they had only barely managed to win—now intended to hold innocent Kruger responsible for their own wrong policies.

Kruger held up the paper again, waving it. "More than that, though, the confees have demanded that we retire this brave old lady for service, along with the rest of our carriers, and turn over peace-keeping duties to squadrons of ConFleet who will police our borders for us to provide a buffer between our 'irresponsible exercise of military adventurism' and the forces of the Kilrathi Empire. What do you think of that?"

Catcalls and hoots answered, and Kruger grinned broadly. "That's about what my reaction was, friends. Out here on the frontier we learned a long time ago that the confees never have and never will follow through on any pledge to protect our borders. We've had to do it ourselves . . . *you* have had to do it, taking this carrier into battle and defeating our enemies with your bravery, your skill, and your ship that refused to die!" He paused again, surveying the crew. "So I say to you, as I have already said to the confees: this carrier, and all the carriers of the Free Republic Navy, shall remain on duty to guard our borders for as long as they need to be guarded. *All* of our borders, and against *whoever* might threaten them. The Landreich is a sovereign nation, and we protect our own!"

With that he turned and entered the shuttle, and the ramp closed behind him to a wave of cheers louder and more sustained than before.

Bondarevsky didn't cheer. He knew all too well what this open break with the Terran Confederation could mean. If the Peace Commission was determined to make an issue out of the matter, it could mean a new war, a war of human against human, with Ragark still waiting beyond the frontier to take advantage of any opening.

But much as he hated the prospect, much as he hoped sanity might prevail so that such a conflict could be averted, Jason Bondarevsky was ready to serve his new people as doggedly as he had ever served the old.

The Landreich's enemies might remain poised to strike the Republic down, but they would find *Mjollnir*, and the Black Cats, and Jason Bondarevsky, all waiting to defend her.

Until the crisis was over, Cincinnatus would not return to the plow.

Jason turned to walk away.

"Jason?"

He looked over his shoulder and saw Geoff approaching.

"Hell of a thanks," Jason growled, shaking his head.

Geoff smiled.

"I take it you're staying here."

"Yes sir, this *is* home now. And you, sir?"

"I'm going back like I said."

"Why?"

"That's where the fight is now."

"Won't you get arrested?"

"Hell, I resigned my commission and was following orders out here. They can't hold me on that."

"I'm curious though, what exactly is this Strategic Readiness Agency?"

Tolwyn smiled.

"A bit of what we talked about before. Did you ever really wonder why I was out here?"

"Yes, sir, frankly I did and still do."

"First-hand look at the situation and also to get out of the way for awhile while certain things clicked into place. Now they're in place."

"I don't get it, sir. Go back to get kicked in the teeth for all you've done?"

Geoff shook his head and chuckled softly. The sound of the laugh was cold and Jason looked at him curiously.

"Ever peel an onion?"

Jason shook his head at the curious question.

"Layer after layer after layer. Jason, what happened here was just a layer of the game. I've been in the service over thirty years. I was there at the very beginning of the war. And I can tell you that what some people thought was the end at Kilrah was just one act in the drama."

"Well, I sure wished it had been the ending."

"No you don't," and the way he said it caught Jason by surprise.

"Who is the enemy? Kilrah? Or is there something else?"

"Sir?"

Again Geoff smiled. "Never mind Jason, never mind. But as to the layers of onions. What happened here was but the game within the game. I realized that long ago, a game within a game within a game," and his voice drifted off for a moment.

"Jason, there are other plans to face the layers. I saw this coming years ago, that what thought might be the ending was but a prelude to something vaster and darker. I've made my preparations and now I must return to see them through."

There was something in Geoff's tone that was troubling but he couldn't quite figure what it was. As he looked into the Admiral's eyes he saw an almost detached look, a gaze he had seen before in the eyes of pilots who had flown one mission too many, or an assault marine who had jumped once too often.

"I'd like you with me, Jason. You might have to lose

a bit of that boyish idealism that I thought years of combat would have washed away. But I think you have the stuff for it. It'll be tough, you'll need stomach and the willingness to fight a shadow enemy, the thing behind the mask."

Jason was silent and suddenly not sure.

Geoff rested his hand on Jason's shoulder and again, for the briefest instant there was the old look again, reminding him so much of the Admiral who had risked all to save his life after the raid on Kilrah, or in that moment of victory in the defense of Earth when all believed that Geoff Tolwyn would be remembered as the greatest hero of the Kilrathi War.

Geoff looked into his eyes and there ever so slowly shook his head.

"Maybe not," he whispered, "maybe not, Jason. Stay here."

"Yes, sir, I think they need me."

"They do. Jason, there might come a day when you might question what I am doing," and for a moment Jason thought that something inside of the Admiral was breaking and then the hard distant look returned.

"Jason, just remember what I was and what I believed in—perhaps then you can help others to understand. Take care, son, and good hunting."

Jason drew back and as Geoff started to turn away he came to attention and saluted. Geoff smiled, his visage sad and filled with an infinite weariness.

"Take care, Admiral, take care," Jason whispered, suddenly filled with the knowledge that never again would he see the Admiral Tolwyn he had so loyally served.

Admiral Geoffrey Tolwyn nodded, and turning disappeared into the crowd.

DAVID WEBER

The Honor Harrington series: *(cont.)*

Field of Dishonor

Honor goes home to Manticore—and fights for her life on a battlefield she never trained for, in a private war that offers just two choices: death—or a "victory" that can end only in dishonor and the loss of all she loves....

Flag in Exile

Hounded into retirement and disgrace by political enemies, Honor Harrington has retreated to planet Grayson, where powerful men plot to reverse the changes she has brought to their world. And for their plans to suceed, Honor Harrington must die!

Honor Among Enemies

Offered a chance to end her exile and again command a ship, Honor Harrington must use a crew drawn from the dregs of the service to stop pirates who are plundering commerce. Her enemies have chosen the mission carefully, thinking that either she will stop the raiders or they will kill her . . . and either way, her enemies will win....

In Enemy Hands

After being ambushed, Honor finds herself aboard an enemy cruiser, bound for her scheduled execution. But one lesson Honor has never learned is how to give up! One way or another, she and her crew are going home—even if they have to conquer Hell to get there!

continued ☞

PRAISE FOR
LOIS MCMASTER BUJOLD

What the critics say:

The Warrior's Apprentice: "Now here's a fun romp through the spaceways—not so much a space opera as space ballet.... it has all the 'right stuff.' A lot of thought and thoughtfulness stand behind the all-too-human characters. Enjoy this one, and look forward to the next."　　　　　　—Dean Lambe, *SF Reviews*

"The pace is breathless, the characterization thoughtful and emotionally powerful, and the author's narrative technique and command of language compelling. Highly recommended."　　　　　　—*Booklist*

Brothers in Arms: "... she gives it a geniune depth of character, while reveling in the wild turnings of her tale. ... Bujold is as audacious as her favorite hero, and as brilliantly (if sneakily) successful."　　　　　　—*Locus*

"Miles Vorkosigan is such a great character that I'll read anything Lois wants to write about him. ... a book to re-read on cold rainy days." —Robert Coulson, *Comics Buyer's Guide*

Borders of Infinity: "Bujold's series hero Miles Vorkosigan may be a lord by birth and an admiral by rank, but a bone disease that has left him hobbled and in frequent pain has sensitized him to the suffering of outcasts in his very hierarchical era.... Playing off Miles's reserve and cleverness, Bujold draws outrageous and outlandish foils to color her high-minded adventures."　　　　　　—*Publishers Weekly*

Falling Free: "In *Falling Free* Lois McMaster Bujold has written her fourth straight superb novel. ... How to break down a talent like Bujold's into analyzable components? Best not to try. Best to say 'Read, or you will be missing something extraordinary.'" —Roland Green, *Chicago Sun-Times*

The Vor Game: "The chronicles of Miles Vorkosigan are far too witty to be literary junk food, but they rouse the kind of craving that makes popcorn magically vanish during a double feature."　　　　—Faren Miller, *Locus*

MORE PRAISE FOR
LOIS MCMASTER BUJOLD

What the readers say:

"My copy of *Shards of Honor* is falling apart I've reread it so often.... I'll read whatever you write. You've certainly proved yourself a grand storyteller."
—Liesl Kolbe, Colorado Springs, CO

"I experience the stories of Miles Vorkosigan as almost viscerally uplifting.... But certainly, even the weightiest theme would have less impact than a cinder on snow were it not for a rousing good story, and good storytelling with it. This is the second thing I want to thank you for.... I suppose if you boiled down all I've said to its simplest expression, it would be that I immensely enjoy and admire your work. I submit that, as literature, your work raises the overall level of the science fiction genre, and spiritually, your work cannot avoid positively influencing all who read it."
—Glen Stonebraker, Gaithersburg, MD

" 'The Mountains of Mourning' [in *Borders of Infinity*] was one of the best-crafted, and simply best, works I'd ever read. When I finished it, I immediately turned back to the beginning and read it again, and I can't remember the last time I did that." —Betsy Bizot, Lisle, IL

"I can only hope that you will continue to write, so that I can continue to read (and of course buy) your books, for they make me laugh and cry and think ... rare indeed." —Steven Knott, Major, USAF

What Do You Say?